FRIENDS WITH EX⌋

A Friends With Benefits Novel
Book Four

LUKE YOUNG

Cover Art by Once Upon a Time Covers
V2

ALSO BY LUKE YOUNG

SHRINKAGE
CHOCOLATE COVERED BILLIONAIRE NAVY SEAL
CHANCES AREN'T

The Friends With Benefits Series:
FRIENDS WITH PARTIAL BENEFITS
FRIENDS WITH FULL BENEFITS
FRIENDS WITH MORE BENEFITS
FRIENDS WITH EXTRA BENEFITS
FRIENDS WITH WAY TOO MANY BENEFITS

The Friends With Benefits Prequel Series:
FRIENDS WANTING BENEFITS

Also Available:
FRIENDS WITH EXPLICIT BENEFITS BOXED SET (Books 1-4 with
select expanded Ian Dalton Scenes)

To contact Luke or to be placed on a mailing list to receive updates
about new releases, send an email to lukebyoung@gmail.com

To find out more about the author and his work, see
http://www.lukeyoungbooks.com/

1

Brian Nash walked out of the bathroom wearing only boxer shorts. Glancing to the bed, he found it empty. He shook his head confused then turned to discover his new wife, Jillian, sitting naked in their sex swing—a wedding gift courtesy of Victoria. His favorite gift by far.

He headed toward her and scoffed. "Hey, I thought you weren't getting in that. And didn't you say you were tired?"

She smiled. "I got a second wind... and I've been kinda mean to you lately, and this is just my way of starting to make it up to you."

He painted on a frown. "You have been really short with me and so preoccupied with all this lawsuit crap."

"I know. I'm really sorry."

"I think it's going to take a little more than one go around in the swing to make up for—"

"Shut-up, get over here and lick me." Jillian shot out as she glared at him.

Brian raised his eyebrows in mock offense.

She smiled, spread her legs wide and ran a finger slowly between her legs. "I mean... Brian, please use your amazing tongue on me."

He rushed over to her while licking his lips. "God, I love you... I kind of like when you order me around during sex, but you should really try to be in a better mood when we're not having sex, too."

Smiling sweetly up to him, she said, "I promise I'll work on it."

"Whenever you start to think about the lawsuit, think about my penis instead."

"I'll try." Jillian licked her lips as she dipped a finger inside her juicy folds. He stared down at her, admiring the sight in a near trance-like state.

She glared impatiently up at him. "What the hell are you waiting for? Lick me now!"

He snapped out of it, grinned, and then moved closer to her. Jillian's legs rested comfortably on the harness supports leaving all the parts of her that he was really interested in exploring incredibly accessible to him. He ripped down his boxer shorts, and his nearly-hard penis sprang before her.

She whispered, "Uhhh... maybe I want you inside me first."

He shook his head no. "I'm tasting that sweet pussy; then maybe if you're lucky, I'll give you the full treatment."

Her mouth dropped open. She enjoyed when he took charge, as well. Brian reached up, quickly unhooked one of the ropes and yanked hard. Jillian's body rose quickly. He stopped pulling when her gorgeous parts were right in line with his face.

She sighed, a little dizzied. "Wow. How the hell did you—"

He raised his eyebrows. "I've been reading the manual."

She grinned as Brian secured the rope. He pushed her legs further apart then shoved his tongue between them.

"Oh my," Jillian groaned. Her eyes rolled back in her head as his tongue slowly explored her delicious folds.

After nearly a minute, he pulled his head back. "This is awesome. No neck pain. I could lick you for hours like this."

She gave him a sad look. "Don't stop now."

He obeyed her request then after almost ten minutes, she came hard, and wave after wave of orgasmic pulses flowed through her. He moved to her thighs and placed tiny kisses over them while she slowly recovered.

She gasped. "Please... lower me. Put it in... I need it."

Grinning, he slowly lowered her until she was in line with his throbbing erection. He secured the ropes, and then carefully slipped inside her. Nodding breathlessly, she stared up at his face. "I love your cock."

He said, "I want to put it in your mouth after. I want you to taste how delicious you are."

She licked her lips. "I want you to cum in my mouth. Will you save it for me?"

Brian nodded as he began slowly pumping in and nearly all the way out of her. He gently held her legs, as she remained suspended in the swing while they continued to make love. Reaching out, Jillian put her hands on his chest. She felt the muscles in his chest straining and wandered to one of his nipples, squeezing it hard.

Faster and faster, he moved inside of her. She closed her eyes, savoring the sensation of him filling every inch of her, while she sat in the swing, feeling almost weightless.

It went on and on until he hit just the right spot. Then her eyes opened wide for only a moment before slamming shut as the huge orgasm swept through her loins. Jillian squeezed the ropes even harder as he kept going. Her eyes rolled back in her head as either an aftershock of the first orgasm or a second mini-climax rippled through her. She wasn't sure which, nor did she care.

He held still, pressed as far inside of her as he could go. She opened her eyes and stared at him for a moment before glancing down to their connection, nodding breathlessly and licking her lips.

Pulling away from her, he stepped between the ropes to move closer to her face. Jillian leaned back and held the ropes while he brought his erection to her mouth. She opened wide, and he slipped inside. She groaned. He began pumping slowly between her lips. Moving one hand to his balls, she squeezed them gently. His head tilted toward the ceiling as he moaned loudly. She kept on pleasing him as he tensed every muscle in his legs, desperately fighting to push it out.

She felt him throb between her lips, then the first gush exploded into her mouth. Cringing, she pulled her mouth from him and finished him with her hands.

He stared down at her face, half in shock and half in ecstasy, as she spit out and then wiped his semen from her lips.

"Hey, what was that?" he asked.

"What?"

"Um... the 'cum in my mouth' stuff. You—"

She grinned up at him while still gently massaging his erection with both hands. "Sometimes you say things in the heat of passion that you don't really mean." She ran her tongue around her mouth with a grimace. "Have you ever tasted that stuff? It's not that great... especially today."

"I did eat a lot of spicy food at the wedding."

"Maybe if you went on an all-pineapple diet, I would really do it."

He smiled. "But you know..." He shut his mouth as she began running her hands over him more forcefully. He sighed. Then after composing himself, he grinned. "This is no way to begin a marriage."

"Really?"

Fighting to keep a straight face, he added, "You, uh, you sit on a swing of lies."

She struggled to hold back a chuckle, and they shared a smile.

She widened her eyes. "How's *this* for a way to begin a marriage?" She quickly pulled him back into her mouth.

He groaned loudly. "Yeah, this is... a great way..."

Reaching up, Brian took hold of the ropes with both hands. He closed his eyes and drifted away in complete ecstasy as the pleasure continued.

Jim arrived at Caroline's dorm at just about the time Jillian was begging Brian to help get her the hell out of that 'thing'. Jim used his key and found the lights out. He saw her in bed, smiled and then stripped down to his boxers and slipped under the covers next to her. Exhausted, he took a deep breath as he struggled to get comfortable.

Pretending to be asleep, Caroline, not wearing a thing, lay on her stomach. She groaned with mock sleepiness when Jim placed his hand on her back. She grinned when he moved his hand lower. When he found his fingers resting on the delicious curve of her naked ass, his heart rate increased. He felt the heat rising inside him as blood rushed to his groin. She moaned as he cupped her ass cheeks gently. Slipping on top of her, he kissed her shoulder. She feigned waking up and whispered groggily, "Jim."

"Yes."

"I missed you."

He kissed her neck. "I missed you, too."

"You body feels so good."

"How's your..."

"Oh, it's ok I think, but you can check if you want."

He grinned as he slipped down toward her ass. She spread her legs and wanted him badly. He began lightly kissing her cheeks, and she responded by shimmying her hips and moaning softly.

He put his chin between the cheeks of her ass and whispered, "You smell great."

"Yeah, I took a bath. I wish you —" She lost her train of thought when he placed a gentle kiss between her cleft.

He pulled up and asked, "Are you sure you're ok?"

"You can kiss it to make it better... if you want."

Spreading her cheeks with his hands, Jim moved his lips lower to her. After exploring her parts with his tongue, she begged him to put it in. He didn't need to be asked twice and slowly kissed his way up her back then slipped inside her. He put his head beside hers and she turned to kiss him. Their mouths connected with their tongues stretching to play together as he began slowly pumping into her.

She whispered breathlessly, "I love you."

"I love you, too."

He lifted his upper body away from her and went up on his toes. She adjusted her hips lower to get even more stimulation where she needed it. She groaned loudly as he slid deeply into her with one long, slow stroke.

"Oh, Jim... harder."

Following her command, Jim began pumping harder and harder. It went on and on, with him driving into her and Caroline rocking her hips up and down as her climax drew closer. Suddenly her orgasm was upon her, big and thunderous. Moments later he exploded, collapsing on her in a heap and kissing her shoulder gently as they both lay there recovering.

She said, "I was waiting for you."

He nuzzled her neck and then whispered, "I could tell."

2

Just as Jim was moving into the spooning position with Caroline, there was a knock at Rob's door. He put on his best fake smile and let Bridget in. They shared a quick casual hug, and once he returned from the kitchen with a beer for each of them, they sat on the sofa next to one other.

"So how was the wedding?" she asked before taking a sip.

"It was good."

"Just good... you were in paradise for Christ's sake."

"Sorry, it was beautiful. I mean after all the excitement. There was a fight and then another fight... oh, and then it rained really hard," Rob admitted and then he guzzled half his beer.

"What the hell happened?"

"You didn't see the TV coverage?"

"TV coverage?"

"Yeah, we—"

"Wait, why does this sound familiar? Wedding in St. Barts with a brawl. Is your mother... Jaclyn West?" Bridget's face lit up.

"That's her," he muttered finding himself still, to this day, a little embarrassed to admit it.

"Seriously... I saw it. So the news said that girl Natalie dated her son, so you dated Natalie?" She stared at him waiting for his reply.

"Yep. That's me."

"Is she really that flexible?" she asked bright eyed.

Rob looked away and sighed.

"Is she?" Bridget repeated.

"Uh-huh," he said, a little disinterested.

Bridget studied his face. "Why are you so depressed?"

"Depressed?"

"Is it the wedding?"

"No, I'm just tired." Turning away from her, he grabbed the bag off the table, opened it and handed her the bracelet.

"You shouldn't have bought me anything." She glanced at the beautiful multicolored jeweled bracelet and smiled. "It's gorgeous."

"Don't worry about it. It's just a little something I saw and thought..."

She studied the bracelet carefully. "This looks a little more expensive than fifty dollars."

"I just... really it's nothing. I want you to have it."

"Thank you. Are you sure you're all right?"

"Honestly?"

"Yeah."

Rob said, "Well, I saw my ex-girlfriend with another guy tonight, and it just freaked me out. We've been broken up a while, but I don't know."

"You mean Natalie?"

"No another ex."

"Oh, maybe she really isn't with this guy. Maybe they're just friends. How can you be sure?"

He said casually, "She had his, uh, penis in her mouth."

She widened her eyes. "Well, I guess then you're sure."

They sat staring at each other for a moment. She smiled at him and asked hesitantly, "Was she your date for the wedding?"

"Yeah, but we weren't back together or anything. She just agreed to go with me."

She held the bracelet up as she asked, "Was this for her?"

He stared at her a moment, unsure how to respond. Then he nodded, embarrassed.

"I can't accept it then."

"Sorry. I'm an idiot. I call you, invite you over here and then act like I'm about to hang myself or something."

Bridget gave him a sympathetic look. "Don't worry about it. But really, I can't—"

"No, it's yours. I really want you to have it."

"Are you sure?"

He nodded. "I think I need to get out of here. Do you want to go to a bar or something and get a real drink?"

"Yeah."

Rob asked, "You mind if I take a shower first? I came right off the beach to the plane and I've been traveling all day. I'm pretty sure I smell like ass."

She giggled. "You don't, but go ahead."

Two minutes later Bridget listened outside Rob's door. She heard the water running in the shower and slipped inside his room, carrying a small black box. Rushing past the open doorway to the bathroom, she caught a glimpse of his body through the fogged glass shower doors. Bridget quickly searched the room until she located his wallet. She found the card key she was after and then slid it through the small black device in order to capture the magnetic strip code.

After replacing the wallet where she found it, Bridget headed toward the hall, stopping briefly to glance at Rob again. She did find him attractive but needed to maintain her distance. Looking down to his midsection, she could tell he was packing an impressive package. She took a deep breath and felt the heat rising up in her loins as she ran her tongue around her lips while she watched him soap his body.

Rob began washing his hair and his penis came into clear focus through the glass door. Sighing, Bridget stared down to it and drifted away while she leaned against the doorframe, caught in the midst of a fantasy of stripping off her clothes and popping in to help him wash.

The squeal from the faucet as Rob shut off the water launched her back to reality. Rushing to the living room, Bridget slumped down on the sofa and tried to remember the last time she'd experienced some good sex—or any sex for that matter. She couldn't remember exactly but guessed she was sadly closing in on the one-year anniversary.

3

Over the next ten days, the newlyweds were tearing things up in the bedroom and at one point almost broke the sex swing. Both sore, they took a much-needed break. After recovering a few days later, Jillian was lying face down in bed, completely naked. It was the middle of the afternoon, and she was staring at document on the screen of her laptop computer. Lazily kicking her legs behind her with a cell phone to her ear, she said, "He should be back any minute."

"Okay, now make sure you don't deviate from the plan. I don't want you screwing this up," Victoria said.

"I won't," she replied while rolling her eyes. "We should be over in about an hour."

"Great, I'm ready."

Jillian paused with a frown then asked, "You don't think were going too far this time do you?"

Victoria scoffed. "No, and remember, he brought this on himself. He's the one who asked me to help him in St. Barts. Look, if he doesn't take the bait now, then he's off the hook. We agreed."

"You're right, but I just feel..." Jillian read a sentence from the screen, smiled, and then said, "This is pretty steamy stuff."

"I think he's really going to like the part with all the ball licking."

"He *does* like that."

"Maybe I should try writing a steamy novel. God knows I've got enough stories floating around in my head."

Jillian said, "Remember, I stole most of yours already."

"That's what you think. I haven't told you everything and some of it—"

"He's back," Jillian interrupted as she heard a noise from the hall.

"Good luck."

Jillian tossed her cell phone to the bed, then placed the ear buds from her powered-off iPod into her ears. Moving to her knees, she knelt with her ass pointed high in the air facing directly toward the open door behind her. She glanced back to check her angle and adjusted the computer screen. Reaching down between her thighs,

Jillian ran a finger slowly around as she waited while wearing a sexy smile.

She shimmied her hips a bit as what she was doing to herself felt really good. She thought, I'd love it if Brian were to slip it in just for a minute. Jillian shook her head as she fought to stay focused. She needed to stick to the plan.

Ten seconds later Brian arrived on the second floor. He called out, "Jillian."

That was her cue and she slipped a finger inside. When he reached the doorway and saw her on the bed touching herself, he stood frozen just watching. His jaw dropped as he witnessed the breathtaking sight of his gorgeous new wife caught evidently in the midst of a masturbatory fantasy.

Now noticing the ear buds, he stood for two more minutes, watching as she continued with her busy finger work. Reaching down to his own growing problem area, Brian adjusted it while he took a step closer to the action for a better look. Jillian could feel him back there, and her smile morphed into a wide grin. He stared, unblinking, from six feet away as she slipped two fingers inside while balancing herself on one elbow.

She moaned loudly, then moved her shoulder to the mattress to support her weight and took her other free hand, coated it with saliva and brought it behind her back to her ass. That was Victoria's idea.

His mouth shot open. Sighing loudly, he watched Jillian slip one wet finger slowly down between her perfect cheeks to her tiny pink puckered hole. His breathing became more labored, and he tugged harder on his penis through his shorts as he leaned in closer still for an even better look. Tilting his head, he held his breath as he focused in on exactly what she was doing.

Jillian turned quickly toward him. Her eyes shot open with convincing surprise as she pulled her hands away from their fun. "Oh, my God, you scared me!"

"Sorry, I, uh... go back to what you were doing."

She climbed quickly off the bed. "No, I'm so embarrassed! I was about to get in the shower before I got *sidetracked*."

"That was just about the sexiest thing I've ever seen." He moved his gaze to her breasts and stared like a lost puppy. "Do you want me to finish you?"

"I'd love it, but we need to be over at Victoria's for dinner in less than an hour."

Composing himself a bit, Brian raised his eyebrows suggestively. "You look to be pretty close. I think I could finish you quic—"

"Sorry, but I've got to shower, shave my legs, do my makeup and hair... and I don't want to be late."

Jillian reached to her laptop and closed the cover. "I'm so embarrassed. I was writing this hot scene, and I just couldn't stop. I was in an erotic zone or something. Then when I was finished I, uh, couldn't help myself." She exhaled deeply, seemingly still trapped in the fantasy and then shook her head to break the spell. "Wow..."

He grinned. "It's okay. Anytime you want me to watch you do that, just let me know."

Jillian smiled. "That sounds like fun." She rushed off to the bathroom, and he stole one last look at her ass before she closed the double doors. His curiosity piqued, he turned to look at the laptop. Jillian watched through the space between the doors as he moved to the bed and hesitantly picked up the computer. She watched, paused a moment, and then shrugged. Covering her mouth to quell her laughter, Jillian shook her head as he opened the cover. The screen lit up, and the document appeared. Jillian turned with a grin as she headed to the shower. Operation "Erection Storm" phase one complete, she thought as she turned on the water.

Brian glanced at the closed bathroom door and then sat against the headboard while looking at the screen. He scrolled up to the beginning of the chapter and began to read:

Jennifer and Brad sat naked, relaxing in Veronica's hot tub. The tub was located next to the pool in her tree-lined, super-private backyard. It was Jennifer's birthday, and Veronica told the couple they could have the use of the house while she was out for the night. In the back of Jennifer's mind, she hoped Veronica would return home early and secretly watch them as they made love in the steamy tub.

Jennifer grinned as she asked, "Have you ever done it in a hot tub before?"

"No."

Running her tongue over her lips, she stood and moved slowly to him. He grinned when she climbed up and knelt over him in the bubbling water with her full breasts pressing gently into his face. He sucked one of her nipples into his mouth. Groaning loudly, Jennifer slowly ran her hands up his thick biceps to his muscular shoulders. He sucked harder at her tender breasts. She adjusted her hips until she could feel his stiff manhood pressing into her entrance. Moving his hands to her hips, Brad guided her down until the thick head of his rigid sex slipped inside her.

She grabbed his head with her hands, pulled him away from her breast, and stared him in the eye. "Not yet. I want to suck you first."

Brad watched breathlessly as she slipped from his lap. She reached into the water, took hold of his erection, and coaxed him up to the surface. She guided his hips to the edge of the tub, then moved between his spread legs. He groaned as she held his erection and placed her tongue at the bottom of his balls, slowly licking all around. Slamming his eyes shut, he enjoyed the feel of the cool air as it chilled his upper body, now free of the steaming hot water.

She moved her head away from him and glanced up at his face, "I love your big, smooth balls. You mind if I just suck on them for a while?"

Nodding breathlessly, his eyes rolled back in his head as she returned her mouth to the hairless twins.

Brian glanced from the screen to the real-life bulge in his shorts and sighed. Grimacing, he adjusted to a more comfortable position and then returned to the story...

Jennifer tongued his sensitive balls like she never had before. The hot water from the tub had dropped them so low away from his body that they hung down almost four inches. She stroked his huge erection as she sucked one of his fleshy globes between her soft lips and gently bathed it with her tongue. Groaning, Brad spread his legs wider.

She pulled her lips from him and said, "I'll bet Veronica is watching us right now."

He glanced toward the house, saw all the lights were out, then returned his attention to her. "You really think so?"

She nodded slowly. "Let's give her a real show."

Moving her hand to his, she pulled him slowly back into the bubbling water. She sat down and leaned back until her head was resting on a towel on the edge of the tub. Next, she guided him to stand on the bench with his legs on either side of her. She looked up at his full balls and huge erection, which hung just above her head as she tilted her neck back.

Brad glanced down at her like he was trapped in a trance as she wrapped both hands around his manhood and slowly stroked it. Opening her mouth wide, Jennifer guided him south by pulling carefully on his penis. He squatted down until she sucked both of his low-hanging balls deep inside her mouth. With her tongue dancing gently around his sack, she continued jerking him off with both hands over her head. He put his hands on his hips and stared dreamily toward the darkened house, wondering if Veronica was actually watching them.

Moaning with delight, Jennifer sucked carefully at his tender skin. Brad was in ecstasy as he stared down at his huge erection while her slow stroking and world-class oral pleasure went on and on. She had never before given his balls this much consideration. It was fucking incredible.

Tearing his eyes from the screen, Brian looked with a painful expression down to his straining loins. He unzipped his fly and struggled to pull it out. He exhaled a long, slow breath, then went back to the screen while he slowly stroked himself. As he continued to read the story, it somehow got even hotter and concluded with Brad enjoying the biggest climax of his life as Jennifer delivered the most sensual blowjob/ handjob combination in the history of hot tub sex.

Brian glanced back down at his erection, then thought, That sounds like the best birthday ever... if not for her than definitely for me. Glancing to the bathroom door, he heard the shower still running. He paused, thinking, then closed the laptop and placed it back on the bed. He stripped and headed into the bathroom with his hardness leading the way.

When he opened the door, Jillian's eyes locked onto his excitement through the glass separating them. She asked as if she didn't already know, "What have you been doing that you're so big?"

"I, uh... I was just thinking about what you were doing before and it—"

"Oh, really?"

He nodded.

"Why don't you come in here for a minute? I think I can take care of that."

Brian slipped in next to her and glanced down to drink in her sexy wet body. Jillian kissed him hard on the mouth then slowly kissed her way down his body until she was on her knees. The hot water from the shower gently ran down his belly and onto his balls. Jillian pulled them carefully, then commented, "Wow, they're really hanging low in here. Must be the hot water."

He swallowed hard, then stammered, "I think I heard something about how hot water does, uh, that..."

She glanced up to his face and said, "They look delicious. I bet I could get them both..." She shook her head then added, "But I don't have time for them now. Maybe just a quick blowjob."

He nodded breathlessly as her hot mouth slipped over him.

4

After a lovely dinner at Victoria's house, Brian, Jillian, and Victoria sat around the dining table enjoying after-dinner drinks. The horny couple enjoyed a beer while their nearly four-month pregnant hostess sipped a glass of apple juice. Victoria and Jillian shared a grin. After giving Victoria a quick wink, Jillian pulled out her phone and glanced at the screen. "Oh, sorry. I've been waiting for this email from my publisher. I've got to run back home and send them a document. I won't be more than twenty minutes."

After Jillian left, Brian and Victoria sat smiling at each other in silence for a few moments until he asked, "So, how's the baby?"

"Fine. I just had a checkup on Friday. Everything is looking good."

"Well, you look great. I've never seen a pregnant woman look better."

Victoria returned an appreciative smile. "So have you thought any more about Jillian's birthday party and how we can—"

"I don't think I want to do it now," he interrupted. "I feel like it wouldn't work, anyway."

Victoria glared at him. "Really! Even after what she pulled on *your* birthday?"

"Well, I—"

"Fine, I thought you had a bigger set of balls down there, but I guess I was wrong."

"Wait. I do want to do it, but I'm not sure we could pull it off." Brian exhaled deeply as he dreaded her reply.

Giving him a tired look, she folder her arms over her chest. "You were going to come up with a plan. Do you have any ideas?"

"Not really. Can we talk about that later? I have something I want to ask you."

Victoria nodded, so he continued, "Do you think Jillian and I could use your hot tub one night? She has this fantasy, and I think I want to help make it a reality, if you know what I mean."

Victoria thought, Here we go as she asked, "Did she tell you this?"

"No, I read it in this new novel she's writing. It was really hot."

"Tell me."

"How's the privacy in your backyard?"

"Only John and Mary can see what goes on back there, and they're so busy screwing each other lately, I'm sure they wouldn't notice, even if you lit yourself on fire and ran around."

He smiled brightly. "Good, I think she wants to give me this... I don't even know how to describe it. Something about how the hot water makes your balls hang down low."

Victoria nodded with a big smile as if she knew exactly what he was referring to. Of course, she did; she wrote most of it, and what she didn't write, she edited. Tilting his head back, Brian put his hands over his head to demonstrate the position described in the chapter. Victoria held back a laugh as he opened his mouth wide and simulated the obscene gesture and then looked at her.

"I think I'm supposed to stand over her while she holds both my balls in her mouth and jerks me off. It sounds really hot."

"Wow, that *is* sexy. It sounds like she wants to give you a Boston double barrel jerk." She nodded. "Yeah, that's the old double. Did she swirl her tongue behind your balls to your perineum?"

Brian nodded slowly with his lips parted. "Uh-huh..."

She added, "Wow, that's a tough one... So, it's a Boston double barrel jerk with a twist. I'm not sure I could even pull that off."

Staring at her mesmerized, he asked, "How the hell do you even know all this crap?"

She shrugged. "I just do... Jillian is smart. You definitely need to get your balls up to about 104 degrees before she could even attempt to pull that off. You better soak them pretty good."

He nodded and watched as her face lit up brightly. "That's it!" Victoria moved to the edge of her seat and added, "The hot tub!"

"What?"

"That's how we get her over here and naked in front of everyone."

Brian looked at her hesitantly as she added, "You tell her you want to give her a massage at my house, and then you want to soak in the hot tub with her afterward. Tell her I'm giving you guys some privacy, since I'll be out... wink, wink. You get her all relaxed on the massage table, then once you're both out in the hot tub, we'll sneak everyone into the house. You go out there with no towels, so when you come back inside... surprise! Yeah, this is perfect!"

He shook his head. "I don't know."

Victoria stared at him with her hands raised. "Come on. It sounds like it can't miss."

"I don't want to spoil the Boston double twist thing."

Victoria exhaled deeply. "Come on. She'll think it's a riot."

"I don't want everyone watching us while she's got both my... you know... in her mouth."

"I promise, no one is going to see that. We won't even be in the house when that's going on. We'll figure out some kind of signal then I'll rush everyone in when you're done."

After curling his lip, Brian said, "Having those women cops ogle me and put me in handcuffs was pretty mean. I was really scared... I mean I really thought I was going to be raped in prison."

"I know, right?" Victoria nodded in complete support.

"I mean look at me, I wouldn't stand a chance in prison."

Victoria widened her eyes. "You would be one popular boy, that's for sure... And they don't even use any lube." Victoria gave him a knowing look. "Backdoor without lube is no picnic."

Brian returned a sickened look. "Okay, thanks for that image."

Summoning up her best acting skills, Victoria painted on a sympathetic frown. "I'm just saying she never should have put you through that. It was just horrible."

Beginning to warm to the idea, Brian said, "She does sorta deserve it."

"No argument here. We can discuss the details of the plan later, but tell me, have you decided on a birthday gift for her?"

He gave her a big smile. "I already bought her a diamond necklace, which matches the earrings I gave her on our wedding night."

She shook her head wearily and said in a tired voice, "A necklace?"

"Yeah."

Victoria just stared at him until his smile faded.

"What? No good?"

She exhaled. "That's so impersonal. You did that beautiful sketch for your wedding, and this would just pale in comparison to that heartfelt, extremely personal gift."

"So... should I draw another picture?"

Victoria glared at him as if that were an even a more horrible idea than the necklace.

He rolled his eyes. "Okay, then what the hell do you think I should buy for her?"

She shook her head, "Not buy, but make." She stood and smiled at him as she added, "The most personal gift you could give a woman. Wait right here." Victoria slipped away and left him pondering what the hell she was referring to. Sixty seconds later she retuned to the dining room with her hand behind her back. She was all smiles as she said, "My husband made one for me and I thought it was just about the nicest gift he could have given me."

Brian stared at her, waiting. Grinning, she pulled the item from behind her back. His mouth dropped as he saw the large realistic-looking dildo she held proudly in both hands.

He asked skeptically, "Your husband gave you a giant dildo and you thought that was a great gift? Here honey, go screw yourself..."

Ignoring the comment, Victoria moved to the chair next to him and stood the dildo up on the table. His eyes locked on it as she began, "No. This isn't just some dildo. It's actually him. It was made from a mold of his beautiful erection. Every vein, bump, and detail, captured perfectly."

Brian picked it up and studied it, blown away. "God, he was a lucky guy."

"I know."

"How do you even make one of these?"

"They sell these kits. You mix up this powder with water, pour it into a tube then insert yourself and wait about ninety seconds. Once the mold hardens, you pour in this rubber compound, and the next day you have your perfect replica."

He looked at her, warming to the idea. Then she added, "You can even inscribe it if you want. Turn it over."

Brian turned it over, and as he read the inscription, his heart melted along with his face. He was sold. "This... this is a great idea."

Victoria smiled. "It really is... but they aren't that easy to make. It's like playing beat the clock. You need to be fully hard and stay hard while you stir up this mixture for two minutes, and then get inside the tube immediately and somehow keep it up for another two minutes with no actual stimulation."

"I think I can do it."

She gave him a skeptical look. "Really?"

"Yes, really," he shot back.

Victoria, unconvinced, shook her head. "I don't know. I could help you. The kit recommends you get a friend to help."

"I don't think Jillian would approve of you getting and keeping me hard so—"

"No, I would do the mixing while you do the... you know..."

"Oh, that makes more sense." He actually appeared to be considering it for a moment before his jaw dropped, and he glared at her. "I'm not jerking off in front of you while you mix up some powder. I'm just not going to do it."

Her face lit up as she jabbed, "Or you could just take another Viagra. That would work."

"No way. I'm never taking one of those again. That's not even a possibility."

"Okay, then you are definitely going to need some help."

He gave her a smug look. "I'll be just fine. I think I can pull this off all by myself."

Victoria turned away with a frown thinking, This is not going according to plan. How to fix this, how to fix this...

He asked, "So where do I get one of these kits?"

Then it hit her. She grinned evilly for a moment while she plotted. She turned back to him with motherly concern. "Let me get one for you. I know a guy. If you order one of these online, you'll be on so many obscene mailing lists, the F.B.I. will be raiding your house to check your computer for kiddie porn."

"Really?" he asked, horrified.

"No, but you wouldn't believe the catalogs you'll get."

Brian nodded. "Okay, great then you get it."

"I'll get us two kits. One backup, just in case you have some trouble."

"I really appreciate it," he said as he handed back the replica.

"I'd better hide this before she gets back," Victoria said. As she headed back to her room, she thought, Oh yeah, I'll get your kit for you all right. A special custom kit... and you will have trouble, a lot of trouble. For a second she almost felt bad, but that emotion soon drifted away, and she couldn't wait to tell Jillian about the success of phase two.

5

By any measure, Victoria's plate was full. On top of assisting Jillian with the preemptive strike against Brian, she was a full-time student buried in course work, struggling to complete her Master's thesis, and also a teacher's assistant for one of her professor's undergraduate classes. She was also, of course, pregnant, which made none of the aforementioned activities any easier. To add to that, the art professor, for whose course she had regularly posed nude, had begged her to sit for his class again, now that she was in her glorious new condition. She pretended to reluctantly agree to do so; secretly, she was enormously proud of being given the offer.

And if all that wasn't enough, Victoria was also playing matchmaker. She had been working on finding a guy for Lisa since they returned from St. Barts but found the assignment more difficult then she originally thought. If she were merely looking for a date for Lisa, that would have been easy, but what she was looking for was a man to take Lisa's virginity, and that was a tall order.

In the class for which Victoria was the teacher's assistant, was a student named Jeff. He was a senior lacrosse player who had been asking her out on a date about once a week since the start of the semester. She considered Jeff for Lisa, because he was charming and attractive, but she was reluctant, since she found him much too full of himself. Victoria found it odd that even as her pregnancy progressed and became unmistakable, Jeff continued to ask her out. She always politely declined.

That is, until the day she met his gorgeous friend, Dale, while walking on campus with Jeff. Dale was tall, muscular, and gorgeous. He seemed not at all cocky like his lacrosse teammate. After meeting Dale, Victoria agreed to go out with Jeff, but only if he could hook Lisa up with his friend for the night. She didn't tell Jeff about Lisa's innocence or what was to be in store for the date. She didn't want Dale going out with Lisa just because it was seemingly a sure thing, because it really wasn't. Lisa needed to be attracted to the guy as well as connect with him on some sort of personal level before she surrendered her virginity to him. Lisa was desperate, but she wasn't about to crawl into bed with just anyone.

Within two hours of the proposal, Jeff called Victoria to confirm Dale was in, and they made plans to get together on Saturday night, which was only three days away. Victoria made a call to Rafael's spa for an emergency waxing for her and Lisa, and he promised to squeeze them in.

Victoria and Lisa were seated in the waiting area of the spa. After twenty minutes of leafing through magazines, Lisa wore a worried expression. "Maybe he doesn't have time for us today."

"He's just running late. We're his last appointment."

"He probably only has time to do you. I'll just watch, and then I can come back another time."

"Why?"

Lisa admitted sheepishly, "I'm a little scared that it's going to hurt. I mean having the hair pulled out of — "

"Do you have testicles?" Victoria glared at her.

"What?"

"Do you have testicles?"

Lisa returned a confused look. "Uh, no."

"I once brought a male friend here and they ripped every single hair off his balls, and he didn't make a sound. He was a trouper," Victoria lied.

"Really?"

"Yes. And do you know how sensitive the skin on the testicles is?"

"No, Not really."

"Well, it's really, really, really freaking sensitive," Victoria said smugly.

"Huh. I didn't know that." Lisa said quietly as if she were suddenly embarrassed about her unwarranted apprehension.

"And this male friend went on to have the best sex of his life after he was freed of all that ugly hair."

"Gee. I..."

"You do want to have good sex don't you?"

"Sure."

"And if you like Dale and want to sleep with him, you'll want his tongue firmly planted on your pussy and your ass won't you?"

"My ass? What?" Lisa gave her a sickened look.

"Sure, your ass. You see, this is your problem. You need to broaden your horizons. Trust me, you'll want a guy to lick it."

"But it's your ass..." Lisa began. Victoria, confused, stared at her, and Lisa added, "That's where you, you know..."

Shaking her head, Victoria gave her a tired look. "You pee from your urethral opening, which is located right between your clitoris and your vagina, and I'm assuming you'd like a guy's tongue floating from one to the other."

"Well, yeah."

"And you don't want him to drink your pee."

"God, no."

"So, what's the difference?"

"I guess it's sorta the same thing," Lisa said, unconvinced.

"Maybe you should just start with the regular oral sex and then later, when you're ready, move on to the other."

"I think that would be best."

Lisa picked up a magazine and paged through it, pretending to read as she thought about Victoria's oral opinions. She felt incredibly aroused down there and suddenly worried if, during the waxing, Rafael would be able to tell if she were dripping wet.

Ten seconds later, Rafael rushed toward them. "Sorry, girls." He continued in a whisper, "I was literally caught in the jungle." He made a sour face. Victoria smiled, and Lisa thought, Oh, no! Am I going to be the story he shares later?

Wearing a wide grin, he turned to Lisa. "This must be your friend."

Lisa returned a weak smile. "Hello. I'm Lisa."

He took her hand into his. "First time?"

Lisa nodded.

Rafael returned a comforting smile and said reassuringly, "Don't worry. I'll be gentle, and you'll love the results."

"I'm looking forward to it." She said with her confidence growing.

Lisa followed Victoria and Rafael into the back of the store. Thirty minutes later, both women walked out of the spa, and there had only been a minimal amount of screaming.

Three days later, Lisa was completely healed from her first Brazilian. It was a few hours from the big date as she studied her new look with a hand mirror, and she was, as Rafael had predicted, enamored with the result.

Lisa met Victoria at her house. From there, Victoria drove to campus to pick up their male companions, and then it was on to the mall. There, the two couples saw a movie and afterward went to a bar sandwiched among all the restaurants in restaurant row. As they drank, Lisa and Dale exchanged some small talk, but they didn't seem to be getting along very well.

Lisa was certainly attracted to him and let it show, but he replied to her questions mostly with one-word answers. He seemed disinterested and didn't bother asking her anything. Victoria was the designated driver as Lisa, Dale, and Jeff began to pound the beers. Jeff was chatting up Victoria, while Dale and Lisa mostly focused on their drinks. In forty-five minutes at the bar, the guys had polished off four beers to Lisa's two. The look on Dale's face was clear evidence that he would rather have been almost anywhere else.

The waitress dropped off another round of beers and a cranberry juice for Victoria. They took big sips of their drinks, and then Jeff smiled as he gazed at Victoria. "Are you really not having any sex until after the baby is born?"

"I'm really not."

Jeff said, "I read that pregnant women can experience some of the most intense orgasms of their lives."

"Where did you hear that?" Victoria asked with a smile.

"I don't know... I read it somewhere."

No one uttered a word for an awkward twenty seconds until Lisa said, "So Dale, you play lacrosse... is that like football?"

Dale gave her a look. "No, it's not at all."

Lisa sighed as she frowned a bit before turning her attention to her beer glass, where she drew a figure-eight design on the side, cutting through the condensation with her finger.

Jeff glared at him as if to say "Be nice, you asshole." Victoria caught the exchange as Dale returned a look, which told Jeff, basically, to fuck off. Dale's eyes locked on Victoria's stare, and he gave her a half-hearted and mostly condescending smile.

Dale exhaled, defeated. "I mean... it's a little like football. The field is pretty much the same size. Guys try to kill each other out there just like football, but the scoring is completely different. We use sticks and a—"

"Ouch!" Victoria grimaced in pain and everyone turned to look at her.

Jeff asked, "Are you okay?"

Fighting to put on a smile, Victoria replied, "Yeah. I think he or she is playing some lacrosse in there right now with my bladder. I really need to pee." She slipped out of the booth and headed toward the restrooms.

Victoria found a line of women waiting outside the women's bathroom. She clutched her stomach and cringed as the baby kicked something potentially vital inside her. Upon noticing the men's room just down the hall, she grinned and headed that way. Victoria opened the door a crack and found the room empty. She rushed toward the stall.

Back at the table, Dale continued, "...we use sticks and a small round ball. There's a goalie, so I guess it's a little like soccer too..." He turned his head to glance at Jeff and punctuated the line with a roll of the eyes, which Lisa couldn't see.

Lisa said, "Wow, I'd love to come watch you play sometime."

"Awesome," Dale said, his statement dripping with sarcasm.

Jeff watched as Lisa frowned. He glared at Dale once again. Dale ignored him and said, "I'm going to take a piss."

Dale took off toward the restrooms, and Jeff gave Lisa an apologetic smile. "Excuse me a second. I'll be..."

Confused, Lisa watched as he rushed off to follow his friend.

In the men's room, Victoria was pulling up her underwear when she heard the door open. Standing frozen, she recognized Dale's voice when he said, "I'm serious. Get the hell away from me."

Next she heard Jeff's voice as he said, "Why are you being such a douche bag? Be nice. You're going to fuck this up for me."

"Dude, she's never going to let you fuck her."

"She will."

Victoria straightened her skirt. She covered her mouth to keep from laughing out loud. The boys began peeing like racehorses as they stood side-by-side at the urinals.

"I can't believe you talked me into this... and over a stupid two-hundred-dollar bet."

"Chase was bragging about nailing her and told me I had no chance. I had to take the bet."

Victoria's mouth shot open. She gasped silently as she thought, Chase... that bastard!

"Chase said she gives the best head," Jeff added.

Victoria widened her eyes but then thought, I do give amazing head. She grimaced, though, when it occurred to her that Chase wouldn't know firsthand, since he'd never had the pleasure.

She listened as Jeff asked, "What the hell is wrong with Lisa? She's kinda cute."

"I wouldn't fuck her with your dick."

Upon hearing Dale's reply, Victoria's jaw dropped.

Jeff scoffed. "She's not that bad. Nobody's saying you need to take her to homecoming. Just be nice to her."

"All right... if she's lucky, I'll let her suck me off."

"That's it. After you blow your load, you can go back to treating her like shit."

"Alright, maybe." Dale let out a huge sigh. He backed away from the urinal, without flushing and then zipped up.

Jeff glanced at him. "Now, Victoria... she's got some great tits. Plus, I've always wanted to nail a pregnant chick."

"You'd better watch out. I'm pretty sure milk is going shoot out of those things when you start messing with them."

Victoria quietly took a step backward. She listened as Jeff zipped up and peeked through the opening to watch both young men as they walked out of the restroom without visiting the sink.

She wasn't sure if she was more upset about their callous attitudes toward women or their blatant disregard for basic general hygiene. Either way, she figured these boys needed to be taught a lesson, probably two.

Victoria flushed, washed her hands thoroughly, and slipped from the restroom without being detected. Moving to the end of the hall, she pulled out her phone. First, she sent Lisa a text message:

These guys are complete assholes. I overheard them talking... Don't let them know we know. When I get back, follow my lead.

Next she dialed her friend in the police force and Jillian's neighbor, officer Williams. He took the call and told her he was on duty but currently on his dinner break. Victoria told him the story, and they quickly assembled a plan. He was more than happy to help.

Victoria returned to the table wearing a bright smile.

"We were staring to worry about you," Jeff quipped.

Lisa gave her a concerned look. Victoria returned a quick wink and then turned her attention to Jeff. She opened her mouth slightly and ran her tongue around her lips sensually. "Jeff, you know I've been thinking a lot about what you said."

"Which thing?"

"The sex and pregnant women... thing."

"Really."

"I want you to show me how good it can be."

"I can definitely do that." Jeff smiled. He shared a look with Dale as Victoria kicked Lisa lightly under the table.

Lisa returned a "what the hell was that for" look, and Victoria returned a wide-eyed stare, which screamed, "Say something!" as she motioned her head toward Dale.

Dale took a big sip of his beer as Lisa stammered, "Dale so, maybe you can impregnate me so that you can, uh, show me, too, how good sex is for a pregnant woman."

Nearly choking, he stared at Lisa, horrified. Victoria kicked her under the table, this time hard.

"Ouch," Lisa called out. Then she painted on a sexy smile. "I mean, let's show them you don't need to be all pregnant to have amazing sex."

Dale glanced over to Jeff nervously and then returned his gaze to Lisa. "Um, yeah... sure."

Victoria raised her eyebrows. "Let's get out of here."

6

Minutes later, Victoria drove with Jeff in the passenger seat and Lisa and Dale in the back. She put her hand on Jeff's thigh. "Is it okay if I give you a blowjob first?"

He scoffed. "Sure."

"I really feel like having a cock in my mouth. It's been so long."

Lisa sat in the back with her hands at her sides, unsure whether she should make a similar comment. While going over possible statements in her mind, she rolled her eyes at her first idea and then shook her head at the second thought to cross her mind. Then on her third attempt, she figured she'd finally come up with the perfect line.

Lisa smiled, but just as she opened her mouth, Victoria yelled out, "Oh my God. It's my elementary school."

Everyone else in the car looked at her like she was nuts as she squealed wheels into the parking lot and slammed on the brakes near the playground. The playground featured a large set of swings capped on both sides with a giant slide and tower combination.

She turned to Jeff. "When I was in seventh grade, my first ever boyfriend brought me here one night." Victoria pointed toward the playground. "I went down on him right up on top of that slide."

Now this was a complete lie, because a) this was not Victoria's elementary school; b) she never blew a guy in seventh grade—it was eighth, but that's not important right now; and c) this playground equipment was no more than five years old, and it had been a lot longer than that since Victoria was in elementary school, although it would be rude to reveal just how long. Suffice it to say, monkey bars and dodge ball were still approved activities.

While staring out the window, ostensibly caught up in the sexy memory, Victoria said, "Yeah, it was over in about thirty seconds." She shook her head and then glanced to Jeff. "But I'll bet you can last a lot longer, can't you?"

Jeff swallowed hard.

She didn't wait for a response; instead, she glanced toward the backseat, beaming. "You guys want to relive a fond memory?"

Jeff's answer was to quickly open his door and rush to the playground.

Lisa and Dale shared a quick awkward glance, and Dale replied, "Uh, okay."

Victoria walked to the playground, slipped into a swing, and began to swing back and forth. Lisa took the swing next to her. Rubbing his hands together, Jeff wore a toothy grin while Dale began warming a bit to the idea as they both stood quietly waiting, in front of their dates.

Victoria glanced up to the stars a moment before she looked at Jeff with her eyes bright. "Now, I remember. Here's how it happened. Billy... um, Billy Clinton... was his name."

Lisa gave her a look. Fortunately, the reference to the former President was lost on the young lacrosse players. Sure, they were dumb, but it was partially because blood was currently leaving their brains and heading to other places where it was urgently needed.

Victoria shrugged. "Anyway, I was swinging, just like I am now, and Billy went up the slide by himself."

The guys didn't make a move. It wasn't until Victoria gave them a tired look and pointed to their respective slides that the walking erections took off.

"That's it. Now climb up there," Victoria bossed as she widened her eyes while giving Lisa a comical look. Lisa covered her mouth to hold back her laugh just as the guys were halfway up their ladders.

Once the guys were in position at the top, Victoria continued, "Billy started throwing his clothes down to me one piece at a time."

Jeff ripped off his shirt and tossed it down. Dale stood confused for a moment, and then the lights finally came on, and he began removing his clothes. He dropped down his shirt, shorts, shoes, and socks as Jeff did the same.

"Now, I was an innocent young girl back then, and I didn't know what the heck Billy was doing. I really didn't."

Lisa and Victoria stopped swinging and watched as Jeff and Dale stripped out of their underwear and tossed them to the ground.

Standing, Victoria gazed up at Jeff. "This is when Billy told me to come up because he wanted to *show* me something."

Jeff stared down at her, wearing nothing but a smile while stroking his prize.

"So say it," Victoria called up.

"Okay... Uh, I need you to come up here because I want to show you something."

Victoria grinned as she raised her hands skyward. "I'll be right up." Lisa gave her an odd look. Victoria whispered, "Come on." Grabbing Lisa's arm, Victoria led her toward the back of the playground, where the ladders to the slides met the ground.

There, Victoria kept hold of her arm and waited while Lisa persisted in giving her a concerned look. A moment later a police car sped into the parking lot with lights and sirens blazing. Victoria pulled Lisa quickly toward a brick building behind the playground. Paralyzed and completely naked, Jeff and Dale stood in the center of their respective towers.

As Lisa and Victoria moved behind the building, they heard officer Williams boom, "Just what the hell are you two boys doing?"

Williams and his partner, Officer Ryan, rushed toward the slides. They each shone a flashlight up at the naked men and then back down at the clothes.

"It seems you boys dropped your clothes."

Jeff said, "Uh, yes sir. We're here with our dates and we, uh, were just—"

"Dates, huh? I don't see any dates." Williams quickly shined his flashlight around the playground and then returned it to Jeff's face. Jeff squinted and attempted to shield his face from the beam with his hand.

"I don't see any dates, either. You sure you're not each other's dates?" Officer Ryan quipped, punctuating his joke with a chuckle.

Dale chimed in, "Oh, no... They, uh, ran off." He pointed toward the building. "That way."

"Okay," Williams replied sarcastically.

"And their car is right there," Jeff pleaded.

"Uh-huh." Williams rolled his eyes. "Why don't you boys come down now? If I were you, I'd take the ladder and not the slide. Wouldn't want anything to get sheered off now, would we?"

The naked pair carefully made their way down the ladders and moved to stand in front of the officers with their hands covering their groins.

"Hands on your heads," Williams said.

Both returned a look that asked, "Really?"

"Get 'em up!" Ryan shot out forcefully.

Jeff and Dale reluctantly obeyed the command. Williams giggled. "Must be pretty cold out here."

Both officers shone their respective flashlights on the two frightened and retracted excuses for male reproductive organs. Ryan broke into a chuckle. "Or maybe that's what scared off their dates."

Victoria and Lisa held back giggles as they listened from behind the building.

Looking down at their junk, Dale and Jeff were visibly embarrassed by their poor showings.

"Mayyybeeee." Williams said, while he and Ryan shared a quick look as they fought to hold back their laughter. Williams paused a moment before he shook his head, put on a serious expression, and loudly said, "Now, do you *little* boys know where you are?"

"Uh, what?" Jeff replied.

Motioning toward the school, Williams said, "That, right there, is a school. Did you know that exposing yourself anywhere near a school, much less on the damn sliding board on the fucking playground, gives you an automatic membership to the sex offender's list?"

"No, we just—" Dale stammered.

"Yeah, you don't even get a trial or nothin'," Ryan yelled out as if he were a hillbilly sheriff.

Jeff began, "Look, officers we were just—"

"Save it." Williams looked at his partner. "Now, should we let them get dressed before we haul them to the station, or—"

"I don't know. They'd be pretty popular down there if—"

"Please, don't arrest us. This is all just a big—" Jeff interrupted.

"Look, college boy. Just shut up," Williams began. "I think we should let 'em get dressed. I don't want their dirty, naked asses on my seats."

The officers shared a nod. "All right, ladies, cover up. I've seen enough Vienna sausage for one night."

Dale and Jeff rushed to put on their clothes as the officers folded their arms, staring at them while wearing irritated looks. Once fully dressed, the two were handcuffed and placed in the back of the police car.

Officer Williams let the two idiots sweat in the back seat as he drove toward downtown Miami. The two officers shared a giggle as they overheard the frightened whispering from the backseat of the car.

A few minutes later, they sat at a red light with the station in view. Williams took a deep breath and glanced at Ryan. "Shit. We're off in five minutes."

"I don't feel like doing all this paperwork, do you?"

The boys shared a tentative grin.

Williams said, "Not to mention the body cavity searches and all that."

Dale and Jeff shared a horrified look.

Williams and Ryan turned to the back seat. Williams began, "If we let you go with a warning, do you promise never to pull this kind of crap again?"

"Oh, God, yes! We promise," Jeff said as both nodded furiously.

Ryan asked, "Where can we drop you?"

In front of the fraternity house, the officers helped the two still-terrified college athletes out of the car and removed the handcuffs.

Jeff said, "Thank you, officers."

The officers nodded before climbing in the car. Williams rolled down his window and called out, "Never mess with Victoria." As Dale and Jeff looked at him, confused, Williams added, "Oh, and for God's sake, wash your hands after you take a piss. What are you, animals?"

Williams sped off, leaving the two drunken idiots staring at each other in utter bewilderment.

Victoria and Lisa sat in the car outside Lisa's townhouse and were struggling to contain their laughter. Suddenly Lisa stopped giggling, put her hand on Victoria's arm, and put on a serious expression. "Gee, thanks for ruining my night."

"Oh, I'm sorry honey... I know you had—"

"I'm kidding. I really didn't want my first sexual experience to be with a drunk asshole lacrosse player who is apparently battling a significant shrinkage problem."

After sharing another chuckle, Victoria said, "He was cute, though. It's a shame he's such a jerk."

"I know."

Victoria turned to face Lisa and looked her in the eye. "You know... You're right. Your first time should really be special. Let's not just find some hard-on with a random idiot attached to it."

Lisa returned a hopeful nod. "What was your first time like?"

Victoria paused. "Oh, it was so... I mean..."

"Tell me. It was probably amazing, right?"

Shaking her head while wearing an uneasy smile, Victoria began, "It was prom night, and after the dance my boyfriend booked a room in a hotel. A beautiful room... there were rose petals, uh, scattered all over the floor and..." Lisa narrowed her eyes as Victoria continued, "...oh, and he picked me up to carry me to the bed, where there were also rose petals and—"

"Was his name Billy Clinton, or was it Georgie Bush?"

After studying Lisa's skeptical expression, Victoria lifted her palms up in defeat. "Okay, you want the real story?"

"I do."

"Well, I was a high school senior, and after school one day I went over to Rodger McCollum's house. His parents weren't home. We went down to the basement. It was horrible and awkward as we fumbled around. It was over in less than two minutes. As soon as he was done, he panicked and threw me out of the house. Said he was worried that his mother might come home. Oh, and he made me take the used condom with me. He was sure his mother would find it or—"

"How awful."

"That's not the worst part."

"What is?"

"I shoved the condom in my purse and forgot about it. My mother found it stuck inside and I was grounded for pretty much the rest of senior year."

"Wow."

Victoria stared straight ahead out the window. "The purse was ruined... there was this big stain and pieces of rubber... It was a mess."

She glanced over at Lisa as her eyes brightened. "But I was a young idiot; you have a chance to really make sure your first time is amazing."

Lisa put her hand on Victoria's arm. "I think I'll stay a virgin, or just maybe I'll give women a try. I don't know."

Victoria gave her a sincere smile. "No, don't give up. There are some decent guys. I'm sure they're out there somewhere."

Lisa exhaled deeply and took in Victoria's hopeful expression. "You're probably right, but I think I'm going to go in and fire up my vibrator. I just bought some new batteries so—"

"I still think Eric is the man for you. I'm going to make it happen, I promise."

Lisa rolled her eyes and sighed.

Staring at her with a determined look, Victoria added, "No, I'm serious... if I need to physically guide his penis into your vagina, I'll do it."

"Okaaayyyy," Lisa replied with raised eyebrows. "I appreciate your help." She opened the door and stepped out of the car.

"Don't use too high a setting with your mechanical friend there."

"Why?"

"You'll get used to having a motorized penis inside you. You'll desensitize your vagina so much that no real man will be able to give you an orgasm."

"Oh, okay," Lisa replied casually.

Victoria watched with a sad frown as Lisa walked slowly away.

7

A few days later, Victoria stood in front of Jillian's house holding a bag. Brian opened the door and smiled at her.

"Are you ready?" she asked.

He whispered, "I haven't done myself in a few days. I should be ready to go."

"Congratulations," she said with a sarcastic grin.

He sneered at her. "I figured that would be a good thing for this, right?"

"It couldn't hurt." Victoria handed him the bag, and he took a peek inside. She slipped past him and asked, "Where's the wife?"

"She'll be right down."

Jillian appeared and smiled at Victoria. "Hey, there. So where should we go?"

"I don't know. You choose."

"Let's walk to the mall and eat there."

"Sounds good."

Jillian glanced at the bag in Brian's hand. "What's that?"

He looked around nervously. "Oh, um... this is nothing."

Smiling, she moved to him and gave him a quick kiss. She put her hand on his chest and ran it slowly down toward his belly button as she whispered, "I can't believe you didn't want to do it this morning."

Brian whispered, "I'm sorry. I—"

Victoria watched them with a grin as she headed to the door. "Come on you two."

Jillian kissed him again. "See ya." She pulled away and followed after Victoria.

Brian called out, "You girls have fun."

When Victoria was out on porch, Jillian looked back at him and smiled. "Let's do something fun tonight, okay?"

"Definitely."

As soon as the door closed, Brian rushed up the stairs with his bag in hand.

Outside, Victoria shook her head. "I can't believe you asked him what was in the bag."

"I was just having a little fun." Jillian held back a laugh as they began walking toward the street.

"You're trying to sabotage this, aren't you?" Victoria asked.

"No, well, maybe... Don't you feel bad? I mean—"

"Oh, lighten up. It's just a little harmless fun."

"I guess."

"Whatever you did to that kit, he's not going to get hurt is he?"

Victoria scoffed. "No, let's just say he's going to have a *hard* time getting the monster into the mold."

Jillian shook her head with a grimace.

Victoria smiled. "Oh don't worry about him. I'll tell you a little something you can do to him in the bedroom that will more than make up for this."

"Really?" Jillian shook her head, unconvinced.

As they crossed the street toward the mall, Victoria began, "You get some ice cubes and some hot tea..."

Brian laid out all the pieces of the "Copy a Cock" kit on the bathroom counter. After reading the instructions carefully, he frowned with the realization that he needed to cut the tube to fit his somewhat impressive—yet sadly modest—manhood, as compared to the mutant-sized male porn superstar pictured on the kit. The kit was designed to produce a replica for a guy up to a shocking foot in length. He stared jealously at the long tube before he readied the scissors and reluctantly cut away the last five inches of the plastic. When it fell to the floor, he momentarily wore a sad expression.

After bouncing back from the crushing realization that he wasn't the largest guy ever to make one of these, he measured out his water and poured the dry mix into the bowl. He placed a laptop computer on the counter, removed all his clothes and spread newspaper out over the floor. After firing up a sex video on the computer, he began working his manhood. He was hoping the erotic stimulation would help him stay as rigid as needed to complete the mold.

As soon as he was fully ready to go, he poured the water into the bowl, set the timer and began stirring the water/powder mixture with one hand as he simultaneously stimulated himself with his other. This was not at all easy. For a moment he wished he had taken Victoria up on her offer. After about sixty seconds, the mixture began to thicken, and he continued on another thirty seconds as directed in the instructions.

He glanced one last time at the timer and then scraped the mixture into the tube. He noticed it felt pretty thick already, almost too hard. He began to panic and in the process lost some of his erection. Glancing back to the computer screen, he quickly went back to work on himself.

Ten seconds later, he grabbed the filled tube and moved to stand directly over the newspaper. While tilting the tube horizontally, he attempted to slip it over his erection. He made it about two inches deep and then everything stopped. He pulled it harder into him and felt a sharp pain where he never wanted to feel a sharp pain, um, ever... He stopped and twisted the tube in a lame attempt to screw himself in further. It wouldn't budge.

He rolled his eyes. "Shit!"

Waddling over to the directions, he scanned them quickly. The paste was supposed to be dripping out all over his thighs as he filled the tube with his penis, but it wasn't happening. He looked down to see not even a third of his manhood inside the tube and he sighed loudly. Brian fought once more to pull the tube further, but it was useless.

"Fuck me," he murmured.

At that moment, Rob was heading up the stairs for an unannounced visit. He called out, "Mom!" When he heard no reply, he followed sounds into Jillian's room. It was mid-afternoon so he thought nothing of walking into his mother's open bedroom door after lightly knocking twice. Brian didn't hear him.

When Rob reached the center of the room and peered into the bathroom, he got an eyeful. Stopping in his tracks, he stared at the spectacle of a completely nude Brian holding some sort of tube over his erect penis. Rob's mouth flew wide open, and he stood there, speechless. Next, he saw the laptop computer playing a scene from a porn movie. He looked back to Brian and shook his head horrified. His first thought was that Brian was jerking off, but he wasn't moving, so that couldn't be it. Brian was standing completely still. It was bizarre.

Brian still didn't see Rob as he stared perplexed down at the tube. Brian rolled his eyes and shook his head in disgust. When he finally looked up and noticed Rob, he nearly had a heart attack.

Rob asked, "Dude, what the fuck are you doing?"

Brian spun away, and now Rob has staring at his ass.

"I'm, uh..."

"Oh, fuck. Thanks. That's a better view," Rob yelled out as he turned quickly away covering his eyes in his hands. "Come downstairs... when you're done," Rob added before he rushed away.

Brian turned to be sure Rob was no longer there and then glanced down, sickened at his failed attempt. By this point, his manhood had shrunk down like a frightened turtle, and he easily pulled the tube away. He exhaled slowly.

Slamming the laptop lid closed, he sat on the floor staring inside the tube at his sorry excuse for a mold. He slid a finger into it and felt around the cast as he shook his head disgusted. It was already completely hard. He didn't bother pouring in the rubber compound, because he thought, Who the hell wants a replica of just the head and maybe an inch more? It would come out as a laughable excuse for a dildo.

He rushed to throw everything away, clean up, and remove any evidence of his secret, slightly embarrassing assignment. As Brian dressed, he resigned himself to the fact that he would need Victoria's help. Then he headed downstairs to find Rob.

Brian discovered Rob sitting out by the pool drinking a beer. Actually he was already on his second after being victimized once again by intense trauma, courtesy of his best friend. Brian slumped down on the chaise next to him, and for a moment there was complete silence.

After taking a big, healthy sip, Rob summoned the courage to look his friend in the eye. "How many times am I going to see your boner?"

"Sorry."

"If you were jerking off, then that must be some new kind of method that I've, uh—"

"I wasn't jerking off."

"What the fuck were you doing then?"

Brian took a deep breath. "Do you really want to know?"

Rob shook his head no and then took another sip of beer. Glancing back to Brian, he grinned. "Okay, yeah I think I need to know... otherwise my mind is just, uh... Tell me."

"I was making a replica of my, you know..."

Rob burst into laughter, and Brian sat there with his eyes closed, just waiting for him to get it all out of his system. Once Rob was merely wearing a smile, Brian continued, "Victoria told me about them. She has one and—"

"Oh, yeah... she showed it to me..." After taking a sip of beer, Rob stared straight ahead. "Whoa, that, uh... That was the night Victoria and I did it." He drew in a long deep breath then let it out. "God, she was really something."

"I'll bet."

"Oh, man..." Rob began. He shook his head as he stared down at his bottle. "I still can't believe that Jim got her pregnant and not me, because I really—"

"I know, I know... you shot like a gallon that night," Brian interrupted. He rolled his eyes. "Actually everyone at the rehearsal dinner knows how much you shot."

Brian glanced at Rob, who was now grinning at him.

"Congratulations on that by the way," Brian added, his words dripping with sarcasm.

"You're just jealous."

Brian scoffed." Of what? How much you shoot or that you slept with Victoria?"

"Both," Rob replied proudly.

Brian broke into a smile. "Okay, maybe I am a little."

They shared a chuckle.

Rob downed a gulp of beer. Choking with laughter halfway through, he coughed, spitting beer onto the patio. He cleared his throat and then broke into hysterical laughter.

Brian glanced at him with a grin. "What so funny now?

"So you were... Why...?" Rob began as he struggled to pull himself together. He coughed once more.

"What the hell is it?"

Rob held back a chuckle. "Why the hell were you making a replica of your dick, anyway?"

"I, uh, was just..." Brian stammered.

Rob's expression morphed into one of terrified confusion as he asked, "Really. Why?"

Sighing, Brian replied hesitantly, "It was kinda for your... mother's birthday."

Rob looked away, sickened. "I think I just threw up *a lot* in my mouth. Oh dude, why did you tell me that? I keep forgetting you're having sex with my mother. It's like I'm in denial or something."

"It was Victoria's idea," Brian pleaded.

"Just stop talking." After taking another deep breath, Rob added, "Note to self: call first."

"If it's any consolation, it didn't work."

"It's not, and really... please, stop..." Rob narrowed his eyes. "Wait. What do you mean, it didn't work?"

"It just didn't work... the mold was too—"

Rob's jaw dropped. "How do you fuck up making a replica of your dick? Are you an idiot? I mean, what...? You couldn't keep it up, or something?"

Glaring at him, insulted, Brian said, "You think it's so easy? I'd like to see you give it a try."

They looked at each, other both feeling creeped out. Brian said, "Now, I'll stop. Can we forget all about this?"

Nodding quickly, Rob switched gears. "So, how about those Packers? Do you think they can go undefeated?"

"I don't know. They have some tough games coming up."

After ten minutes of football discussions, which just about returned the testosterone to the proper level, they began discussing Jillian's upcoming trial and then moved on to the depositions, which had already begun.

Rob asked, "Have the lawyers been able to contact any of the other guys Natalie dated to back up our story?"

Brian shook his head. "No."

"The only person I could think of who might know the names is Natalie's old roommate, but they already interviewed her, right?"

Brian nodded. "Cindy's deposition was yesterday. She told them she didn't know any of the names. Claimed that Natalie never shared any of that with her."

Rob scoffed. "They were so close. They were always together. Can they force her to reveal the names?"

"Evidently not."

"This sucks. So, it's just her word against ours, and we're both going to look like we're just trying to protect my mother."

"I know." Brian stood up. "I'm going to get a beer. You want another?"

"I really need one. I can't get that image of you —"

"Seriously, shut up."

"Okay."

Brian took off into the house.

When he returned with beers for each of them, Rob told him he had been in Miami visiting a client and figured he would stop by, since he wanted to speak to his mother about his upcoming deposition. Brian promised to have Jillian call him. There wasn't another mention of Brian's boner or replicas or anything relating to the bathroom incident. Rob knew it would be another Brian memory that he would not soon forget.

8

After Rob left, Brian took a quick shower and waited in bed for Jillian. He quickly dozed off, and when Jillian returned, she found him still asleep. Lifting up the covers, she discovered he was naked. She grinned, then headed downstairs.

A few minutes later, she returned with a glass of ice and a mug of steaming hot tea and placed them on the nightstand. She pulled the covers completely off him and admired his young, tight body as he was lying face down. She removed all her clothes as she licked her lips and struggled to remember if Victoria told her to use the ice or the hot tea first. She recalled she needed to move from one to the other gradually, to avoid damaging her teeth, but was a little fuzzy on the suggested order.

Shaking her head in confusion, Jillian decided to go with the ice. She slipped a cube between her lips and sucked on it as she climbed on the bed and got between his legs. The ice melted in her hot mouth as she swirled her tongue all around it. Jillian stared at his hairless penis and balls as she moved her head down to his manly parts. She spread his legs apart gently.

Stirring awake, Brian turned to look at her. "Hey, you're back. What are you—"

She grinned. "Just relax."

He smiled and placed his head back down.

Jillian grabbed another cube and spun around until her ass was hovering over his shoulders, with her knees on either side of his head. She let this cube melt in her mouth a little more, then slipped it between her teeth and held it there as she moved closer to him. Brian felt a cold drop of water land on his balls, and he shuddered.

"Wow, what was—"

Before he could finish the question, she placed the edge of the cube directly between his balls and moved it slowly around.

"Holy fuck," he groaned.

He held onto his pillow for dear life as Jillian danced the ice all around his sensitive sack.

"Oh, my God. This is..."

By this time, Brian's penis had quickly expanded to full size. She ran the cube all the way down the length of him as he lay there with his eyes rolling back in his head. Over and over, she trailed back and forth as the ice melted all over him.

Once the ice had melted away completely, she used her ice-cold tongue to lap up the tiny trail of water that remained on him. She slid her tongue over his parts while he moved his hands to his head, tugging at his hair as he slowly died with pleasure.

Moving lower, she pressed her face to the mattress and took him into her cold mouth. The slight pain from the awkward way she was bending his manhood behind him was completely overshadowed by the intense pleasure of her attention. Brian would have jumped off the bed, if not for her gorgeous body resting on top of him. Instead he cried out, "Jillian!"

After pleasing him with her cold mouth some more, she had him turn to his back, then grabbed the mug and took a tiny sip of the tea. She let her mouth acclimate slowly to the change in temperature and then gradually took larger and larger sips, swirling each around with her tongue. She took one big sip and held it there and while it warmed her mouth, she began teasing him with another ice cube.

"Oh, my God... That feels amazing."

"Um, hmm," she said with her lips closed before swallowing the tea.

Jillian took one last big sip and held it again in her mouth. After placing the mug back on the nightstand, she moved into position over him. She leaned down and rubbed what was left of the ice cube all over his erection. When it had melted fully, she swallowed the tea and plunged her piping hot mouth down over him.

Brian's eyes rolled into the back of his head as his mouth shot open wide. He moaned, "Wow!"

She kept going and going over him. While she pulled up to warm her mouth once again, he shook his head in awe and asked, "Where did you learn this?"

She gave him a wide-eyed look with her lips tightly pursed and her cheeks bloated with the tea.

He grinned. "Oh, you can't answer... Was it Victoria?" She nodded and began running the ice all over his parts.

Brian watched her breathlessly. "She has the best damn ideas."

Jillian grinned before moving the cube down under a particularly sensitive area and holding it there. He gasped. She swallowed the tea and plunged her hot mouth over him once again.

"Oh, fuck!" he yelled.

After her mouth tired, she began teasing him again by running ice all over his manhood. Then Jillian moved over him, guiding his manhood to her entrance before pressing down. His cold erection was a completely new feeling inside her steamy loins. While they were going at it, he grabbed an ice cube of his own and let it melt a little before slipping what was left into an unmentionable place on her. Immediately she cried out with a huge climax, and seconds later, he cried out in ecstasy as well.

Collapsing on him, she asked as she struggled to catch her breath, "Where did you... get that move? Victoria?"

He shook his head with a grin. "No, I kinda came up with that on my own."

2

The next morning, Brian woke up early. Jillian was sleeping soundly next to him as his mind shifted into high gear. He was really feeling guilty about the revenge surprise party he was planning for Jillian, especially after the events of the previous day. Thoughts swirled through his mind... Was he going too far? She was so adorable. Could he actually go through with it? Would he regret doing that to her, or would she think it was hilarious? Could he take that chance?

He watched as she breathed in and out slowly. God, she was gorgeous. Jillian was lying on her side, curled up with a pillow, and he lifted the sheets to drink in her naked body. He shook his head as he studied her perfect ass.

Slipping out of bed, he leaned over the side of the mattress for a better look. His lips parted, and he tilted his head as his eyes locked on her tiny pink seam. He'd love to go down and begin kissing her there, but she probably wouldn't want to be woken up to that. Or would she?

He moved his lips toward her and stopped short with the guilt suddenly becoming unbearable. He thought, I've got to put a stop to this party. I'd better talk to Victoria now. Taking one last look, Brian grinned and then placed a gentle kiss on her pale ass cheek before covering her up. Jillian stirred, and Brian grimaced as he waited for a moment to see if he had disturbed her. She took a deep breath and rolled over without making another sound. He breathed a sigh of relief and then headed for the bathroom.

Brian left Jillian a note telling her that he was going out for a run. He headed straight for Victoria's house. When he arrived, he checked his phone and found it was only 8:38 a.m. He wondered if she was still sleeping. He stood in front of the door, contemplating whether to knock, and then thought better of it. He noticed movement through a nearby window and, without thinking, moved to it.

The window happened to be to Victoria's bedroom, and inside she was lying in bed wearing only a bra as she pleasured herself with her late husband's replica dildo. Her five-month pregnant belly was still quite small, and she looked pretty freaking sexy. When he saw her through the slightly open blinds, he gasped in shock. He quickly pulled away, but Victoria had already spotted someone there and was angrily heading to confront the intruder.

Standing off to the side of the window, contemplating exactly what to do, he paused a moment and then shrugged. One more look wouldn't hurt. She'd spied on him once when he had, uh, well... you know. He turned back to the window and was stunned to find the blinds fully open and the half nude Victoria standing there with the giant dildo pressed up against the glass. With his heart leaping around his chest, he jumped away from the house and fell to the ground after tumbling over a bush.

Victoria's angry look morphed into a smile as soon as she recognized him. Brian clutched his chest as he stared wide-eyed up at her face. She opened the palm in the one hand as if to say, "To what do I owe this surprise visit?" His glance traveled to the giant dildo, and her eyes followed. Grinning, she shrugged without bothering to cover anything up. His eyes next traveled down to her tiny coiffed pubic hair then quickly back up to her face. He shook his head with a wide, slightly embarrassed smile as she motioned for him to meet her at the door.

Now wearing a robe, Victoria opened the door with a grin. "What the hell are you doing?"

"What are *you* doing?"

"Well, I *was* about to have a big orgasm."

He grimaced. "Oh, sorry."

Victoria and Brian sat in the living room, holding mugs of tea. She was curled up with her legs on the sofa, and he sat across from her in a big, comfortable chair. Her robe was riding up a bit, so he could see a little too much of her thighs. She still looked amazing, and he fought to maintain eye contact with her.

After taking a sip, she held the hot mug close to her face. "So what is it?"

"I've been thinking, and I can't go through with it."

"What?"

"Jillian's surprise party thing. I don't want to embarrass her like that... I don't want to do it."

Victoria gave him a disappointed look. "Come on, she really got you good last time. You need to get her back—"

"I just can't do it. She's the love of my life, and I don't want her to be mad at me."

"That's understandable," she replied, her voice dripping with sarcasm.

Brian took a sip of his tea and glanced down at her thighs. Her robe had moved up a little more, and he could clearly see the gentle curve of her ass. He shook his head as he thought, How the hell does she still look like this being five-months pregnant? He caught himself and returned his gaze to her face.

Victoria grimaced as she asked, "So how'd it go yesterday?"

His face contorted into a look of intense pain. "It didn't work. It was—"

"I know. Sorry."

"How did you know?"

"I got an email late last night that those kits I bought were defective. They're all being recalled. Some problem at the factory, or something."

"I wish you'd called me. I almost broke my dick off."

"It was after you already... and I was afraid to call. Sorry about that."

Brian exhaled deeply, and then he grinned at her. "I see you were enjoying yours."

"Yeah, I just woke up early. Early and really horny... so I grabbed it."

"Jillian and I had some amazing sex last night."

"Did she use the tea and the ice cubes?"

He nodded with a big grin. "Thanks for that."

"Don't mention it. The company is shipping me out a new kit. I'll get it this week."

Brian shook his head and made a face like a child staring at a plate of Brussels sprouts. "I don't know."

"Don't tell me you don't want to make it now." He glanced down at her thighs, then pointed out to her that she was exposing herself. Looking down, she grinned. "Sorry." She covered up with the robe.

"I found it really hard..." He grinned. "To stay *hard* while mixing up the stuff anyway. I don't think I can pull it off."

"I told you I'd help. I won't even look. I'll mix it in one room and you can get yourself *ready* in another. I'll just hand you the tube and you'll be all set."

"Are you sure this kit won't send me to the hospital?"

"I promise." She nodded. "My guy assured me they've fixed the problem. You've got to make one for her. If you do it yourself, you won't make the best impression, I can assure you that."

He looked at her, contemplating.

"You do want yours to, you know, show all that you've got in your full glory, right?"

"Well, yeah."

"I love mine," she said.

"I saw that." He raised his eyebrows and gave her a look.

"She'll go nuts for it. You can even play threesome with it."

He stared at her, a little put off.

"I mean, imagine filling her up with two of you?"

"What? That sounds a little creepy."

"Whatever." She shrugged. "Are you in or not?"

Brian exhaled. "Okay. Let's do it."

Victoria smiled brightly. "Great. How about next Saturday, in the afternoon, about four? I have exams all week, and I have an appointment in the morning on Saturday. But after that, I'm free."

"All right."

"I'll tell Jillian I need you to help me move some boxes, or something."

"I guess it'll be fun," he admitted hesitantly.

She gave him a slightly evil grin as she thought, It will be. She said, "Jillian will love it."

He nodded, now completely on board. Shifting position, Victoria inadvertently flashed him a view of her spectacular private areas. He closed his eyes.

She covered up and smiled. "Sorry." She widened her eyes with a realization. "Oh, I'm glad you're here. Can you look at something for me?"

"Is that outlet in your bathroom not working again?"

"No, my ass."

"Your ass?"

"Yeah," she replied casually.

"Really?" He cringed.

"Yes, look I read that when you're pregnant your anus can get really hairy. I feel the hairs down there, but I need you to tell me if they are those fine blonde hairs or those dark ugly ones."

"Seriously."

"Yes. I was trying to get a look at them with a hard mirror, but I can't really see. I need your help."

"So you want me to stare into your ass and tell you what color the hair is?"

Victoria gave him a tired look. "Yeah, unless you think *that's* too much for you."

"What exactly are you going to do with this information?"

"Oh, don't worry. I'm not going to ask you to shave me or anything like that. If it's a nightmare, I'm going to make an appointment at the spa. I just can't stand to not know if I'm hairy back there. What if I get in an accident or something?"

"I don't think they'll be studying how hairy your ass hole is if you're in the hospital."

"You don't know that... they might be." She gave him a tired look. "Can you do this little thing for me or not?"

"Okay."

Victoria smiled.

Looking up at the ceiling, Brian breathed out deeply. "So where do you want to—" He shut up when his gaze traveled back down, and he discovered she was already bending over with her hands on the sofa, the robe pulled up and her gorgeous ass staring him right in the face.

"Okay, so right here then," he said while rolling his eyes.

"Yes, here. Come on."

Brian made his way to her and glanced down between her shapely cheeks. "You look fine to me."

Victoria craned her neck around and glared at him. "You aren't even looking. Get down there and really look at it."

He sighed and moved to his knees.

"So, what does it look like? Wait, let me..." Resting her head on the cushion, Victoria used both hands to spread her cheeks apart. All her lady parts were splayed out before him and he stared at them mesmerized. He swallowed hard and felt something move in his shorts.

"Wow," he exclaimed.

"What? Are the hairs dark, or not?"

Brian's expression went from one of admiration to clinical concern. "You know, you are a lot hairier then when I drew you that time in class."

She groaned. "I knew it."

"Are they dark hairs?"

He nodded. "They are, but you still look cute." Brian felt blood heading south as his eyes glanced down to the pink lips of her vagina. She was pulling her cheeks so far apart that her hole was also pretty wide open. Inside, he spotted how absolutely wet she was. His mind went quickly to Jillian. He wondered if she was still sleeping and exactly how wet she was at that moment.

"But would you lick it?"

"What?" The question brought him back to earth. "Are you *asking* me to lick it?"

She let go of her cheeks, stood, covered up everything with the robe and turned to sit on the sofa. She gave him a serious look but said in a tired voice, "Yeah, I want you to lick my ass. Do you want to do it here or should we go to the bedroom?"

"Sorry." He grinned.

"I meant if you were dating me and saw the condition of it would you lick it or be horrified."

"Oh, I'd lick it."

She gave him a look like she didn't buy it. "You're just saying that."

He nodded confidently with a completely straight face. "I would be all over it. You wouldn't be able to keep my tongue out of there."

She grinned and then began to chuckle. He lost his serious expression and laughed along with her.

Victoria said, "Thanks, but I'm still going to make an appointment. You want to go with me?"

Giving her a horrified look, he said, "No f'ing way."

She widened her eyes. "Do you need me to check your ass?"

He scoffed. "No, my ass is probably fine. I'm taking care of everything myself. I'm having good luck with a razor for the front parts and they might not be perfectly baby smooth or anything, but I'm never letting wax touch my junk again."

She grinned. "That was a fun day."

Brian shook his head and opened his mouth to comment but decided against it. "So, are you dating anyone?"

"Oh, God no. But there is this professor I keep seeing around campus. I get so wet when I see him." She paused and then added, "But then again, with the pregnancy, I'm always wet."

He mumbled softly, "I know."

"What?"

"Oh, nothing."

Brian adjusted his shorts. Glancing down to his problem area, Victoria grinned. "Why don't you run along and go see your wife?"

He chucked and stood. "I think I will. I'll let you get back to what you were doing, too."

Victoria gave him a sexy look. "Yeah, I am a little stressed out."

She walked him to the door. As he was stepping off the porch, she said, "Bye. Oh, and, uh, thanks for looking at my ass."

He turned back, smiled for a moment then his face contorted as he realized how strange that sounded. "Okay. I'll, uh, see you."

"Remember Saturday."

Brian nodded, turned and took off running to see his wife. Victoria watched him with a grin for a moment before closing the door. She slipped off her robe, climbed back into bed and then glanced down at her David replica. She reached for it, smiled, and then decided to make a call first.

10

Jillian was awake, but still naked and lounging in bed when the phone rang. "I'm glad you called. I decided against having the party."

"What? Why?" Victoria shot back.

"I don't know. It just doesn't seem right. You really think it's a good idea to march my new husband out with a full erection in front of a group of our friends?"

Victoria cracked up. "I think it would be hilarious."

"I don't know. I'm just—"

"Look, I need this. I've had one night of sex in the last five months, and it lasted maybe twenty minutes. I haven't even seen a real, actual penis in almost six weeks. I was doing the math the other day. I have a lot of time on my hands... I don't sleep much. In five months, there are two hundred sixteen thousand minutes and in all that time I've only had a cock in my mouth for about six minutes, and the remaining fourteen minutes it was in my, you know..."

"Oh my, I, uh—" Jillian began.

"And not one minute in my ass. You know how much I enjoy anal sex."

"I know. I know, but—"

"Do you know what percentage twenty minutes is of two hundred thousand?"

"Uh, no. What is it?"

"Well, it's... it's... I don't know exactly, but it's a really, really, really small percentage."

"I'm sure," Jillian replied hesitantly.

"I've never had such a low percentage of penis time versus non-penis time since probably high school." Victoria continued on with an edge to her voice. "My hormones are raging... I'm constantly horny. I feel like fucking just about every guy I see. Even the not-so-attractive ones. I literally have no excitement in my life right now. I—"

"But how is doing this going to solve your problem?"

"I don't know, but I put a lot of work into this already. It took me hours to retype the instructions for the penis kit. Not to mention all the planning and everything. Now, I've got everything set for this Saturday. Everyone is invited, and Brian is coming over at four. In fact, Brian was just here. We were going over the details of the whole hot tub thing he's planning to pull on you."

"Really?"

"Yes, really. He can't wait to get you back. He was practically foaming at the mouth."

Jillian remained silent as she contemplated. Victoria shook her head, then added, "Okay, fine. I guess I'll tell him that your party is off. I'll make up some excuse. He'll probably figure out some other way to get you back, so don't come whining to me when he does, because I'm done. That's it. I keep giving and giv—"

"Wait a second. Maybe we—"

"Just have him call me when he gets in."

"No, wait. Let's do it."

Victoria didn't say a word as a grin spread across her face.

Jillian repeated, "I'm serious. Let's do it."

"Are you sure?"

"Yes."

"Don't you dare pull out of this now."

"I won't."

"Great. I need to go and take care of something, but I'll call you later to confirm all the details."

Jillian shook her head, suddenly regretting her decision.

Victoria glanced down at her dildo, then remembered, "Oh, by the way, I'm pretty sure your husband is coming home to have sex with you."

"How do you know?"

"We were talking about sex, and his shorts seemed to be a little crowded, if you know what I mean, when he walked out of here. Actually, I think he was running."

Jillian heard the front door open. "There he is. I'd better go."

She hung up the phone and grinned.

Jillian pushed the covers down to her thighs and lay face down on the mattress with her legs spread wide. Brian arrived at the bedroom door and stopped in his tracks when he saw the sight of his gorgeous wife's breathtaking ass.

He softly said, "Jillian."

She didn't move and just wiggled her hips a bit as she groaned as if in the midst of a spectacular sex dream. Moving closer, he pulled off his shirt and whispered, "Jillian are you awake?"

Jillian moaned softly and turned her head to the side. Her eyes remained closed, and she breathed out deeply. He grinned and slipped his shoes and the rest of his clothes off.

"Oh Brian," she cried out quietly. He moved closer, and she finished that thought when she whispered, "... lick me."

He grinned. He didn't need to be asked twice. After pulling the covers off her completely, he carefully climbed over her so his penis was hanging down on her back. He studied her beautiful parts for a moment before plunging his head down between her legs.

She remained in her faux dream state for about five minutes while he explored every inch of her with his tongue and fingers. After that, she pretended to awaken as she felt his erection slipping down past her cheek. She took him into her mouth, and they performed some acrobatic style sixty-nine for the next ten minutes or so, which resulted in huge climaxes and stiff necks for both.

Afterward, as they lay in bed together, she nuzzled up on his chest. He stared at the ceiling while running his fingers gently over her lower back. The guilt washed over him as he replayed the conversation with Victoria in his mind.

Jillian placed a gentle kiss on his chest. "That was amazing. I love you."

"I know," he replied in an irritated voice. Realizing his inappropriate tone, he said softly, "I mean, I love you too."

After taking a deep breath, he said, "There's something I need to tell you."

Jillian stared up at him, waiting.

"You know how we planned to go to Victoria's on your birthday, and I was going to give you that massage, and we were going to get naked in the hot tub."

She sat up in bed and listened intently. "Yeah."

He gave her a hesitant look. "Well..."

"What is it? What's on your mind?"

He grimaced and then stammered, "It... it was all a trick to get you over there and get you back for the whole policewoman thing."

Gazing up at her apprehensively, he waited, dreading her response.

She painted on a surprised look. "Really?"

"Yes, I'm not proud of it. I was going to get you to go back into the house, and it was going to be full of all your friends. Victoria, of course, was going to help."

She glared at him in mock anger. "You're a very bad boy."

"I know. I'm sorry."

"And what... the way I just took care of you made you decide just now not to do it?"

"No, I decided last night."

"Really."

"Yeah, I already spoke to Victoria and called it off."

"But she... Wait. I just talked to her on the phone, and she said you were foaming at the mouth to do it. She said it was still on."

Brian gave her an incredulous look. "She told you about this? That little witch." Shaking his head, he stared across the room. "I even looked at her asshole for her, and she —"

"You looked at her ass?" Her eyes widened.

He replied casually, "Yeah, she just wanted me to check how hairy she was getting."

Jillian nodded matter-of-factly and then looked confused. "Wait... what?"

He ignored the question. "I wonder what the hell she's planning. If she's lying about this, maybe she's trying to get us both in some —"

After exhaling deeply, Jillian said, "I know exactly what she's planning."

"You do. What is it?"

"I have a confession of my own." She gave him a sorrowful look as she asked hesitantly, "So, how'd it go yesterday when you, uh, tried to make that replica of your penis?"

Brian's face dropped. "She told you!"

Jillian nodded. "Did you hurt yourself?"

He scoffed. "Almost."

"She did something to your kit."

"Holy shit. Are you serious?" Brian asked as he sat up on the edge of the mattress.

"Yes, she did. She changed the directions, or something."

With the gears turning in his brain, Brian's face morphed into one of realization. "She wants to help me make this thing. I *knew* she was up to something."

"Did you really?"

"Well, no, but—" he admitted, feeling like a giant idiot.

She paused a moment. "You know that policewoman thing was ninety-nine percent her idea also."

"She told me it was mostly your idea."

Nodding, not at all surprised, she added casually, "She lied. And I'll bet this hot tub thing was her idea."

"It was!"

"She was going to parade you out in front of everyone with an erection... somehow."

He shook his head and took a deep breath. "We're a couple of morons, and she's this genius puppet master. We're just pawns in her little evil game."

"She's a little bored. She's not getting laid."

Brian narrowed his eyes. "I don't give a shit if she's not getting any action. She shouldn't go around screwing with people like this. She needs another freaking hobby."

Jillian nodded her head in agreement as they stared at each other, both feeling stupid. As the anger boiled up in Brian, she looked away, contemplating their options.

He said, "I'm going over there right now to give her—"

"No."

"Why not?" He stared at her gape-mouthed.

Returning an evil grin, Jillian said, "Don't say anything to her. She wants you over there on Saturday, right?"

"Yeah." He gave her a confused look.

"Here's what we're going to do..."

Brian was all ears.

Over the next few days, Jillian and Brian spent hours planning their mission, code-named Operation Erection Shield. The name was Brian's idea; since the previous one was called Erection Storm, it just made sense.

Jillian avoided seeing Victoria for the entire week because she feared, in person, she would probably give something away. She did, however, spend a lot of time on the phone with the pregnant schemer as they plotted the events of Victoria's original master plan.

11

That Friday afternoon in Philadelphia, Caroline fidgeted in her seat, bored out of her mind as her professor droned on about social media's impact on marketing in the Internet age. Pulling her phone from her purse, she checked the time. Still fifteen minutes to go. She scrolled through pictures and stopped on an image of Jim, shirtless, playing tennis. She stared closely at his firm, muscular, sweaty body as she ran her tongue around her lips. The previous night, they were supposed to do it but didn't. They ended up falling asleep instead, but now she wasn't tired, and she wanted to do it. She really wanted to do it.

Switching to her messaging screen, she sent Jim a text, asking what he was doing and telling him she missed him.

Caroline glanced up at the professor and pretended to listen as she waited for Jim's reply. After a few minutes and no response, she sent another text, this one detailing exactly what she wanted to be doing with him right at that moment. Closing her eyes, she began to fantasize about her steamy message while she unconsciously and slowly ground her hips into the chair. After a few minutes, she pulled herself back to reality and glanced around the room to be sure no one was staring at her.

Finding no one the wiser, she sat up straight and let out a long, slow breath. With a naughty fire in her eyes, she sent one last graphically explicit message about what she was going to do to him when she returned to the apartment in just ten short minutes. He was instructed to be ready.

In the apartment they shared, Jim was wearing only a towel as he sat on the sofa, wearing a big smile in the midst of a phone conversation with Victoria. She had just finished telling him all about the trick she and Jillian were planning to play on Brian. He couldn't believe his brother was actually falling for it, and he promised not to give it away if they spoke. Next they discussed the recent checkup with her OB GYN and how both baby and mother were doing fine. Jim had ignored the three beeps he received for new text messages, as he was engrossed in Victoria's captivating story.

After sharing what he and Caroline were up to lately, Victoria started telling him about her experience with the two lacrosse players in the bar and her attempt to help Lisa lose her virginity. It was at this time that Caroline strolled through the door.

Taking in the vision of Jim sitting on the sofa wearing only a towel, she grinned, thinking he got her messages and that he had cleaned himself up properly in order to experience the pleasure she'd spelled out in her final text. Upon hearing him laugh out loud, she glanced up to his ear, saw he was on the phone, and frowned a bit. He smiled at her with a quick motion that indicted to give him a minute, and Caroline slumped down in a chair, tossing her backpack beside her.

Jim widened his eyes as he said, "Oh, Victoria. No, you—"

"Is everything okay?" Caroline asked, concerned.

He ignored her as he listened intently. Caroline moved to the edge of her seat.

Jim asked, "What the hell were you doing in the men's bathroom?"

After listening, he shook his head with his jaw gaping. Caroline stared at him now, both confused and worried.

"What's going on? Is she okay? Is the baby okay?"

"He said what...? No.... Okay, yeah." Keeping the phone to his ear, he looked at Caroline with a dizzied expression and said softly, "She put me on hold for a second. Her tea water is boiling or... Sorry, I'm almost done. She's in the middle of this story."

"Is everything okay with the baby?" Caroline asked.

"Oh, yeah."

"And she's fine, too?"

"Sure."

"Thank God."

"She's just telling me all these stories about--" Jim held his finger up to her once more as Victoria returned to the phone. Caroline exhaled deeply before slumping back into the chair.

He giggled as he listened intently. Caroline stared out the window at nothing in particular as her frustration grew.

"No way! The police... Sure, I remember Officer Williams."

Caroline frowned. She stared at Jim as he glanced back at her with a look that screamed he wanted to tell her all about this. At that moment, she couldn't care less.

Moving to the edge of her seat, she whispered, "Did you get my texts?"

He narrowed his eyes at her, and she repeated the question.

"Hold on a second," Jim said into the phone before pulling it away and covering it with his hand. Giving Caroline his complete attention, he asked, "What?"

"You didn't get my text messages, did you?"

"No, sorry. I heard the beeps, but I've been so... Sorry. I swear, I'm almost done. Two minutes."

"Sure."

Jim put the phone back to his ear. "I'm back."

After listening a moment, he chuckled then asked, "They were both naked?"

With her jealously slowly boiling over, Caroline rose from the chair and walked to him while wearing a sexy expression. Slipping to her knees in front of him, she placed her hands on his towel, and Jim looked at her, surprised.

"They didn't take them to jail, did they?" Jim asked.

Caroline pulled the towel open and gazed down at his manhood lying there sparkling clean and flaccid against his thigh. She licked her lips, grinned and then plunged her head down.

With his eyes widened and his jaw slackened, Jim stared down at her in disbelief.

"Uh-huh," he muttered into the phone. "What was that?"

His eyes locked on Caroline's head as she worked her magic over his quickly responding penis. "Oh, yeah. That's really, uh, crazy stuff."

Caroline slipped a finger under a particularly sensitive area and Jim cried out, "Caroline!"

Startled, his eyes opened wide. "Um, yes, she just walked in... um, okay hold on."

He covered the phone with his hand, swallowed hard, and then said, "She wants to speak with you."

Tilting her head up with her mouth still occupied, her eyes met his. She shook her head slightly no, and he stared down, mesmerized at the sight of her enthusiastically doing what she was doing.

Caroline quickly plunged her head down, taking more of him unto her mouth and leaving him struggling to breathe. He looked at the phone, confused, then placed it back to his ear. "Uh, she can't talk right now, she's... Actually, I kinda really need to go. I have this thing that, uh.... Okay.... Bye."

Abruptly, he ended the call and stared down at her dreamily. A few minutes later, when she had finished him off, her eyes traveled up to his face. "You really shouldn't ignore my texts."

He nodded quickly in wholehearted agreement as he struggled to catch his breath.

12

The next day in Miami, Jillian and Brian spent the day at home, poring over the final details of Operation Erection Shield. At 3:00 p.m. they headed up to the bedroom for some last-minute preparations, as in, repeated sex, designed to render Brian's penis un-erectable. Then at 3:52 p.m., Jillian gave him one last *preparation* as he stood with his back pressed against the front door. Brian held on for dear life with his mouth wide open, letting out a silent scream as Jillian brought him to orgasm, albeit a small and mostly painfully strained one, for the fifth time inside of an hour. He was literally and figuratively spent.

She stood and wiped her lips as he zipped up while panting like he'd just completed a marathon. Jillian opened her mouth wide and shifted her jaw from side to side to work out a kink before she glanced up at him and smiled. "That should do it."

Squeezing his groin suggestively, he gave her a sexy smile. "I don't know. I might need just one more."

She simply shook her head ruefully and scoffed.

"I'm kidding."

"Just get the heck out of here."

Brian opened the door and stumbled out. On the porch, he wobbled a little before turning back to her. "I'm dizzy." He shook his head and widened his eyes as he clutched his chest.

Jillian frowned. "Geez, you guys complain that you don't get enough sex, and then when you do you—"

"I'm not complaining. I just probably should have made sure my will was in order before we did all that. If I go down during the walk over there, just remember I love you."

"I love you, too. Now go, or you're going to be late."

Moving to her, he gave her a kiss.

She asked, "You have the pill?"

He patted his pants pocket and then smiled. "I do."

"Good luck."

He turned and headed down the path toward the street, weaving a little. A bit concerned, she watched him and called out, "Be careful crossing the street."

Ten minutes later, Brian was fully nude and sitting over a towel on a chair in Victoria's bedroom with a completely flaccid penis. He was working it and working it without result as she prepared the kit in the bathroom.

Victoria poked her head through the doorway. "Ready?"

"Not yet."

She narrowed her eyes as she failed to see what she was expecting and checked her watch. "Hurry up."

Victoria disappeared into the bathroom for thirty seconds then rushed out and asked, "Anything yet?"

"No, I'm sorry. I don't know what—"

Storming over to him, she got down on her knees. She stared down at his pathetically unresponsive, shrunken penis and lightly tapped it with the back of her hand. "What the hell is wrong with you?"

"I don't know. Maybe we could try it another time."

Victoria stood and rubbed her chin. "No, it's got to be today, or it won't be ready for her birthday party next week."

"Why not? It only needs, like, two days to set up right?"

"Um..." She stammered as the gears in her head turned. "That's right, but I'm completely slammed the next few days with school and just everything that—"

"Okay, okay," he interrupted while fighting back a grin.

"Wait. I think I have something that might help."

She rushed over to her night table, opened the drawer, and began pulling out various sex paraphernalia. He grinned and nearly broke into laughter while he stared at her back as she pulled out items one by one: a dildo, handcuffs, condoms, another dildo, and then, finally, a spray bottle. "Okay, here it is. Wait, no... this is desensitizing spray. You definitely don't need that."

When she returned her attention to him, his smile morphed into a frown, and he began pulling on his penis again.

"I think, uh, I felt something." He glanced up at her and nodded. "Yeah, maybe."

"Really?" she asked hopefully.

"Yeah, I think it's starting to happen."

She took a few steps toward him and glanced down at it with her eyes narrowed. "It looks the same to me."

"No, I felt it... really."

She widened her eyes. "Why don't you just take the Viagra?"

He shook his head. "No way. Last time I nearly ended up in the hospital. Do you know they need to stick a needle in your penis to drain the blood when that happens? I'm not having a needle shoved into it. No way!"

"Oh, you big baby."

Victoria frowned as she stared down at him. Brian kept jerking his completely flaccid and thoroughly overworked penis. He was pretty sure that Jillian's repeated attention made it virtually impossible for him to attain another erection for hours, possibly days.

She glanced at her watch before staring back down at his manhood and shaking her head in frustration. "Pathetic." She widened her eyes. "You had sex today, didn't you? I told you not to."

"No, I swear."

She gave him a skeptical look. "When's the last time you did it then?"

"Like three days ago. I'm just nervous. Maybe because I almost hurt myself last time."

"I told you, this is a new kit. They assured me—"

"Wait, I have an idea." He gave her a confident smile. "When I was over here last week, and I watched you through the window, touching yourself, that was so hot."

She gave him a hesitant look. "Yeah...?"

"Maybe if you do that in front of me, I could, you know, get it up."

"Seriously." She exhaled and just stared at him.

He nodded. "It's worth a try, isn't it?"

"I don't think that—"

"Okay, then." Brian stood. "How about if I come back tomorrow in the morning? Then we can—"

"Just sit your ass back down," Victoria shot back.

Turing away from her, he covered his mouth to keep from laughing out loud. When he could finally contain himself, he sat down and continued to tug on his unresponsive manhood. Victoria slipped her skirt and panties off as she shook her head in disbelief. She still wore her blouse but was naked from the waist down as she climbed into bed only five feet from his chair. He watched as she pulled the David replica from her nightstand. She took a moment to study it before slipping it in her mouth to moisten it with saliva.

For a moment, Victoria became fully immersed in giving passionate head to the replica until she spotted Brian's wide-eyed stare. Then she quickly pulled it from her lips, looked at him as if almost embarrassed, and said, "Sorry."

It was just about the sexiest thing Brian had ever seen, and he swore he actually felt his exhausted penis move as he half-heartedly massaged it.

"Are you ready?"

"Yeah."

She glared at him. "Concentrate, okay?"

He watched Victoria move the sizeable replica down between her legs with her eyes tightly closed. He mindlessly worked himself as he stared at her, mesmerized. He was married, but he wasn't dead.

When he glanced down to find his penis growing, he pulled his hand away from it and attempted to focus on something else. He glanced at the ceiling but quickly returned his eyes to her, finding it incredibly difficult to look away as Victoria went on, blindly engrossed in pleasing herself as if he weren't even there.

Slipping the dildo inside her, she held it still a moment while blowing out a long slow breath. When she opened her eyes and found his hand nowhere near his penis, she gave him an angry look. "Hey, Brian, what the fuck are you doing?"

He grimaced and pretended to work a kink out of his right hand. "Sorry, I uh... my hand was cramping."

"You do have two hands."

He smiled uncomfortably, began working himself with his left hand, and replied, "I think I'm starting to feel something."

Victoria glanced down at his lap and noticed a definite increase in size. She gave him a satisfied smile before closing her eyes and getting back to work. She took a long, deep breath, held it, and when she exhaled, she moaned loudly. She stared at him and said in an almost scary voice, "God, I really miss a real cock... I really miss it."

He believed her. He really fucking believed her. His penis twitched excitedly, and his eyes widened as he watched her closely.

"This is okay, but nothing like the real—" Victoria lost her train of thought as she pushed the dildo as far into her as she could.

Finding himself totally caught up in her sexy show, Brian stopped moving his hand completely. He stared for another few seconds then shook his head to pull himself back to reality. He shielded his eyes as he repeated the mantra in his head: Stick to the plan, stick to the plan.

After collecting his thoughts, he took a deep breath and began the final phase of his mission. He began moving his hand over his manhood again, but faster now as he said, "Yeah this is doing it, but could you take off the rest of your clothes? I really think if I saw you completely naked, that would help."

Victoria glared at him. "Are you serious?"

"Yeah." He painted on an apologetic look.

Sighing, she dropped the dildo to the bed, quickly unbuttoned her blouse, and removed it, along with her sexy bra. Brian swallowed hard while thinking, I should have gone for that sixth orgasm, after all.

Victoria went back to work with the dildo and Brian looked down at his erection, which was at half-mast and climbing. She glanced over to him as well, noticed his condition, and smiled. "Good, it's working."

"Would you mind turning around, so I could see your ass?"

Victoria was so caught up in her activities that she followed his command without giving it a second thought. Turning around, she held the dildo against the mattress as she adjusted her position and gradually slipped on top of it. Slowly she began riding it up and down. He stared at her, getting lost in the show.

He whispered, "Holy fuck," with his eyes locked on the amazing sight and his erection closing in on three quarters full. And while this was an image of Victoria he would never forget, he almost forgot what he was supposed to do next. He watched her bouncing up and down in a trance-like state until Victoria craned her neck toward him and asked breathlessly, "How are you doing?"

"Uh, okay."

Then it hit him. He said, "I, uh, think I need to take the Viagra."

"Good," she moaned. "It's right over there on the dresser."

Brian walked over and grabbed the pill and the bottle of water as Victoria kept going without skipping a beat. Returning to the chair, he slipped the Viagra in his pocket and pulled out the replacement pill. He somehow maintained his composure, even though he found himself unable to look away from Victoria's spectacular live demonstration.

He asked, "Could you do one more thing for me?"

"Uh-huh," she replied while barely paying attention to him.

"Would you finger your ass? That would really —"

"What?" Victoria turned to glance at him.

"Your ass. Would you finger it a little?"

She noticed he was fully hard and grinned. She was still caught up in her own fantasy at that moment, turned away from him, and simply replied, "Okay."

Brian watched as she bent over further and slipped her other hand behind her back and between her legs. He stared in awe as she ran a finger between her legs with the dildo still in position. Slipping it in, she drenched it with her juice. Victoria moaned loudly, and Brian watched the action closely, suddenly feeling his mouth full of saliva. Like a drooling dog, he ran his tongue around his teeth and then swallowed hard. Brian glanced down at his now-massive erection and then back to her as she slowly moved her finger to her ass.

"Wow," he murmured, as he felt his heart pounding out of his chest. He gasped, finding that he now also needed to remind himself to breathe. Slapping himself in the face, he fought to break free of her spell, but when Victoria circled her finger around her seam, Brian leaned closer to the action. She slipped her finger inside and moaned quietly while she continued pumping her hips up and down.

Completely captivated, Brian watched Victoria but somehow now remembered to both swallow and breathe. He was still working his manhood, and he began feeling the heat rising up through his erection as if he were about to climax.

He stopped touching himself, glanced down at his penis, and then shook his brain free from the trance. His eyes shot wide open as he remembered what the hell he was supposed to be doing. After quickly popping the replacement pill into his mouth, he reached for the bottle. He took a tiny swig of water just as Victoria's body shuddered with the release of a huge orgasm. She pushed her face into the mattress to avoid screaming out loud as her body convulsed wildly.

Brian chewed the pill up in his mouth, and the foaming quickly began. He grinned and then collapsed on the floor with a loud thump that sent Victoria popping up on her knees and looking around the room, struggling to get her bearings. Her eyes first went to the chair, but she didn't see him. She called, "Brian?"

She heard moaning and followed it to the source. Glancing down, she discovered him on the floor with white foam dripping from his mouth. He was shaking like he was in the midst of a seizure.

"Oh, fuck." She jumped off the bed and knelt next to him. It was all he could do to stay in character as he fought to not open his eyes and burst into laughter. Victoria put her head to his chest and then rushed to her feet.

"Shit, shit... fuck," she mumbled quietly. Then she screamed, "Call 911!" as she headed to the bedroom door and grabbed her blouse along the way.

Thirty-seven of Victoria's closest friends waited in the living room, which was decorated all in pink and blue for her baby shower. They all watched, grinning, as the red-faced and panting panic-stricken woman tore into the room, attempting to cover her naked body with a tiny blouse, which she held over her breasts. The garment was nowhere near up to the task. As the stunning pregnant beauty bounced up and down on her feet with her hand shaking nervously, the men in attendance stared open-mouthed while the women looked on jealously.

"Did someone call 911?" Victoria yelled out without noticing the themed decorations.

Jillian tried her best to act surprised. "What the hell happened?"

"It's Brian... I think he's having a heart attack or a seizure or something."

"What?"

"He took a Viagra, and I found him on the floor, and he —"

"No, I didn't." Brian said cheerfully as he appeared behind her, fully-clothed and wearing a huge grin.

Victoria turned to him quickly in absolute shock, which delivered the crowd a view of her bare ass. She stared at him a moment with the gears turning in her head. "Brian, how the..." Her jaw dropped as the realization hit her, and she turned to Jillian.

Jillian wore a huge smile, as she said, "Don't mess with us."

Brian patted Victoria's bottom as he headed past her to Jillian and repeated, "Yeah, don't mess with us."

Victoria broke into a chuckle as she clutched the blouse to her chest.

Brian added, "Nice ass Victoria."

"Thanks," Victoria replied as she shook her head and fought back her laughter.

Jillian said, "Now, hurry up and get dressed. You don't want to miss your baby shower."

"You guys... you guys are good." Smiling, Victoria took in the decorated room. A tear fell from her eye as she nodded to her guests. "This is really nice." She glanced down almost self consciously and then held her head high. "If I knew you all were coming, I would have dressed up."

The crowd broke into a laugh and Victoria added, "Now if you'll excuse me, I'll be back in a few minutes. I probably should at least put on some underwear for this."

She turned and walked slowly and unabashedly to her bedroom as everyone looked on wearing bright smiles.

Twenty minutes later, Victoria slipped out of her room looking drop dead gorgeous as she joined the first baby shower ever to be kicked off with a live sex show and fake heart attack, and featuring semi-frontal and full 'backal' nudity from its guest of honor. Jillian was able to convert her birthday party into a perfectly-catered and fabulous affair for her best friend in less than a week. Everyone had a wonderful time, and despite the inappropriate start, Victoria received all completely baby shower appropriate gifts.

After the party, Brian sat between Victoria and Jillian on the large sofa. He had one foot of each of his favorite women in his hand. Both women's eyes were fluttering dreamily as he worked his magic fingers over their aching heels.

Victoria said, "No wonder you married him."

"I know. He gives the best foot rubs," Jillian replied.

Brian said, "So, Victoria, no hard feelings about the whole production today?"

She glared at him a moment and then broke into a chuckle. "No, none."

Jillian asked, "Do you think we can call a truce? Planning all this stuff is exhausting."

"Truce." Victoria nodded.

"Definitely truce for me," Brian added.

Jillian stared at Victoria with a serious expression. "Really, can we stop all this, before someone has a real heart attack or gets arrested?"

"I'm done. I swear. I'm lucky I didn't go into labor today. I have a baby coming, and I'll need to be a more responsible person."

"You really should," Brian joked.

Victoria grinned. "Oh, and you're such a proper adult. Who was it directing me to finger my ass earlier?"

Brian's eyes widened and he turned his face slowly to Jillian.

Jillian said, "He what?"

"I thought you planned all this with him. Now that I think about it, it all seemed pretty rehearsed with getting me to turn away so you could pretend to take the Viagra."

"I was pretty good in there," Brian said a little too proudly for Jillian's taste.

"Back to her ass," Jillian said.

"Uh, yes," Brian replied.

"I thought you were going to do it exactly like we said."

"I was, but I had an inspiration and I just went with it."

Victoria smiled. "I'm glad he did. That was a nice touch, Bri."

"Thanks." He looked at Jillian. "You can't really be mad about this. I mean, you mapped the whole thing out with me getting her naked and to 'do' herself, and just because I brought her ass into the mix—"

Jillian cracked up. "I'm just messing with you..." Her expression changed to deadly serious. "Just don't do it again."

Brian trembled a little. "I won't."

Victoria shook her head. "You two are way too cute. I could just eat you both up."

13

Brian and Jillian lounged on the sofa in the great room, watching television. On screen Darcy Gray, justice-themed interview/debate show host, appeared, sitting in front of the camera with her big hair and signature bright pastel-colored pleather jacket. On this night, Darcy's jacket of choice was a loud sea foam green.

"Bombshell tonight in the Brookhart v. Grayson and New Perennial Press lawsuit. Brookhart's attorney, Josh Roth, has successfully argued to have the defendants split into separate trials. He wanted his shot at Jillian Grayson first with plans to go after her publishing company at a later date. Ms. Grayson's novel, The Leg Thing, has been number one on the Amazon and USA Today bestseller lists for the past ninety-eight days. It's sold millions of copies and has truly been a runaway success. With us tonight is attorney Joe Whitaglia."

Jillian said, "I can't believe she already knows the trials were split."

The image shifted to where Darcy's frowning face occupied half the screen, while in one quarter appeared an image of a Joe wearing a suit, and the final quarter showed a loop of the St. Barts wedding video where Brian punched Albert Brooks in the jaw.

Joe began, "I think this is a smart move Darcy –"

"Hold on," Darcy interrupted. "This is my favorite part."

Darcy grinned at the camera as the punch was replayed with Albert tumbling to the grass after Brian decked him.

In the Grayson home, Jillian grabbed Brian's hand. "There you are again. I never get tired of watching that, either."

Darcy said, "Sorry, Joe. Please continue."

Joe said, "Yes, Darcy, I think this is a smart move. I believe that Roth fully expects to win against Ms. Grayson and will then use that result to force the publishing company into a huge settlement."

"Sounds like a risky strategy to me," Darcy replied.

Joe began, "Not really. I believe he has a good chance to win a huge judgment against Ms. Grayson, and if he somehow loses this initial trial, separating the trials gives him a shot to regroup and give it another go against the publishing company. It's a win-win for Miss Brookhart and a nightmare for the defense."

"Thank you, Joe."

"Any time, Darcy."

Darcy's face now occupied three quarters of the screen with the Brian Nash punch video filling the remaining quarter. When Albert again hit the ground, Darcy shook her head and smiled dreamily.

"If only Ms. Grayson were facing a criminal trial. Why, then she might serve some jail time, and I'd have my shot at the gorgeous hero, Brian Nash."

Jillian growled, "Hey."

Brian blushed. "Well, I'm not really a hero."

Darcy said, "Good luck with your upcoming trial, Ms. Grayson. My thoughts and prayers will be with you and that husband of yours." She *winked at the camera and then added, "Just kidding about stealing your man, but I'll say it again, make sure you treat him right."*

Narrowing her eyes at the screen, Jillian grabbed the remote and turned off the television. She said, "Can you believe the nerve of that woman?" She turned to Brian, who now wore an arrogant smile.

"She's just joking around."

"Yeah, I'll bet," Jillian said sarcastically.

"But it's not bad advice, you know."

"What?"

"Treating me right, because sometimes you ignore me and, uh..."

Jillian grinned, tossed the remote to the cushion and slipped to her knees in front of him. "What kind of treatment, exactly, do you need?"

"Um, well—"

He shut his mouth when Jillian moved her hand to his zipper and pulled it down slowly as she said, "Do you need this kind of treatment?"

"That's, uh, great kind of treatment."

Brian leaned back and put his hands behind his head as Jillian extracted his equipment and began working it with both hands.

She said, "That woman really has me angry. I've got a good mind to call in to the show some night and let her have it."

Brian glanced back to Jillian, who now wore a determined look as she angrily worked over his shaft. He grinned. "Go with that emotion. You really are much more passionate when you're angry."

"Yeah," Jillian replied as she began moving her hand faster and faster over him.

Just to egg her on, Brian stammered, "She's completely out of line... um... here you are..." He sighed, closed his eyes caught up in the intense pleasure Jillian was delivering then glanced back to her and continued, "... um, facing a major trial and..."

Staring at him with her passion boiling over, Jillian shook her head and sneered.

Brian teased, "... and this Darcy Gray woman is threatening to, uh, steal me from you. It's not right at—"

He shut up when Jillian plunged her mouth over him.

After just over six minutes of expertly performed super passionate oral pleasure, Jillian rose to her feet, wiped the corner of her mouth and stared down at Brian, wearing a proud smile. "Send Darcy a video of that!"

Glancing up at her with his eyes glassy and while struggling to catch his breath, all Brian could mutter was, "Huh?"

"Never mind. Do you still feel neglected?"

"Uh-uh." He shook his head no. "Wow, where did you learn that swirly thing there at the end?"

Jillian plopped down next to him on the sofa, exhausted. "I read an article in some women's magazine."

He nodded quickly. "That was amazing." He slid off the sofa and unbuttoned her shorts.

Giving him a look, she muttered, "Uh, what are you doing?"

"Returning the favor."

She shook her head with a grimace.

"Really?" he asked.

She returned an apologetic nod. "Sorry, I just don't feel like it."

"Since when don't you feel like having me lick you? You usually beg for—"

She snapped, "I just don't feel like it, okay?"

"Alright, sorry." He moved to sit next to her. "I just thought it might help relax you. You've got to meet with the lawyers tomorrow, and—"

"You know, sometimes I just want to please you. You don't always have to be shoving your tongue places."

"Geez, okay. Got it." He turned away, frowning.

Regretting her harsh tone, she tried to repair the damage. "It's not you... it's just... I don't know."

Turing back to her, he painted on a sympathetic smile. "I understand."

"I think I'm going to go up to bed."

"It's only nine."

"I'm just tired."

He was unsure whether to offer to go up with her or not. After studying her expression, he asked hesitantly, "You want me to give you a back rub or anything?"

She gave him a half-hearted smile. "No, but thanks."

"Okay, I'll be up later."

After he watched her walk out of the room, he rubbed his hands over his face, slumped into the sofa, and began mindlessly channel surfing as he thought of nothing other than Jillian.

Over the next three weeks, Jillian became more and more engrossed in her case. She spent hours at her lawyer's office, going over strategy and her upcoming deposition testimony. In between meetings, she was flying off to do book signings and interviews with the media, and she was up to her neck in all sorts of book promotion tasks. This left little time for writing or spending time with Brian. The two definitely didn't have time for tennis together during this time, so Brian took to hitting against the ball machine in order to work out some of his pent-up frustration.

During the times that the newlyweds were intimate, Jillian didn't feel at all like herself. She still wasn't in the mood for Brian's tongue between her thighs. She just didn't feel right down there and worried something was medically wrong. After two visits with her gynecologist, who ran a battery of tests, she was given a clean bill of health.

Relieved nothing was physically wrong, she arranged an intimate night, featuring wine and candles, with her husband. Things went well until they slipped up to the bedroom, where she begged Brian to go down on her. She lasted less than a minute before pulling away and nearly bursting into laughter.

Apologizing profusely, she used the excuse that she shouldn't have taken such a hot bath that day and promised to make it up to him. Her solution was to shower him with a lot of her own oral attention, but he found that it was a poor substitute for the satisfaction he received in delivering to her what he thought was the ultimate pleasure. He missed the connection that they used to share and knew something wasn't quite right, although he found it a little hard to complain with his gorgeous wife's lips wrapped around his manhood.

Upon reflection, he concluded that since Jillian's deposition was scheduled for the next afternoon, her nerves were simply getting the best of her. And that night, as he struggled to sleep, thoughts of his own early-morning deposition clouded his mind.

14

The next morning at 10:00 a.m., Brian sat in a conference room with Jillian and her attorney, Stanley Parrish, on one side of the table. On the other side, Josh Roth sat next to the scowling Natalie Brookhart. At the head of the table was a young and attractive stenographer with her pad ready.

After a few minutes of softball questions, Josh asked, "Mr. Nash, at the start of the Fall semester in your sophomore year, did you meet a woman named Ann Brown?"

Brian gave Josh a surprised look and stammered, "Um, yes."

"Could you characterize your relationship with Miss Brown?"

"We had actually met the previous year. We sat together with friends in the dining hall and that kind of thing."

"So, you were friends?"

"Yes."

"Uh-huh." Josh nodded. "Was there any night in particular when your relationship with Miss Brown changed, became more intimate, perhaps?"

Brian glanced around the table nervously, first to Stanley, who was staring down at a note pad, and then to Jillian, who returned a supportive smile. He turned back to Josh and began, "We, um, were at a bar with a group of people and then ended up talking a lot that night."

"And afterward?" Josh asked with his eyes widened.

"Afterward... I walked her back to campus, and I believe she went back to her dorm."

"You didn't stop at your suite first?" Josh fired back accusatorily.

Swallowing hard, Brian glanced at Natalie, who was grinning evilly at him. He looked down to the table. "How do you know about that?"

"Just answer the question, Mr. Nash."

"How is this even remotely related to the trial?"

Stanley asked, "Mr. Roth, where are you going with this?"

"We're just trying to explore a little of Mr. Nash's dating life prior to his relationship with my client."

Stanley exhaled deeply. "Brian, please answer the question."

"We did go back to my suite."

Josh smiled. "And you rushed her into your room. Is that correct?"

"Well, yes."

"And what happened then?"

"Nothing, really. She left pretty quickly."

"Why'd she leave?"

"I'm not sure."

Josh gave him an impatient look. "Isn't it true, Mr. Nash, that Miss Brown rushed out of your dorm room after you quickly stripped off all your clothes and exposed yourself to her?"

Jillian stared at Brian in mild shock as Natalie covered her mouth to keep from laughing out loud.

Brian began, "Hey, look, we were both drunk. Like, really drunk, and I don't remember everything that happened at the bar, but we were getting along really well, and we must have both been feeling like we wanted to, you know, so..." He glanced toward Natalie's bright-eyed expression then shot back, "Look, it's not like I was date raping her or anything. She just left. I didn't touch her."

"While you were stripping all your clothes off, was Miss Brown doing the same?"

Brian answered in a tired voice. "No."

"So, you exposed yourself to Miss Brown, and she ran away, terrified."

"I wouldn't say she was terrified." Brian scoffed.

"So, was she laughing, then?" Josh asked calmly.

Brian glared at him. "No. I don't think she was laughing either."

Brian looked at Stanley, who widened his eyes and cleared his throat. "Mr. Roth, could you please move on?"

"Sure." Josh glanced down to his legal pad. "Mr. Nash, at the end of your sophomore year, did you meet a woman named Jessica Bell?"

Brian searched his memory for a moment then replied, "I'm not sure."

"You met her at a bar..." Josh glanced down to his legal pad. "Chubby's. And it was the night after the last final exams. You accompanied Miss Bell back to her apartment, isn't that correct?"

Brian paused a moment to run his hands through his hair. "Yes, I think I remember Jessica."

"What happened when you returned to Miss Bell's apartment?"

"We, um, had sex."

"And you had never met Miss Bell before that night, correct?"

Brian returned a sarcastic look. "Yes, it's what you call a one-night stand."

"Thank you," Josh replied snidely. "The next morning, Miss Bell claims that she was awakened to find you on top of her and having sex with her again."

"That's not true."

"So you didn't have sex with her again in the morning?"

"We did."

"While she was asleep?" Josh shot back.

"No, she wasn't asleep!"

"Do you often rape women in their sleep?" Josh asked casually.

"I didn't rape her. Jesus, where are you getting this information?"

Josh stared down at his legal pad. "We interviewed Miss Bell, and she said, quote, 'I woke up to find him inside of me, like, pumping away, and I was hungover, and I could barely feel him.'" He glanced up at Brian, grinning, and then returned to the pad. "She went on to say, 'I probably would have stopped him, but I just wanted to get it over with and get him out of there.'"

Stanley frowned. "Is there a question in there somewhere?"

Josh replied, "We're just trying to establish a pattern of Mr. Nash forcing himself upon women and being aggressive."

"I was never aggressive with any women." He sighed. "Look, I was a shy guy. For some reason, usually at the start and end of each school year I would somehow get lucky and, you know, meet someone. And yes, we usually met at a bar, and yes, I was usually drunk, but I never forced anyone to do anything."

"Alright, Mr. Nash," Josh said.

Brian looked at Josh in shock. "You're not planning on bringing all this up during the trial, are you?" Without waiting for a response, he looked to Stanley and asked, "He can't ask me all this at the trial, can he?"

Josh interrupted, "We may very well explore these issues at trial."

Stanley looked at Brian. "They'll be required to submit a witness list prior to trial, so there won't be any surprises." Then he turned to Josh. "Do you have anything else for Mr. Nash?"

Josh glanced down to his pad, and Natalie leaned in as Josh pointed to a line near the bottom. Natalie stretched up to whisper in his ear. He nodded, and they shared a grin.

Brian stared at them. Concerned and craning his neck to get a look at the pad, he whined, "Who else do you want to ask me about? Come on."

Josh glanced up to him with a grin. "Uh, I think that's all we have for now on your previous relationships."

"Good."

Opening a folder, Josh pulled out a photo and slid it over to Brian. It was a full-color image of a naked man hiding behind a tree. It was slightly grainy and shot from above, but it was unmistakably Brian.

Brian's jaw dropped. He pushed the photo toward Jillian, and her eyes widened as she took it in.

"Is that a picture of you?" Josh asked matter-of-factly. "It looks just like you."

"Um, I, uh..." Brian stammered.

"Take your time, Mr. Nash. Here, I have another. In this one you can see the street sign that's just a block away from your house." Fighting back a grin, Josh added. "If it's not you, it's someone who looks an awful lot like you." He slid toward Brian the second photo, which showed the street sign clearly.

"How did you obtain these pictures?" Stanley asked.

"Let's just say that one of Ms. Grayson's neighbors is an active member of the neighborhood watch committee, has a very expensive security system, isn't a big fan of Ms. Grayson's books, and really hates her neighbor's landscaping choices."

Jillian's jaw dropped. "What's wrong with my landscaping?"

Opening his hands, Brian shot her an incredulous look.

"Sorry," Jillian replied.

Stanley glanced at the photo for a moment before pushing it away, embarrassed. All eyes returned to Brian and he nervously scanned the faces at the table.

"Is that you in the photo, Mr. Nash?" Josh asked.

Closing his eyes tight, Brian exhaled, paused and then began, "We were locked out of the house, okay? And I was walking, actually running, to Jillian's friend's house to get the key, and—"

"Do you often run around naked through the neighborhood?"

"What? No, we... What? No, I..."

Josh grinned. "Wait, I have one more." He pulled out another picture. This one was a close-up of frightened, tiny male genitalia.

"Was it cold that night, Mr. Nash?" Letting the picture fall from his hand, it slid across the table until Brian slapped his hand down on top of it. Natalie let out a loud chuckle as Brian stared down at the picture in horror.

Slowly, his angry glare traveled up to Josh's face. "Cold... I'll show you how cold it..." Biting his lip, Brian cut off that thought. It took everything he had to not dive across the table and choke the life out of Natalie's weasel attorney.

Josh widened his eyes and pushed his chair away from the table. Stanley put his hands up. "I object to this. There is no way you are introducing these pictures at trial."

"We'll see what the judge has to say about that," Josh announced.

"He can't show these in court, can he?" Brian pleaded to Stanley.

"Don't worry about this. I'll take care of it," Stanley said.

Clearing his throat, Brian looked at the stenographer. "Um, I'd just like to note for the record that I'm a grower."

Stanley looked confused, and Jillian nodded enthusiastically. "He really is."

The stenographer stared back like a deer in headlights until Brian motioned with his finger for her to actually record his comment. After she finally did, he nodded and almost smiled in celebration of the small victory.

Stanley glared at Josh. "Do you have anything else for Mr. Nash?"

"No, I think that just about does it."

Brian looked around the table, dizzied, before he rubbed his hands over his eyes.

"Who's next, Mr. Roth?" Stanley asked.

"We'd like to depose Ms. Grayson now."

"Fine."

"And we're going to need a lot of time," Josh added.

Sighing, Jillian looked at Brian. He was staring down at the picture of his shrunken manhood. She gave him a sympathetic look. "Brian?"

When he didn't reply, she repeated, "Brian."

"What?"

"You can go home now, if you want. I'll get a ride back with Stanley." Jillian glanced to Stanley, who returned a supportive nod.

Rising slowly from his chair, still shell shocked, Brian said, "Yeah, I think I'll go. Yeah. Okay."

Hours after sunset, when Stanley dropped Jillian off at home, she found Brian in the great room with seven empty beer bottles on the table and one in his hand. She gave him a hesitant look. "Are you okay?"

"Oh, yeah sure. I'm just fine," he shot back, his voice dripping with sarcasm. "How was your deposition? Any naked pictures of you, or—"

"It was a nightmare, but no pictures. I'm so sorry about today."

Jillian slipped down next to him on the sofa. After taking a big sip of beer, Brian motioned to the kitchen counter. "Oh, and we made the local paper."

She cringed. "What's it say?"

"Just that I'm your unemployed, boy-toy, loser husband. There is good news, though, along with some bad news."

Brian took another sip and looked her in the eye, waiting.

Jillian grabbed his beer, finished it off, then asked shyly, "Um, what's the good news?"

"The article doesn't feature a picture of my shrunken penis."

Jillian nodded as if that were actually a victory, albeit a small one. "And the bad news?"

"The story was picked up by CNN, USA Today..." He ran his hand over his face and then added, "Oh, and we're trending on Twitter. I've been getting text messages from friends all night and, uh, I accidentally dropped my phone in the garbage disposal."

"Wow."

"I'll need a new phone."

"Okay."

"And we'll need a new garbage disposal."

"Huh."

"Of course, you'll need to pay for both, because I'm a big, giant, unemployed boy-toy loser."

Placing her hand on his shoulder, Jillian said, "You're not a loser."

Rising up from the sofa, he headed to the kitchen. Seconds later, he returned with another beer and glared at her. "Why can't you just settle this lawsuit? Give her whatever she wants. Shut her up before—"

"I can't."

"Great. So my little flaccid penis picture will be displayed for the jury and then go viral on the Internet, and maybe David Letterman can use it in one of his Top Ten Lists."

"Stanley assured me that the picture would never be admitted into evidence."

"Great," Brian replied sarcastically. "But why can't you settle the lawsuit?"

"Because..."

"Because why?"

"It's great for book sales."

He stared at her, dumbfounded. After taking a big gulp of beer, Brian glared at her. "Book sales."

"Look, I know everything is stressful right now. I've been going crazy with the lawyers, and I've been a little grumpy, but we'll—"

"Grumpy." He glared at her. "This has turned our lives upside down. We don't have sex like we used to. I know we still do it and all, but you used to like when I, you know..."

"What?" She narrowed her eyes.

"When I licked your, you know… The last three weeks, you keep telling me you're ticklish down there, and you've been stopping me after, like, one minute."

Jillian shook her head, defeated. "I'm sorry. I've been in a rut."

"You used to beg me to lick you, and now…"

"I know. I just need some time."

After taking another gulp of beer, Brian frowned at her before staring up at the ceiling. "How many times have we had to cancel the Scottsdale trip? Like, three?"

Closing her eyes, Jillian let out a long, slow breath. "I'm sorry."

"When are we going to go, huh?" Brian shot her a frown.

"Soon, I promise."

"Soon. Great. How about next week?"

"I can't. I have meetings with the lawyers starting tomorrow for the next few days, and then I leave for a book tour."

"Well, just let me know when you want to go. God knows my schedule is wide open."

Jillian looked at him, unable to find the words.

He shrugged. "I'm going to bed."

She widened her eyes and gave him a hopeful smile. "Brian?"

"Yeah."

"You want to lick me tonight? I'll let you do it as long as you want."

Narrowing his eyes at her, he scoffed then walked out of the room without saying another word.

She slumped down on the sofa and shook her head. After staring straight ahead for a moment, her eyes brightened. Her jaw fell open, and she smiled and reached for her phone.

Jillian was up until two in the morning, confirming strategy with her attorney, rearranging her schedule, making reservations, and packing for the both of them. She set the alarm for 10:00 a.m. and slipped into bed next to the snoring Brian, almost too excited to sleep.

The next morning when the alarm blared, Brian groaned and punched the snooze button. Springing from the bed, Jillian smiled at him. "Get up."

"Why?"

"The car will be here in one hour."

"What car?"

"The car to take us to the airport." She climbed in bed and straddled his hips. "Get up."

Fighting his way to consciousness, he glared up at her face. "What the hell are you talking about?"

"We're going to Scottsdale."

"What about your meetings and the book tour?"

"It's all worked out. I've packed everything. We're booked and ready to go."

"Really?" Brian's jaw dropped.

She gave him a bright smile. "And you can lick me all you want on this trip."

"Are you serious?"

"About the trip or about letting you go down on me?" she asked with a grin.

"The trip."

"Yes."

"Great." He narrowed his eyes. "Are you also serious about the you know... ?"

She slipped off the bed, pushed down her panties and replied, "I'm really serious about that. So serious that I need to shave before we go. Now get your ass in the shower."

Grinning, Brian sprang from bed and rushed to the bathroom. Jillian followed right behind.

15

During the ride to the airport, Jillian assured Brian she would not mention the lawsuit during the trip, and she told him she would return to her normal happy self immediately. She promised to keep her legal distractions to a minimum and go back to being his blissfully happy wife. That was exactly what he wanted to hear.

About an hour into the flight, Jillian was staring at the restroom in the front of the first-class section of the plane. She was in the midst of a fantasy featuring their return flight from St. Barts, when they joined the somewhat exclusive Mile High Club. Brian was lazily looking out the window as Jillian turned to him and eyed him up and down. She was wet and horny and desperately wanted to screw her sexy husband in the bathroom again but decided the danger was just too great. Doing it on a plane she had paid to charter was one thing, but banging on a commercial flight was quite another.

Brian turned to her and smiled. "I'm going to read a little." He pulled out his Kindle and fired it up.

"Okay," she murmured, a little disappointed.

Jillian glanced across the aisle at a woman who was sleeping under a blanket, and an idea hit her. She grinned. "Are you cold?"

"Uh, no. Not really."

"I think I'm going to get a blanket."

He nodded and went back to his book as Jillian located a flight attendant. After the plush blanket was delivered, Jillian covered her lap, lifted up the armrest between them, and leaned toward Brian. "You mind if I sleep on your shoulder?"

He shook his head and smiled at her.

"You sure you're not cold?"

"No, I'm fine."

Closing her eyes, Jillian leaned her head up against his shoulder. Her hand slid down to his bare knee, just below the leg hole of his shorts, and she slowly swirled a finger around his inner thigh. Electricity shot through his body, and his brain quickly sent blood down to that general area.

He swallowed hard and opened his mouth to tell her to wait until they were in the hotel, but as Jillian's finger slipped into the leg hole, and she drew little circles over the soft hair on his legs, he instead closed his eyes in order to simply enjoy her touch. Brian glanced nervously around the cabin and breathed a sigh of relief as he realized no one was watching them. He placed his Kindle in his carry-on bag and smiled.

Jillian stretched up to his ear. "Are you sure you aren't cold at all... not even maybe your lap?"

"Why, yes, I am a little cold down there."

She grinned and covered his important parts with the blanket. She glanced over to check if they were being watched, smiled, and returned her head to Brian's shoulder. Moving her hand up to his penis, she felt that it was already nearly hard and let out a long, sexy sigh. Jillian heard rustling in the cabin and quickly pulled her hand from him. A flight attendant rushed by as they both held their breath.

When the coast was clear again, he whispered, "Okay, she's gone."

Jillian returned her hand to his groin. He exhaled softly as she squeezed his bulge carefully through his shorts.

"Oh," he moaned softly.

With her eyes rolling back in her head she squeezed him more firmly.

"Ouch," he whispered.

"Sorry."

"It's just all squished up in there."

She grinned. "I'll fix that."

Jillian worked one leg of his baggy shorts up his thigh slowly as Brian stared out the window, fighting to not give anything away. He curled his lips as she slipped her fingers through the leg hole and stroked his manhood as it fought to break free from his boxer briefs. Jillian gasped when she felt how hard he was. God, she wanted him in her mouth! She desperately wanted to taste him, to lick every inch of him, but this would just have to do.

Sliding two fingers through the leg hole of his briefs, she took hold of him and carefully pulled until his penis slipped through the open leg hole of his shorts. Brian groaned softly, "Oh, man."

His penis now two-thirds exposed, lengthened further down his leg as Jillian wrapped her fingers around it and slowly began pumping it.

Brian glanced once more around the cabin as Jillian lost herself in her task.

She leaned in and whispered, "You're so hard... and slick."

"Uh-huh."

Jillian moved her fingers over him as Brian slipped his hand into her lap. She whispered, "No, just let me take care of you."

He squeezed the armrest with a white-knuckle grip as he shut his eyes tight and gripped her knee with his other hand.

She kept moving her hand over him, as his breathing became more and more labored. She knew he was close and opened her eyes in search of something to contain his impending explosion. Grabbing a napkin with her free hand, she slipped it under the blanket over his head as she stroked him faster and faster. Brian pushed back against his chair as he lifted his ass off the seat a half-inch. He brought his hand to his mouth and covered it just as he exploded.

Jillian's heart pumped right along with his, as she pictured she was riding him at that moment. Her fingers kept sliding over his sensitive flesh, as Brian moved his hand to the armrest and squeezed hard again. She slipped her index finger down, touching a part of him that was unusually sensitive at that moment. Gasping silently, he quickly brought his hand down over hers to stop her from moving.

This pulled her from the fantasy, and she gazed up into his eyes dreamily. "How was that?"

He nodded with a smile, and his glazed-over look answered her query. She blindly swiped the napkin on his thigh in an attempt to clean him off. Reaching further into his shorts, she slipped the boxer briefs over his manhood and then pulled his shorts down completely.

"Wow," he said before exhaling a long, slow breath.

Jillian gave him a smile. "Be right back. I'm going to clean up."

She slipped out of her seat, and he watched as she moved toward the restroom, wishing he could go with her.

They arrived at the hotel just after 8:30 p.m., checked in, and went to the restaurant for a late dinner. After dinner and a few adult beverages, they stumbled up to their suite, where they shared a bath in the large two-person tub.

Brian carried her to the bed, placed her down gently, and then crawled between her legs to return the favor she had so sexily delivered to him at thirty-thousand feet. She experienced two mind-blowing orgasms courtesy of Brian's tongue, combined with a random finger here and there, and even right near the end of orgasm number two, he just happened to have fingers both here and there at the very same moment. As Brian was doing it he thought, Sometimes you need to bring out all your weapons at once.

Shortly after Jillian received her pleasure, she offered to put him to bed. He smiled brightly, because he knew exactly what that meant. She slipped under the covers and put him to bed all right. Ten minutes later they were both in REM Stage Five while wearing huge smiles.

Brian woke up early the next morning. He lifted the covers to drink in his wife's sexy body before dressing in shorts and a t-shirt and heading out for a run. After putting in more than two miles around the gorgeous grounds of the resort, he came upon an older gentleman giving a tennis lesson to two kids who looked to be about ten years old. Brian stood and watched, impressed, as the kids pounded the ball forcefully back and forth over the net while the older man stood beside the court, calling out instructions.

"Keep your eye on the ball... Come on, use good footwork... That's it, nice shot."

After a few minutes, the instructor told the pair to get a drink and take a break. Brian moved to the fence and said, "They're good. Are they your kids?"

The man turned to him and replied, "No, I'm one of the instructors."

"The boy... what's he, like, a 4.5 player?"

The man smiled proudly. "Now he is. When I started with him, he was about a 3.5."

"Awfully young to be that good. I wish I had been, back then."

"Don't we all?"

"Out of curiosity, what does it take to become an instructor?"

"You need to be certified by the USPTA."

The kids walked back onto the court. The instructor turned to his students and said, "Let's work on your serve." He glanced at Brian. "Gotta get back."

"Have fun."

They shared a smile, and Brian jogged away.

Jillian was still sleeping when he returned. He took his laptop onto the balcony and Googled USPTA certification programs. He located the United States Professional Tennis Association's site and searched until he located a page on how to acquire a certification as a Little Tennis Specialist. As he read the description, his face lit up. This is what he wanted to do, at least to start with. He could get a job that didn't seem at all like a job. He could teach, and maybe it eventually would lead to something bigger. He figured, what could be more fun than teaching the game to children and their families? He read up on the certification program, such as where to apply and take the necessary classes. Brian performed another Internet search and was able to find a location in Miami where he could become certified. He wore a smile as he completed the online application process.

Brian quietly slipped back into the room and found Jillian still asleep. He went into the bathroom, closed the door, and filled the sink with super hot water. He grabbed Jillian's travel bottle of baby oil and placed it in the steaming water.

Picking up the hotel phone, he ordered them both breakfast to be delivered in thirty minutes and then waited while the oil warmed. A few minutes later, he carried the oil out to the room and climbed into bed.

Jillian stirred and glanced up at him with a sleepy smile. "What time is it?"

"About ten thirty?"

"I'm starving."

"I ordered us breakfast."

Rolling over onto her back, Jillian stretched her arms up languidly and let out a big yawn. "Grrrreat."

"Can I interest you in a full-body rub while we wait for breakfast?"

Jillian smiled and turned onto her stomach. He pulled the covers down to fully expose her exquisite body and drank it in as he blindly removed the cap from the oil.

Brian held the bottle about a foot over her back and dripped a few drops onto her skin. Once the warm oil touched her, she exhaled deeply then said, "You heated it up?"

"Uh-huh."

She turned to glance up at him. "I'm so going to take care of you later."

He grinned.

She relaxed back into position as Brian dribbled warm oil all over her back, legs and breathtaking rear end. Jillian melted with his touch as he worked every inch of her. After twenty minutes of heaven, Jillian slipped into the shower while Brian waited for room service. They enjoyed a spectacular breakfast and then made spectacular love before they got ready for their 1:00 p.m. court time.

Their match was tied one set all and five games apiece in the third set. They sat on the bench taking a much-needed break from the steamy Arizona weather and sipped water.

Jillian smiled. "Would you like to make it interesting?"

"Sure, what do you have in mind?"

"How about whoever wins gets to choose what we do in bed later."

Brian gave her a skeptical look. "Whatever we want... I mean nothing is off the table?"

She placed a hand on his knee and replied, "Nothing is off the table."

A big smile spread over his face. "If I win, you do know what I want to do, don't you?"

She gave him a sexy grin. "I can guess."

"You'd probably be right... you're not planning on cheating, or anything?"

Jillian gave him an innocent look as her hand traveled up his leg to his groin, and she gave it a quick squeeze. After noticing some swelling, she grinned. "You'd better get your head in the game if you hope to win."

He stood. "I'm ready. Just tell me you're wearing underwear."

"I might be." She picked two tennis balls off the court and got to her feet. "Don't forget your balls."

He gave her a smile. "When I win, you won't be forgetting them later."

"We'll see. I hope your tongue isn't sore from all that work last night."

Brian headed toward the service line and called back, "It's a little sore, but I don't think I'm going to need it for the rest of the day and night."

Jillian positioned herself to return serve. "Oh, you'll need it all right."

Both played some high intensity tennis, and each won their service games to send the match to a tiebreak. Jillian tried to derail his win with a flash of her thong-covered ass when he was up six-five in the tiebreak and serving for the match. He grinned and called her to the net. They met there, and he whispered in her ear. Jillian's heart skipped a beat as he took twenty seconds to describe all the things he was going to do to her with his fingers, his penis, and, yes, even his semi-tired tongue. He wrapped up his erotic narrative by pointing out that everything he had just mentioned was only going to happen after she performed one particularly specific act on him.

He turned and walked to the service line, leaving her dizzied and standing at the net, fantasizing about all he had just told her. After a few moments, Jillian shook herself back to reality and slowly made her way into position while still more than just a little preoccupied.

"Ready?" he called out.

"Uh-huh," was all she could muster.

Brian hit a decent serve, but it was still returnable. Jillian was in pretty good position but swung badly and drove it out of the court.

He grinned proudly while he headed toward the bench. As Jillian walked over to join him, she thought, Maybe I let him win because his victory plan sounded so well-thought-out, not to mention a whole lot more fun than what I had in mind.

Jillian and Brian returned from Scottsdale, relaxed, refreshed, and with Jillian's female parts somehow back in perfect working order. He had spent just about as much time with his tongue exploring her as he they did together on the tennis court, and they played an awful lot of tennis. It was precisely the balance he was looking for.

As they settled back into a normal routine, she kept her word and was less focused on the case. After completing her rescheduled two-week book tour, she returned to Miami for a series of four meetings with her legal team, which ironed out the final trial strategy. Afterward, the horny pair celebrated with a three-set tennis match followed by a long bedroom romp. Brian won the tennis match two sets to one; however, Jillian led in the sex department, edging him out two orgasms to one. She enjoyed her victory a bit more.

16

Over the last few months, Rob had been completely consumed with work and earning tons of money as he sold shares in Wealth Stone. His clients were showing big returns, on paper anyway, and all were ecstatic. He and Bridget had been dating casually over that stretch and seeing each other once a week or so, but the relationship had not yet become physical.

For months, they had been talking about catching their Georgia State Bulldogs at a football game. Well, they were Rob's bulldogs anyway since Bridget actually graduated from Clemson. He, of course, didn't have a clue. Bridget had recently been sidetracked with another more pressing matter at work, until a priority shift returned her attention to Rob, Wealth Stone, and Carl Rodgers.

Now with her focus fully back on Rob, they were together in a bar just outside of Orlando, watching the game on the big screen. She wore a GSU t-shirt and jeans and looked amazing. Rob spent a lot of time stealing glances at her body when he wasn't watching the action on television. He was on his fifth beer, while she was only on her second. She needed him a little drunk for what she had planned later.

After the game, dinner, and a few more drinks, they returned to Rob's apartment. He took Bridget on a tour of the building, which began in the gym. There were only two practically naked young women working out while six guys eyed them hungrily. Bridget found this extremely amusing. Next, they moved to the pool area, where they began sipping yet another beer. Rob was already loaded, and his conversational filter was pretty much gone.

Bridget asked, "So your boss, Carl, also owns this building?"

"Yeah, and he lives here too."

"Do you see him much?"

"Not really. He seems to have a lot of girlfriends and spends most of his time in his penthouse apartment."

"Have you seen it?"

"No."

Frowning a little, Bridget glanced around the pool area, where a number of attractive young women were relaxing in the hot tub. She shook her head with a grin. "It's amazing how many women are living here. I mean, compared to the number of guys, it's just... unusual."

"Let's just say Carl subsidizes their rent a little." They shared a grin, and Rob continued, "He knows a lot of girls. We actually threw my mother's new husband's bachelor party here. Carl put everything together."

"That was nice of him."

"Yeah, they have this large party room downstairs with a big screen TV. Carl had it catered with all this food, and it rocked."

Bridget grinned. "So, how was the stripper?"

Rob gave her a tentative look.

"It's okay; you can tell me. I have a few brothers who share way too much. I've sorta heard it all."

"Actually, he had two... entertainers there. They put on this somewhat interactive two-girl show."

She scoffed. "A sex show?" Rob nodded with a big smile. She asked, "What do you mean 'interactive'?"

"Uh, well, the girls were trying to involve Brian in their little act, but I took the bullet for him," he announced proudly.

"God, I hope you wore a condom."

Widening his eyes, Rob lifted his hands in his defense. "No, I didn't have sex with them. They just used me as sort of... some kind of apparatus."

Bridget gave him a curious look.

"It's hard to explain... let's just say that none of my parts were involved and there was literally no touching... really. I did it all to protect my friend, Brian."

"Huh." She gave him an unconvinced smile.

He grinned and leaned over closer to her. "The girls were doing, you know, each other on this black lounge chair thing. It looked really cool, like it was made for sex, or something... I don't know. I have the security code to get in the room. Do you want to see it?"

Bridget's face lit up. "Yeah."

Rob guzzled the rest of his beer before he led Bridget into the building and directed her down the long corridor to the party room. As he walked behind her, he stared at her ass the whole time. That last beer was really taking its toll and putting his libido in high gear. All he could think of was having sex with her on that chair, in the steam room, in his apartment, in the pool, hell anywhere would do just fine. Once they reached the door, Bridget watched closely as Rob keyed the code into the button lock.

Inside the party room, Rob gave her a tour of the kitchen, the bar, and the main lounge area. As they stood by the large black chaise lounge chair, her eyes wandered to the other large steel door with its identical push button lock.

She asked, "So what's behind that door?"

"There's a big safe back there. More like a bank vault. I think Carl keeps some of the company's assets in there."

She stared at him, intrigued. "Have you been in it?"

"No, but I did see inside once when I was down here with Carl."

"Do you have the code for that door?"

"No." Rob moved closer to her. She glanced up at him in surprise. He put his hands on her shoulders and leaned in for a kiss. Bridget kissed him back until it grew more passionate.

She pulled away. "I just got out of long-term relationship, and I—"

"Sorry..." Rob backed away a few steps and rubbed his hands over his face. "No, it's my fault. I thought you, um, we were..."

Bridget gave him an apologetic look. "Rob, I really like you, but I just need to take it slow."

He nodded. "I understand. So, do you want me to walk you out?"

"No, I think I'd rather go up to your apartment and have another drink. Unless you're tired, or something."

"No. Sure let's go." Rob smiled as he turned and headed for the door. Bridget glanced back for one last look at the door in front of the vault.

After two more beers each, in Rob's apartment, Rob was pretty hammered. Sitting next to him on the sofa, Bridget gave him a smile. "I think I'm going to go."

She stood, wobbled a little bit, and then tumbled back into the cushion. "Wow, sorry. I don't think I should drive home."

"You can sleep here if you want. You can have my bed. I'll sleep on the sofa."

"Really, you don't mind?"

"No."

"I'll stay, but I don't want to kick you out of your bed. I'll sleep out here."

Rob set her up with one of his t-shirts, supplied bedding for the sofa, and then climbed into his bed. Bridget waited on the sofa under the covers while she stared at the ceiling. Two minutes after she heard the light snoring begin, she snuck into Rob's room to confirm his condition. His chest and shoulders were uncovered as he lay there peacefully sleeping. She paused a moment to admire his bulky masculine frame before sighing and then heading back to the living room. Bridget quickly put on her clothes and slipped out the door, making sure to leave it unlocked.

She took the elevator down to the bottom level and made her way to the party room. There, she stood outside the door and glanced down both sides of the corridor. Just as she reached for the doorknob, Carl Rodgers appeared at the end of the hall.

Pulling her hand from the knob, Bridget stared at Carl, confused, as he walked toward her. She shook her head and gave him a ditzy look. "I'm so lost. Is this the gym?"

Carl wore a smug smile. "No, but I can show you where it is."

"Thanks. Rob gave me a tour earlier, but I got all turned around." She put on an airheaded look with her hands raised.

Carl's face lit up. "You're Rob's girlfriend?"

"We're just friends."

"Oh, I thought, uh..." Carl began as his eyes shot down to her breasts for a long time before returning to her face. "It's kind of late for a workout."

Bridget stammered, "I, uh, couldn't sleep and just thought I would walk on the treadmill or something."

"It's right this way."

Bridget followed Carl as he led her to the gym. Once inside, she climbed on the treadmill and began to walk slowly. She felt Carl staring at her with a look that screamed I want to kill you or rape you, or possibly both.

He said, "You know what's really good for insomnia?" She widened her eyes, and he added, "A steam."

"You have a steam room? That sounds—"

"It's unisex," he interrupted.

She stared at him for a moment trying to not appear completely creeped out. "Oh, I didn't bring my suit."

Moving toward her, Carl put his hands on the rail of the treadmill. "It's also clothing optional."

She nearly lost her balance. Carl grabbed her arm to steady her. She looked at him, a little shocked, and hit the button to stop the belt. "I, uh... I break out in hives in a steam room."

"That's a shame." Carl kept hold of her arm.

Glancing down at his hand, she grimaced. He rolled his eyes and pulled his hand away.

Bridget stepped off the treadmill. "I think I'm just going to try to sleep now. I feel tired now."

"Okay, then."

They stood staring at each other for a moment. Bridget painted on a fake smile. "Thanks for helping me find the gym."

Carl nodded and stared at her as she backed away slowly and then slipped out the door. She rushed down the hall with her heart beating out of her chest and slipped quietly back into Rob's apartment and onto the sofa. Rob never knew she was gone.

17

The next morning, Rob stood in the living room staring at Bridget as she slept. He was shirtless and wearing a pair of gym shorts. Wearing only his t-shirt and panties with one of her shapely legs sticking out from under the sheet, she looked amazing. He took a deep breath, stole one more glance, knelt down next to her and then gently touched her shoulder. "Bridget."

She flipped over quickly, cried out, and stared up at him, terrified.

Rob moved back. "Sorry."

Glancing around the room nervously, she caught her breath and then looked back at him. "No, I, uh, was just having a bad dream."

He raised his eyebrows. "You should have slept with me then."

After giving him a chuckle, she said. "Thanks again for letting me stay over."

"Any time. You want to get some breakfast?"

"What time is it?"

"A few minutes after eight."

She shook off the cobwebs as Rob leaned in closer to her. She could feel the heat boiling up between them. Bridget's eyes traveled up from his large pecs to his broad shoulders. She breathed in deeply and was dizzied a bit by his scent; it was clean, yet manly. They looked into each other's eyes.

She began, "I, should really get going. I have..."

He moved his lips to hers, and they shared a gentle kiss. He pulled up and smiled at her. Exhaling deeply, she lifted back up to reach his lips. Rob came down to meet her, and they shared a long, passionate kiss. Her hands wandered all over his muscular back as he slipped a hand under her t-shirt. She moaned as he began squeezing her full breasts and sucking at the flesh on her neck.

Bridget put her hand on his knee. After lifting her shirt over her breast, he brought his mouth down to her nipple. As he sucked it into his mouth, her eyes rolled back in her head.

"Oh, Rob."

Rob moved to the other breast as her hand wandered up his thigh to the bulge in his shorts. When her hand reached his nearly hard penis, Rob feverishly bit down hard on her nipple.

"Ouch!"

He pulled away from her. "Oh, sorry."

"It's okay."

Sliding up on the sofa, Bridget took a deep, calming breath. Her glance traveled down to his large bulge. She ran her tongue around her lips with her eyes still locked on it. God, she wanted him, but she needed to stick with the plan.

Rob grinned and began lowering his mouth back to her chest. She grabbed his head with both hands. "Sorry, I really should go."

"Really?"

He leaned back as she pulled her shirt down and then curled her legs up to her chest. "Yes. I can't do this. I'm not ready."

He sat next to her and stared straight ahead for a moment before glancing back at her and noticing she was staring right down at his lap. He followed her eyes, noticed his excited condition, and quickly grabbed a pillow to cover up. They shared a smile.

Bridget tore her eyes from the pillow. "Sorry about getting you all, uh..."

"Don't worry about it."

"I just don't want to rush into anything. I really like you, but I've always had bad luck when I let things get physical too soon."

"You're right. We should take it down a notch." He shook his head in unenthusiastic agreement.

She painted on a tentative smile. "Not that it wouldn't be amazing. I think it would totally be amazing."

"Oh, definitely."

"But I need to get to work."

He nodded as Bridget stood and quickly grabbed her shorts. Rob stared at her tight ass while she put them on.

After slipping on her shoes, she smiled at him.

Rob asked, "Do you want to do something later?"

She gave him a sorrowful look. "I can't. I've got to work late and I've got this big project going on at work. I'll be buried in it up until Christmas. Then I need to go home for the holidays..." She rolled her eyes. "But can I call you when I get back on January third?"

"Oh, yeah. Sure." He stood and dropped the pillow to the sofa now that the swelling had been mostly reduced. "I have a lot going on at work this week myself, so..."

"Okay, good."

Bridget picked up her purse, and he followed her to the door. She turned back quickly and knocked into him. They shared an awkward grin as she once again drank in his scent.

"I, uh..." she began, and Rob moved his lips to hers. Wrapping her arms around his neck, Bridget pressed her body to his. She felt his excitement rising up again and could sense her own body begging for his touch.

She pulled away and tried to catch her breath. "Wow... When I get back, uh, let's definitely do something."

He nodded quickly. "Something."

They stood for a moment, just staring at one another.

"Bye," she said, and then she opened the door and slipped into the hall.

Bridget took a deep breath and leaned against the wall as he did the same on the other side of it. Glancing down at his groin, Rob decided he needed to relieve the pressure... and as soon as possible. He rushed toward the bathroom, as Bridget remained slumped against the wall, still struggling to catch her breath.

<u>18</u>

Just before Christmas, with the trial only a few short weeks away, the once again happy newly married couple planned a spur-of-the-moment ski getaway. Badly needing a break from all of it, Jillian was looking forward to a relaxing weekend away with a few close friends.

Brian, Jillian, Victoria, and Lisa drove together to Gatlinburg, Tennessee, the location of the only ski resort in the southeast. Two other couples, along with Eric, whom Lisa had met at Jillian and Brian's wedding, were also on their way to meet them at the five-bedroom house they rented for the weekend. Eric was still recovering from his recent breakup with Annette, and after Brian's begging wore him down, he finally agreed to go. The plea came from Jillian through Victoria on behalf of Lisa, but Brian could not disclose any of that. He made up some story about how much fun it was going to be and also included a joking reference to Eric owing him one, since Eric broke his CD player during their freshman year at college.

Gatlinburg was a thirteen-hour drive from Miami, but Victoria's doctor had given her the approval to make the trip as long as she stayed off the slopes. Victoria loved to ski and had fond memories of a trip she took the previous year to this same resort. She was disappointed that she wouldn't be able to ski but wanted to go for two reasons: first, to celebrate her successful completion of the Master's program, and second and most importantly, to help Lisa finally lose her virginity.

Everyone settled in at the house just after 7:00 p.m., and Brian went to town to pickup dinner. Victoria was sitting on the bed, waiting for Lisa to model a sexy outfit she had picked out for her to wear that night.

Lisa slipped out of the bathroom, wearing jeans and a tight pink sweater, which was unbuttoned just enough to put Lisa's push-up bra-enhanced cleavage on full display.

"Now that looks good." Victoria said. "Let me see the back." Lisa turned, and Victoria gave her a wide smile. "Your ass looks spectacular."

Craning her neck to get a look, Lisa replied, "You think?"

"I'd be surprised if Eric doesn't get hard the minute he sees you."

"I hope." Lisa stared at her reflection in the full-length mirror.

"Now remember to avoid all political discussions."

"Okay. Sure."

"Alright, let's get out there." Victoria said. As she stood, she clutched her belly with a grimace. "Ouch."

Moving quickly, Lisa took hold of her arm. "Are you okay?"

"The baby must be kicking my bladder again. I need to pee, like, every ten minutes."

Lisa guided her to the bathroom. "I'll wait for you."

"No, get out there and show him your ass. I'll be two minutes."

In the dinning room, a huge selection of wings, ribs, and corn on the cob were spread out before the group. When Victoria entered the room, she instantly spotted Lisa gnawing on a chicken wing. She looked at Lisa in shock and then glanced at Eric to find him staring at the spectacle as well.

Lisa was slurping and sucking the meat off the bone with expert precision, as Eric looked on, slightly horrified.

"Lisa!" Victoria called out. Glancing up at her, Lisa continued enjoying her wing. Victoria gave her a look. "Uh, can I see you for one second?"

Victoria pulled Lisa into the powder room and closed the door. After sighing, she began, "Um... we already talked about this, didn't we?"

"Talked about what?" Lisa replied. Then she sucked the wing sauce off two fingers with a loud pop before staring at Victoria, confused.

Victoria made a face, paused, and then said, "Yeah, that."

Looking down at her hand, Lisa eyed another glob of sauce and began raising the finger toward her mouth. Victoria grabbed her arm by the wrist and rolled her eyes while shaking her head.

"Remember the conversation about the way you enjoyed the food at the wedding?"

"Sure," Lisa replied casually.

Victoria nodded with her eyebrows raised until Lisa returned an embarrassed smile. Lisa began, "Oh... I thought you were only referring to shrimp."

"No, this eating rule covers all foods. Honey, I'm sorry I wasn't clearer on this. When a man sees you devouring food like a buzzard attacks a deer carcass on the side of the road, he understandably gets concerned. Look, when a guy watches you eat, he's picturing you performing oral sex on him."

"Really?"

"Yes, really. He imagines that what you're doing to that wing, you'll be doing to his penis when he places it between your lips. And now, this penis of his is very important to him. Do you understand that?"

"Yeah, sure."

"And the way you went to town on that wing, the only conclusion he could logically reach is that after you're finished with his penis, he'll be pulling back nothing more than a bloody stump, and that scares the shit out of him."

"Oh, okay. I get it." Lisa nodded with a slightly confused stare.

"So I would skip the wings, at least for tonight."

"No problem."

"What else do they have out there to eat?" Victoria asked.

"Ribs, um... corn on the cob, and salad, I think."

Victoria shook her head once again with the concern screaming out loudly from her intense facial expression. "I don't want to see you anywhere near a rib or the corn, for that matter."

Lisa gave her a perplexed look. "Why?"

"I'm not even going to answer that." Victoria frowned.

"What can I eat, then? I'm really hungry."

"You should stick with the salad."

"That's not going to fill me up."

Victoria shook her head. "Sweetie, if you want to have any chance of *really* getting filled up this weekend, then you've got to focus on the penis a little more and the food a lot less."

"That makes sense, but I do need my strength. If I don't eat, I get cranky."

Victoria pondered this for a moment. "Okay, you can have the ribs, but eat them with a knife and fork. Got it?"

"I can do that."

"I mean it. If I see you sucking on a rib or slurping sauce off your fingers you'll be finding yourself a new sex coach."

Lisa nodded with an embarrassed smile.

"Just remember we want him to *want* to put his genitals near your mouth."

"I've got it now."

"Good, now wash the rest of the sauce off your hands and get back out there."

During the rest of the meal, Lisa was able to control her table manners—for the most part. After dinner the three couples and Lisa, Eric, and Victoria sat in the great room to watch a movie and enjoy some cocktails. Brian whipped up his semi-famous cosmos for the women, while the men guzzled beers, and Victoria sipped cranberry juice.

They watched the George Clooney movie, *The Descendants*. Even though it was currently still in theaters, Victoria had in her possession an Oscar screener DVD copy of the film. The copy was courtesy of one of the producers of the movie, with whom Victoria had had a brief, yet passionate, fling eighteen months earlier, while he was on location in Miami. The two still kept in touch despite that fact that he was now married. Victoria figured that although she could no longer enjoy his body, she could still enjoy an early movie release in the comfort of her own home or while on vacation, as the case may be.

It turned out to be the wrong film choice as far as Eric was concerned, since it was a story about a husband who learns of his wife's secret affair while she's in a coma. One hour into the film, Eric was on his seventh beer, and his comments sprinkled throughout the viewing made it evident he had recently discovered that Annette was cheating on him.

After the film, the three couples retired to their bedrooms while the three singles stayed behind in the great room, talking. As Eric polished off beer number nine, Victoria shared a look with Lisa. Then Victoria asked, "So, what should we do?"

Lisa shrugged her shoulders.

Victoria paused, thinking, and then her eyes brightened. "Hot tub? I'll just put my legs in, but you guys could get in."

"I'm up for that," Lisa replied excitedly.

The women looked at Eric for his reply, but he was merely staring down into the bottom of his empty beer bottle.

"Eric," Victoria called out.

"Huh?" he replied.

"Feel like going in the hot tub?"

"Why not," he mumbled half-heartedly.

Victoria smiled. "Great. Go put on your suit and we'll meet you out there in a few minutes."

Victoria pulled out her see-through white bikini and handed it to Lisa. Lisa put it on, and Victoria adjusted her breasts for maximum cleavage display.

"He won't be able to resist you. When this gets wet, your nipples will come shining through, if you know what I mean. He'll be so hard that his bathing suit will explode off his body."

Smiling, Lisa stared in a mirror at her bikini-covered breasts.

Victoria added, "After you two get settled, I'll excuse myself. Just keep the twins underwater until I leave, and then sit up and put them on display. After that, I'm going to guess your bed won't be slept in tonight." Victoria winked at her.

"Gosh, I hope so."

Victoria slipped on bikini bottoms along with a hooded sweatshirt, and they headed out to the great room to wait for Eric.

After a few minutes, when Eric still hadn't appeared, Victoria lightly knocked on his door with Lisa standing behind her. When he didn't respond, Victoria opened the door, and they found him face down on the bed, wearing only boxer shorts and snoring loudly.

Victoria moved to him and called his name a few times before pushing on his shoulder to jar him awake. When he did nothing more than groan and turn over, they shared a sad look and slipped out of his room.

"I guess you're getting a roommate tonight," Lisa said.

"Don't worry about it. We'll try again tomorrow."

19

Just after 10:00 a.m., Carl sat in his office at Wealth Stone watching a video on his PC. Rob knocked on the open door. "You wanted to see me?"

"Yes, Rob. Please come in and close the door."

Carl motioned for him to sit in a chair opposite from his desk. Rob took a seat and asked, "What's up?"

"I want to show you something."

After Carl clicked the screen, a video began running of the empty party room at the apartment building. A few seconds later, Rob and Bridget came into view and stood near the black chaise.

Rob's face turned a pale white. "Oh, sorry. I was just show—"

"Don't worry about it." Carl narrowed his eyes. "She's hot."

"Who?"

"Your girlfriend."

"Thanks, but it's not really all that serious."

Carl stopped the video. "You're fucking her, aren't you?"

Rob's mouth opened wide, but Carl didn't wait for a response. "I would really love to watch you have sex with her. I'll bet she's really..." He shook his head with a faraway creepy look. After a few moments, Carl returned from whatever freaky place his mind had gone and stared back at Rob. "I record everything that goes on in that room. Everything... I have the bachelor party and also this..."

Carl clicked on another video, and it began playing. He clicked again on the screen, and the video jumped to Rob getting a blowjob from Carl's date on that black chaise on the night that Carl was off in the other room with the guards.

Rob tried to mask his horror. "Wow, that's... I didn't know you had that recorded. It's not, uh, going to be on the Internet or anything, is it?"

Carl scoffed. "It's for my personal collection. So what's your girl's name?"

"Bridget."

"I want to watch you have sex with her. Do you think you could bring her down to the room and put that together?"

Rob stared at him, dumbfounded, and stammered, "I'm really not sure. We're trying to take it slow, so..."

Carl shook his head, disappointed. "She looks like she's got great tits. How are her tits?"

"They're, uh, pretty great... yeah," Rob replied softly.

Carl smiled. "I met her a couple nights ago."

"Bridget?"

"Yeah, she was wandering through the building looking for the gym at around one in the morning."

"Really? I didn't—"

"I tried to get her to try out the steam room, but she's a shy one."

"Yeah, she is." Rob tried to process this information as he thought, What the hell was Bridget doing wandering around the building after they supposedly went to sleep?

Carl's phone buzzed. He hit the speakerphone. "Yes."

"David Walters has arrived."

"Okay," Carl shot back.

Rob stood. "So, I'll just—"

"Hey, I've got to go to this lunch meeting, but you stay... you've got to see the video of the bachelor party."

"Uh, I—" Rob began.

"It's so hot the way those chicks rode your face. Here. Stay." Carl didn't wait for a reply. He selected another video, hit play, turned the PC screen to face Rob, and then smiled. "Try to get Bridget down there. I'm serious."

A very clear shot of Rob being used as an apparatus began playing on the PC. Rob stared at the screen with his heart pumping wildly. Carl grinned. "Maybe you could get her to do that to you."

Carl slapped Rob on the back and then headed for the door. Rob turned to find the door left wide open. Rob rushed to close it and then returned to the desk. He sat in Carl's chair, turned the screen back toward himself, and stopped the video. He sat there holding his head and struggling to catch his breath.

"Fuck."

Turning to the window, he watched as Carl climbed into a car with another man and then drove away. When he turned back to the PC, he pulled up the directory list of videos and saw that there were hundreds. He selected one at random and played it. He fast-forwarded to a scene of Carl having sex with two girls on the chair.

He stopped the video and selected another; this time, it was of Carl pleasuring himself while he watched two girls lying on the floor and making out. He selected yet another, but this one was a shot of the safe door. He watched as Carl unlocked the safe, opened the door, and disappeared from view. From the camera angle, Rob could see the bottom edge of a large stack of gold. A few moments later, Carl returned into view, pushing a hand truck containing a stack of gold bars.

Pausing the video, Rob stared straight ahead while rubbing his chin. He exhaled deeply and closed his eyes. When he opened them, he glanced at the PC monitor and noticed a number of other minimized applications at the bottom on the screen.

Turning back to the window, Rob glanced out at the parking lot and then nervously toward the door. He clicked on a spreadsheet and began studying it. It was a listing of gold purchases with dates going back almost four years. At the top was an entry for the current price of gold. It held the number 1,739.22 per ounce.

The sheet was also broken down into two sections, one labeled "Wealth Stone" and one labeled "Blue Stone." He scrolled down the Blue Stone list to the bottom. There, he saw the most recent purchase was 600 pounds with a date less than a week old. He looked at the bottom line total of 20,250 pounds of gold with a value over 563 million dollars.

Rob ran his fingers through his hair with his mind racing. Pulling out his cell phone, he selected a number and hit send.

A man answered. "This is Gary."

"Gary, it's Rob. I'm, uh, out with a client, and he's asking about the fund's current position in gold. Can you check for me?"

"Sure, hold on a sec... Um, looks like it's two point three million."

"Really? And what's the total value of the fund right now?" Rob asked.

"Seven hundred fifteen million and change."

"Thanks." Rob ended the call. He turned back to the computer screen and shook his head. Scrolling to the Wealth Stone section of the spreadsheet, he checked the bottom line. There he found the total listing just over 10,000 pounds of gold with a value of over 278 million dollars.

He leaned back in the chair and stared at the ceiling, thinking, How the fuck does Wealth Stone have over eight hundred fifty million in gold, and virtually none of it is on the books?

20

Back in snow country after breakfast, Lisa removed her bra and panties as Victoria looked on, holding a one-piece coral-colored ski suit. Victoria said, "Just forget about last night. Nothing is better than outdoor sex on a cold, crisp day out on the ski slope. I take that back; oral sex while riding on a ski lift is pretty fucking amazing, not to mention somewhat dangerous."

"How would you know?"

Victoria gave her a tired look, and Lisa returned a casual nod.

"Giving or receiving?" Lisa narrowed her eyes.

"Giving. I tried receiving, but the logistics of it are just impossible."

"Huh." Lisa frowned as she asked, "You sure this is going to work?"

"It can't miss. Just do it exactly like we discussed, and when you get back, your virginity will be gone."

"I never pictured that my first time would be standup sex out in the middle of a snow-covered mountain."

"Just go with it. If it gets too uncomfortable, tell him you want to go back to the house and finish him properly. He'll follow you like a lost puppy."

Putting her hand on Victoria's shoulder, Lisa stepped into the legs of the suit. The sex coach pulled it up over her student's shapely hips, and Lisa squeezed her breasts together by curling her shoulders as Victoria zipped her up in front.

"You look great. He won't be able to resist you."

"Okay. Thanks," Lisa added, semi-convinced.

"My God, would you smile... you're about to be on the receiving end of a big, hard cock, and look at you!"

"I'm worried that I'll—"

"We've been over everything. You know what to do. I've given you the benefit of all my experience. Well, some of it, anyway. If you're not ready for this now, you'll never be."

"I'm sorry. You're right."

"And you're a great skier right?"

"Yeah, I'm pretty good."

"Eric isn't, so he'll be looking to you for some guidance up there. You'll guide him, all right." Victoria widened her eyes and glanced down between Lisa's legs. "Guide him right into—"

"Okay, enough with the sex pun jokes. You're making me nervous."

"Sorry."

Lisa took a look at her outfit in the mirror and then began, "Are you sure about Eric's skiing experience, because I heard he was like an expert or something."

"I'm sure. I spoke with him about it last night. You remember where to lead him, right? Next to the snow tubing run, there's this little path."

"You're positive no one will see us? I mean, I'm not going to end up in jail, or anything?"

"Positive. Last year, I took this guy I was seeing there, and we did it with our skis still on for more than a half hour. We didn't see anyone. There are a lot of big trees. Just do what I told you, and everything will be fine."

"Okay, I can do this." Lisa painted on a smile.

"That's it. Now go get you some man meat!"

Lisa returned an uncomfortable look.

"Sorry." Victoria rolled her eyes and added in a haughty Italian accent, "Go make love to him."

They both broke into laughter.

At the base of the mountain, Eric and Lisa stood with Jillian and Brian.

Jillian said, "Well, we don't want to slow you two down. We're starting on the bunny slopes."

"But we're definitely going to move to the more advanced ones right?" Brian asked hopefully.

Jillian leaned over and whispered in his ear. Lisa and Eric looked on as Brian's jaw dropped a bit.

"Well, maybe, uh, we'll see you two up there later," Brian said.

"Or maybe not," Jillian added.

"Yeah." Brian smiled, and they shared a sexy look.

"You two have fun," Jillian said as she and Brian headed off.

Widening his eyes, Eric gave Lisa a look. "Newlyweds."

She nodded with an embarrassed smile. "So, I heard this is only your third time skiing."

He scoffed. "Who told you that?"

"Oh, I thought I just heard..."

"I mean I haven't skied in, like, three years, but my parents had me on black diamond slopes when I was six."

"Wow," she replied, suddenly concerned.

"So how about you?"

She stammered, "Me, too... I'm totally black diamond." She scoffed. "Anything else is, like, a complete bore."

He smiled, "Awesome. Finally, a girl who can ski. You'll probably be a little bored here... this isn't Colorado or anything. A black diamond on this mountain is probably like an intermediate slope at Vail."

She nodded with an uneasy smile. "No doubt."

"Great. Let's do the Grizzly." Eric took off toward the lift as Lisa whispered with her brow furrowed, "The Grizzly?"

At the top of the run, Eric looked down the slope, smiling. "You want to go first?"

Lisa stared down the steep run with an anguished look. "No, I'll follow you."

He nodded and pushed off down the run. After taking a deep breath, she followed after him. Lisa held her own, and at one point, Eric glanced back at her and smiled, which caused her nearly to wipe out. After regaining her balance, she survived the first run, and on their second run, Lisa began scouting out the slope to find the trail to the secluded spot that Victoria had mentioned. On the third run, she finally located it, and while riding up the lift, she said to Eric, "Follow me this time. I want to show you this special trail."

"Okay."

At the top of the slope, Lisa stood next to Eric while wearing a goofy smile. She waited for a few other skiers to begin their runs, so they were alone. She pulled her zipper down, exposing a whole lot of cleavage. Eric glanced down at her breasts, and his mouth opened wide.

"Follow me," she said excitedly.

Lisa took off down the hill at high speed and left Eric grinning at the top. He took a deep breath and rushed after her. She glanced back at him, smiling as he punched his poles into the snow in an effort to catch her.

"Come on," she screamed.

"Where are we going?" Eric yelled as he caught up to her.

"I'll show you."

"Aren't you cold?"

"I won't be after you warm me up." She glanced at him with sexy grin.

Smiling excitedly, Eric stole one more look at her nearly-exposed breasts. One of his skis hit an icy patch and slipped out from under him. He lost control and went tumbling off to the right and toward a line of trees, all the while screaming loudly.

Lisa watched in horror as he barely avoided slamming into a tree and flopped down hard onto the snow in a giant heap. While attempting a sharp turn toward him, she lost control as well, crashing to the slope with mounds of snow pilling into her open jumpsuit.

She shrieked loudly as the shock of the icy cold snow felt as if it were burning her skin. A group of skiers went to check on Eric; others rushed to her and gave her a strange look when they spotted her snow-covered breasts.

Five hours later, after Eric's sprained ankle was wrapped in the emergency room and Lisa's mild case of frostbite was treated, everyone returned to the house. Eric and Lisa didn't have a chance to discuss the incident, mainly because he was hopped up on painkillers.

Eric retired to his room, and Lisa spent the night pouting about her embarrassing day. Victoria tried her best to cheer her up, but nothing worked, and everyone went to sleep early. After midnight, Lisa woke up and struggled to get back to sleep. She glanced over at her sleeping roommate/sex coach and sighed. With no one to stop her, she decided to go to Eric's room to apologize.

She knocked on his door once and then opened it slowly. She found him sitting up in bed, watching television. After giving him a sympathetic smile, she whispered, "Mind if I come in?"

"Sure."

Lisa closed the door and sat with him on the bed. He turned off the television. She began, "Sorry about today. I was just trying—"

"To kill me." He gave her a serious look, paused for dramatic effect, and then broke into a smile.

"No, I was trying to... I don't know exactly. It was Victoria's idea."

"Thanks for showing me your breasts, but I would prefer if you did that when we weren't going forty miles per hour down an icy ski slope."

"Again, sorry about that." She returned an embarrassed smile.

"Don't worry. It's a memory I won't soon forget."

They shared a laugh.

She asked, "Can't sleep?"

"Yeah, I went to bed too early. The drugs wore off, and I don't know... I'm just wired."

"Are you in any pain?"

"A little."

"Can I get you anything?"

"No, I'm good."

They shared an awkward silent moment until he said, "They're nice."

"What?"

He smiled. "Your breasts."

"They were. Now they're all red from frostbite."

They shared another laugh.

Eric asked, "What exactly were you trying to do out there?"

Lisa bit her lip for a moment and then stammered, "Well, um, I guess I was hoping to..."

"To what?" he asked.

"To have sex with you out there."

He grinned. "And get frostbite over your entire body and mine, for that matter?"

"Something like that." She looked away from him shyly.

"That sounds like fun. I've never had sex outside while wearing skis. In fact, I've never done it outdoors before."

"I've never done it, either."

"Outside?"

"No... sex. I've, uh, never actually done it," she admitted in a low voice.

Staring at her in disbelief, he asked, "You've never had sex?"

"Nope."

He smiled and scoffed. "Come on. You're kidding."

Lisa glared at him. He reacted to her look by putting on a straight face. "Sorry, I'm not making fun of you."

After she made eye contact with him, he broke into a smile. He covered his mouth, but a laugh escaped anyway. Frowning, Lisa got up and headed toward the door.

"Wait," he called after her. "Sorry. I swear I'm not laughing at you."

"What are you laughing at then?" She moved to the bed and glared down at him.

After holding his hand out with his lip curled, he put on a silly grin and began, "So wait, let me see if I understand. You wanted your first sexual experience to be outside on a ski slope in twenty degree weather. Most people go for something romantic... dinner, some flowers, maybe a nice hotel room, but you think snow, skis, all with a chance of being arrested for indecent exposure."

Widening his eyes, he stared at her with a serious expression, waiting. When Lisa finally broke into a laugh, she slumped down next him on the bed and grinned. "Well if you hadn't passed out drunk last night we could have had our romantic night. You should have seen me in that see-through bikini."

"See-through bikini?"

She sat on the bed, nodded, and glanced at him with a smile before turning away coyly.

"Sorry about that." Eric moved his hand to her face and brushed the hair away from her eyes. "You're beautiful."

Lisa turned to look him in the eye. He leaned to her and she moved closer to him. They closed their eyes, and their lips met briefly. They pulled away from each other and opened their eyes for only a moment before Lisa slammed her lips back to his, kissing him hard. Wrapping his arms around her, he pulled her body on top of his with her legs still dangling on the carpet. She slipped a leg up onto the bed, striking his ankle.

"Ouch," he moaned.

"Sorry. Sorry."

"It's okay. Maybe if you moved to the other side."

Lisa pushed up from him carefully and walked around the bed. She stopped and stared down at him while she pulled off her t-shirt, exposing her slightly frostbitten, pink—but still beautiful—breasts. "I promise I'll try not to hurt you anymore."

He watched, mesmerized, as she removed her pajama bottoms and underwear. His eyes traveled down to her completely shaved pubic hair. He swallowed hard and pulled off his shirt.

"Do you want me to help you with your shorts?"

He nodded. "Just watch my ankle."

Taking hold of the waistband of his shorts, she pulled them down as he lifted his hips off the bed. Then she pulled his boxers down and carefully slipped them off while avoiding his sprain.

She drank in his body, and then her eyes settled in to watch his quickly rising erection. Climbing over him carefully, she settled her knees down on either side of his chest.

Lisa leaned down slowly and kissed him. Slipping her tongue into his mouth, she kissed him more passionately. Her eyes rolled back in her head as she ground her hips into his groin.

Craning her neck, she glanced down at his penis. "Wow, you're so big."

Raising an eyebrow at her, he moved his hand to her breast. She pulled back in pain.

"Sorry," he said.

"Neither of us is one hundred percent."

They shared a giggle.

Lisa moved her hands down and wrapped them around his penis. She began massaging it as he closed his eyes and enjoyed the feel of her touch. Lifting up, she positioned his thick head at her entrance and held her breath.

"Wait. Should I get a condom?" Eric asked.

She took a deep breath and held still over him. "I'm on the pill." He gave her a look, so she explained, "I know, a virgin on the pill sounds weird, but it helps regulate my period, and it really cleared up my skin."

"Huh."

"Ready?" Lisa asked.

He nodded, and they stared into each other's eyes. She opened her mouth wide as she fought for the right angle while still holding his shaft.

"Oh..." he groaned.

Finally she found it, and the tip pushed up quickly inside of her.

"That's..." Lisa began. She held her breath again and then slipped down onto him, her virginity now a thing of the past. Groaning in mild pain, she pushed down slowly until she was resting completely on him.

"Are you okay?"

"I think so," Lisa replied. She wore a slight grimace as her body adjusted to the fleshy intruder. Circling her hips slightly, her expression shifted to a sexy grin. "Oh, my," she moaned. "She was right."

"Who?"

"Victoria."

Lisa began moving her hips up and down over him.

"Right about what?" Eric asked breathlessly.

"How amazing this feels."

He smiled. Leaning down, she pressed her lips to his while maintaining her rhythmic gyrations.

About six minutes later, Eric exploded inside of her with a thunderous orgasm. Lisa didn't have an orgasm that night but still went to sleep thoroughly satisfied with the matter of her virginity safely behind her. The next day, they took a bath together, and she experienced her first male-induced climax courtesy of what Lisa would refer to, when she shared every single detail with Victoria, as Eric's magical tongue.

21

Jim and Caroline decided to return to the place where they first met, the Borgata in Atlantic City, New Jersey, for a New Year's Eve getaway. Jim was able to book a reservation in a suite similar to the one where they spent that memorable night during the previous summer. The plan was to relive their experiences pretty much as they had on the night they met, except for a few minor role-playing adjustments. Jim didn't know exactly what she had planned, but he was told to go to the casino and then search for her in one hour. He was instructed to retrace his steps exactly as he had on that fateful night.

Jim slipped down to the casino and experienced absolutely none of the luck he had previously. When he found himself two hundred and fifty dollars down at the blackjack table, he checked the time and found he still had forty minutes to kill. While strolling around the casino, he noticed the roulette wheel and grinned. He pulled the remaining forty dollars' worth of chips from his pocket and placed them down on twenty black, just as he had during his last visit. Jim waited while wearing a confident smile as the wheel spun round and round.

The ball bounced around from slot to slot until it finally landed on double zero. His smile morphed into a frown as he vowed to never gamble again. He checked the time and discovered he had used up all of three minutes since he last checked. He spent the remaining time watching other lucky gamblers win at blackjack and then wandered around the casino while he waited for the real fun to begin.

When it was time, he glanced around the casino, trying to recall what his next move should be. His eyes brightened as he remembered that after gambling, he'd enjoyed a drink at the bar.

As he entered the Gypsy Bar, he discovered a woman facing away from him and dressed in a tight spaghetti strap black dress. She looked incredibly sexy with her hair up and Jim stood staring, his eyes followed her long neck as it tapered down to her slim shoulders. From there, he cocked his head to one side as his glance headed further south to the woman's tiny waist and slightly curvy hips. It, of course, was Caroline.

Grinning, he moved to the bar and sat across from her. Aside from the bartender, there were only a few other people around. The bartender approached Jim and took his order, a gin and tonic. Jim made eye contact with the slender beauty, and they shared a smile. When his drink arrived, Caroline moved to the seat beside him.

She began in a mock Russian accent, "I Tatiana."

Jim looked around nervously as if she were speaking to someone else and then glanced back at her. He replied, "I'm Jim."

She leaned closer to him with a big smile. He glanced down at her cleavage and narrowed his eyes.

"Will you buy me drink?" she asked.

"Uh, sure."

"Seven and seven."

Jim relayed the order to the bartender.

Caroline smiled at him and asked, "You staying here?"

"Yes. Why, yes, I am," Jim replied a bit awkwardly.

Caroline gave him a sexy look. "Are you looking for company tonight?"

The drink arrived as Jim stammered, "Uh, sure. Well, I mean... I have a girlfriend, but—"

"Five hundred for an hour or two thousand for the whole night." His eyes widened, and she continued, "For that price, we can do anything you want. Well, except the anal. If you want that, it another thousand."

He gave her a casual nod. "That seems pretty reasonable." Jim paused a moment to let the offer sink in. "So, for three thousand dollars, I can have anal sex with you all night long."

Caroline leaned in an inch from his face and fought desperately to hold back her laugh as she said, "And you never forget it."

He pulled back a little. "Look, you are gorgeous, but I can't. I'm actually sorta pre-engaged so—"

"So, you haven't actually asked her to marry you?"

He shrugged. "Well, not technically."

"You're not really engaged then."

"I guess you make a good point."

"Does your precious girlfriend do everything?"

"What are you asking?"

"Does she give you the anal?" Caroline said in a soft, sexy voice as she ran her hand down his shirt to his lap.

Jim's eyes followed her hand down. "Oh, well, um sometimes."

She squeezed his package hard. He grimaced in pain and then glanced around the bar nervously before looking her in the eye.

"Yes, she does. She's a real trouper about that. I mean, like, you know..."

"When is your girlfriend supposed to meet you here?"

"She should be here any minute."

Caroline gave him a tired look and then asked in her regular voice, "Are you sure, Jim?"

Shaking his head, confused, Jim said, "I mean, she was supposed to meet me here, so—"

She put her fingers gently to his lips to stop him from speaking. "Would you excuse me for one second?"

Turning away, Caroline pulled her cell phone from her purse. She smiled at him and then began typing a text message.

Jim, sorry running late. I'll be there in one hour.

She turned back to him and smiled. "Now, where were we?"

His phone beeped, and he pulled it from his pocket. "Sorry. Do you mind?"

Caroline shook her head and waved her hand at him to proceed.

After reading the message, Jim gave her a big smile. "That was my girlfriend."

"Really?"

"Yes, she won't be here for an hour." A smile spread across his face as the lights finally came fully on. "Ohhh... She won't be here for an hour."

They shared a smiling nod. "You see, I didn't get a lot of sleep last night, so I'm a little slow today."

Caroline jumped out of character and said, "That's okay, just try to keep up."

"I will."

"Ready?"

"I think so."

She placed her index finger on his arm and traced it slowly in a circular shape as he smiled and stared down at her hand. After a moment, she widened her eyes and glared at him. He glanced up at her face and shook his head. "I forgot where we were."

Caroline said, "Here, I'll start again... So, it sound like you will be all alone."

"Oh, yeah... I've got it." He attempted to put on a confident grin as he asked, "So, how much did you say for an hour?"

"Five hundred."

"Would I have to wear a condom?"

She broke character for a moment and nodded approvingly at the sexy question while wearing a bright smile. Then she jumped back into her role and frowned. "Of course."

"Even for a blowjob?"

"You must."

"What if I had a little more money?"

Caroline nodded casually. "For seven hundred, I'll suck your big cock slowly for a whole hour, no condom."

"Will you swallow?"

Glaring at him, Caroline lost the accent completely. "Don't push it."

He widened his eyes. "Okay, gee, I was just having some fun with it."

"So, do we have deal?"

Jim nodded.

Two minutes later, they were in the elevator heading up to the twenty-fourth floor. A couple in their early sixties stood next to them. The wife glared at the scantily-dressed Caroline, and the husband's jaw dropped as he eyed her up and down.

After catching the woman's judgmental gape, Caroline shot Jim a quick look. Then she said softly, "Remember, you must pay first."

Jim's eyes shot to the woman, and he spotted the look of horror on her face. The man was grinning. Jim murmured uncomfortably, "Okay."

Caroline looked directly at the woman. "Trust me, you've got to get the money up front. Once they finish, they don't feel like paying anymore."

Gasping, the woman turned to her husband. She found him leering at the supposed hooker. The wife narrowed her eyes as she punched him in the arm. The elevator doors opened, and the woman dragged her husband into the hall.

As the doors were closing again, Jim and Caroline broke into giggles. Jim said, "That was mean."

"It was, but she was giving me a look. She totally deserved it."

"You probably ruined her evening."

"I don't care." Her frown morphed into a smile. Moving to him, she wrapped her arms around his neck. She pushed her body against his and felt his near erection pressing into her stomach. "You're already hard!"

"A little."

Caroline moved her hands down to his groin and squeezed. Jim groaned, "Yeah."

"I feel like pulling you out right here and —"

"They have cameras, you know."

"Yeah, right." She pulled her hand away and glanced at the ceiling of the elevator with an apologetic smile. "I think I can wait."

The elevator doors opened, and the horny pair rushed to their room.

Once inside, Caroline stayed in character. Pushing him against the wall, she slipped down to her knees and began running her hands over the bulge in his pants.

Jim leaned his head back against the wall, closed his eyes tight, and exhaled. "Oh, wow."

She unzipped his fly, reached in, extracted his nearly-hard equipment, and began massaging it with both hands.

Caroline smiled up at him with one eyebrow raised. "You have nice size cock."

Jim glanced down at her. "Gee, thanks."

Her silly expression changed to a more passionate look just before she plunged her mouth forward, swallowing half his length all at once. Jim spread his hands out wide and grasped for something to hold onto. After finding nothing but the wall, he brought his hands back and put them on the sides of his head. He stared down, dizzied at the sight of Caroline's passionate attention.

She kept running her mouth over his length, back and forth, slurping and sucking, as he stood completely still and gasping for breath. Moving his hands down to the straps of her dress, he pushed them over her shoulders. He slipped his fingers to her breasts and worked the fabric down to uncover them. She groaned as he squeezed her nipples firmly. He gazed down at her breasts and began pumping his hips back and forth in small strokes to drive his erection deeper into her mouth.

Her eyelids fluttered as she floated away in ecstasy, imagining that they were fucking right at that moment. He pushed too fast toward her and caught the back of her throat, causing her to gag. After recovering, Caroline gave him a mock-scolding look as she shoved him hard against the wall and held him there with one hand.

Jim stared down at her, open-mouthed and panting, as she used her other hand to unbuckle his khakis and pull them down to his ankles. After bringing both hands to the waistband of his boxer briefs, she tugged them down to his knees. She stared at his hovering erection before opening her mouth wide and taking him back inside.

Groaning loudly, Jim brought a hand to her face and brushed it against her skin. He closed his eyes as she went on pleasing him. After a few minutes more, he couldn't take it any longer.

"I've got to taste you," Jim said as he gently took her head in his hands and coaxed her carefully away from him. Sliding back from him, she followed his lead and remained on her knees, just glancing up at him patiently. He kicked off his shoes, slipped down to join her, and kissed her wildly, shoving his tongue deep into her mouth.

He moved his lips to her neck and sucked at her tender flesh for a moment before sliding down to her breast. He nibbled roughly on her hard nipple before opening his mouth wide and sucking it between his lips. Closing her eyes, she ran her fingers through his hair as she took in a long, deep breath.

Jim pulled up and drank in her sexy body as the tiny black dress fought to cover her. Her large, firm breasts and creamy thighs were exposed, the fabric bunched around her torso as she remained in that kneeling position, simply waiting breathlessly for what was to come. Staring deeply into her eyes, he moved his hand to her back and gently guided her to the floor.

Jim took hold of her dress and pulled it up over her hips to expose the tiny black thong that covered her. She spread her legs wide as he moved his mouth lower. He placed his tongue directly on the tiny strip of black satin between her legs and licked hard.

"Oh, Jim!" she cried out.

After pushing her panties down, he plunged his head into her and went to work. Using his lips, mouth, fingers, and tongue, he pleased her as if they'd been separated for months.

Minutes later, she had more than enough of his teasing. She desperately wanted to be filled up and not with more fingers or tongue. She wanted him deep inside her.

"Put it in," she moaned softly.

Pulling up, Jim gave her a curious look.

"Put it in," she repeated sternly.

He knelt up and frantically fought with the buttons of his shirt as she tore the dress up and over her head. He kicked his khakis and boxers off as she spread her legs, waiting for him to take her. Jim moved over her, and her hands quickly went to his manhood. He pressed his tongue deep into her mouth as she guided him to her entrance.

Caroline sucked on his tongue just as he pressed his hips down and slid inside. Wrapping her hands around his back, she pulled him closer.

He stared into her eyes as he began pumping back and forth, with her pulling him harder into her body with every downward thrust. Soon they climaxed together for what seemed like the first time. It was the perfect beginning to a special night.

Twenty minutes later, Jim and Caroline relaxed together in the large soaking tub. The toes of her left foot toyed with one of his nipples as he worked his fingers into the heel of her right foot. Caroline cocked her head back and closed her eyes. "God, that feels amazing."

"You like that?"

"Uh-huh."

"I read there are all these pressure points in the feet."

"Really?"

Moving his attention to her toes, he said, "Like, if I touch a certain part, I can take away a headache, or another part will stimulate your clitoris in some strange way."

"Do you know which spots do what?"

"Sorry, I didn't get to the end of the article."

She chuckled. Jim moved his fingers to the ball of her foot and worked it firmly.

Opening her mouth wide, she leaned her head back against the tub. "Wow, I swear I just had a little orgasm... I think you actually reached my G-spot."

Jim grinned. "I'll try to remember what I just did there."

He moved forward to take her big toe into his mouth. She lifted her head and giggled. "You know I don't like that."

He pulled his lips from her toe and said, "I love your feet."

"You're weird."

"Oh, you like it."

"Maybe a little." She grinned as he took another toe between his lips. He massaged it harder as he ran his tongue around her second toe.

"You can keep sucking them if you keep rubbing them hard."

Grinning, Jim kept working them with his hands.

Caroline slumped her head back and closed her eyes, melting into complete relaxation.

Reaching over to a towel on the edge of the tub, he slid his hand between the folds. Jim pulled out the diamond engagement ring he'd been holding on to for months. He glanced back to Caroline's face to be sure she was still mesmerized by his foot massage and found she was. He grinned with her toe still held captive between his lips.

He pulled his head back and then slipped the ring onto her second toe. While staring up at her face, he began planting gentle kisses on each of her exquisite toes. He rubbed her foot with both hands as he waited for her to notice the pear-shaped diamond ring.

"Don't stop," she said.

"That's what you said before."

Caroline glanced up at him with a smile. "I know. We should definitely role play again."

He kept rubbing her foot with a silly look on his face as she continued to be oblivious to the ring. "That was fun."

"We should sleep naked tonight... want to?"

"Sure."

Finally glancing at her toe, she spotted the ring. "What's that?"

"Caroline Ryan, will you marry me?"

She shook her head with a grin. "Are you seriously asking me in the bathtub with the ring on my foot?"

He nodded. "Stupid, huh? I was going to ask you at dinner, but I couldn't wait."

After shrugging her shoulders, she smiled brightly with tears welling up on her face.

He pulled the ring from her toe, gently placed her foot back into the water, and moved until he was kneeling next to her. "Let me do this right." He stared into her eyes. "Caroline, I love you. I know that things won't be easy with Victoria and the baby coming and everything, but I'm committed to making this work. I can't stand to be away from you. From the moment that I met you, I've never been happier in my life."

She stared up at him with her lip quivering.

Jim asked, "Will you marry me?"

Caroline moved her hand to cover her mouth as Jim stared unblinkingly at her with the concern starting to show on his face. "Do I need to repeat the question?"

"No."

"No, I don't need to repeat the question or no, you don't want to—"

"Yes, I will marry you."

He smiled brightly. She held her left hand out to him, and he slipped the ring on her finger. Looking down at the sparkling diamond, she beamed. "It's beautiful."

"I picked it out myself."

Caroline looked up at his face. "I love you."

"I love you."

She reached up, wrapped her hands around his neck and pulled him to her for a kiss. Pulling her lips from his, she said softly, "Why don't we stay in and order room service instead of going out?"

He nodded with a sexy smile as he moved his lips back to hers.

22

Back in Orlando, Carl sat in his lavish penthouse apartment in front of his large PC screen. After selecting a camera showing the pool area, he grinned when he spotted Rob and Bridget as they stood in the pool next to each other, enjoying a drink and talking.

He clicked the mouse to move the camera and zoomed in on Bridget's cleavage. He sighed a long, creepy sigh. Shaking his head while licking his lips, he reached down to pull at his zipper. His cell phone rang.

"Fuck." He groaned and zipped back up.

Carl answered the call in a tired voice, "Yeah."

A voice on the other end began, "Mr. Rodgers, I have the information."

"Well, what is it?"

"Her last name isn't Foster, it's Marshall. She's with the F.B.I."

"Shit... what else do you have?"

"We've got a guy inside. They've been building a case against you. He says they're a few days from filing charges."

Carl hung up the phone. Grabbing a vial of cocaine off the desk, he opened it and took a quick hit.

Bridget climbed out of the pool with Rob's eyes glued to her ass as he followed her to the pool deck. She wore a tiny bikini, and Rob struggled to control his body's inadvertent response to how amazing she looked in it. His case of blue balls was getting worse by the second and climbing dangerously near the highest threat level. No way could he ask her to join him in the steam room with the current problem brewing in his trunks. He'd surely be hard during the whole nude experience unless, of course, he could relieve the pressure at least twice beforehand.

As he pondered how to slip away, she dried herself with a towel. Holding his towel over his groin, Rob stood there dripping wet. Bridget paused a moment and then asked, "How do you like working at Wealth Stone?"

"The money's good. It's okay, I guess." Rob's eyes brightened with a memory. "You made quite an impression on Carl the night you stayed over."

"When?"

"Carl said he found you wandering around after midnight and—"

Bridget eyes widened, and she stammered, "Um, I couldn't sleep so I went down to the gym."

"I would have gone down with you."

"I didn't want to wake you up."

Rob paused, deciding if he should grill her on the subject some more. He thought better of it and then shrugged it off. "He wants us to have dinner with him one day next week."

"Okay. That sounds nice."

"We were going to try to do it tonight, but Carl had to go to Atlanta today."

Bridget glanced at him, concerned. "He's in Atlanta today?"

Rob gave her a look, so she tried to repair the damage. "So, he went to Atlanta. I love Atlanta... When's he coming back?"

"Tomorrow."

She exhaled as her mind raced.

Rob continued, "I meant to tell you my mother's trial starts tomorrow, so I need to head back to Miami pretty early in the morning. I'm not sure when I'll be called to testify; I'll be there for a few days."

"When are you coming back?" Bridget asked.

"Maybe not until late next week."

She looked around nervously and mumbled under her breath.

"Are you okay?" Rob asked.

"I, uh... I think I just got my, you know." Rob stared at her, confused, until Bridget glanced down at her stomach and then back to him.

"Oh."

"Can I get your keys? I need to..."

He handed over the keys.

"Be right back."

Rob watched as she grabbed her cell phone and headed toward the building. He fell back into a lounge chair, adjusted his swim trunks, and let out a big sigh as he thought, Great, so she's got her period. We're definitely not going to do it tonight, and I can't even stand up without getting wood.

Bridget dialed a number. "Shit... answer your phone."

"This... Adams."

She heard the call breaking up.

"Vince, can you hear me? Rodgers is in Atlanta *today*. We've got to move now."

"Can't... West now."

"What? Hey, I can't hear you."

Bridget moved closer to the door in an attempt to get better reception.

"Marshall I'm... boat and—"

She waited a moment and then said loudly, "Vince we need to go in tonight. Wednesday is a no go."

"I..."

"What?"

"... Key West and—"

"You're in Key West?"

"Yes and—"

"Vince... Vince."

The line went dead. After hitting redial, Bridget rubbed her head as she listened to the cellular network's "cannot-reach-the-subscriber" message. She dialed once more, heard the same message, and then stood in the hall, staring at the phone as she pondered her options.

She whispered to herself, "I can do this. It's got to be done today." She put on a confident grin as she headed up to Rob's apartment.

Carl scrolled through security camera views inside the building until he located Bridget walking down the hall toward the party room. He watched as she stood in front of the door wearing only that tiny bikini and holding some kind of small black box. She punched in the code, glanced down either side of the corridor and then quickly slipped inside.

Carl stood, grabbed the gun off the desk, and slipped it into the waistband of his pants before pulling his shirt over it.

Inside the party room, Bridget made her way to the second locked door and pulled out the black box. After opening the box, she pulled out an earphone and secured it to her ear. Next, she pressed the box against the lock mechanism and began punching codes.

Ninety seconds later, she smiled as the lock clicked open. She pulled the earphone from her ear just as the gun barrel pressed into her back.

"Miss Marshall," Carl said. Bridget held perfectly still. He added, "Can I help you find something?"

When, after ten minutes, Bridget hadn't returned, Rob walked into the building and went to his apartment. He found the door locked, and after knocking a few times, headed back down to the ground floor. After glancing out to the pool and not finding her, he went to the parking lot and found her car was still there. He headed back into the building.

Rob spotted Carl coming out of the party room. Their eyes met for a moment, and Carl gave him an evil smile. "Are you looking for someone?"

"You haven't seen Bridget have you?"

"She's right in here." Rob returned a tentative smile as Carl held the door open while staring at him casually.

Rob paused a moment and then shook off his concern as he began walking toward the room.

"She's waiting for you," Carl added.

"Aren't you supposed to be in Atlanta?"

"The trip was cancelled."

Reaching the door, Rob gave Carl a confused look as he asked, "She's in here?"

Carl nodded, and Rob entered the room. Rob glanced around the room but didn't see Bridget anywhere. As he began to turn back, Carl slammed the butt of the gun hard against the side of Rob's head. He slumped to the floor.

23

Rob and Bridget lay on the floor of the large safe wearing only their bathing suits. Their hands were tied tightly behind their backs, and their ankles were also bound. She struggled with her ropes as Rob continued to lay unconscious. After thirty seconds, she gave up her fight and sighed.

"Rob," she called out, but there was no response.

Bridget wiggled her way over to him and pushed her head against his shoulder. She called his name again, pushed into him once more and called again, "Rob, wake up!"

He groaned as his eyes fought to open. He shook his head slowly, opened his mouth, and looked at her, bewildered. "What the hell happened?"

"Carl dragged you in here."

"My... my fucking head hurts." Struggling against the ropes, he gave her a puzzled look. "Why?"

"Did he hit you with something?"

"I don't know... I." Rob turned his head and grimaced in pain. "Shit... Why is this happening?"

"Rob, I—"

"Why the hell would he tie us up and—"

"Look, I'm actually... I'm with the F.B.I."

"What?"

"We've been building a case against Carl Rodgers for the last ten months."

Rob narrowed his eyes. "What the hell are you talking about?"

"He's running some kind of ponzi scheme, and we been trying to gather enough evidence to arrest him."

"You're with the F.B.I. So, you've been fucking lying to me this whole time?"

"I had to."

He sneered, and Bridget returned a sorrowful look. "I wanted to tell you, but I couldn't blow my cover or risk putting you in danger."

After staring at her a moment, he said slowly, "You mean, like the kinda danger I'm in right at this moment?"

"I know. I'm sorry."

With her eyes wide open, she looked around the room at the stacks of shiny bars. "There must be, like, two hundred million dollars' worth of gold in here."

"Five-hundred eighty-three million," he said with some confidence.

She gave him a curious look.

He narrowed his eyes. "Or maybe it was 584 million."

"How do you know?"

"I saw a spreadsheet on Carl's computer a few days ago. I mean, it could be worth more or less now with gold prices fluctuating. Plus, he's got another smaller stash at the office. All together, it's a little over 800 million."

Bridget said, "We believe he accepted about six hundred million in investments. If he's got that much, there's enough here to pay the investors back their principal and more than his promised return. There's probably still enough left over for the company to make a ton of money. I wonder why the hell he's doing this?"

"I'll tell you why... He's a crazy, coked up, sex-addicted, lunatic psycho... I mean, I like sex as much as the next guy, probably more, but he's, uh... out of his fucking mind. And now I'm going to die surrounded by almost a billion in gold."

"I'll get us out of here. I promise."

Bridget struggled with her ropes, and Rob did the same. After less than a minute, they gave up. She said, "Carl told me to have a good night... like maybe he isn't coming back until morning. All we need to do is get untied, then—"

"Then what? We just blink our way out of this safe or wait for him to find us sitting on the gold, then blow us away?"

"Let's just get free. We can worry about the next step after that."

Rob glared at her, "You know, I can't believe you pretended that you liked me just so you could stake out the building. You could have told me what you were up to, and I would have agreed to help you."

"I was not authorized to tell you. There was a plan in place, and I couldn't deviate from it."

"Great plan."

"It wasn't supposed to happen this way. When you told me Carl was in Atlanta, I kind of went rogue or, I don't know, I just..."

"Great, I'm trapped in here with the freaking female John McClane."

"Who?"

"*Die Hard*," he shot back.

She stared at him, confused.

"Oh, just forget it."

"I'm sorry."

"Me, too."

Bridget paused. "Let's move back-to-back; then I can try to untie your hands." After sharing a nod, they both began shifting around until their backs were pressed against each other. They moved close and she went to work on his ropes. After two minutes of fruitless struggle, she realized she was getting nowhere.

She said, "I can't get it. Shit. Try to untie mine."

Rob went to work fumbling with her ropes. He kept at it for another minute then groaned. "This isn't working."

They turned to look at each other, their faces only a few inches apart. She smiled at him. "I really began to like you. It... it started out as a case, but... I don't know. I wanted to tell you. I just—"

"Really?"

"Yes. If we get out of here... I mean, *when* we get out of here, we should go on a real date."

"I'll be unemployed, so I should have lots of free time," Rob quipped.

"I think I will, too," she said, and they shared a grin. "Why don't you try to use your teeth on my ropes? Maybe that'll work."

Rob nodded. She twisted around as he moved lower. The string of her tiny bikini worked its way untied on one side as she turned. The fabric fell open, and half of her beautiful ass was staring him right in the face.

"Uh, your bathing suit, it—"

"Just focus on the ropes."

"Okay," he said as his eyes locked on her adorably pale-white ass cheek with his penis quickly expanding in his swim trunks. Moving his mouth to her hands, he worked at getting the rope between his teeth. He tried and tried, but it was no use.

She said, "Spit on the rope."

"What?"

"I mean, spit on my wrist where the rope is, and maybe I can slide my hands through."

"Okay," he replied unconvinced.

After working up a nice batch of saliva in his mouth, Rob blew a huge wad unto her wrists. She cringed then broke into a chuckle. He did it again, and she began to squirm. Her bikini bottom had practically fallen all the way off now. He stared at her ass and the spectacular back view of all her parts with his swim trunks quickly crowding. He spit again, and this time she laughed out loud. He asked, "What the hell are you laughing at?"

"It tickles, and it's kind of gross. I can't believe I'm asking you to spit on me. This is like bad porn or something."

Rob chuckled.

She said, "Okay, now use your tongue to push it under the ropes."

"Push what?"

"The spit!"

"Seriously?"

"Yes."

Moving in, he did as she asked, tasting the bitter nylon rope as he fought to work the saliva in really well. He finished the chore and then pulled back, spitting out rope fibers as he cringed. "Okay, give it a try now."

He moved back a little further, and she fought to pull her hands free. She struggled and struggled, thrashing around. Her bikini bottoms now fell completely off. He stared at her with his manhood sticking straight out and tenting his trunks impressively.

"Fuck," she cried as she gave up. She flipped over to look at him and her eyes immediately went to his huge erection. "Why the hell are you hard?"

"Well, I'm down here staring right at your vagina and spitting into your wrists and then licking it. It was kind of hot in a totally bizarre way."

Bridget couldn't take her eyes off his trunks. While parting her lips, she felt her vagina moisten as she said, "If we're going to die like this, uh..." She glanced up at his face then back to his bulge. "... the least I can do is give you a blowjob."

Rob nodded in enthusiastic agreement as she flipped around until her face was in line with his trunks. She plunged her mouth on his bulge over the fabric of his trunks, and he stared down at her breathlessly. Her hips were only a foot from his face and his eyes quickly moved to her vagina. He stared at it, desperately wanting to taste her.

Moving her mouth to the bathing suit tie, she clamped down on one end with her teeth and pulled the knot free. She smiled proudly and pushed her face into his abdomen. There, she used her teeth to grip the waistband of his trunks, and she struggled to pull them down. It wasn't working. She tried again, then once more with no luck before finally giving up and groaning in frustration.

Bridget flipped around breathlessly then scooted up until her still-secured hands could reach his trunks. After grasping the waistband with her fingers, he moved one way and she moved the other. Working together, they pulled the flexible waistband down. He moaned, relieved as his manhood sprang free. Bridget pulled his trunks down a little more then quickly flipped back and moved into position with her face inches from his groin and her parts just a foot from his lips.

She took him into her mouth and sucked him enthusiastically, punctuated with a loud groan of delight.

"Oh, fuck..." he moaned. Glancing up between her thighs, he narrowed his eyes. He moved to her and pressed his lips just over her pubic hair. She got the message and spread her knees apart as best as she could with her ankles still bound. Wedging his head between her legs, he shoved his tongue inside.

Moaning, she worked her mouth over him as he licked her like he'd never wanted to enjoy anything more. They each kept going and going with what may have been the first-ever bound sixty-nine session in a safe full of almost one billion dollars in gold.

Suddenly, Bridget was struck mid-lick with an epiphany. Her eyes opened wide as she pulled away from him and asked breathlessly, "How much do you ejaculate?"

He kept licking her until she repeated, "Hey, Rob! How much do you ejaculate?"

Pulling his mouth from her, he glanced at her face while wearing an odd expression. "Um, the normal amount, I guess. I'll tell you before I come, so—"

"No, that's not... I want you to come on my wrists."

Rob looked at her like she was out of her mind. "I've heard 'come on my tits' and even 'my ass,' but—"

"Look, we can use it to loosen the ropes. I hope you shoot, like, a gallon."

He raised his eyebrows. "You've been giving me blue balls for the entire week, and I haven't jerked off even once. It should be a lot."

"I'm proud of you," she said with a smile.

"Thanks."

"Okay. I'm going to go back to work, but you tell me when you're close. Give me some notice. Then we'll switch around so I can finish you with my hands, and if everything goes as planned..."

"Okay, I'd better stop what I'm doing so I can focus, and I don't... But God, you taste amazing! Just one more..." He plunged his face back between her thighs and licked her wildly. She groaned and let him go on for twenty seconds before she closed her legs and said, "Okay, wow. Just uh, you have to stop, or..."

Shaking his head in an attempt to focus, he pulled away from her. "Sorry."

She slid her lips back over him and started again. He watched her, completely turned on as she appeared to lose herself entirely in the experience.

After ninety intense more seconds, he moaned, "Oh, fuck. I'm ready."

She quickly spun around then backed up until his manhood was pointed right at her wrists. She used both hands to massage him as he pumped his hips back and forth into the makeshift double-handed vagina-like receptacle. Groaning loudly, he flexed every muscle in his body to push out the orgasm. He cried out as he blew a huge load right into her wrists. She moved a few inches away from him until she cradled only the head of his penis in her hands just as shots two, three and four splattered against the ropes. Thrusting his hips, he pushed his erection back to her wrists, letting out one last huge groan.

Bridget kept on milking his manhood between her aching fingers in an attempt to pull every last drop to her wrists. He made some strange noise before holding perfectly still as he struggled to catch his breath.

"Are you done?" she asked.

"Yeah."

Bridget rolled onto her stomach to keep the semen from escaping to the floor. She shook her hands while pointing them to the ceiling to drive the liquid freedom where it needed to be. She cringed as the strange feeling of his thick liquid dripping down her arms and wrists and onto the ropes overcame her.

Once she felt the dripping had stopped, she commanded, "Turn around." They moved back-to-back again as she added, "Use your fingers to get it in there."

Following her instructions, he began to work it in while wearing a disgusted look. He said, "This is gross. I'm telling you right now that I'm not using my tongue to work that in, so don't even ask."

She chuckled as he pushed the semen all over her wrists and under the ropes. He announced proudly, "I think I did shoot a gallon."

Bridget said, "Okay, let's try it."

He moved away as she began twisting her wrists back and forth and thrashing on the floor. She called out, "Come on!" He watched her with a hopeful look, then she cried out once more, pulled harder, struggled, and finally pulled one hand free. Grinning, Bridget moved her hands down to her feet. She glanced at him, and they shared a brief smile before she went to work on the knots by her ankles.

Free from all her ropes she went to him with her lower half completely uncovered and her coiffed landing strip just eighteen inches from his face. His eyes roamed over her body as she worked on the ropes around his wrists. Once his hands were free, she moved to his ankles and untied his feet.

Lying in front of her with his swim trunks around his ankles, his penis was still nearly hard. She wore only her bikini top, and they stared at each other with a fire burning just below the surface.

She moved to him, and he pulled her close, rolling on top of her, their lips slammed together with unbridled passion.

Rob ran his hands down to her ass and moved to his knees. Then he pulled her up until her legs were wrapped around his back with her hands clutching his neck. They kept kissing as he got to his feet while still holding her, and he searched for a place to put her down. Spotting the waist-high stack of gold bars, he moved toward it.

He gently rested her spectacular ass on top of the brightly glowing stack. Placing his hands on her bikini top, he pushed it up to expose her breasts. He looked at the twin beauties for the first time, narrowed his eyes, then leaned down and took one of her tiny pink nipples into his mouth.

He licked and sucked passionately as she ran her fingers through his hair with her eyes tightly closed.

"Oh, God..." Bridget cried out as he moved to her other nipple.

Pulling up from her, he stared down hungrily at her tight body. He had to have her. She wanted him badly. All at once, he slipped inside and they fucked for what seemed like forever.

After they both enjoyed tremendous climaxes, she moved away from him, collapsing to the floor, panting and spent. He slipped down to join her and they lay there curled up together, naked, exhausted, thirsty, and struggling to recover.

24

On Friday, January 6th, in the Superior Court of Miami-Dade County, the trial of Brookhart v. Grayson began. At 9:00 a.m. the rigorous process of jury selection kicked off, and it wasn't until almost two hours later that the pool of more than two hundred was narrowed down to the final twelve. The jury consisted of seven women and five men who ranged in age from twenty-three to sixty-one. After lunch, everyone assembled in the courtroom. Jillian sat at the defense table with her lawyer, Stanley Parrish, and another attorney from his firm. On the plaintiff side, Josh Roth sat next to the conservatively-dressed Natalie Brookhart.

Behind the defense table, Brian and the not-entirely-conservatively-dressed Victoria Wilde sat with the other spectators. She wanted to show off her newly abundant mid-pregnancy cleavage, and the blouse she chose that morning did the job well.

Josh Roth moved to the front of the court to deliver his opening statement. He began, "Jillian Grayson is a bestselling author of fifteen novels. Her latest novel, *The Leg Thing*, is a breakout success. It's a story of an older woman who falls in love with a younger man who just happens to be the best friend of her son. Anyone who reads the book and knows the Grayson and Nash families can plainly see that the characters in the novel are based on these real people. And this is fine. What's not fine is that my client, Miss Natalie Brookhart, is also depicted in the novel completely and wholly without her knowledge. No attempt was made to contact my client to obtain her permission, and for this, she is entitled to damages."

Josh moved closer to the jury as he continued, "What's more, Natalie is reflected in an extremely unflattering light. She's been defamed and has suffered emotional distress and pain as a result of her unauthorized portrayal in this racy and scandalous work."

Next he moved over to a large flip chart and revealed a blown-up image of the book cover. The jury stared at the image of the young, slim, and attractive woman performing that now-famous and difficult ballet move as Josh added, "This is the cover of the book, which depicts a woman in the midst of a complex ballet position. And sure, there are a number of ballerinas who can perform this move, but the novel isn't based on any of those other ballerinas, because none of those others ever dated both Ms. Grayson's son and her new husband. Natalie Brookhart can perform this move; Natalie Brookhart dated both Rob Grayson and Brian Nash."

Glancing over to the defense table, he continued, "We're here to prove that this isn't really a novel at all; it's actually a memoir based on the life of the defendant and those around her. A true accounting of her recent past, with the lone exception of how Miss Brookhart is portrayed in the story as a manipulative, lying, conniving, scheming woman of loose morals. Ms. Grayson was incredibly jealous of Miss Brookhart and—"

Jillian scoffed loudly, and all eyes went to her. She returned an apologetic nod, and Stanley leaned over to whisper in her ear.

Josh said, "Ms. Grayson set out in the book to destroy Miss Brookhart's character. We will prove that this was done with malice and premeditation, and for these reasons, Miss Brookhart is entitled to punitive damages."

Josh returned to his seat.

Judge Maxwell said, "Mr. Parrish."

Stanley moved to stand before the jury and began, "We're here today because of jealousy all right, but not on the part of Ms. Grayson. We're here because when Miss Brookhart doesn't get what she wants, she gets mad. So mad that she's here today in an attempt to destroy a marriage, purely because she was rejected by Ms. Grayson's husband, Brian Nash, a young man she tried to manipulate and possess, like she had so many others before."

Glancing at Natalie, Stanley shook his head before returning his attention to the jury. "We will prove a pattern of behavior on Miss Brookhart's part, which clearly shows the type of spoiled, vindictive, manipulative personality she embodies."

Natalie glared at him as if she might jump up and rip his face off. She felt a juror's eyes on her, glanced over, and painted on a smile.

Stanley continued, "*The Leg Thing* is a fictional story, based loosely on actual events in Ms. Grayson's life. There is no malice here. This is a case of a young woman who sees her opportunity to simultaneously get revenge and shamelessly cash in on the success of another."

Stanley nodded to the jury before returning to his seat.

25

At Wealth Stone, Carl paced nervously around his office. The room was a disaster with stacks of papers on the desk, documents strewn across the floor, and empty soda cans falling out of the overflowing trashcan. He dropped a folder into a box that sat on his desk. Pulling a vial of cocaine from his pocket, he opened it, pushed his pinky inside, and snorted it quickly.

After rubbing both hands over his chin, Carl lifted a cell phone off the desk to check for any missed calls. He cursed then checked the battery level and the number of bars. He shook his head and cursed again.

There was a knock at the door. Turning quickly toward it, he ran his hand over his face to wipe away the sweat.

He cleared his throat as he tried to compose himself. "Yes."

Carl's secretary opened the door. "Carl, the staff meeting's in five minutes. You wanted me to—"

"Call it off," he fired back gruffly. "Actually, cancel everything I have today."

The secretary didn't bat an eyelash, since his erratic behavior was commonplace, and replied, "Yes sir."

After she closed the door, he rushed over, locked it, and then sat in front of the desk. He opened a drawer, moved a gun aside, pulled out a vial of cocaine, and took another hit. The cell phone rang. Rubbing his nose, he sniffed, glanced at the phone display, and took a deep breath. He pushed the button before putting the phone to his ear and said, "Mr. Sampson."

"Rodgers."

"I've been trying to reach you all night."

"What is it?"

"I need to move the gold today." Carl waited for a response and after a few seconds of silence added, "Sampson, I need you to take it today."

"I can't do that. We're all set for Friday. I don't even have—"

"It must be today. There's no deal if we don't do it today."

Sampson sighed loudly, and Carl could hear his breathing as he again waited for a response. Finally he replied, "Let me get back to you... but Carl, if we do this today, I can't pay twelve hundred."

"Come on Sampson. We had a deal."

"Hold on."

Carl struggled to listen as inaudible dialog spilled through the phone while Sampson apparently conferred with an associate. He waited and after hearing a few seconds of silence on the other end, Carl began, "Sampson, do we —"

"A thousand an ounce."

"What? It's worth over seventeen hundred."

"A thousand," Sampson shot back loudly.

Carl stared out the window, thinking.

"Rodgers, do we have a deal?"

"Fuck it. Okay. But it's got to be today."

"Call you back."

After tossing the phone onto his desk, he reached once more for the vial of cocaine.

26

In the courtroom, Natalie was seated on the witness stand as Josh approached the jury.

Josh began, "Miss Brookhart, how did you learn about this book?"

"I was walking past a bookstore, and something caught my eye in the widow. I noticed the cover, since it was very unique and had a picture of the ballet move that was very familiar to me."

She smiled sweetly at the jury. "I went into the store and read the jacket. I knew that Rob's mother wrote as Jaclyn West, that's her pen name, and then I read the book description."

The men in the jury were studying the cute little Natalie as she testified. They wore distant smiles, completely captivated as they hung on her every word.

"When did you realize that this Rebecca character in the book was based on you?"

"Still in the store, I read the chapter where Brice meets Rebecca for the first time. He was watching her do this ballet move, and it was exactly the same as how I met Brian for the very first time."

"You're referring to Brian Nash, who is now Jillian Grayson's husband?"

"Yes."

"Go on."

"So at that point, I realized the Rebecca character seemed to be based on me. I scanned through the book and looked for references to this Rebecca character, and what I found horrified me..." She stopped, covered her mouth with one hand, and looked to be on the verge of tears.

"Do you need a minute?" Josh asked.

In the otherwise silent courtroom, Jillian scoffed, and all eyes went to her. She slumped down in her seat.

"No, I think I can continue." Natalie took a calming breath and then added softly, "Next I, um, read a part where Rebecca said she was a 'technical virgin' and I had no idea what that was so I read more, and the character went on to explain that she only had a certain kind of sex, a kind, uh, which I find to be utterly appalling."

"What kind of sex?" Josh asked in an innocent voice.

"Natalie glanced at the jury and then hesitantly over to the judge. Her eyes went back to Josh. She paused and then whispered, "Anal."

Everyone in the room leaned in and all eyes narrowed as they struggled to hear. The court reporter raised her hand and blurted, "Sorry, Your Honor, but I did not get that."

The judge said, "Please repeat that Miss Brookhart."

Natalie curled her lip and then took a deep breath. Giving her a sympathetic look, the judge said, "Take your time. Just begin again when you're ready."

Jillian scanned the crowd with dismay. Everyone was staring at Natalie as if they wanted to either comfort her, have sex with her, or both. Jillian's mouth was wide open as she wore an expression, which screamed, "Can you freaking believe this?"

"Okay, sorry this is just so..." Natalie moved closer to the microphone and said loud and clear as day, "ANAL SEX." The words reverberated around the courtroom and were punctuated by loud screeching feedback from the microphone. Then the room fell silent as the men grinned, and the women inaudibly gasped. A moment later, the only sound heard was both Jillian and Victoria chuckling. All eyes went to Jillian; she covered her smile before catching the judge's disapproving glare.

After shooting Jillian a dirty look, Natalie returned her sad, pouting face to Josh.

"Please continue, Miss Brookhart."

"I went on to read more, and the book made this Rebecca character out to be a horrible girl who manipulated men and treated them terribly. She's portrayed basically as a slut, and, um, but mainly what struck me over and over through the entire story was that it seemed to follow exactly my relationship to Jillian Grayson's son, Rob, and her boyfriend back then, Brian."

Jillian stared at the jurors who still appeared to be completely captivated by the loveable Natalie. Shaking her head, she exhaled, defeated, before returning her eyes to the witness.

Natalie continued, "I've had calls from people who've read the book... I mean even the title screams that it's about me. I practically invented the term, 'The Leg Thing.' That's what everyone called it at school. She even stole the title from me."

Natalie squeezed the bridge of her nose as her eyes became weepy. She sniffled, and her gaze slowly traveled to Jillian as she curled her lip, fighting back tears. She glanced back to the jury with a puppy dog look. They were all with her, shaking their heads, frowning and glaring at Jillian.

"You poor thing," one female juror whispered.

Josh said, "Okay, Natalie, are you aware of anyone else that either Rob Grayson or Brian Nash know who can perform this ballet move shown on the cover?"

"No. There are very few people who can," Natalie announced smugly.

Nodding, Josh turned to the judge. "Your Honor, if it may please the court, we would like to demonstrate how Miss Brookhart can perform this ballet move and how it is identical to the book cover image."

Maxwell pondered this for a moment. "Yes, Mr. Roth. I believe that we would all like to see this."

The men in the jury all sat up just a little straighter.

"Miss Brookhart needs to change into a leotard, if that's okay. It'll just take a minute."

Nearly every man in the courtroom moved to the edge of his seat with his eyes glimmering.

Maxwell said, "Certainly. She may use the restroom attached to the courtroom."

Natalie stood and made her way to meet Josh at the plaintiff's table. He pulled a bag from his briefcase and handed it to her. She headed off to the restroom as Jillian whispered something into Stanley's ear.

Two minutes later, Natalie appeared wearing a black leotard and looking absolutely drop dead spectacular. Slowly she waltzed her perfect rock hard body in her bright pink sock-covered feet toward the front of the courtroom. The men's pulses quickened as they all stared at her. All women (well, except for two) looked on jealously.

Glancing up at the judge, Natalie said softly, "I just need a minute to warm up."

He nodded while wearing an awestruck smile.

Natalie brought one leg up halfway and held it for a few seconds and then returned it to the floor. Next, she repeated the identical stretch with the other leg. After taking a deep breath, she slipped down quickly into a perfect split. There was an audible gasp from the jury. After languidly stretching her body out along one leg, holding it briefly and then the other, she moved her torso back to the center and quickly popped up. The jurors looked on, impressed.

She smiled. "I'm ready."

Maxwell said, "Proceed."

She glanced at Josh, and he returned an approving nod. All eyes were on her, and no one made a sound. Natalie stood perfectly still, took another deep breath, and slowly and gracefully lifted her right leg until it was pointed straight at the ceiling, while the other remained firmly planted on the floor but up on the ball of her foot. She held her leg there with one hand, almost effortlessly, as nearly everyone looked on, completely blown away, their jaws slacking.

The male jurors' eyes all got lost in Natalie's crotch area as the fabric of her leotard struggled to cover all her important parts. Most tilted their heads, caught up in a dream-like state. Glancing at them, Josh held back a smile.

Jillian scoffed, and Victoria held back a laugh as Josh walked slowly over to the flip chart. He asked, "Are you doing okay?"

"I'm fine," Natalie replied.

Josh flipped back to the large image of the book cover as he said, "And once again, here is the book cover, so an accurate comparison can be made."

Most jury members' eyes moved between the cover image and the live demonstration, although a few of the men never looked away from Natalie's crotch as the leotard appeared to be slipping away right before their eyes.

The judge took a deep breath as he glanced quickly to the flip chart, and then his eyes traveled slowly down Natalie's lithe body. He sighed while a dreamy smile spread over his face. Shaking his head, he fought his way back to reality, painting on a more appropriate professional expression.

Brian found himself staring at the demonstration, as well. For a moment, his mind drifted back to when Jillian had performed that move for him bare-ass naked, and while she held that sexy position, they had actually done it. Closing his eyes, he pictured the way her calf rested against his shoulder as he was making love to her on that spectacular day. It was a sexual experience he would never forget.

He pulled himself from the fantasy just as Jillian turned to him and rolled her eyes. Brian shook his head in disgust, and they shared a grin.

Glancing at her attorney, Jillian found him staring at Natalie's body along with every other owner of a penis in the room. She scoffed and then bumped her knee into his under the table.

Stanley's eyes shot to Jillian's angry stare. He shook his head and yelled out, "I object."

The judge gave Stanley a confused look as all eyes in the courtroom went to him. "On what grounds?"

"I, uh... to the inflammatory nature of this demonstration."

Maxwell shook his head and grimaced. "Overruled."

All eyes returned to Natalie. Josh's stare traveled down her body slowly. After ten seconds of drinking in her amazing body, he fought his way back to Earth and said, "Okay, Miss Brookhart. Thank you."

Natalie slowly returned her ceiling-pointing leg to the floor and looked up at the judge with a gentle smile.

The judge stated, "Let's take a ten minute recess while Miss Brookhart changes." He leapt out of his seat and rushed to his chambers. He was glad he was wearing a big freaking robe.

Brian stood with Jillian outside the courtroom. Leaning in close, he whispered, "When she was doing that, all I could think about was you in that position when we did it."

"Really?" Jillian grinned.

"Yeah, I had to stop myself from thinking about it, because I was getting worked up."

Jillian wiggled her hips. "God, I just got wet myself." She put her hand on his waist. "Maybe later you can help me work off some of the stress of the trial."

They shared a grin until Jillian's smile faded. "Hey, have you seen Rob yet today?"

"No, I haven't."

"He was supposed to be here by ten."

Stanley Parrish walked up to Jillian and said, "Can we have a word?"

Jillian nodded then looked at Brian. "Try to find him okay?"

Brian said, "I will."

Brian headed down the hall as he dialed Rob's number. The call went directly to voice mail, so he left a message. When he turned back to Jillian, Stanley was heading away from her and into the courtroom.

Brian walked back to Jillian. "He's not picking up. I left him a message."

She gave him a concerned look.

He added, "But I'm sure he's on his way."

"Yeah, maybe he's in traffic." She shook her head. "Stanley tells me I'm being called next. I'm not sure I can do this."

"You'll do fine."

She stared up at him. He opened his arms, and she slipped inside.

27

Josh stood glaring at Jillian as she sat nervously in the witness chair. He paused a moment. "Ms. Grayson..." He grinned. "... or should I call you Mrs. Nash?"

She squirmed in her chair. "I'm keeping my name, you know, for my career and—"

"Ms. Grayson, isn't it true that the Rebecca character in your novel is wholly based on my client, Natalie Brookhart?"

"It is not."

Exhaling deeply, Josh flashed the jury a skeptical look before returning to Jillian. "Rebecca in your novel is an ex-ballet dancer, and Natalie is a ballet dancer, isn't that correct?"

"If you say so."

A few members of the jury held back a giggle, but Josh was not amused.

With an edge in his voice, he asked, "Ms. Grayson, in your novel is Rebecca an ex-ballet dancer?"

"Yes."

"And are you aware that Miss Brookhart once studied ballet?"

"Yes," Jillian replied sarcastically.

He continued, "In your novel, the Rebecca character was dating your Brice character, and you wrote how she attended his tennis match and then disappeared in the middle of it. Is that correct?"

"Yes, that's right."

"And Miss Brookhart actually attended one of your husband's tennis matches and, in fact, did disappear. She was also dating him at the time. Isn't that correct?"

Jillian widened her eyes. "She was dating him and half the men on campus."

Almost everyone in the attendance roared with laughter. The judge cracked a smile until he caught Josh's angry stare and banged his gavel hard against the wood block. The room fell silent.

Judge Maxwell said, "Quiet! I will have order in this courtroom."

Josh cleared his throat. "Ms. Grayson... and one of those men she was dating was your son, Rob. Is that correct?"

Jillian glanced down at the floor then back up at Josh. "Well, yes."

"And there is a character in your book named Ryder, based on your son, who dated the Rebecca character. Isn't that correct?"

"Yes, it is."

Josh smiled. "I'm going to take you through a few of the plot points and you just answer yes or no if these events are, in fact, in the book." He asked snidely, "Can you do that?"

She fought back an evil look as she replied, "Yes."

"Mr. Nash admitted to Natalie that he read a diary entry he believed to be about him, and in your novel Brice admitted the same fact to Rebecca. Is that correct?"

Jillian grit her teeth quickly then composed herself. "Yes."

"Miss Brookhart can get into the ballet position known as 'developpe leg devant ala derriere,' and in your novel, Rebecca gets into that same position. Is that correct?"

"Yes."

"Mr. Nash met Miss Brookhart at a Super Bowl party, and in your novel, Brice and Rebecca meet at a party. Is that correct?"

Jillian gave him a tired look. "Yes." She folded her arms and leaned back defiantly in her chair.

Josh stared at the jury while wearing a shit-eating grin as he said, "Miss Brookhart drove to Miami during Spring Break to see your son, Rob, and in your novel, the Rebecca character drives — also during Spring Break and also to Miami — to see your Ryder character. Is that correct?"

Jillian remained back from the microphone as she said softly, "Yes." Josh returned his eyes to Jillian and waited with his eyebrows raised. "Could you repeat that?"

She leaned in and said loudly, "Yes, it is."

"All right... And Ms. Grayson, even the title of the novel, *The Leg Thing*, is, in fact, derived from the name of Miss Brookhart's ballet move."

"Well, yes, but—"

"You stole her likeness without her permission didn't you?" Josh interrupted.

"I did not!"

"Now, isn't it fair to say that your entire novel is based on true events surrounding Miss Brookhart's life, and you made no attempt to secure a release from her to use these events or her likeness?"

Folding her arms, Jillian stared Josh down. "It is not fair to say."

"Well, then, how do you explain the title and the ballet move and the diary and the tennis match and everything else that—"

"There is one thing that *is* based on your Miss Brookhart," Jillian interrupted as her blood boiled.

"Yes, what's that?" Josh asked.

"My Rebecca character is an anal whore, and so is your client." The crowd gasped, and the judge gave Jillian a surprised look. The jury stared gape-mouthed at Jillian as she breathed heavily while glaring down at Josh as if she wanted to snap his neck like a twig.

Natalie looked up, appalled, pointed at Jillian and screamed, "You little bitch!"

Judge Maxwell slammed his gavel into the block twice. "Miss Brookhart, you will not speak in my courtroom unless you are in the witness stand."

Natalie stared angrily at Jillian. The judge asked sternly, "Miss Brookhart, do you understand?"

Natalie shook her head. "She can't call me—"

"Ms. Grayson can say whatever she likes while she's on the witness stand." Maxwell made a face and shook his head as he glanced at Jillian. "Even if it's to her detriment." He returned to Natalie. "Keep your mouth shut now, Miss Brookhart, or I'll have you removed."

"Yes, Judge." Natalie sat back in her chair and stared at Jillian like she wanted to pick up the fight right where they left off in St. Barts.

Judge Maxwell said, "Continue, Mr. Roth."

"Ms. Grayson, so not only did you create a character solely based on Miss Brookhart, but you also chose to paint that character in an unflattering light."

"That's not true. The characters in my novels are usually a combination of my imagination with bits and pieces of some people I know, have observed, or may have heard about."

Sighing loudly, Josh looked back to Jillian. "How can you explain all the similarities between Natalie and the Rebecca character in your novel?"

"Coincidence."

"Coincidence," Josh replied as he nodded his head just staring back at Jillian. He turned to the jury and scoffed before repeating, "Just a coincidence."

"Yes," Jillian shot back confidently.

"The diary..." Josh held his fist up and counted the items off one-by-one on his fingers while speaking loudly with a sarcastic tone."... the tennis match, the dating of the son, the trip to Miami... all coincidences."

"That's right."

Josh studied the jurors' skeptical expressions. He repeated snidely, "Okay." He grinned then turned back to Jillian.

"Wasn't it true that you were upset when Mr. Nash left Miami with Miss Brookhart after he had begun an affair with you while vacationing in your home?"

"We were not having an affair!"

"Not having an affair."

"No, we weren't."

Josh narrowed his eyes. "So, do you generally go skinny dipping with men you are not sleeping with?"

Jillian's mouth flew open as she stared back at Josh. She glanced at Brian, and he shrugged his shoulders, confused. She returned her gaze to Josh. "How did you—"

"Answer the question."

"We were not sleeping together."

Josh grinned. "So, after you smoked that joint together, you were not swimming naked in your pool?"

Jillian narrowed her eyes at Josh before glancing to Stanley for some assistance. He stared back at her, helplessly shrugging his shoulders.

Glancing down at his legal pad, Josh began, "It's all in the deposition testimony of a Miss Victoria Wilde... she is a friend of yours, is she not?"

Jillian glanced to Victoria who returned an apologetic look and mouthed the word, "Sorry."

Josh repeated, "Is she a friend of yours?"

Jillian paused and then said without a hint of emotion, "She was."

Several members of the jury chuckled and even the judge managed a smile.

Josh continued, "Remember, you are under oath, Ms. Grayson."

After closing her eyes for a moment, Jillian stared back up at Josh.

He began again, this time in a tired voice, "After you got high with Mr. Nash, isn't it true that you swam naked with him in your pool and were so in love with him and jealous of Miss Brookhart that when he returned to college, you began to write a novel based on my client as an attempt to make her pay for stealing your—"

"All right, the novel is based on her!" Jillian interrupted with her blood boiling over. "She's a man-hating, manipulative little bitch. Her name was changed, the college was changed... no one would have known this had anything to do with her if she hadn't filed this lawsuit."

Jillian took a quick breath. Everyone stared at her in complete shock as she continued her rant. "I can't stand her. She's a money grubbing, lying, spoiled little—" Jillian caught Stanley Parrish's horrified glare, shut up, and closed her eyes tight.

Widening his eyes, Josh glanced to the jury. He turned back to Jillian. "Thank you for your candor, Ms. Grayson." He smiled brightly as he headed back to the table. "I believe I'm finished with this witness."

The judge looked at Stanley. "Redirect, Mr. Parrish?"

"No, Your Honor," Stanley replied sheepishly.

"You're excused, Ms. Grayson."

Jillian appeared woozy as she stood and made her way back to her chair. Josh slipped in next to the smiling Natalie, and they shared an evil smile. Natalie leaned over to Josh, and he moved his head closer to her. She whispered in his ear, "I've never wanted to suck a cock more than I do yours right now."

He turned to her with his eyes opened wide.

The judge announced, "Mr. Roth, you can call one more witness before we break for lunch."

Natalie moved her hand to Josh's lap and squeezed his penis through his pants. He nearly jumped out of his seat. He cleared his throat and began, "Your Honor, I would like to, uh, call—"

Natalie leaned back over to him with her hand still resting in his lap and whispered, "I want to lick your balls, too."

Maxwell narrowed his eyes and asked, "Mr. Roth, your witness?"

"I, uh..." Josh stammered as he took a quick peek at Natalie's breasts. He glanced up to her eyes and watched as she licked her lips and mouthed the word *now*.

He turned to the judge. "Your Honor, would it possible to break now? I, uh..."

"For what reason?"

Natalie pulled her hand from his lap as he replied, "I, uh, need to confer with my client before proceeding. We have what you could all a, uh, situation that needs immediate attention."

The judge shook his head. "All right, court adjourned until 1:15."

Natalie wore a grin and innocently folded her hands in front of her on the table as the judge left the courtroom. As the bailiff delivered instructions to the jury, she leaned over, cupped her hand over Josh's ear and slipped her tongue inside. He held his breath, moved his hands to his pants for a quick adjustment, and glanced at her with a dreamy smile.

While shaking his leg nervously, he watched the jury begin to make their way from the room. Josh glanced down at his lap and suddenly became concerned about the logistics of getting out of the courtroom while sporting a huge bulge in his pants.

After the jury had filed out, Jillian, Brian, and Stanley stood and began leaving the room. Natalie glared at Jillian. Josh held his briefcase in front of his groin as he followed his client toward the hall.

28

Josh and Natalie slipped into a conference room, and she pushed him hard against the door. He held his briefcase in one hand as he stared down at her, half never more excited in his life and half scared to death.

"She really blew it," Natalie said with a bright smile.

"I know. Her attorney probably is doing damage control right now."

Running her fingers over the bulge in his suit pants, she said, "You were amazing in there."

"Thanks." He nodded shyly.

"Now I'm going to show you how amazing I can be."

She slipped to her knees as her eyes locked on the currently swelling area. Grinning, she pulled down his zipper and reached in to grab his penis. She pulled it through his fly and slowly massaged it while she licked her lips.

Natalie held it at the base as she stared up at his face and whispered, "You're never going to forget this."

"Uh-huh," Josh stammered.

Staring back down at his growing manhood, she opened her mouth slowly and blew her hot breath over him. Natalie extended her tongue teasingly, almost to his head, but stopped short of licking it.

He held his breath as he waited desperately for her to begin. She blew on it once more before taking him into her mouth.

"Oh, fuck," he moaned.

She gave it all she had, and he was more than rewarded for his courtroom performance. With her enthusiasm in high gear, it didn't take long, and when she finished him, he slumped against the door, struggling to recover.

29

Jillian, Brian, and Stanley Parrish were walking out of conference room B just as Natalie and Josh entered the hall. After adjusting her skirt, Natalie looked up to see Jillian glaring at her. Natalie grinned as the groups approached each other down the long corridor. As they moved closer, Stanley put a supportive hand on Jillian's shoulder.

"Where's your son? Is he too scared to testify?" Natalie quipped.

Moving to Natalie, Jillian got right in her face. "If you've done something to him, I'll..." Brian rushed to Jillian and pulled her away.

Natalie glared at Jillian. "I don't know what the hell you're talking about." She looked at Brian. "Better keep that crazy bitch away from me."

Josh pulled Natalie aside, and they continued down the hall as Jillian pressed her body close to Brian. She said softly, "Jesus, I think I'm losing it." After talking a deep breath, she said, "Rob might be a lot of things, but he's never late. He would have called."

"Natalie's nuts, but you don't really think she could —"

"No." Narrowing her eyes she considered the possibility. Then she bit her lip and looked Brian in the eye." I don't know, but I just have a bad feeling about this."

"I'll try to call him again," Brian replied.

"Okay, okay. Yes, please —"

"Jillian, they're waiting," Stanley interrupted.

Glancing at Stanley with tears forming in her eyes, she nodded. Josh and Natalie stood waiting for the elevator at the end of the hall. Natalie stared back, grinning at Brian.

Jillian turned to Brian. "Call him now. I'll meet you back here in a few minutes."

"I will. Are you going to be okay?"

"Just find him."

He returned a supportive look as Jillian turned away. Pulling out his cell phone, Brian headed toward the conference room as Natalie looked on. The elevator doors opened, and Josh and Natalie slipped inside. Her grin widened. She stepped out of the elevator, as Josh watched her, confused. She glanced at him as the doors closed. "I'll meet you down there."

Inside the conference room, Brian stood near the far wall with the cell phone to his ear. He listened to Rob's greeting and then began, "Look, Rob, we haven't heard from you, and you know... look, Jillian's worried sick... we both are so—" Just then Natalie slipped into the room. Brian turned and watched as she moved toward him while wearing a sexy yet evil smile.

He pulled the phone from his ear. "What do you want?"

She moved close to him. "It's not what I want. It's what you want."

"What the hell do you mean?"

Placing her hand gently on his chest, Natalie stared into his eyes as she whispered, "You know."

"Look I'm trying to find Rob. He's missing, and—"

"Seriously, she thinks..." Natalie scoffed. "I don't kill men, I please them." She slowly ran her hand down his chest to his belt and placed a finger on top of the gold buckle.

He took a step back from her.

She smiled. "I know you're with that old hag just to make me jealous."

"You're out of your mind."

Natalie began, "I'll bet she can't do this." Turning quickly to face away from him, she went down on her hands, flipped her legs in the air and did a perfect split just a foot from him. Her skirt fell around her midriff and Brian glanced down at the vision of Natalie's absolutely flawless body, as her legs remained perfectly horizontal to the floor. She wore a tiny thong, and he could clearly see her ass, as it was displayed right in front of him. His eyes went to a large birthmark almost directly between her two private areas. He glanced at it for a moment before averting his eyes to the ceiling.

Without a hint of any struggle in her voice, despite the difficult position she held, she said, "Imagine your cock slipping inside my tight ass while I'm in this position."

Gazing back down, momentarily sidetracked, Brian stammered, "I, uh, you, uh..."

She flipped back up and moved to him. "Do you know how flexible I am?"

He nodded like a moron with his lips parted and his eyes glassy.

Shaking her head slowly, she began, "I don't think you do. I can get into a position where you're actually deep inside me and while you are fucking me..." She placed her hand between his legs and cupped his balls. "I'm curled up and actually licking your balls."

Brian tried to process this for a moment. "Wow, that sounds, um, impossible. You can really do—"

"Just ask Mitchell Garrett. I did that to him."

"Your roommate Cindy's boyfriend?" Brian asked, surprised.

"Oh... yeah. He played hard to get... just like you."

"Aren't they engaged?"

Brian took a step backward, and his body struck the wall.

"Not after I was done with him. He got so hung up on me that he left that chubby thing."

"Does she know?"

"What do you think?"

Brian narrowed his eyes. "You're a fucking monster. You just make me..."

Slithering up, Natalie pressed her body to his. "When the trial's over, let's run away together. You're the only man I could ever love. I—"

"You're incapable of loving anyone except yourself." Brian glared at her.

She whispered. "That's not true."

He slipped away from her and headed around the conference table. He opened the door and shot her a hateful look. "Just stay away from me, you completely freaking insane, delusional freak."

He rushed down the hall and turned around a corner. Slumping against the wall, he stared at his phone, shook his head, and whispered, "Fuck... Rob where are you?"

His eyes widened, and he dialed another number.

"I'm trying to reach Rob Grayson is he in... Do you, I mean, is there anyone else that can—Wait, is Carl in? It's Brian Nash. It's an emergency."

At Wealth Stone, Carl Rodgers stood staring out the window while nervously rubbing his hands together. The office phone rang. He leaned over and punched the speakerphone button. "Sampson."

"No..." Brian replied.

"Who's this?"

"Brian, Brian Nash... Rob's friend."

Carl froze as his mind raced. He had almost forgotten about Rob.

"Carl... Carl?"

Carl moved around the desk and fell into the chair. He looked down at the phone and hit the mute button. After taking a deep calming breath, he hit the mute button again.

"Brian, what's up?" he said while wearing a fake smile.

"We're trying to find Rob."

"That was some bachelor party, wasn't it?" Carl asked as he pulled open a drawer, grabbed papers, and tossed them into a box.

"Uh, yeah... Have you seen Rob? He's not answering his phone, and he's supposed to be testifying this afternoon in Miami at —"

"No, he, uh, didn't come in today."

"Have you seen him at the apartment? Did you see him this morning?"

Carl slammed the drawer shut, stood, and packed more things in the box as Brian repeated the question.

Carl finally answered, "No I didn't. I'm heading over to the building in a few hours. I could check for you and call you back."

"That would be great."

Laughing for no apparent reason, Carl rushed to file cabinet and made a lot of noise as he searched inside.

Brian said, "Let me give you my number." He heard nothing but more noise on the other end of the phone. "Carl... Carl, let me give you my number."

"I, uh, see it right here on my phone. I'm sure Rob's not in any danger, or you know... He's probably just banging that hot new girlfriend of his. Have you met her?"

"No."

"She's smokin'... I'll get back at ya."

Brian began, " Okay, great. I would — "

Carl's cell phone rang. "Gotta go."

Carl hit the button to end the call and quickly pulled out his cell. Checking the display, he took a deep breath before answering the call.

"Do we have a deal?"

"Tonight at six," Sampson replied.

Carl cracked his first genuine smile of the day. "You'll have all the money?"

"Yes."

"Six."

He ended the call, leaned back in his chair, and exhaled deeply.

Brian stared at his phone with concern before slipping it in his pocket. He stood there shaking his head as Jillian rushed around the corner and spotted him. "There you are. Did you talk to him?"

"What?"

Jillian asked angrily, "Did you find Rob?"

"Um, no... just got his voice mail again."

Jillian studied his faraway look. "What's wrong?"

"I just spoke to Rob's boss, Carl Rodgers. Something's not right with that guy. Last time I spoke to Rob, he said was concerned about his job, that Carl might be on drugs and doing something sketchy with the investments. He didn't give me any details... he had to go to a meeting or something. He said he'd call me back, but he didn't."

"When was this?"

"Maybe two days ago."

"Why didn't you tell me?"

"You were so busy with the trial, and I didn't want to worry you." Brian put a hand on her shoulder, and she moved closer to him. They stared at each other for a moment, both thinking the worst.

"You met the guy; you don't think he could have done something to Rob, do you?"

"No..." Brian wore a skeptical expression until he saw the concerned look on Jillian's face. He shook his head and continued, "I mean, no... No way, but I think I'm going to drive to Rob's apartment and check it out."

Jillian nodded.

Brian asked, "Will you be okay?"

"I think so. Be careful."

As Brian drove south, court resumed. Natalie searched the room for Brian and was surprised when she could not find him. Josh called a number of character witnesses, who all testified about what a level-headed, sweet, and innocent girl Natalie was. Josh decided against calling Rob or Brian to the stand that day, wanting instead to wait and cross examine them both when they were called to testify for the defense. He felt the trial was going so well for him now, and he clearly had all the momentum. Josh believed this strategy gave him the best chance to make Rob and Brian look like fools on the stand. He was also hoping to wrap up his case by the four o'clock that day and give the jury a favorable opinion of him as they headed home for the weekend.

As Josh Roth was grilling Albert Blair, Jillian's former agent, Natalie's mind floated away from the case, and she began thinking of ways to seduce Brian. She stared straight ahead, not paying attention at all as she tried to recall if she had ever seen Brian fully naked and what kind of lover he might actually be.

Mr. Blair mostly told the truth about how he failed to obtain the proper release forms from Natalie and how he failed to inform the publishing company about Miss Brookhart being the inspiration for the character in the book. He claimed he felt that there never was a potential issue with using her likeness, so that's why he didn't disclose it. He wasn't asked if he had been responsible for sending Natalie a copy of the book or inviting her to Jillian's wedding in St. Barts.

After nearly an hour of questioning from Josh, Stanley took his turn but hardly asked him anything at all. After Albert returned to his seat, the judge asked, "Mr. Roth. Please call your next witness."

Josh stood. "Your Honor, we have no further witnesses."

"So, do the plaintiffs rest?"

"Yes, Your Honor."

"Very well."

Checking his watch, Judge Maxwell said, "We will resume with the defense Monday at 9:00 a.m."

30

As Jillian was walking from the courtroom, Brian pulled into the parking lot of Rob's apartment complex. He saw a large rental truck backed up to the side of the building. Glancing around, he thought he spotted Carl Rodgers behind the truck before he disappeared through a doorway into the building. He headed that way. Inside, he found Carl dialing the combination into the door to the vault.

"Carl," Brian called out.

Carl turned toward him, clutching his chest. "Fuck, you scared me."

Eyeing the giant safe intently, Brian shook his head in confusion and then turned back to Carl. "Hi. Sorry. Did you get a chance to check Rob's apartment?"

"What... uh, yeah. He's not there."

Brian looked away, thinking as Carl stared back at him, trembling and sweating. Glancing back at him, Brian noticed his condition and asked, "Are you okay?"

"What? Yeah. Sure." Carl shot back quickly.

"Would you mind if I took a look at his place? His mother is really worried, and maybe I can find a note or his cell phone or something."

Carl stared at him. A glimmer of a frightening look crossed his face before he painted on a gentle smile. "No problem. We'll go through the building this way."

Brian stepped into the middle of the room. After taking a deep breath, Carl hit the button to close the rolling back door. Once the door was closed, he pulled out a gun and pointed it at Brian's chest.

"What the hell?" Brian stared at him, shocked.

"Shut the fuck up."

"What are you doing?"

Brian stared down at the gun in Carl's shaking hand. "Hey, I'm just looking for Rob. I don't care what you're doing here or —"

Carl shouted, "Shut up and turn around!"

Brian turned toward the vault.

Jamming the gun into his back, Carl said, "Get against the wall."

"You don't have to do this, I—"

"I said shut up."

While holding the gun to Brian's back, Carl dialed in the combination to the safe. Brian glanced at him from the corner of his eye as his heart pounded out of his chest. He thought, This deranged lunatic is going to kill me... I'm going to fucking die right here.

Carl messed up the combination and cursed. He pushed the gun harder into Brian's back and started again. After clearing his throat, Brian began, "Uh, that, uh, bachelor party was amazing, I—"

Carl yelled, "I need to concentrate here! Shut the fuck up or I swear I'll kill you right here!"

Brian bit his lip nervously as Carl successfully dialed the combination. He pushed down the handle and pulled open the vault. A gold glow shimmered through the door onto Brian's face, and he tilted his head for a better look. As the door opened further, Brian saw the huge stack of gold bars, and his jaw dropped. Next, he looked down at the floor of the safe and spotted a large pair of bare feet. He held his breath.

Pressing the gun to Brian's back, Carl pulled the safe door open fully. It smashed loudly against the steel wall of the vault.

"All right, let's go."

Rob was ducked down behind a stack of gold, holding a brick in his hand.

Brian said, "I won't tell anyone about—" Upon hearing Brian's voice, Rob mouthed the word, "Fuck." He took a silent deep breath as he contemplated a change in plans.

"I told you to shut up," Carl shot back.

Carl led Brian into the safe with the gun at his back. As they moved past a stack of gold, they both spotted only Bridget's lower half sticking out from behind another stack of bricks. Her bikini bottom was off, and her hands and ankles were tied behind her back. Carl stared down at the breathtaking sight of her perfect female curves while wearing a dirty smile, not for a moment wondering where Rob might be.

Watching out of the corner of his eye, Brian saw Rob lunge at Carl while holding a gold brick high above his head. Brian's expression changed, and Carl noticed. Turning, Carl caught sight of the danger and attempted to duck out of the way as Rob swung down. The brick caught Carl in the head, hard, but a little off the mark. He staggered woozily as the brick flew out of Rob's hand and skidded across the floor.

Losing his balance, Rob dropped down to his knees as Carl stood still for two seconds before collapsing to the floor in a heap. Carl moaned and began to lift his head up as he slowly raised the gun, pointing it toward Rob.

Springing into action, Brian stepped on Carl's arm, smashing it back to the floor. The gun went off with a huge bang that reverberated through the steel walls of the vault, and the bullet lodged into a stack of cash.

Crying out in pain, Carl dropped the gun and fought to move to a sitting position as Brian remained with his foot trapping his arm to the floor. Rob leaned forward toward Carl and punched him hard in the jaw, knocking him out cold. He glanced up at Brian with a grateful smile as he struggled to catch his breath.

Raising his eyebrows, Brian stared back at the naked woman's ass. "I don't think you really needed my help. He was a little preoccupied and didn't see it coming."

Rob said, "I know, her ass is spectacular isn't it?"

Bridget called out, "Okay, seriously. Please untie me."

"Do I really have to?" Rob grinned.

"I'd better wait out there." After stealing one more glance at Bridget, Brian stepped out of the vault.

Thirty seconds later, Bridget with her bathing suit re-secured, emerged from the vault with Rob. She gave Brian an embarrassed smile. "Hi."

Rob said, "It was my idea to have her bottoms off."

Brian shook his head with an approving grin. "Good thinking."

"Brian, this is Bridget," Rob began. "Bridget, this is actually my stepfather."

Looking at him, a little shocked, Bridget said, "Really?"

"Yes, that's me, his old man..." Brian grinned. "Oh, hi, nice to meet you."

A loud moan spilled out from the vault. They all turned to look through the door at Carl lying face down on the floor. Brian said, "You tie him up, I'd better call Jillian."

While Brian was on the phone with Jillian, Bridget called the F.B.I., and agents were en route immediately.

Almost two hours later, Brian and the now-fully-clothed Bridget and Rob were finishing up their interviews with officials as F.B.I. and local police swarmed the apartment building. At the Wealth Stone headquarters, another group of federal agents located the safe in the basement of the building and were in the process of opening it. When the contents were finally totaled from the safes in both locations, a little more than eight hundred million dollars worth of gold and ninety million in cash were recovered and transported safely away.

After their interviews and after promising to remain available for further questions, the three went up to Rob's apartment. Bridget headed to the bathroom as the boys slumped onto the sofa together. Rob asked, "So, how's the trial going?"

Brian just shook his head.

"That bad?"

"They destroyed your mom on the stand. They made her out to be some revenge-seeking witch. I think they're talking about settling the case to avoid some huge judgment against her."

"Shit. So, do you think I still need to testify?"

Brian shrugged. "Maybe you should call Parrish."

Nodding, Rob picked up his phone and checked the display. "Someone from the law office just called. I'll check my messages."

Rob began listening to voice mail. When he reached Brian's second message, he heard something interesting. After listening to it while wearing a grin, he opened his mouth wide and said, "Holy fuck."

Brian asked, "What is it?"

"Natalie."

"What?" Brian moved to the edge of his seat.

Rob put his finger up. "Shhh..." As he listened to more, his smile grew wider right along with his eyes. Returning to the room, Bridget stared at both of them, perplexed.

"You've got to hear this." He replayed the message on the speakerphone as Bridget and Brian looked on. It began faintly, until Rob turned up the volume, and Brian's voice filled the room.

"Look I'm trying to find Rob. He's missing, and — "
"Seriously she thinks... I don't kill men, I please them... I know you're with that old hag just to make me jealous."
"You're out of your mind."
"I'll bet she can't do this."

After hearing some soft rustling and then a faint gasp out of the speaker, Rob stopped the message and stared at Brian. "What'd she do?"

"She did this handstand with her legs spread wide and her skirt flipped up. I could see pretty much everything. Did you know she had this birth mark right by her — "

"Of course, I know about that."

Brian nodded casually.

Rob asked, "So what kind of panties was she wearing, or wait was she *not* wearing any?"

Bridget looked on horrified, as Brian replied, "No she was wearing just this tiny little — "

"Jesus, guys! Can we get back to the message?"

The boys shared a "what's-gotten-into-her" look and a smirk.

"Sorry," Rob said sarcastically as he hit a button on the phone. The message continued with Natalie speaking:

"Imagine your cock slipping inside my tight ass while I'm in this position."

Dropping her jaw, Bridget stared at Rob, horrified. "Who the hell is this?"

Rob stopped the message, but Brian beat him to it as he casually replied, "Oh, just Rob's old girlfriend."

"No, it's *your* old girlfriend."

"At least I never had sex with her," Brian shot back.

"You wanted to, you freaking douche bag."

"Guys, knock it off," Bridget interrupted.

As Rob began to play the message again, the Brian in the room conceded, "Good point," while the Brian in the phone said:

"I, uh, you..."
"Do you know how flexible I am? I don't think you do. I can get into a position where you're actually deep inside me, and while you are fucking me... I'm curled up and actually licking your balls."

Bridget wore a sour look; conversely, the boys were almost panting. With a sickened look, Bridget said, "This is your ex-girlfriend? She sounds like a skank."

"Oh, she is." Brian said.

Rob nodded matter-of-factly. The message continued:

"Wow, that sounds, um, impossible. You can really do – "
"Just ask Mitchell Garrett. I did that to him."
"Your roommate Cindy's boyfriend?"
"Oh yeah he played hard to get... just like you."
"Aren't they engaged?"
"Not after I got done with him. He got so hung up on me that he left that chubby bore."

Rob stopped the message once again. "Do you really think she can do that ball-licking thing when you're in her...?" Rob glanced down like he was actually trying to picture the logistics of it. He began again, "She's... How can – "

Bridget stared at Rob in disbelief.

"I know, I was thinking of that on the drive here, and then I remembered... Have you ever seen those videos of the guys who can suck their own dicks?"

"Oh, yeah, yeah."

"So, I think it's a little like that," Brian concluded.

"But the guys who can pull that off are, like, a foot long, so she would have to..." Rob shook his head, confused, as he processed this. Bridget stared at both of them with a wide-eyed look that screamed, "You've got to be fucking kidding me!"

Brian wore a serious expression. "I see what you're saying, but when you're facing away from her..." After jumping to his feet,

Brian spread his legs and squatted down, demonstrating, as Rob hung on every word. He added, "... like this, then it could work, since she wouldn't really need to reach her pu —"

"Okay, stop," Bridget demanded.

Rob ignored her request. "I would so never leave the house if I could do that."

Brian nodded in complete agreement as Bridget stared them down.

Brian's eyes went to her slowly. "Sorry."

"Yeah... sorry," Rob added.

Shaking her head in disbelief, Bridget sighed. Then they all remained in silence for a few moments.

Brian's expression brightened. "I can't believe we have this recorded. Would we be able to use this in court?"

Bridget replied, "Probably not."

"Well, at least now we know a name of another guy she had sex with." Brian paused for a moment. "And maybe if I played this for Cindy, she would actually..." he made quote marks in the air as he continued, "... 'remember' some of the names of the guys Natalie dated. At the very least, she could help us find Mitchell."

"Yeah, if this message doesn't make her realize that Natalie is a complete psychotic bitch, then nothing will."

Brian nodded in agreement.

Rob's eyes brightened. "Wait, I know. I'm friends on Facebook with a couple people, who I'm sure have Cindy's number."

Rob rushed to his computer and after successfully retrieving the number, he emailed a copy of the voice message to Brian. Brian called Cindy and received her voice mail greeting, but he didn't leave a message. Instead, he decided to keep trying to reach her while driving back to Miami.

Rob called Stanley Parrish and found he was needed in Miami on Monday to testify.

Bridget called to check in with her office, and was told she was being placed on administrative leave pending an investigation of the day's events. This suited her fine, as she was beginning to question her career decision and very much wanted to accompany Rob back to Miami.

Brian dialed Cindy's number every half hour as he drove. On the fifth call, she finally answered with an angry, "What?"

He hesitated a moment before he replied, "Um, Cindy?"

"Yeah."

"It's Brian Nash from Georgia State."

"If this is about the lawsuit, I really don't have—"

"Listen, I really need to talk to you. Sorry... One second. I'm driving, and I..." Brian quickly pulled the car onto the shoulder. After taking a moment to collect his thoughts he said, "Look, I know you and Natalie are, like, best friends, and I hate to be the one to tell you this, but she... she—"

"What?" Cindy asked in a tired voice.

"She slept with Mitchell while you guys were still together."

"She did not. You're lying—"

"I'm not."

"You just want me to testify against her, and I won't do it."

"Look, I have a recording of her admitting it. Just listen to it."

Cindy didn't say a word. After ten seconds, Brian asked, "Cindy, are you still there?"

"Yeah."

"I really am sorry to be the one to tell you this, but it's true. I swear. Let me email you the voice message... please."

"Okay."

Cindy supplied her email address and ended their conversation with a promise to call him back. Brian got back on the highway and began to worry after nearly thirty minutes went by without a return call. After another ten minutes, the phone finally rang.

"Cindy?"

"Sorry it took so long, but I called Mitchell, and that bastard admitted it."

"She called me a chubby bore, and she actually had sex with him." Cindy began to sob.

"I know. She's a horrible person."

Cindy sniffled and blew her nose with an ear-piercing blast that had Brian cringing on the other end. Then she said, "I've always known it, but she gets in your head and makes you feel special, even though half the time she's treating you like shit."

"I know. I know," he agreed.

"Brian?"

"Yeah."

"I should apologize."

"For what?"

After pausing a moment, Cindy began, "I knew she was messing with your head. I knew, and I didn't tell you. You're the only one of her boyfriends who didn't treat me like her fat, ugly friend, and I—"

"You don't need to apologize. I was a moron. I should have seen what she was really like."

She took a deep breath. "What do you need me to do?"

"Will you testify?"

"I don't think I can. At the deposition, I told them I didn't know anything... I think I can get in serious trouble if now, all of a sudden, I change my story."

"I don't really know anything about how that works. Let me ask the lawyers, and I'll get back to you. I'll keep your name out of it until I can make sure you won't get in any trouble."

"Okay, thanks," she replied.

"Aside from that, can you help us find some of her old boyfriends?"

"Some. I think I know the names of a few of them."

"Do you think Mitchell will testify?"

She scoffed. "I can get him to do pretty much anything right now."

"Great."

"Oh, and Brian?"

"Yeah."

"If they can figure out a way for me to testify, wow, do I have a lot of stories to tell. I read the book, and I know she looks bad in there, but in actuality she's even worse than the book makes her out to be."

Brian smiled brightly. "Wow, that would really help. We just want the truth to come out, so..."

"So do I."

"Thank you so much. I'll get back to you soon."

31

Both starving and desperate for some fresh air, Rob and Bridget picked up carryout from a local restaurant and ate by the pool. When they returned to Rob's apartment, they sat on the sofa, both exhausted. He turned to her and smiled. "Well, that was fun."

"Yeah, I've never had such a good time," she replied with a grin.

"I still can't get that image out of my mind of you tied up with your ass in the air," he said while sighing and looking away. He shook his head coyly then asked, "Any chance I could see you that way again?"

"Maybe tomorrow."

"Oh, okay." He asked innocently, "You want me to run you a bath?"

She gave him a skeptical look.

Rob's jaw dropped as he stared at her. "No, I, uh... just thought you might want to relax. You could stay over, if you want. I'm not trying to have sex with you or anything."

"Okay. I'd like to stay."

"I mean, if I get to see you naked one more time, that'll be a bonus, but..."

She grinned. "A bath might be nice. If you behave yourself, I'll even let you get in."

"Cool," he said with a smile. He rushed off to the bathroom, and she watched him while wearing a wide grin.

About an hour later Bridget and Rob were lying in bed, watching television. On the screen, a reporter appeared as the news began:

"The founder of Wealth Stone Investments was arrested today and will be charged with fraud as the mastermind behind an apparent ponzi scheme, which had taken in a more than five hundred million dollars in client investments. It is being reported that a substantial amount of gold and cash was recovered during the arrest. Rodgers was captured as he was preparing to move the contents of a safe from an unnamed location in Orlando. It's not known if the recovery is enough to pay back all the defrauded investors. A press conference is planned for noon tomorrow.

As the reporter moved to another story, Rob turned off the television. Bridget said, "Those bastards didn't even mention you."

"I know, here we save the day, probably recover everyone's money and then some, and no one gives a shit."

They shared a laugh.

She wore one of his t-shirts, and he couldn't help but stare since she looked pretty fucking amazing in it. The gentle curve of her breast stood out deliciously beneath the thin fabric.

"Well, I guess we should go to sleep," he said a little sarcastically as he slipped down to lie flat.

Following him down, she gave him a grateful look. "Thanks again for saving me."

They stared into each other's eyes with their noses nearly touching.

"Don't mention it." Pausing a moment, Rob looked toward the ceiling, seemingly reliving the horrifying experience, but wearing an expression which told her he was just trying to get some sympathy action. "But I could have been killed, you know. It was, uh..."

She grinned. "I promise I'll make it up to you tomorrow."

"I'm just kidding."

"Well, good night. I'm wiped out."

"Me, too." Rob turned off the light, then they both adjusted their pillows before turning onto their backs.

In the pitch darkness of the room, they both lay staring up with their eyes wide open and their minds racing. Rob could feel he was rock hard, but he tried to focus on something else. Taking a deep breath, he put his arms behind his head and closed his eyes.

After ninety seconds, Bridget moved her foot to his and slowly ran it along his ankle.

"Hey, that's not helping me sleep," he said.

"I don't think I can sleep."

"Well, that's making me ha—"

Before he got the words out, her hand was holding his erection through the fabric of his boxer shorts. He moaned as she extracted his length through the flap and gently massaged it with one hand. Rolling over, she placed her head on his chest. "You did risk your life for me today, and maybe I should try to pay you back at least a little tonight."

Bridget tossed off the covers and trailed kisses down his chest. He stared down at her and said, "I guess, if you really wanted to, you could—"

He shut up when her wet lips plunged over his erection. After ten minutes of that, Rob slipped it inside of her. Five minutes later, they both came and two minutes after that, they were both out cold.

32

After Jillian called Stanley to relay the new developments, he was overjoyed and called an emergency meeting of the legal team. Stanley promised to protect Cindy Taylor's interests in the matter and directed a team of lawyers to review her deposition testimony for any possible legal exposure if she were to now "recall" some pertinent facts and become a witness for the defense. The lawyers worked until after 2:00 a.m. and found what they needed.

On Saturday, Stanley and his team, along with Brian and Jillian, met to discuss this new breakthrough in the case. They held a conference call with Cindy. She was assured that she would be protected and offered legal services—fully paid for by Jillian Grayson—related to any issue arising from her testimony. She was thoroughly satisfied with the arrangement and proceeded to tell them everything she knew.

First, Cindy supplied the names of eight of Natalie's previous boyfriends. Two members of Stanley's team were immediately dispatched to track them down. Next, Natalie's longtime roommate shared stories of deceit, male manipulation, and unnecessary heartbreak, all caused by the she-devil herself, Natalie Brookhart. After the new witness had shared all that she could, everyone in the conference room smiled brightly and was fully confident that this would turn the trial in their favor, although they stopped short of opening a bottle of champagne.

Afterward, arrangements were made for Cindy and Mitchell to travel to Miami so they'd be available on Monday to testify.

The legal team spent the rest of the weekend preparing documents and filing briefs in preparation for the firestorm that awaited Miss Brookhart's case come Monday morning. Jillian thanked Brian publicly at the meeting, and as they drove home she fantasized about how she would really thank him in private. The sun was setting, and as they drove past a store that sold pools and hot tubs, it hit her.

Her mind raced as she went over the details. As she daydreamed, she found herself getting a little worked up. She shook herself out of the fantasy and sent a text message to Victoria. After she received the reply she was looking for, she grinned.

"Mind if we stop by Victoria's for a few minutes before we go home?"

"Sure, why?"

"Oh, I just need to pick something up."

He nodded, oblivious. They were still thirty minutes from Victoria's house, and as Brian drove, Victoria was already rushing to put Jillian's plan in motion.

33

By the time Brian pulled the car into Victoria's driveway, she was already gone. The front door was unlocked, and Jillian went inside first with Brian right behind her. On the table was a large platter of gourmet seafood from a local restaurant.

Jillian removed her shirt and bra as Brian stared at her, confused. "What are you doing?"

Turning to him, she gave him a sexy smile. "Thanking you."

"Thanking me?"

She kicked off her shoes, pulled down her shorts and underwear and then made her way to him.

Brian glanced around the room, "Where's Victoria?"

"Out."

He asked hesitantly, "A group of our closest friends aren't going to pop out and make fun of my penis or anything, are they?"

She shook her head slowly. "Who would make fun of it? It's perfect."

"Seriously, what are—"

Jillian put her fingers to his lips and said slowly, "I need to thank you properly for saving Rob and for saving me today." She ran her tongue around her lips as she lowered her hands to the bottom of his shirt and then pulled it up over his head.

Slipping down to her knees, she unbuttoned his shorts then pulled them down, along with his boxer briefs. Jillian placed a tiny kiss on his already growing penis and then stared up at his face. "You see that platter of delicious food over there? It's from McNulty's"

Brian glanced at it quickly before returning to her. "Uh-huh"

"We're going to take it out to the hot tub. There, we're going to enjoy it, and then... I'm going to enjoy you." She licked her lips seductively.

Swallowing hard, he craned his neck to look at the platter. "Do I see their famous broiled scallops?"

"You do."

His excitement was now on full display, and Jillian placed another tiny kiss on it.

"Oh, wow. You really give me great, uh... when you eat scallops."

"That's why I requested it special."

Jillian stood and turned away from him. Reaching back, she gently took hold of his erection and slowly led him outside to the hot tub. At edge of the water, Jillian let go of her 'leash' and motioned for him to get into the tub. Brian wore a silly grin as he slipped slowly into the hot bubbling water.

She pointed to the twin bottles of expensive champagne chilling in ice next to the tub. "You pour, and I'll be right back."

Jillian rushed to the house and returned with the platter. After placing it on the patio, she slid into the tub next to him. Brian handed her a glass of champagne, and they clinked them together before each taking a sip.

Jillian proceeded to feed him shrimp, scallops, lobster and McNulty's famous fresh baked bread as he lounged back in the tub. As she took her last bite of scallop, and he watched how she savored it in her mouth, he knew what would come next. Blood rushed to where he needed it. After emptying her champagne glass, she directed him up out of the tub. He sat on the edge as she remained in the water.

Grinning, she moved to him, grasping his nearly-hard penis around the base with both hands, and guiding it to her lips. She carefully plunged her mouth over the head, and Brian groaned loudly.

Jillian proceeded to thank Brian for saving both her son and her case in one of the most sensual ways possible. She even explored some of the techniques she and Victoria had come up with for the erotic hot tub story she had tricked Brian into reading. In Victoria's hot tub, truth just about matched fiction on this happy day, and it was absofuckinglutely out of this world.

34

In Judge Maxwell's courtroom on Monday, Natalie Brookhart was the first witness called by Stanley Parrish.

Stanley glanced at a legal pad and then up at Natalie. "Miss Brookhart, isn't it true that you manipulated both Rob Grayson and Brian Nash into some sort of love triangle during the spring of last year in order to pit one against the other?"

"No, that's not true. Yes, I dated them both, but I did not pit them against each other."

"Was either Mr. Grayson or Mr. Nash aware that you were dating the other and at the same time?"

"Well, no."

"So if your intention wasn't to pit one against the other, then what was your intention?"

Natalie glared at Parrish. "My intention... I was just dating them at the same time. I liked them both."

"Uh-huh. But you drove down to Miami during Spring Break to see Mr. Grayson, and after Mr. Nash and Mr. Grayson had a fight, you ended up driving back with Mr. Nash to school, where you began seeing him again."

"Yes."

"You enjoy having men fight over you, don't you, Miss Brookhart?"

Folding her arms, she put on an icy stare. "I do not."

Stanley shook his head skeptically toward the jury, glanced at his legal pad and then took a deep breath. "Let's back up a little to the winter of 2011. You began dating Mr. Nash in early February, and then things cooled off a bit."

"That's correct. He wanted to take our relationship to the next level and get physical, and I wasn't ready. Back then, I was still a virgin. Brian said we could take it slow."

"There was a night in February when you left Mr. Nash alone in your room, and he read your diary. Is that correct?"

Turning her head to find Brian, she glared at him before replying with an edge to her voice, "Yes, I remember that." She returned her gaze to Stanley.

"Isn't it true that you left him alone in your room, the diary sitting out in plain sight, with the intention for him to read it?"

"No. Those were my private thoughts and —"

"Isn't it true that this so called diary was not your *real* diary but a separate *fake* diary you created just to get Mr. Nash more enamored with you?"

"No, that's not true."

"But the diary only had a few entries in it. How do you explain that?"

"It was new," Natalie shot back. "I had just filled up my old one."

Stanley shook his head in disbelief, picked up a document and began, "Okay. But you left it open on your bed to a page which read, '*I think I'm falling in love with him, but I just can't give myself to him yet because of you know... There's too much pressure. I need some space now, but I hope he will wait for me because I know I will get there soon.*'"

"Yes, it may have been on the bed, but I did not intend for Brian to read that."

"Wasn't it your intention that Mr. Nash read this so-called entry in your *new* diary, since you felt he was slipping out of your grasp, and you wanted to give him some false hope as to your feelings toward him?"

"No, I didn't. Everything was fine with Brian and me at that point."

"Isn't it true that you left him in your room for over forty minutes with the diary sitting right there?"

"Well, yes."

Stanley narrowed his eyes. "And who were you with while Mr. Nash was waiting?"

Natalie stared back nervously. "Um, just a friend."

"Isn't it true that you were out with another one of your many boyfriends while you set this trap for Mr. Nash in your room?"

"That's not true!" She furrowed her brow and added, "And this was not a trap."

"The diary was a fake, wasn't it, Miss Brookhart?"

Shooting up from his seat, Josh Roth yelled, "Objection, Your Honor! He's badgering the witness. This question has been asked and answered."

Maxwell said, "Sustained. Move along, Counselor."

Stanley cleared his throat and then glanced at his legal pad. "A few weeks after the diary incident, you had occasion to attend one of Mr. Nash's tennis matches. Is that correct?"

"Yes."

"And you had never gone to one before, correct?"

"That was my first."

"And since the diary incident, you two had not seen each other or spoken. Is that correct?"

"I think that's right."

"So you show up for his match, and then out of nowhere, you disappeared right in the middle of it. Could you tell us what happened that day?"

Natalie took a deep breath. "Well, an old boyfriend from high school showed up at the match and said he wanted to talk. So we went to talk."

"How did he find you?"

She folded her arms. "I don't know, he just did."

"How would he have known to look for you there?"

"I really have no idea," Natalie replied smugly.

Sighing, Stanley let his gaze wander to the jury and then back to Natalie. "Isn't it true that you set up this *coincidental* meeting with your old boyfriend in order to further manipulate Mr. Nash and to make him jealous?"

"No, I would never—" Natalie began and then covered her face with her hands.

The jury gave her a sympathetic look and then glared at Mr. Parrish. Stanley caught the jurors' stares, then his eyes moved to the floor before glancing back at Natalie. It almost looked as though he felt sorry for her as well. Shaking off that emotion, he waited, just staring at the witness while wearing an impatient expression.

"Do you need a break, Miss Brookhart?"

Natalie composed herself. "I'm okay... I would never do anything like that to Brian. I liked him a lot back then. I just wanted to watch him play."

"But you left and didn't come back to the match, correct?"

"No, I was too upset."

"Too upset," Stanley repeated as he looked out over the jury with a skeptical look.

Returning to Natalie, he rubbed his hands together as he appeared to be carefully considering how to ask his next question. After a pause, he plowed ahead, "Okay, Miss Brookhart, are you familiar with the term 'technical virgin'?"

"I wasn't before I read Ms. Grayson's book," she shot back angrily.

"You weren't?" Stanley asked, his words dripping with sarcasm.

She sat up straight. "No, I had never heard of it before that day."

"That term is used for a woman who believes she can remain a virgin by abstaining from vaginal sex while enjoying other types of sex, including oral and anal sex."

"Yeah, now I know that, but..." Natalie frowned at him. "Before, I'd never heard of it."

"So you didn't inform both Mr. Nash and Mr. Grayson that you considered yourself a 'technical virgin'?"

"I did not." She stared at him with a disgusted look.

"Did you ever have anal sex with Mr. Grayson?"

"No, I didn't."

"Didn't you offer to have anal sex with Mr. Nash, and he turned you down?"

"No, that's ridiculous."

"Didn't you tell Mr. Nash that you had had anal sex with four guys when you two had a conversation about this exact subject during the month of April in 2011?"

She folded her arms and glared at Stanley. "I most certainly did not. I told you, back then, I was a virgin. Not this kind of virgin or that kind of virgin. A virgin... I had never had sex of any kind."

"And now, are you still a virgin?"

Josh called out, "Objection. Miss Brookhart's current sex life is not at issue here!"

"Sustained."

After taking a deep breath, Stanley continued, "So, Miss Brookhart, anyone who would testify that they had sex with you of any kind during the spring of 2011 would be lying?"

"That is correct, they would be lying."

"And anyone who would claim that you were deliberately trying to manipulate Brian Nash into believing that you had strong feelings for him would also be lying?"

"I've never tried to mislead Brian. I was always honest with him. So yes, that person would also be lying, or mistaken, I guess."

Stanley smiled at her. "Thank you, Miss Brookhart. You're excused."

Natalie sat motionless as a confused look slowly spread across her face.

Judge Maxwell said, "Miss Brookhart?"

Natalie glanced at the judge. "Huh?"

"You're excused."

"Oh, okay." Natalie looked back to Josh, who was now staring down at a legal pad. She stood, headed back to her table, and sat down next to Josh.

The judge said, "Call your next witness."

"The defense calls Miss Cindy Taylor."

Cindy emerged from the last spectator row in the back of the courtroom and walked toward the witness stand. Natalie watched her in complete shock and then whispered in Josh's ear.

Josh stood. "Judge, we object to this witness. She isn't on the defense's list, and we had no prior knowledge of her —"

Stanley interrupted. "She's on the plaintiff's list, Your Honor."

"Mr. Roth?" Maxwell scolded as he glared at Josh.

"Well, yes, but I still object to —"

"You had no objection when you placed her on your witness list."

"Yes, but..."

The judge said, "Objection overruled. You are free to cross examine this witness."

Slumping back in his seat, Josh shook his head and sighed. Natalie leaned to him and again whispered in his ear.

After Cindy was sworn in, Stanley asked, "Miss Taylor, could you tell us your relationship to Miss Brookhart?"

"I was her roommate at G.S.U. for three years until she transferred this past fall."

"And how close were the two of you?"

"Very close."

"Are you aware of any instances where Natalie, in your opinion, mistreated any of the men she was dating?"

Cindy scoffed, "I couldn't name a guy she didn't treat like crap."

"Could you give us some examples?"

"Uh, well... with Brian she totally —"

"Brian Nash?" Stanley asked.

"Yes, with Brian Nash, she invited him over to our dorm one night and planted this diary with an entry, designed to make him believe she was in love with him but just needed more time."

"How do you know this?"

"Well, she had me help her write the entry. I'm not proud of it, but I was always trying to gain her approval. I, uh... she had me in her spell just like half the male population on campus."

"Did she tell you anything else about that night?"

"She told me that she was sure Brian had read the diary when she left him in the room for so long. She said he was acting strange when she returned. She set the whole thing up. Natalie actually laughed about it. I'll never forget that night... we were lying in bed with the light out, and she was joking about how when Brian was in her room alone, she was in the library with some guy and, uh..."

Cindy gave Stanley a hesitant look as everyone in the room sat on the edge of their seats. Even Judge Maxwell leaned in close.

"It's okay, just tell us what she said," Stanley encouraged.

"Natalie said that while Brian was reading her diary, she was giving some guy a, uh, blowjob."

Many in the crowd gasped. Josh leapt up. "Objection! Hearsay."

Maxwell said, "Overruled. You'll have your chance to impeach this witness."

Cindy took a deep breath, and Stanley gave her a sorrowful look. "I know this makes you uncomfortable, but please continue."

Glancing around the room nervously, Cindy said, "Another time, Natalie told me that she thought her old high school boyfriend wasn't paying enough attention to her. Brian had been giving her some space, as well, and she didn't like it. She enjoyed getting calls from lots of guys and telling them no, like, uh, ninety percent of the time. Soros, her old boyfriend, hadn't called in a few days, so she wanted to make him jealous. Brian was always asking her to go to his tennis matches, but she never would. She hated tennis."

"She hated tennis?" Stanley asked with a surprised look as if this, in and of itself, were some sort of crime.

"Yeah... she couldn't stand it."

"Go on, please."

"Well, this one day, she knew Brian had a match, so she invited her old boyfriend over to meet her at the dorm. When Soros showed up, she wasn't there. She had asked me to wait in the room for him and to bring him to the tennis court, so she could create some kind of scene between the both of them."

"And what happened?"

"Well, I walked him to the court, and there wasn't a scene, but Soros got mad at her and led her away, so they could talk. After that, she told me she got him all worked up and angry, and he left. And then after that, Natalie told me she waited on the trail back to Brian's dorm, so she could mess with him, too. Sure enough, Brian saw her, and they had a fight."

"At the deposition, you testified that you had no direct knowledge of Natalie's boyfriends other than Brian and Rob."

Cindy gave the judge a distressed look. "I, uh... well, I didn't want to say anything bad about my friend and —"

"You knew you were under oath?" Stanley asked.

"Yes, I'm sorry, but there are some things that I didn't know when I testified back then that I know now."

"Like what?"

Cindy stared angrily at Natalie. "Like that... Natalie had sex with my boyfriend, Mitchell, behind my back."

"I hate to ask you this, but are you aware of the type of sex that she had with your boyfriend?" Cindy glanced around the courtroom shyly and then looked to Stanley for support. He smiled apologetically. "It's okay; just take your time."

After taking a deep breath with tears forming in her eyes, she said softly, almost inaudibly, "Anal."

Stanley widened his eyes as everyone leaned closer to hear the witness. "Could you move to the microphone and repeat that?"

Cindy moved forward and said loudly, "Anal sex." The words blasted through the courtroom. Pointing directly at Natalie as the anger boiled over inside of her, she added, "That bitch let my boyfriend, you know, do her in the ass."

The members of the jury looked at one another as the spectators began gasping, laughing, and murmuring.

Judge Maxwell banged his gavel. "I will have order in this courtroom!" As the disruption continued, the judge stood glaring at the crowd as he slammed his gavel down hard, sending the block shooting to the floor. The room quieted as the bailiff scurried after the wood block.

Maxwell remained standing with his eyes floating angrily around the room. He shook his head before returning to his seat. "Miss Taylor, while I realize this trial is rather *unique* in its subject matter, please… watch your language."

"Yes, Your Honor. Sorry."

Maxwell motioned to Stanley. "Continue, Mr. Parrish."

"Thank you, Your Honor." Stanley returned to the witness. "How did you come to learn this?"

"I heard a recording of Natalie admitting it, and then I asked —"

Josh jumped up. "Objection."

Glaring at Parrish, completely annoyed, Maxwell said, "Counsel, approach."

Josh and Stanley made their way to the bench. The judge covered his microphone, and the three discussed the matter for almost two minutes. Everyone looked on curiously as they conferred while the courtroom speakers emitted white noise. Afterward, the lawyers returned to their tables, and the judge said, "We will break for ten minutes."

Brian, Jillian, and her legal team followed Judge Maxwell, Natalie, and Josh into the judge's chambers.

The Judge began, "Mr. Nash, you made this recording?"

"Yes, Your Honor. I was leaving a voice mail for Jillian's son, Rob, and Natalie stormed into the room and confronted me."

"So, you did this without her permission?"

Brian raised his hands up. "I didn't know it was recording. I thought I had disconnected after I left the message. It wasn't until later that I realized—"

"Do you know recording someone without their permission is a violation of the law in this state?"

"As I said, Judge, I didn't even know it was recording."

Stanley Parrish said, "We believe Miss Brookhart should have reasonably assumed that her conversation with Mr. Nash was being recorded. She interrupted him on the phone, and he clearly stated to her that he was trying to locate Rob Grayson."

Maxwell scoffed. "That's a stretch, Counselor."

"We would like to play this recording for the jury," Stanley said.

Josh grumbled, "You can't be serious! There is no way—"

Putting his hand up to silence Roth, Maxwell stared at Stanley, "Do you have the recording with you?"

"Yes."

"Okay, let's hear it."

Stanley pulled out a digital tape player and started the recording. Natalie seemed unfazed by all of it, as Jillian looked on, half smirking and half mock-horrified. Josh was a little more than turned on.

When the recording finished, the judge glared at Natalie. "Miss Brookhart, is that your voice on the recording?"

"Uh, well you see..." she began. She switched gears almost psychotically and stared angrily at Brian. "You unemployed boy toy! I can't believe you would—"

Jillian interrupted, "Look, Butt Girl, call him a boy toy again, and you'll be spitting out teeth."

"Knock it off," Maxwell growled. "Control your clients."

Both Josh and Stanley whispered into their respective client's ears.

After shaking his head, Maxwell made eye contact with Natalie. "I'll ask again. Is that you on the recording?"

"Yes," she replied sheepishly as she stared down at the carpet.

Maxwell sighed. "I'm not sure if you're having trouble with the semantics here, but when defense counsel asks if you have ever had sex, and you testify *under oath* that you haven't, that you were still a virgin at the time in question, then if you are lying, that is perjury, and my dear, I assure you the court does not look upon that lightly."

He stared at her until she looked him in the eye. "Now, I know a former President seemed to be a little confused as to what constitutes a sex act, but in my courtroom if you've had a man's penis in your mouth, your vagina, and yes, even your anus, that does qualify, so to avoid a perjury conviction, I suggest you answer future questions about your sex life truthfully."

"Yes, Your Honor."

Stanley said, "We have a new list of witnesses as a result of Miss Taylor's, uh, memory returning to her."

"Let's see it."

Stanley produced a list consisting of a half page of names. He handed a copy to the judge and one to Josh.

Natalie snatched it out of his hands and began reading. Nodding, she studied a particular name curiously and smiled. "Oh, I forgot about him."

Natalie glanced up and found everyone giving her an odd look. She snarled back, "What?"

"What? What do you think?" Jillian shot back.

"Why don't you go f—"

Maxwell interrupted, "Shut up, Miss Brookhart, and keep your comments to yourself, Ms. Grayson."

"Yes, Your Honor," both women replied softly.

Maxwell said, "Why are we just seeing these now?"

"As I said, we've just been made aware of these names ourselves. We've been working the entire weekend to track some of these witnesses down," Stanley replied.

"What kind of relationship do these witnesses have to the plaintiff?"

"They are all former boyfriends of Miss Brookhart."

"I wouldn't call them boyfriends," Natalie shot back.

Maxwell ignored her comment and then asked, "And why weren't these names revealed during discovery?"

Stanley said, "Miss Brookhart failed to provide the names."

Returning his gaze once more to Natalie, Maxwell gave her a tired look. She simply shrugged. "I didn't even know some of their last names. I..."

Maxwell shook his head and then turned to Stanley. "So, who gave them to you?"

"Miss Taylor."

"And why did Miss Taylor fail to provide these names previously?"

Stanley cleared his throat. "Well, Your Honor... for instance, she had no previous knowledge of her ex-boyfriend's involvement with Miss Brookhart until she heard the recording and confronted Mitchell with it. Once she did, he was able to provide some other names, and well, there may have been some lapses in memory —"

"I suggest you stop talking, Mr. Parrish!" Everyone sat silently while Maxwell took a moment to ponder all of this. He shook his head in disgust and then finally said, "The recording is out. I will not allow it to be played." He glared at Stanley. "Do not reference it again in my courtroom, got that?"

Josh began, "Then I move for a mistrial on the grounds the jury has been prejudiced by the mention —"

"Shut your mouth, Mr. Roth. There will be no mistrial. If you have an issue with this, I suggest you take it up on appeal."

"Yes, sir."

Maxwell continued, "It sounds like we've had way too many issues with lapses in memory during this case. I would suggest, counselors, that you inform your clients and witnesses of this little thing we like to call perjury and how damn serious it can be."

"Yes, Judge," Stanley replied.

"Yes, Your Honor." Josh nodded.

Maxwell said in a loud voice, "We'll deal with these perjury issues after this case is finished, but if I even have the slightest impression that such behavior is continuing on either side, some of you will be spending the night in jail. Got that?"

All nodded in unison.

After studying the list once again, Maxwell glanced up at Stanley with a weary expression. "How many of these witnesses do you actually plan on calling?"

"At least five. We have people trying to locate the others now."

"Let's wrap this up as quickly as we can, Mr. Parrish."

"Yes, sir."

Josh glanced at the list and frowned. "Judge, I'll need some time in order to properly prepare to question these witnesses."

"How much?"

"A week."

"I'll give you two hours."

"Two hours?"

Maxwell narrowed his eyes. "Oh, do you not want the two hours?"

Swallowing hard, Josh stammered, "No, uh I think I can—"

"Good, now let's go back out there are try to act like adults and finish this. We'll wrap up Miss Taylor, and then Mr. Roth can take his two hours."

35

The Judge instructed the jury to disregard what they heard about the recording and that no such recording was entered into evidence, nor should it be considered during their deliberations. Josh cross-examined Cindy Taylor, blasting her with questions about why she had changed her testimony since the deposition. He accused her of lying now in order to hurt Natalie. The jury appeared to have sympathy for her, and Josh's bullying left her credibility only slightly damaged.

During the two-hour recess, Josh sat with Natalie in a conference room, poring over the potential witness list. She was aloof and bored during the discussion and offered little, if anything, that might help him during his cross-examinations. What she did tell him left him mostly holding his head in disbelief.

When court was back in session, the defense called its next witness.

After Mitchell Garrett was sworn in, Stanley asked, "How do you know Miss Brookhart?"

"I was dating her roommate, Cindy, and that's how I met Natalie."

"While you were dating Miss Taylor, did Miss Brookhart ever make a pass at you?"

"Almost from the first day we met. Whenever Cindy would leave the room and I was left alone with Natalie, she would make me feel uncomfortable."

"How so?"

"She would change right in front of me. One time she took off all her clothes and got into her bed completely naked."

"With you watching?"

"Yes."

"And this began when?"

"I'd say in the fall of 2009."

"And you never mentioned any of this to Miss Taylor?"

"No, um, it was all kinda harmless flirting at first, and, I mean, I felt weird about it, but I didn't think Cindy would've believed me. She was crazy about Natalie, and Natalie just seemed so innocent and pure, you know... At one point, I thought that maybe I was misinterpreting what she was doing. She never touched me or said anything inappropriate. She was just naked a lot. I thought maybe that's how she was raised or something... I don't know."

Stanley asked, "Did things escalate at some point after that?"

Mitchell glanced at Cindy, who was sitting with the other spectators. He cleared his throat. "Um, yes... one night we had all been drinking and Cindy had way too much and was pretty drunk. Natalie and I helped her back to the room and put her in bed. She was out cold. "

"And then what happened?"

"Natalie took off all her clothes and began touching herself. I, uh, told her I was going to leave and when I went to grab my coat, she moved in front of the door and sorta blocked it. She did this thing..." Mitchell's eyes bugged out of his head as he continued, "She did this reverse hand stand with a split thing... I mean, I knew she was flexible and all, but my God, she... remember, she was completely naked. I'd never seen anything like that in my life. She has a perfect, like... dancer's body, you know."

Natalie beamed as Jillian sneered at the comment.

Mitchell said, "So there I was looking down at her, you know... that way... and I was drunk, and I just..." Mitchell gave the crowd an embarrassed look.

"Just tell us what happened."

"Then Natalie got back on her feet and kissed me. I didn't stop her. She moved down to her knees and started rubbing my, you know... penis, and I was really drunk and not thinking clearly. She pulled my pants down and began kissing it.... After that, she led me to her bed."

"And all the while, your girlfriend, Cindy, Natalie's roommate and best friend, was passed out just a few feet from you?"

"Yes," Mitchell said softly.

"And then what happened?"

"She told me we could have anal sex, only anal sex. She said she was some kind of a virgin thing that I don't remember exactly, but that she only did it that way."

Stanley glanced to the jury and then returned to Mitchell. "Mitchell, did you have anal sex with Natalie that night?"

"Yes."

After pausing for ten seconds to let the weight of that reply sink in, Stanley asked, "Did you notice anything unique about Miss Brookhart while you were with her?"

"Yes, she has this birthmark right between her... I guess you could call it her vagina and her..." He continued a little softer with everyone listening closely, "... assho— I mean, her 'anus,' is the proper term."

"And could you characterize it?"

Tilting his head, Mitchell appeared to be daydreaming.

With Josh's mind wandering far away—and more specifically to Natalie's ass and the birthmark he was suddenly remembering--his jaw dropped. He, too, was trying to figure out exactly what it looked like, and if it hadn't been for all this, he might have objected to this line of questioning.

"Mr. Garrett?" Stanley prompted.

Mitchell's eyes brightened. "Uh, yeah... it looks a lot like the state of Texas. It's shaped, you know, just like it."

Josh nodded in happy agreement before catching himself and painting on a solemn look.

A few random chuckles spread throughout the courtroom. Maxwell even found that comment comical. He let the interruption slide.

Stanley plowed ahead. "What happened after you had sex with Natalie?"

"Natalie told me if I ever told Cindy, that she would claim that I was the one who came on to her."

Shooting the jury a confident look, Stanley said, "I have nothing further."

Maxwell said, "Mr. Roth, your witness."

Natalie whispered into Josh's ear. He paused a moment, then approached the witness stand.

"Mr. Garrett, isn't it true that you became obsessed with Miss Brookhart?"

"Well, yes, but... that was after she seduced me that night."

Josh gave him a skeptical look. "Oh, it was after... Isn't it true that you were the one pursuing Natalie all those months and that you took advantage of her that night when you got her drunk?"

Sitting up straight, Mitchell narrowed his eyes. "No, that's not true at all."

"Come on, Mr. Garrett, you two were together, you both were drunk, and your girlfriend was passed out. You took advantage of my client, didn't you?"

"Objection," Stanley called out. "Asked and answered."

Maxwell groaned, "Move on, Mr. Roth."

After taking a deep breath, Josh glanced at Natalie. She returned an angry nod, and he continued, "On the night in question, weren't you so drunk that you had trouble performing... sexually?"

Mitchell was taken aback by the query as everyone stared at him, waiting for a reply. He glanced around the courtroom nervously and then began, "I, uh, well... I mean, I wasn't at the top of my game, but..."

Members of the jury grinned as an audible chuckle spilled out from the spectators.

The Judge banged his gavel once. "Quiet down."

Shooting up out of his seat, Stanley said loudly, "Objection, Your Honor. Mr. Garrett's sexual performance is not at issue here."

Mitchell gave Stanley a grateful look.

"Sustained."

Josh shook his head in disgust at Mitchell. "I have nothing else for this witness."

Next up Rob, testified. He accounted his sexual experiences with Natalie. He described her now-famous birthmark. He testified how she only seemed interested in him once she found out that he had a longtime girlfriend waiting for him in Miami. He admitted he felt guilty about dating Natalie behind Brian's back and recounted what he could about his impressions of Natalie's manipulation of members of the opposite sex.

Josh tore into him with accusations of lying to protect his mother's reputation and fortune, a fortune he was destined to inherit. He survived mostly unscathed. The jury appeared to believe him, and Josh's constant attacks on the witnesses appeared to be tiring the members of the jury.

Brian Nash took the stand next. He repeated the tennis and diary stories. He also described the birthmark but admitted that he did not see it during any sex act with Natalie. He told the story of the circumstances which led him to see the birthmark, but no mention of the recording was made.

Just as he'd done with Rob, Josh grilled him about lying to protect Jillian and wanting to hurt Natalie now, since she had rejected him back at college. He performed brilliantly, answering every question calmly, and also came across as a credible witness.

Next up was Soros Demopoulos, Natalie's high school boyfriend. Mr. Parrish asked questions about his relationship with Natalie. Soros confirmed Cindy's story about Brian's tennis match. He elaborated on the nature of their sexual relationship; it was looking more and more like Natalie wasn't a technical virgin or any other kind of virgin, for that matter. The jury appeared to be captivated by the way the trial was now progressing.

Josh again blasted this witness for lying in order to get back at Natalie for some wrong he perceived that she committed. When that tactic didn't seem to be working, he excused Soros and then walked sheepishly back to his seat while Natalie glared at him, completely disappointed.

After that. Stanley paraded out two of Natalie's former boyfriends along with a one-night stand Natalie had enjoyed a drunken romp with, which the legal team was somehow able to locate. Each of the two former boyfriends recounted similar stories of Natalie only seemingly being interested in them after she learned they were dating someone else. Both had similar experiences in the bedroom, although neither had been given the opportunity Mitchell had been given, to enjoy Natalie's incredible contortionist moves. Neither had any idea what they had missed out on.

Natalie's one-night stand attempted to recall his experiences with her, and although he admitted everything from that night was a bit hazy and he wasn't sure exactly which hole of hers he had become intimately familiar with, he was sure he had become familiar with at least one.

Josh Roth struggled to impeach the three and failed pretty miserably. Natalie barely paid attention to the more than one-hour spectacle, while Jillian watched it all, totally riveted. As one-night-stand boy headed off the witness stand, Josh headed back to his seat, looking utterly defeated.

Jillian glanced at Natalie as she lazily stretched her neck from side to side. For some reason, she found it amusing. And then Jillian's mind raced. She narrowed her eyes, and her jaw dropped with an epiphany. She whispered in Stanley's ear.

Maxwell said, " Mr. Parrish, call your next witness."

Stanley gave Jillian a skeptical look. She nodded and then returned to whisper again in his ear. When she pulled away and gave him a hopeful look, Stanley paused, thinking, before shaking his head in reluctant agreement.

"Mr. Parrish," the judge said with an edge to his voice.

"Yes, Your Honor. I have a motion to bring before the court and feel it would be best if not done in front of the jury."

Maxwell glanced at his watch. "It's after four already." He gave Stanley a tired look and added, "The jury is excused. We will resume at 9:00 a.m. tomorrow."

After the jury left the courtroom, Stanley stood and began, "We would request that photos of Miss Brookhart's birthmark be taken so that we may have our witnesses positively identify her."

Josh leapt to his feat. "What the hell?"

Maxwell glared at him. "I take it you object?"

"Sorry, Your Honor. Yes, I object."

Maxwell asked, "Why is this necessary?"

Stanley said, "Uh, we feel that if we can corroborate the testimony that our witnesses have, in fact, been intimate with Miss Brookhart, it can put to rest any question as to the state of her virginity during the spring of 2011."

Josh said, "Judge, this is ridiculous. There is no precedence for this."

Stanley fired back, "Yes, there is. In the People of the State of California versus Michael Jackson trial, Jackson was ordered to have pictures taken of his, uh, genitals in order—"

"That was a criminal matter," Josh scoffed.

"Would you prefer we did an ass line up?" Stanley quipped.

Jillian broke into a chuckle and quickly covered her mouth. Maxwell scowled down in displeasure at Stanley's comment.

Josh pleaded, "Your Honor, please, this is absurd. In the Jackson case, the jury was not permitted to view those pictures."

As Maxwell pondered this a moment, Natalie sat deep in thought with a slight smile brewing on her face.

The Judge said, "I'll expect both your motions on my desk at 8:00 a.m. tomorrow."

Shaking her head no, Natalie motioned for Josh to come to her. He leaned in, and she whispered into his ear. Josh looked at her as if she were out of her mind.

She nodded adamantly, glared at him, and whispered, "Just do it."

Turning his attention to Maxwell, Josh exhaled deeply. "Judge, uh, we will consent to the pictures."

Stanley and the judge both raised their eyebrows in shock.

Maxwell smiled relieved. "Great. It is so ordered. Bailiff?"

The Bailiff approached the bench as the attorneys conferred with their clients.

About ninety minutes later, Josh supervised the picture taking by a photographer hired by Jillian's defense team. Natalie endured; well, actually, she embraced the whole experience. What began as evidentiary quickly morphed into something a hell of a lot more like a Playboy photo shoot. As Josh watched Natalie strike a particularly sexy pose, all he could think of was the lurid and graphic descriptions she provided on Brian's voice mail recording. He was more than a little worked up, as was the male photographer.

36

After the photos were taken, Natalie stood outside the courthouse with Josh. He stared at her like a lost puppy as she returned a bothered look. He began, "On that recording you said you could put yourself in this position where I could be inside you and you'd be licking my..." he glanced around to be sure no one was near and then continued, "... balls. Can you really do that? Because that sounds really amazing."

Natalie maintained a completely straight face before she put on a sexy smile. Then she opened her mouth wide to reply, said nothing, and closed her lips.

Josh whined, "You can't be upset with me about the way the case is going, are you?"

She just stared right through him.

He opened his palms to her. "I mean, I was blindsided by all this. You didn't share any information with me about this string of relationships. Had you, I could've been at least somewhat prepared."

After glaring at him a moment, Natalie shook her head, turned, and walked away.

He watched her with sad eyes. "Seriously, Natalie... Natalie. Aren't we still going to dinner?"

She never looked back.

As Josh sulked, the makeshift ass photo lineup was being prepared for use the next day. A graphic artist was hired to mock up six additional images of similar birthmarks Photoshopped into the private areas of images of the actual Natalie and attractive posteriors that looked quite similar to hers.

Judge Maxwell's clerk was on hand to supervise, to ensure the fairness of the proceeding, and to guarantee that no attorney from either side knew which picture was the real one and which were the fakes. Each picture was letter coded by the clerk to identify the real image from the decoys. The clerk then created a key, slipped the page into an envelope with the photos, and sealed it securely. Only he and Maxwell were to have access to the images until the trial resumed.

That night, Brian waited in bed while Jillian was in the bathroom. As the Darcy Gray show began on the television, he called out, "It's starting."

Jillian rushed from the bathroom, wearing nothing but a huge smile.

His eyes were pulled from the screen to her breasts as she approached. "Wow, you look cute."

"Thanks."

"Do you feel like doing that mermaid raft thing in the pool tonight?"

"Shhh, I really want to watch this."

"Okay," he whined.

She slipped onto the bed and sat up on her knees. Glancing at the delicious curve of her ass, he shook his head, rolled his eyes sadly, then returned them to the television.

Darcy appeared on screen, wearing not only a scowl but a bright orange pleather jacket and a little too much jewelry.

"*Bombshell in the Grayson Brookhart trial... If the birthmark fits, you must acquit... today in the* — "

Darcy grinned at the camera. She bit her lip fighting to contain the laugh that was desperately trying to break free. She held one hand over her mouth and the other up to the camera.

"*Sorry, I just need a... you see someone on our staff came up with that line and I, uh laughed my ass off at the meeting... please excuse my language.*"

Darcy shook her head quickly. "*Let me try that again.*" *She cleared her throat, painted on a straight face, and then began again.* "*Bombshell in the Grayson Brookhart trial. If the birthmark fits you must acquit... today in the defamation suit against my favorite author, Jaclyn West, the defense carted out witness after witness, all of whom testified under oath that they were intimately familiar with Miss Butt Girl's most private of areas. As you know, Butt Girl claims to have been a virgin during the period in question, but every witness recalled seeing the same — now, get this — birthmark near her nether regions, and all describe it as looking like the great state of Texas.*"

Widening her eyes, Darcy took a moment before plowing ahead. "*So, it seems like Miss Brookhart has what looks like an image of the Lone Star*

State just north of her star-fish." Darcy clenched her lips tight. She turned and glanced off screen. "I bet you thought I would lose it there."

She smiled and returned to the camera. "Sorry, folks."

In the Grayson bedroom, both Brian and Jillian wore even bigger smiles as they watched, although Brian stole a few glances of Jillian's flawlessly coiffed pubic hair as he wondered if it had been recently trimmed. It sure looked different. He looked down at his own and shook his head thinking, Time for a trim. Then Brian returned his eyes to the screen.

Darcy said, "What was looking just a few days ago like a slam dunk for the plaintiff now looks like a scramble. There's a rumor floating around that a picture of the said Lone Star birthmark... might be requested from Miss Brookhart when the trial resumes tomorrow morning."

The television screen split to Darcy on one half and Darcy's favorite random legal expert, Joe Whitaglia, on the other.

Darcy asked, "Joe... how can the plaintiff's attorney still be sticking to the story that Miss Brookhart was a virgin, when countless witnesses can recall such an intimate detail about her most intimate of areas?"

Joe began in a confident voice, "Well, Darcy, just because a witness can identify her in that regard is no proof that the witness has had sex with Miss Brookhart. Also – "

"Uh, yeah..." Darcy interrupted as she shook her head comically at the camera. "I have a long list of men who have seen that area on me that I've not slept with... uh, like, maybe my doctor..." she widened her eyes to the camera and then continued, "Joe, you've got to be kidding me. You'd have to be a moron to – "

"Look, Darcy. The jury needs to consider this new evidence among all the – "

"Hold on. Hold on, Joe. Let me see if I've got this straight... the jury is supposed to believe that six guys and counting can positively identify a birthmark on Miss Brookhart's tiny, little, perfect, super-flexible backside and that not a single one of them has had sex with her? They're supposed to buy that she's a virgin?"

"That's right; show us the video tape of actual penetration, and then – "

"What?" Darcy stared at the camera unblinkingly. "You want actual video evidence of Miss Brookhart fornicating in order to believe that she's not a virgin?"

Darcy's face now occupied the whole screen as she said, "We need to break. While we're gone, we'll have Joe's head examined... We'll be right back with more."

Jillian grabbed the remote and turned off the TV. "I trimmed for you."

"I thought so." Brian smiled.

She glanced down at his groin. He had been at half-mast since she appeared naked from the bathroom. Jillian licked her lips, and Brian followed her eyes. "I could use a trim, myself."

Grinning, she slowly leaned down to his lap. "I don't mind."

He looked toward the ceiling with a big smile as he drew in a long, slow breath. As Jillian enthusiastically went to work, Brian's mouth shot wide open, and his hands clenched the sheets on either side of him.

37

The next day, the picture packet was delivered and placed on Judge Maxwell's desk just before 8:00 a.m. Maxwell arrived at 8:02 that morning, the earliest by far that he had ever reached the courthouse. It wasn't a coincidence; he was psyched.

At 9:05, Maxwell emerged from his chambers, slightly flushed and carrying the envelope. The jury remained out of the courtroom as the attorneys met with the judge at the bench. White noise emanated over the sound system as the three spoke.

It was decided that the jury would not be allowed to view the pictures, but they would watch as the witnesses paged through the images and made their selections.

Each of seven eyewitnesses to Natalie's distinguishing mark were brought to the courtroom one-by-one as the others remained sequestered in order to ensure the legitimacy of the proceeding. Brian went first and quickly selected the correct image, which was not only fresh in his mind, but an image he would not soon forget. Rob, Mitchell, Soros, and the two other 'boyfriends' were also able to identify the correct birthmark photo. Only one-night-stand-boy was unable to make the correct selection, and Josh took great pleasure in this victory, small as it was. The jury didn't take much stock in his failure, since they all remembered that this was the young man who also wasn't quite sure which of the plaintiff's orifices he had actually experienced.

As Josh was heading back to his chair, a member of Jillian's legal team whispered into Stanley's ear. He was told that although they located six of the other potential witnesses, two were out of the country, and none of the other four could be in Miami to testify any sooner than the following Monday.

Jillian turned back to Brian, and their eyes met. He clenched his fist to her as a show of support, and they shared a smile. Jillian glanced at Natalie, and when Natalie met her gaze, Jillian's smile disappeared. They stared at one another for a brief moment before Natalie sneered and then turned away.

The judge glanced at his watch. "Defense, call your next witness."

After studying the tired looks on the juror's faces, Stanley figured they had had enough. He stood. "Your Honor, the defense—"

Jillian grabbed his arm. Stanley leaned down, and she whispered in his ear.

Looking at her with concern, he asked, "Are you sure?"

She shook her head and whispered again in his ear. Stanley widened his eyes, and Jillian returned a confident nod. Maxwell glared down at them, his patience tested.

"Mr. Parrish."

"Sorry, Judge. The defense would like to recall Jillian Grayson." Jurors four, seven, and twelve rolled their eyes. Many of the others just shook their heads and checked their watches.

38

Stanley approached the witness stand as Jillian sat up straight while wearing a slightly worried expression. He asked, "Ms. Grayson, what is the name of the ballet move depicted on the front cover of your novel, The Leg Thing?"

"The official name for the position is developpe leg devant ala derriere."

Stanley nodded as if he actually were interested in the name.

"Miss Brookhart isn't the only person you know who can perform this advanced ballet move, now, is she?"

Moving closer to the microphone, Jillian replied, "No, she isn't."

"Who else do you know can?"

"I can."

Natalie scoffed loudly, and all eyes went to her. She slumped down in her seat with an embarrassed look.

The jurors perked up a bit. Turning to the judge, Stanley began, "Your Honor, Ms. Grayson would like to demonstrate this move, if she may, for the jury in order—"

"Objection," Josh called out as he shot up from his seat.

The male jurors' bored expressions evaporated. Maxwell glared at Josh. "On what grounds?"

Josh glanced at Stanley and then at Jillian before he stammered weakly, "Uh... on the grounds that it would be, uh, prejudicial to the jury."

The Judge sighed, "Overruled."

Josh slumped down in this seat as Maxwell directed to Stanley, "Let's make it quick, Counselor."

Three minutes later, Jillian slipped out of the adjoining bathroom and into the courtroom, wearing a black leotard over white tights. The outfit showed off her perfectly tone body, but no skin, unlike Natalie's previous nearly R-rated demonstration. The male jurors moved once again to the edge of their seats and wore big smiles.

Making her way to the center of the courtroom, she looked around nervously before taking a deep breath. She glanced at Brian and Victoria, who both returned confident nods.

Jillian rose up on the ball of her left foot, and then began slowly lifting her right leg and following it up with her right hand. She kept going until it pointed straight up to the ceiling, and her right elbow rested against her right knee. Her forearm ran along her leg, with her hand holding her ankle.

Everyone looked on in astonishment as Jillian held the position seemingly effortlessly, but inside Jillian muscles were straining. Natalie watched gape-mouthed until she caught herself, grimaced, and slumped down in her chair.

The Judge stared down at Jillian, smiling and shaking his head in mild shock.

Jillian slowly returned her leg to the floor and then glanced at Stanley while wearing a wide smile.

"Thank you, Jillian," Stanley said proudly.

She nodded. As she headed past Stanley, Jillian stuck her tongue out at Natalie. Natalie's jaw dropped in shock. Then Jillian turned, shared a smile with Brian and Victoria, and made her way back to the restroom.

Turning toward Maxwell, Stanley smiled. "And on that... the defense rests."

The judge held back a chuckle but grinned instead. "Good." He moved his eyes to Josh. "Mr. Roth, do you wish to recall anyone?"

"No, sir."

"Adjourned until two o'clock, when we will begin closing arguments."

After the break, Josh Roth approached the jury. He held the fingertips of both hands to his chin for only a moment before he began, "Ladies and gentlemen, Jillian Grayson held a grudge against Natalie Brookhart. That is clear. She was jealous of her youth and the fact that both her son and her boyfriend were obviously still smitten with her. The Rebecca character in her novel, *The Leg Thing*, was undoubtedly based on Miss Brookhart. Both her character and Natalie have similar physical appearances, both were college students and both were ballerinas who could perform this advanced pose.

Josh smiled at Natalie and then glanced back to the jury. "It has been established that the novel is torn from Ms. Grayson's real life. Characters based on herself, her son, and her new husband are all central to the narrative. You heard Jillian Grayson herself testify to this fact. The actual events of early 2011 are also depicted in the novel. Miss Brookhart was the catalyst of those events. Without her, none of this would have happened. There would have been no novel. She dated both Rob Grayson and Brian Nash in real life and in the novel. The evidence is abundantly clear."

Josh turned away from the jury and took a few steps toward the defense table. He turned back. "Albert Blair, Jillian's former agent, is being blamed for not securing the proper release from Miss Brookhart. And while Ms. Grayson claims that she had no knowledge of what Mr. Blair was planning, he certainly knew what he was doing; he's a smart publicist. Now whether Ms. Grayson knew or didn't know that Albert had obtained a release doesn't matter. Ultimately it is not Mr. Blair's responsibility; it is the responsibility of Ms. Grayson herself to ensure that the proper release is granted."

Josh stared at Jillian. "There was no such release, and that's why we're here. After Mr. Blair's little publicity stunt in St. Barts, sales of the novel exploded."

Moving his attention to the jury, he paused a moment to emphasize the point with his hands mimicking an explosion. "The book's been number one on Amazon for months. Over three million copies of *The Leg Thing* have been sold worldwide, placing seven and one half million dollars into Ms. Grayson's pocket and earning her publisher approximately another fifteen million dollars."

Josh scoffed and shook his head slowly as he looked at the jury. "Twenty-two million dollars." He pointed to Miss Brookhart. "Twenty-two. So they have all that money, and what did Miss Brookhart get out of all of this?" He paused for effect and repeated, "What?"

"Humiliation, embarrassment, and ridicule, that's what." Josh stared at Natalie, who painted on a sad face as he continued, "Somehow, that just doesn't seem fair. My client was defamed in this novel. Lies were spread about her; she was mischaracterized with clear malice on the part of Ms. Grayson. And for this reason, we feel punitive damages are also due to Miss Brookart. Put yourself in Miss Brookhart's shoes... How would you feel if someone got rich while they destroyed you, or perhaps your daughter, in their novel and just sat back and collected millions?"

Josh glared at Jillian, and she returned a sneer. Turning back to the jury, he said, "Maybe you should send Ms. Grayson a message before she... she writes a book about you." Josh's eyes traveled over the jurors as he shook his head slowly.

"Thank you."

He moved to his seat and gave Natalie a supportive smile before placing his hand atop hers and giving it a gentle squeeze.

Stanley Parrish stood and slowly made his way to the front of jury box. He began, "This case is not about Miss Brookhart being defamed in Jillian's novel; it's about revenge. Miss Brookhart's revenge for not getting what she wanted. She wanted Brian Nash, that was clear. She still appears to want Brian Nash, based on his testimony of her confrontation with him just a few days ago. There was no malice here; there was no attempt to defame or libel Miss Brookhart. All that you have here is a writer who wrote a fictional story inspired by..." Stanley paused a moment as he glanced at Jillian and then back to the jury. "... a fictional story inspired by true events."

Motioning to Natalie, he continued, "What's truly amazing here is that many lies have been told during this trial that have been proven false. You've all watched it unfold. Miss Brookhart is arguably a man-manipulating, lying, spoiled woman who's used to getting her way with anything and everything she desires."

He scoffed. "And she was anything but a *virgin* during the spring of 2011. It could be argued that Miss Brookhart was painted in a slightly more positive light within Jillian's novel than she actually was in reality."

Stanley paused a moment to let that sink in. "As absolutely ridiculous as that sounds, it's true. The definition of libel is a false and unprivileged publication, which exposes any person to hatred, contempt or ridicule. The circumstances in this case in no way rise to meet this burden. Additionally, the plaintiff's attorney was required to prove that a reasonable person reading the book would recognize that the fictional character in the novel represented Miss Brookhart. They didn't even come close to proving that. No one would have recognized Miss Brookhart as the Rebecca character in the novel, without her announcing it to the world. The only reason we are here is that Miss Brookhart herself decided to bring this to the attention of everyone who would listen. In addition, no proof was presented as to the damages that Miss Brookhart has suffered as a result of this supposed representation of her in the book."

After taking a deep breath, Stanley added, "Miss Brookhart is angry that she didn't get a chance to break Brian Nash's heart for a second time back in the late spring of 2011. That's when he decided to break up with her, and this is her desperate way of getting him back. No one breaks up with Natalie Brookhart... no one."

Stanley glanced at Natalie, who returned an evil look and the jury caught the exchange. He turned back to the jury. "Natalie... always gets what she wants... always... but you, you can put a stop to that."

Stanley's gaze traveled over the twelve jurors with a determined nod as he repeated, "You can put a stop to that."

He returned to his seat as the jurors sat in quiet reflection.

Judge Maxwell read the jury instructions, and the jurors were led from the courtroom to begin deliberations in the late afternoon. When no decision had been reached after nearly three hours, the jury was dismissed and told to report the next morning.

39

The next morning, the chosen twelve returned to the jury room. About an hour later, several jurors (the men) requested the pictures of Miss Brookhart's photo shoot, but Judge Maxwell denied the request.

Deliberations continued until just after noon, when a vote was taken. The results were nine to three on one of the questions and eleven to one on the remaining question. The jury broke for lunch and returned for another hour-long discussion. Afterward, they put in a request to confirm the retail price of Jillian's hardcover novel. Once this information was delivered, another vote was taken. This time, a unanimous agreement on both questions was reached.

All parties were contacted and assembled in the courtroom. The jury took their seats, and when the room was quiet, the judge made his way to the bench. The foreman handed the written verdict to the clerk, who brought it to Judge Maxwell. Maxwell read it and said, "The verdict appears to be in order."

As the clerk returned the verdict to the foreman, Jillian sat at the defense table with her heart pounding. Behind her, Brian rubbed his hands together nervously as Victoria held her hand over her mouth to hide her worried expression. The foreman stood and read, "On the issue of defamation, we, the jury, find in favor of the defendant."

Jillian turned to Brian, and they shared a smile. The foreman said, "On the issue of invasion of privacy and appropriation, we, the jury, find in favor of the plaintiff and award compensatory damages in the amount of $125,000."

Jillian's head dropped in despair as Natalie and Josh's faces both brightened. Stanley didn't react but listened closely as the foreman continued to read, "... and punitive damages in the amount of $26.95."

Natalie's jaw dropped as Josh scoffed at the odd figure. Jillian lifted her head up, confused. Stanley leaned over and asked, "Twenty-six ninety five?"

Jillian's eyes widened. "That's the price of the hardcover." A huge grin spread across both their faces while behind her, Victoria and Brian shared a hug.

The Judge thanked the jurors and released them from service. After court was officially adjourned, Jillian jumped up and hugged Stanley. Brian rushed over, and they shared a kiss. Next to them, Natalie began letting Josh have it.

Jillian and Brian turned to watch as Josh put his hand on Natalie's shoulder. She pulled away from him and headed out of the courtroom. Jillian and Brian turned to one another and fought to suppress their smiles. Lifting Jillian into his arms, he squeezed her tightly.

An hour later, Jillian, Brian, Victoria, Rob, Bridget, and four members of Jillian's legal team were sitting around a large table at the Sunset Grill in Key Biscayne, just outside of Miami. The mood was, of course, festive. Jillian stood and held her glass high. "I realize I've been a bit moody for the last few months, and I'd like to apologize and thank you all for your support. And even though it wasn't a complete victory, with the fact that Butt Girl was awarded damages today, I think this is the best possible outcome."

Brian lifted his glass. "It's over."

"It is," Jillian added, and then she paused. "Well, I was thinking of writing a sequel, and—"

"Oh, no. Please, don't," Brian said with a grimace.

Victoria smiled and shook her head in complete agreement. Stanley called out, "Brian, we already discussed this, and there will be no sequel without a signed release from... Butt Girl."

Everyone cracked up. When they composed themselves, Jillian lifted her glass and said, "Cheers."

Adam Rawlings, the owner of the restaurant, was moving from table to table to check on his guests. He stopped at Jillian's table and smiled brightly. "Excuse me for interrupting. I hope you're enjoying your evening."

Jillian replied, "Yes, everything is wonderful."

"I'm glad. If there's anything else you need..." Adam began and glanced around the table. When his eyes met Victoria's, he stopped for a moment and then added, "Please, don't hesitate to ask."

"Thank you," Jillian replied.

Nodding, Adam returned his attention to Victoria. He moved to her and smiled. "Have we met?"

Victoria smiled up at him. "You do look—"

Adam's eyes brightened. "I know. I met you on a flight back from Philadelphia."

She smiled. "Yes, I remember."

"Adam Rawlings, and you're... Victoria, right?"

"Yes." Victoria glanced to Jillian who returned wide eyes, which screamed, "*He's cute.*"

Victoria looked back to Adam as he added, "You said you might stop in, but that was, what, last summer? I figured you would a little sooner."

"Sorry, I've been a little busy." Victoria looked down to her round belly and pointed.

"I can see that."

"It's great to see you again."

"And you."

Adam glanced down at her hand and noticed the absence of a wedding ring. He moved closer to her, leaned down, and said softly. "You look spectacular. I mean, pregnancy really agrees with you. Just stunning." He shook his head and smiled.

Victoria blushed. "Thank you."

Glancing quickly around the table, Adam said, "But I'm sure you hear that a lot from your boyfriend."

"No boyfriend."

"Husband?"

She shook her head no.

"Well, you look fantastic."

Victoria smiled up at him. "Thank you."

Adam stood just gazing down at her, wearing almost a silly look. "It's really great seeing you again."

"You also."

Adam gave Jillian a polite nod and slipped away. Jillian looked at Victoria and opened her mouth wide. She leaned over and whispered, "He's gorgeous. Why didn't you grab hold of him on the plane?"

"I was sorta throwing up."

"Oh... He likes you."

"You think?" Victoria gave her an unsure look. "I'm huge."

"He's right; you look amazing."

Victoria glanced over at Adam as he chatted with another party. Her eyes traveled down his body. She took a deep breath and smiled. God, she missed being with a man, but seeing one that attractive made her remember exactly how much.

Adam sent over complimentary after-dinner drinks along with dessert, and when Jillian and her group were ready to leave, he was working behind the bar. Victoria walked up to him and smiled. "Thank you for everything."

"My pleasure, Victoria. I would love to see you again."

"I'd like that."

"Perhaps I could take you out to dinner sometime?"

She glanced down at her pregnant form and then back up to his face. "You really want to be seen out in public with this?"

He chuckled. "I do. You're sure the baby's father won't mind?"

"No, we have an... understanding. He's a great guy, but we're not going to ever be together. No..." Her expression grew solemn until she shook it away and painted on a smile. "How about I call you after I get settled with the baby and everything and can actually fit into some normal clothes?"

"Sure, whatever works for you."

"It was good seeing you again," Victoria said.

Adam nodded as he stared deeply into her eyes. She looked away, embarrassed. When she looked back at him, he said, "Sorry, I'm... I'd be lying if I said I haven't been hoping you'd walk through that door since we met."

The good-looking restaurateur and the single, hot pregnant woman exchanged cell numbers, and when Victoria finally made her way to the car, Jillian grilled her all about him.

Adam called Victoria a few days later, and for the next week they spent a lot of time chatting on the phone. Victoria shared the details with Jillian, and Jillian decided to invite Adam to Victoria's somewhat-surprise fortieth birthday. Victoria had already been invited to Jillian's under the guise of a small dinner on that Friday night, but she wasn't told it was a party until about an hour before the event. They didn't want to shock a woman in such a fragile state once again, especially after what they put her through at her baby shower. Rob and Bridget were leaving for a two-week cruise to the Mediterranean, which they booked to celebrate her promotion, using the generous donations sent to Rob by several of Wealth Stone's most affluent and now grateful ex-investors. All told, he had collected just over one hundred and fifty thousand dollars.

40

In New York, Jillian and Stanley Parrish waited in a conference room in the law offices of Albertson, Wyatt, and Price. Josh and Natalie entered the room, and the two women exchanged evil glares. After the lawyers shared polite greetings and settled down at the table, Stanley began, "We understand you are considering appealing the decision."

"That's right. I feel that the appeals court will easily find that there was actual malice under the New York Times standard, and the ridiculously-low punitive damages award will be thrown out," Josh said.

Natalie nodded confidently with her arms crossed over her chest.

"We believe you'll lose on appeal."

Josh shot him an incredulous look. "Mr. Parrish, then why are you here?"

Opening his briefcase, Stanley pulled out a document. "If you move forward with the appeal, Miss Brookhart won't be seeing the settlement money for many years. We would like to make an offer that will enable both parties to resolve this matter and move on with their lives."

"We're listening."

Stanley glanced at a document. "The jury awarded $125,000 to Miss—"

"*And* twenty-six dollars and ninety-five cents," Natalie shot back sarcastically.

Stanley smiled, "Oh yes, sorry. You are correct... one-hundred twenty-five thousand *twenty-six dollars and ninety-five cents*. We're prepared to double that figure and have a check cut tomorrow if you agree to accept the jury's decision and cancel the appeal, and if Miss Brookhart will sign a release to permit Ms. Grayson to publish a second book in this series featuring the Rebecca character, which, as we know, is based on Miss Brookhart."

Natalie's mouth shot open, and she glared at Jillian. "You want to write another book? After all this crap, you want to write another book?"

"I do," Jillian replied smugly.

Natalie shot back sarcastically, "What does Rebecca do in this one? Kill someone... or maybe she could screw the entire—"

"Okay," Josh interrupted, and he put a hand on Natalie's shoulder. She glared back at him, fuming. "I don't think a quarter million dollars is going to do it. I'm not going to permit Ms. Grayson to continue trashing my client."

Stanley slid a stack of papers to Josh. "In this release, we've outlined the context in which the Rebecca character will be portrayed throughout the rest of the series. We believe Miss Brookhart will find it acceptable."

After pushing another document to Josh, Stanley added, "And here is the settlement agreement. As I said, accept this, and we're prepared to cut a check immediately, or you can take your chances with the appeals court and wait years for this to be over."

Josh glanced at Natalie and found her still seething. Sighing, he looked down at the release agreement and began reading. Moments later, he shook his head with a frown. "There is no way you're getting off the hook for a quarter million dollars when the value of future books in this series is worth at least fifty times that."

"Ms. Grayson will be publishing the next book with or without this release," Stanley shot back.

"Well, then, prepare for another lawsuit."

"Mr. Roth, bring it on. The publicity from Miss Brookhart's first suit still has the book on the bestseller's list. We're quite confident that Miss Brookhart is now herself a celebrity as a result of this ordeal. And as a celebrity, we believe that her image is fair game, and you'll lose at the next trial. Either way, we would relish the publicity another sensational trial such as this would bring."

Natalie whispered in Josh's ear, "They can't do this, can they? She can't write about me again. I—"

Josh softly said, "Calm down. I'll take care of this."

"We're going to require final approval of the manuscript, and you're going to have to come up with something in the seven-figure range for this—"

"Mr. Roth, it's not going to happen," Stanley interrupted. "We're not turning over editorial approval to your client. You have our offer. It's good until the end of the month." He stood and Jillian followed him.

Josh rose from his chair and left Natalie sulking at the table. Josh and Stanley shook hands. Josh nodded to Jillian before she and Stanley slipped out of the room. Turning back to Natalie, Josh said, "I think we can at least get them up to half a million."

She stared at him with her expression unreadable.

With a hopeful expression, he asked, "Would you like to go to dinner tonight to discuss it?"

Shaking her head, Natalie gave him a tired look before standing and heading for the door.

"Natalie... Natalie!" Josh called after her.

She turned back, "Are you like the worst lawyer on the planet?"

"What? No, I... Look, we won and—"

"We won?" she said sarcastically. He opened his mouth to reply, and she held her hand up to stop him.

"We didn't win."

"I'm sure I can get a better offer."

Natalie shot him a tired look.

"Dinner?" Josh pleaded pathetically.

Glaring at him, she slowly turned and left the room.

Two days later, Josh sat in his office, wearing a bright smile. He glanced at the clock then called out to reception for the third time in the previous twenty minutes. "Is she here yet?"

"Mr. Roth, no. She... Wait, yes, she just walked in."

"Send her back."

Josh stood, straightened his tie, cupped his hand over his mouth, blew into it, and checked his breath. He shook his head with a grimace, thinking he should have skipped the coffee. Quickly, he opened a desk drawer and fumbled for a pack of mints.

Just as he slipped one into his mouth, Natalie took a step into his office.

He smiled at her as he quickly tried to suck the mint down.

"I..." he began then choked on the mint. Natalie stared at him with an incredulous look.

He coughed, cleared his throat, then plowed ahead, "I have great news."

"They increased the offer?" Natalie asked.

Josh approached her. "No, but..." She turned to leave. He put his hands on her shoulders and guided her to a chair. "It's better."

After closing the door, he swallowed the mint, checked his breath again, and rushed to his chair. Josh sat down and gave her a big, goofy smile.

She frowned. "What the hell is it, Josh? I hope you didn't bring me all the—"

"You'll never guess who called me last night from L.A.?"

She gave him a tired look. "I don't know... Snoop Dogg?"

Narrowing his eyes, he scoffed. "A Mr. Hugh Hefner."

"No way." Natalie's mouth shot open, and she moved to the edge of her seat.

Josh nodded. "Evidently, you have a big fan in the Playboy mansion. They want you to be the centerfold in the June issue."

"How much?"

He widened his eyes. "Seven-hundred-fifty thousand."

"No freaking way." She beamed as she jumped up and began pacing around the room.

"Heff followed the trial. He heard about the pictures, and they want you do a nude pictorial of all the ballet poses. Plus, they want to do a full article about the trial and the book, all of it. This is big."

Natalie turned to him. "And the settlement?"

"They won't budge. But I read the release, and it's fair. They've outlined how you'll be portrayed, and it really isn't that bad. I mean, actually much better than you already were in the first—"

"Stop talking before I walk out of here," she said with a grin.

"Sorry... So, are you happy?"

Natalie gave him a sexy smile as she slowly made her way to him. Rolling his chair out from the desk, Josh spun toward her.

"I've missed you so much," he whined.

"I don't think I hate you anymore." Natalie slipped down to her knees in front of him.

"That's, uh, good."

She placed a hand on each of his thighs and slowly ran them up toward his fly. "Do you think you could get Heff up to a million?"

Josh began, "I'm not sure if they..." He stopped talking when she pulled her hands away from his pants.

She frowned. "Oh, I think there's room for negotiation."

"There might be some," Josh said slowly.

Placing her hands over his growing erection, she massaged it a bit. He closed his eyes as she unzipped his fly and pulled out his manhood. She worked it until it was fully hard, opened her mouth, and moved down until she was within a millimeter of his hot flesh before she glanced up at him. "Tell me you'll get them to a million."

Josh opened his eyes and stared down at her. Natalie's warm breath tingled his sensitive skin. Her lips were so close to it as she breathed out once more, waiting for his reply. He fought to speak.

"Tell me," she repeated.

"Uh, I, uh..." he murmured as he wished he were just a half inch longer, for then he'd be inside her lips.

"A million... Say it," she whispered.

He nodded, mesmerized. "I'll get them to a million."

She grinned before wrapping her lips around him.

The night of Victoria's birthday party, the crowd gathered in Jillian's backyard out by the pool. Adam and fifty of Victoria's friends were in attendance, and the event was catered with delicious food and featured a bartender and wait staff. Victoria was just entering her thirty first week of pregnancy. Looking at her from the back, you could barely tell she was pregnant at all, especially in her stylish, short maternity dress. The front was another story. There, she carried the baby beautifully in a fairly large, yet compact, ball.

Her breasts were, however, enormous. They had somehow expanded even further since the trial. All the other women looked her over jealously as nearly all the men who glanced at her imagined what she'd look like naked. A few even enjoyed a pregnant woman sex fantasy as they watched her mingle with the crowd.

Victoria and Adam stood together, chatting. Just as the cake was being carried outside, Victoria grimaced in pain and clutched her stomach. Adam grasped her elbow; she smiled and shook her head as she rubbed her hand over her belly.

"Wow that was different." She exhaled deeply. "It didn't feel like a normal kick by my little friend here."

He held her, and she was fine for a moment until her mouth opened wide, and she doubled over again. Jillian rushed over, concerned, as Adam put his arm around her waist and helped her to a chair.

"I'm fine, really."

Adam and Jillian knelt down next to her as the guests stared on in silent concern. Brian came over and put his hand on Jillian's shoulder. "Is she okay?"

Jillian said, "We should take you to the hospital."

"No, really I just need to sit for a—" Victoria's words dropped off as she moved her hand down between her legs. "I'm a little wet down here. This can't be my water, right? It's too early for that. Jillian, what's going on?"

"Don't worry. Brian, get the car," Jillian said calmly.

Brian rushed off as Jillian directed two male guests to help Victoria to the driveway. Jillian sat in the backseat with Victoria as Brian drove quickly to the hospital.

She was whisked up to the maternity ward, where a number of tests were performed. Both Victoria and the baby's vital signs were stable. Victoria had experienced a premature rupture of the membranes, which led to a leak of the amniotic fluid. She was given antibiotics to fend off any potential infection and corticosteroids to help the baby's lungs mature faster, in the event that a premature delivery would be required.

Brian called Jim and updated him on the situation. Jim was ready to get in the car and make the twenty-four hour drive to Miami, but Brian talked him out of it. Brian promised to keep him informed of any change.

Victoria spent the night in the hospital, and her OB GYN arrived the next morning. Dr. O'Reilly met with the staff doctor and both were in agreement that the baby was probably going to come early and soon, but there was no way to know when. Victoria remained in the hospital for one more night before going to stay with Jillian and Brian, so she could stay off her feet as much as possible.

The next morning during a routine exam, Victoria was found to be already two centimeters dilated. The baby was beginning to enter the birth canal and was in a good position for delivery. There was no stopping it now. Brian called Jim immediately, and twenty minutes later both he and Caroline were driving to the airport.

As Jim and Caroline sat together on the plane, he glanced down at her engagement ring and asked if she wouldn't mind taking it off until they returned to Philadelphia. He explained that he wanted to announce the happy news under less stressful circumstances and Caroline reluctantly agreed. Just as their plane was taking off, the two and a half pound baby was delivered without complications. The lungs were only partially developed, so the tiny baby girl was rushed off and placed on a breathing machine. Victoria was able to only steal a brief glimpse of her daughter before she was whisked away.

Jim and Caroline arrived at the hospital a few hours later and discovered Brian and Jillian sitting next to Victoria's bed as she slept.

Jillian quietly got up and met Jim near the door. She gave him a big hug, and the four slipped out to the hall.

"How is she?" Jim asked.

"She did amazing, and she's fine," Jillian replied.

"And the baby?"

"She's on a breathing machine..." Jim sighed and then rubbed his hands over his face as Jillian continued, "... but the doctors think she's going to be fine."

"I have a daughter?" he began before his eyes filled with tears. Caroline looked on, touched by his reaction, and then moved close to him. He wrapped his arm around her shoulder. She smiled up at him and placed her hand on his chest.

After pausing a moment to pull himself together, Jim asked, "Can I see her?"

Brian nodded. "I'll take you."

Caroline and Jillian returned to Victoria's room as Brian led Jim to the NICU. Before entering, Jim was given instructions for proper hand washing and a hospital gown to put on over his clothes. Once he was ready, a nurse escorted him to the small isolette, where his daughter lay connected to the ventilator.

Kneeling down, he stared through the clear plastic to the tiny, beautiful baby with his eyes dripping and his lip curled up as he fought to hold back his emotions.

The nurse said, "She's doing really well."

Jim nodded to her with a smile before wiping his eyes. "Can I hold her?"

"In a day or two, probably, but for now, you may hold her hand or stroke her head. A gentle, consistent touch is what she needs right now."

"She's gorgeous."

"She is." The nurse smiled and took a step back from him. Jim reached into the isolette and gently extended his finger to her tiny hand. The baby reacted to his touch and wrapped her little fingers around his seemingly giant one.

He blinked his eye, and a tear streamed down his face. Moving his hand to the baby's forehead, he gently stroked her skin. He ran his other hand over his face and stared at the baby that he and Victoria had made and began to really lose it.

Jim said with his voice cracking, "Mommy and I... are so happy that you're here."

He shook his head with tears streaming down his face. He wiped them away and glanced around the room nervously.

The nurse spotted a doctor scrubbing up in the outer room and said, "The neonatologist is coming in now to insert a feeding tube. But you can come back and see her later."

Moving away from the isolette, Jim took one last look at his daughter. He smiled. "Okay, thanks."

Victoria was now awake in her room with Jillian and Caroline standing on each side of the bed.

Jillian said, "She's perfect. They think she'll be breathing on her own in a day or two."

"I want to see her."

"You can soon."

Moving her gaze to Caroline, Victoria asked, "How are you doing?"

Caroline chuckled. "Me... I'm good. How are you feeling?"

"Tired. I'm sorry you guys had to rush down here."

"Don't worry about it."

"I was hoping to put this off until you were on Spring Break, but, uh..." Victoria widened her eyes. The three women shared a smile.

After a slightly awkward silent moment, Victoria added, "This isn't too weird, is it?"

Caroline put her hand over hers. "No, it's really not."

Jim and Brian returned to the room. Jim and Victoria's eyes met, and he moved to her. Caroline took a few steps back in the now-crowded room.

"Are you okay?" he asked.

Victoria nodded. "Did you see her?"

"Yes. She's beautiful."

Caroline narrowed her eyes, watching the new parents with concern.

Jillian and Brian shared an awkward glance and then asked, "Caroline, we're going to head up to the cafeteria, did you want to come?"

Caroline looked confused by the question as her mind raced. Then the lights came on. "Yeah, sure." She glanced at Jim and asked, "Do you want anything?"

Jim didn't respond to the question. Caroline repeated, "Jim, do you want anything?"

"What?" He turned to look at her while wearing a faraway smile.

"We're going to the cafeteria."

"Oh, no... thanks."

He returned his attention to Victoria as Caroline followed Brian and Jillian from the room.

After moving to the chair next to Victoria, Jim placed his hand atop hers.

She curled her lip. "I want to see her."

"The doctor is with her right now. Let's give them a couple minutes, and then I'll check."

"Okay." She fought to brighten her expression. "So, who does she look like?"

He smiled. "You. She's all you. Let's hope, anyway."

They shared a chuckle.

Victoria took a deep breath with her eyes closed. When she opened them, she gave him a serious look. "Do you think Caroline is really okay with all of this?"

After pondering that briefly, he shrugged. "We're going to make it work somehow."

They shared a silent moment as Jim stroked her hand.

Victoria smiled and looked up at him. "I can't believe she's really here."

"Do you have a name picked out yet?"

"No, I wasn't ready for her. I do have a few ideas, though."

"Like?"

"Elizabeth."

Jim grimaced immediately as a memory flashed into his brain. He shook his head. "The first girl I ever kissed was named Beth. After we did, she laughed at me, told me I didn't have any lips, and then told everyone how bad of a kisser I was."

"That bitch." Jim nodded in agreement, and Victoria continued, "You have lips... They're pretty great lips too."

"Thanks."

"So, no Elizabeth, then."

"Well, I think I could get over it and move on."

She gave him a supportive look. "You shouldn't have to."

"Thanks. That's probably best. What else do you have?"

"Kaylie."

"I like that." Jim smiled.

"You think?"

"Yeah, it's pretty." He nodded. "That's a good name."

Victoria nodded along with him as she adjusted her position in bed. She grimaced in pain.

"Are you okay?"

"Yeah, it just really freaking hurts when you deliver a baby. I didn't realize... I mean, I know she was small, but you try squeezing something even that size out of your vagina, it's not too much fun."

He chuckled. "What did you expect?"

"I don't know... I just thought with all the sex I've had, it would be... Like this one time, I had sex with this guy. He was..." She extended her fingers and put her hands together forming a huge circular shape. "... this big around and —"

"No way." He looked at her, both shocked and a little horrified.

Victoria held her fingers in that position as she added with her eyes wide, "I swear, he was that big, and —"

Putting his hand to hers to break up the show and tell, he wore a distasteful look. "Please, don't tell me any more."

She smiled. "I just thought I'd be better prepared down there."

"Did they give you drugs?"

"Yep, but I think I got them too late."

He shook his head and gave her an incredulous look. "I think they're taking effect right about now... A guy as big around as a freaking grapefruit. You're —"

"Okay, maybe he wasn't that big."

They shared a chuckle.

"Do you think I could see her now?"

Jim said, "I'll go check." He headed toward the door.

"Jim." Victoria called. He turned back, and she gave him a serious look. "I'm glad you're here."

He gave her a sad nod as if he were again on the verge of tears. "Me, too."

They stared into each other's eyes for a few seconds until he covered his mouth with one hand, turned, and got the hell out of there before he really started to lose it. As the door closed slowly, Victoria let out a big sigh.

41

Victoria and Jim stood beside the isolette on either side of the baby, wearing proud smiles. She now had both the breathing and feeding tubes connected to her.

Jim said, "She does look like a Kaylie."

"I think so, too." Victoria leaned in for a closer look. "I think she has your nose."

"No." He scoffed.

Victoria reached her hand in and let Kaylie wrap her tiny fingers around her extended finger. "She's strong."

Jim smiled. "Just like her mom." Victoria didn't feel so strong right at that moment, and she curled her lip as she stared down at the beautiful baby and wondered how the hell she was going to pull off being a parent all by herself.

"And now comes the hard part, right?" Jim said.

"I know," Victoria replied. She grinned up at him as if he were reading her mind.

"As soon as I graduate, we want to move to Miami so we can help."

"That would be wonderful. And Jillian told me she wants to babysit every single day."

"Take her up on that. I read they don't sleep much for the first couple months."

They shared a smile. Jim gently stroked Kaylie's head. "Are you going to breastfeed?"

"She needs to be on this high calorie formula for a few days, but I'm going to try." Victoria looked down to her swollen breasts and grinned. "They're killing me."

Jim glanced up. "They look huge."

"Thanks, but they're kind of ugly, all full of veins and everything right now. They also really hurt."

"I don't believe they're ugly for a second."

"You haven't seen them." Victoria stared up at him, thinking, I really do want you to see them.

"I'll take your word for it." He gave her a curious glance, and they shared a smile.

They spent the next hour bonding with the baby, singing and talking to their little creation until it was time to let Kaylie sleep. Afterward, Victoria returned to her room and quickly fell asleep herself.

Jim and Caroline went to Jillian and Brian's house to spend the night. In the great room, Brian opened a bottle of wine to celebrate Kaylie's birth, and Caroline drank nearly half of it. A second bottle was opened, and Caroline's apparently unquenchable thirst continued.

The four sat around chatting and enjoying the wine. Caroline said, "The baby is beautiful. I knew it would be. You both, uh... I mean with, uh, you two, it would have to be."

"She is adorable," Jillian said. She glanced at Brian, whose eyes were drooping and fighting sleep. "I think we're going to bed. It's been a long day."

Brian's head jerked up, and his eyes opened wide. "What?"

"Are you tired?" Jillian asked while rolling her eyes.

"Yeah." He nodded.

"We're all getting older, some of us before our time," Jillian quipped.

"Hey!" Brian frowned.

"Oh, just get upstairs." Jillian smiled. She stood and glanced at Jim. "You guys know where the guest room is, so just make yourselves at home."

"Goodnight." Jim nodded, and he watched as Jillian and Brian headed toward the stairs.

Leaning over, Caroline placed her head on Jim's chest. "I really feel like doing it tonight. Do you want to do it?"

"Sure."

Jim asked, "Do you feel okay?"

She smiled. "I think I just drank a little too much."

"Are you okay with everything... you know, the baby and Victoria and—"

Caroline moved her lips to his and kissed him. Placing her hand over his groin, she squeezed it softly. Jim kissed her back. She pulled her lips from his. "Let's not talk about it. I'm okay, I guess. I just feel like going to bed."

Jim and Caroline retired to the guest room. That night Caroline was more passionate in bed than he had ever seen her before. After she gave Jim his third orgasm and started to work on a fourth, he had to delicately ask her to stop. He claimed he was exhausted, which he actually was, but in actuality, it felt like his dick was about to fall off.

A few minutes after that, she passed out, and Jim watched her sleep. His mind raced with thoughts of Kaylie, Caroline, and Victoria all swirling in his head.

42

The next morning Caroline, Jim, Brian, and Jillian ate breakfast together at the house. Brian prepared his famous pancakes. Caroline looked a little pale, and after her third bite, she rushed upstairs, went into the bathroom, and threw up. A minute later, Jim followed her and found her slumped on the bathroom floor. She decided to stay behind while the others returned to the hospital.

Jim asked to borrow the car, and after he dropped Jillian and Brian off at the main entrance, he went to run an errand.

As Jillian was browsing in the gift shop, she caught Brian's bored expression and sent him up to the maternity ward. In Victoria's room, the doctor was in the process of delivering the good news that Kaylie was progressing well and informing the new mother that the plan was to remove the baby from the ventilator and have her breathing on her own by the end of the day.

When the doctor left, Victoria took a deep calming breath, and for the first time since she arrived at the hospital, she was relieved. She finally felt that everything would be okay. She smiled, thinking, Maybe it's time to stop worrying about everything and just focus on getting back to living.

Glancing down at her swollen breasts, Victoria shook her head with a grin. She missed her old ones. She had always fantasized about having really big ones, but now that she had them, she really, really wanted to go back.

Sliding her hand down, she touched her belly. It was still swollen, and she pondered how much work would be involved in getting some semblance of her old body back. She would need to exercise twice as hard. She moved her hand lower. She wondered if sex would feel the same now that she had delivered a baby through there. Not that she could even really remember what it was like, because it had been so long since her last time.

Victoria moved her hand down between her legs just to see if it still felt as she remembered. She carefully ran her fingers around her parts and began to frown. Something felt completely different. Pushing the sheets down, she craned her neck as she lifted up her gown and struggled to get a look at her vagina. That's exactly the position Brian found her in when he entered the room.

He caught a glimpse of her and closed his eyes. "Sorry." He began backing through the door blindly.

Victoria glanced up at him and smiled. "Good. You're here."

He stopped in his tracks but kept his eyes closed. "Can I open my eyes now?"

Victoria gave him a look. "It would help."

Brian opened his eyes to find her staring at him with her legs spread and her gown still pulled up. He turned away quickly and whined, "I thought you were going to cover up."

"Oh, just get over here."

He shielded his eyes halfway as he smiled at her. "I'm really afraid to ask what you're doing."

"I need a favor."

"Okay," he replied hesitantly.

Victoria smiled. "Oh, by the way Kaylie will be coming off the ventilator today."

Brian beamed. "That's great news, but could you cover up a little?"

Victoria rolled her eyes and pushed down her gown. "I was kinda hoping I'd have a C-section."

"Jillian told me."

"I need you to look at my... you know... and tell me if everything looks the same, or am I like some kind of freak show down there now? Something doesn't feel right. It's like I have a giant flap now, or something."

"A flap?" Brian asked with a cringe.

"Yes, a flap."

Putting his hand up, he held it in front of her as he furrowed his brow. "How would I even know what it's supposed to look like?"

She glared at him. "Have you forgotten when you tricked me into touching myself in front of you?"

The realization hit his face. "Oh, yeah." His look morphed into a sexy smile. "That was fun."

"It was, wasn't it?"

"Plus you spent hours looking at it when you drew it that time."

"Now, that I forgot about."

"How could you?" She smiled.

He wore a serious expression. "You see one vagina up close, you've seen them all." He smiled. "I'm kidding. Yours was pretty nice."

"Gee, thanks. I need to know if it still is." She stared at him hopefully.

Brian moved to her. "But I don't know if I should, really."

"I think it'll be okay." She gave him a wide-eyed look. "Besides, if you don't do it, I'm going to have to ask Jim."

"Jim, really?"

"Yeah, you two are the only guys who know what my vagina is supposed to look like."

"Can't I just get you a hand mirror or something?"

Victoria rolled her eyes. "Okay, yeah. Go out to the nurses' station and ask for a hand mirror. Tell them that I'm so vain that I need to look at my pussy immediately."

Brian stood. "Be right back."

"Uggg. Get over here. I was kidding."

"Sorry."

"Will you do it?"

Glancing out the window, he rubbed his hands through his hair. "All right."

Victoria grinned, pulled her gown up and spread her legs wide apart.

"Okay, but let's do it quickly."

"I'm waiting on you."

Brian moved between her legs and took a look as Victoria asked, "Is there a new flap?"

"I don't see it." He narrowed his eyes.

"Right here," she said as she ran her finger over one side of it.

"That just looks like a normal lip thing, you know. Like a regular one."

"Okay, good."

"Can you see the bottom?"

"What?"

"The bottom. I've heard of women who rip all the way to their anus."

Glancing up at her, Brian asked sarcastically, "Wouldn't you have felt that?"

She glared at him. "Just look for me."

He moved his head closer to the mattress. "I can't really see. Can you lift up or something?"

Just as Victoria lifted her ass off the bed, Jillian popped into the room carrying flowers and took in the scene. Her jaw dropped. "What the hell are you doing?"

Victoria glanced up casually. "Oh, hi, Jillian."

Lifting up, Brian turned to his wife. "Don't just stand there. Help me look at her vagina."

"What? Why?"

"She asked me to."

Victoria smiled. "I want to make sure everything looks the same down there."

Jillian shook her head. "And he's the one you chose for this mission?"

"He's seen it before. Thanks to you both."

Nodding matter-of-factly, Jillian moved to the bed and got down on the other side of Brian to check everything out.

Brian turned to Jillian. "Kaylie is coming off the ventilator today."

Jillian smiled. "That's great." She turned to look at the target area as an almost clinical look spread across her face. "I've never been this close to it, but it looks okay to me."

Pointing to a particular area down there, Brian said, "Huh."

"What is it?" Victoria asked, suddenly concerned.

"I don't know, but that looks new... different."

Victoria craned her neck down. "What do you mean?"

He furrowed his brow and pointed. "That little thing right there."

"What?"

He stared up at Victoria and smiled. "I'm kidding."

"You bastard."

Brian shrugged. "I think everything looks pretty much the way I remembered it. Maybe just a little more hairy."

Victoria said, "The hair grows like crazy when you're pregnant."

"I can see that," Brian shot back with a smile.

"Does my asshole look darker?"

Brian and Jillian narrowed their eyes as Victoria lifted up a bit more.

They both shook their heads and nodded reluctantly. He said, "It's a little hard to tell through all that hair."

"Look away. I'm hideous." Victoria slumped down and covered up.

Brian and Jillian stood and gave her a sympathetic look. Brian said, "You look great down there. Nothing a little waxing won't cure."

"I'm getting a waxing *and* a bleaching as soon as I get out of here."

Jillian said, "I think you're overreacting."

"Overreacting... uh, how hairy is your ass?"

Brian smiled. "It doesn't have a single hair on it. I was just recently in that general area, so I know."

Jillian and Brian shared a knowing chuckle as Victoria stared back at them, a little irritated. "Can you knock off the lovey dovey shit around me? I haven't had any sex in, like, four months, and it's pretty much killing me."

"Sorry," Jillian replied.

Moving to her, Brian said sincerely, "I'm sure as soon as you shave your ass, men will be back all over it. I promise."

"Gee, thanks." Victoria gave him an angry stare before breaking into a smile. The three began to chuckle.

Victoria said, "That was a good one, Bri... You got that one out with a straight face and everything."

"I've been working on my delivery," he said proudly before adding, "In all seriousness, I'm pretty sure men will be chasing you around soon enough."

"I sure hope so."

Jim arrived at the hospital twenty minutes later and made his way up to Victoria's room. He carried a small jewelry store bag and tucked it into his pocket before entering Victoria's room.

When he found her alone, he smiled. "Where are Jillian and Brian?"

"They went for coffee."

"When will they be back?"

"In a few minutes."

Victoria smiled. "Have you seen the baby yet?"

"No."

"They're going to take her off the ventilator today. They think she's ready to breathe on her own now."

He smiled brightly. "Thank God! I was so worried."

"Me, too."

Jim moved quickly to her. "I'll go see her in a minute, but I want to do this before they get back. I got you something."

Jim pulled the bag from his pocket. Victoria smiled as she stared down at it, and her heart skipped a beat. Her mind instantly went to engagement ring, but when Jim pulled out a box a little too long for a ring, she sighed, feeling both stupid and silly.

After handing it to her, he waited while she simply held the box looking up at him with a confused stare. After pausing she said, "You shouldn't have gotten me anything."

"All new mothers need a gift."

Victoria felt her emotions getting the best of her. Jim glanced at the door. "Could you open it now before they get back? I don't want to—"

"Oh, sorry."

Opening up the box, she pulled out the beautiful amethyst bracelet. She looked it over with her mouth open, shaking her head. "Wow, it's..."

"When Brian and I were born, my father bought one just like that for my mother with our birthstones in it. This is Kaylie's birthstone."

She stared at him, absolutely blown away. "It's so beautiful. I, uh... you didn't have to."

"Could you not tell anyone that I bought it for you? I wouldn't want Caroline to get the wrong idea. I mean... I'm not sure what I mean. It's just—"

"Sure, sure. I'll tell people I bought myself a gift from the baby."

"Thanks."

She stared down at the bracelet. "Help me try it on?"

Jim placed it around her wrist and struggled with the clasp. As his fingers brushed her skin, she felt the heat of his touch. Her gaze traveled up to his eyes, and she watched him, mesmerized. Victoria breathed in deeply to capture his scent. He turned his head slightly and found their lips were just a few inches apart just as he secured the clasp. "Got it."

They smiled at one another for a slightly awkward moment before he pulled back to a safe distance. Looking down, he found her still staring at him.

Jim asked, "Are you okay?"

Tearing her eyes from him, she shook her head. "Oh, yeah."

He looked down at her wrist. "It looks nice."

Victoria stared straight ahead while wearing a lost expression. "What?"

Jim rolled his eyes. "The bracelet."

Snapping out of it, she smiled down at the gems. "Sorry, I think the drugs are still working through my system... I love it. It's perfect."

"I'm glad."

"So, where's Caroline?"

"She wasn't feeling well, so she stayed back at Jillian's." Jim smiled to her. "I'm going to go see my daughter now." He chuckled. "That sounds so weird to say... my daughter."

Victoria grinned. "Okay, bye, Father."

"Be back soon, Mother." Jim's smiled disappeared. "That sounds a little creepy."

"It does."

"Let's not call each other that."

Victoria nodded and Jim turned to leave. Glancing down at the bracelet, she said, "Wait! You better hold this for me, if you don't want anyone to see it. I'd hate to lose it. Just slip it into my jewelry box at home. Jillian has the key. Just tell her you need to pick up something for me."

"Good idea."

After unclasping the bracelet, she handed it to him. He tucked it away and slipped out of the room. She stared at the door until it was fully closed and then returned her gaze to her now-bare wrist.

Closing her eyes, an image flashed in her brain of Jim, her, and the baby. They were lying in her bed on their sides with the baby between them, and all three were giggling about something. She opened her eyes, and the image faded away. She turned, curled up with her pillow, and began to cry.

43

Twenty minutes later, Jim returned to Victoria's room with a nurse, who was carrying their adorable baby.

Kaylie still had the feeding tube coming out of her nose and taped to the side of her face. Her eyes fluttered open a bit and were a pale blue. She was awake, but groggy, as she waved her arms around slowly. Victoria smiled brightly as the nurse gently placed Kaylie into her arms.

"Oh, my God... She's perfect."

Moving closer, Jim stared down at mother and child while desperately fighting back tears. Brian looked at him while struggling to hold back a chuckle. Jillian glanced at Jim and shook her head, touched by his emotion. Shifting her glance to Brian, she gave him an incredulous look. Brian caught her stare and curled his lips as he pulled himself together. Jillian shook her head at him, returned to the baby, and smiled.

"You are such a pretty girl," Victoria said softly.

The nurse smiled. "I'll return in a few minutes to take her back. This is her first big girl trip, so just a short one today. After that, we can work on pumping some milk for her."

Victoria replied, "Okay."

Brian shot Jim a juvenile smile as the nurse left the room. Rolling his eyes, Jim returned a look that screamed *"Grow up."* Jillian caught Brian's expression once again but this time fought to hold back a laugh. After composing herself, she elbowed him gently in the stomach before giving her new husband a proper head-shaking, disapproving grin.

Holding his hands up as if to say he would behave, Brian fought to suppress his own grin. Jillian shook her head once more and then turned her attention to the baby. "She's precious."

Victoria glanced up at Jillian with her heart melting away. "She's so tiny." She looked to Kaylie and said, "You are so cute."

Kaylie's eyes blinked open, and she appeared to be staring up at her mother. Victoria smiled brightly as she said, "Yes, you know your mommy. We are going to have so much fun together. We can pick out clothes and toys, and your daddy can help."

Kaylie's eyes drifted closed as Jim leaned in and said, "You are such a beautiful girl."

Jim extended a finger to the baby, and she blindly waved her hand at it. "I think she wants to give me five. She's, like, so advanced already... like a little genius."

While still fighting his juvenile reaction to seeing his little brother as a father, Brian leaned in for a closer look. His gaze traveled up to Jim then back to the baby as the silly smile melted away from his face.

Victoria flashed her eyes to Jim. "She's really tired."

"She's been through a lot," Jim replied in a soothing voice.

Jillian glanced up at Brian, who now appeared to be on the verge of crying his own tears. Reaching out, she ran her fingers along his arm before taking his hand. He looked at her, embarrassed, then rubbed his hand over his mouth before clearing his throat. Leaning over, she whisper in his ear, "You're just like your brother."

Brian shook his head no, and Jillian smiled as she nodded yes. They both returned their gaze to Victoria, Jim, and the baby and then glanced at each other feeling a little awkward, like they were crashing this new family's first truly intimate moment.

After motioning to Brian with her eyes, Jillian took a step back. Brian followed. Jillian said softly, "We're going to give you guys some privacy."

"Especially if you're going to be pumping." Brian quipped as he held back a chuckle.

Jim glared up at him, and Victoria shook her head with a smile. Then the new parents both returned to making over their precious baby as Jillian and Brian headed out of the room.

Once they reached the hallway, Jillian checked to be sure they were alone. She moved to Brian and kissed him deeply. When she pulled away, he asked, "What was that for? I thought you might be mad, but seeing my brother as a father just, uh..."

"I'm not mad. I mean you are being a little immature, but..." She smiled. "I don't know I, uh, got so wet just seeing you all emotional." She placed her tongue between her teeth, glanced around to be sure the coast was clear before leaning to him and whispering, "I kinda feel like blowing you or something."

He gave her a bright smile. "Really? There's a bathroom over there where the door locks."

"You're kidding, right?"

"No."

"We can't, can we?" Jillian glanced up at him with a half-innocent, half-naughty look.

"Or we could go to the car." He lifted his brows with a sexy smile.

Jillian stared back at him, shaking her head. "I really don't want to end up on the evening news. I think you're just going to have to wait until tonight."

"Seriously? You've got me all hard and everything."

Redirecting her eyes south to the problem area, her jaw dropped. "Gee, you are... wow."

"You see."

She glanced down both sides of the hall and then pressed her body to his, kissed him more passionately this time before pulling away. "I'm so horny, myself, but we're just going to have to wait."

After giving her a disappointed look, he adjusted his pants. "Okay, but you've really got to stop doing this to me. It's not healthy for a guy my age to get all worked up and then left hanging."

Jillian smiled and grabbed his hand. "I know. I'm sorry. You're just so cute."

They began walking toward the elevator, and she added, "I'll give you the full treatment later."

"You better."

"And maybe we could even do... *everything*."

"Are you serious?"

Jillian smiled. "Yeah, I kind of feel like it. Don't you?"

He nodded quickly. "When don't I? Geez... now I think I'm going to need to sit down." Brian glanced down to his bulge, and Jillian followed suit. It was unmistakable now.

Her eyes widened. "You know... we could go home now and check on Caroline. She probably needs a ride to the hospital." She winked at him.

"Okay, yeah... perfect."

"I'll go tell them and be right back." Glancing at his lap, she rolled her eyes. "Try to settle down or something so we can get out of the hospital without attracting too much attention."

Jillian broke into a grin before she turned. Brian watched her head back to Victoria's room while wearing a wide smile.

44

Twenty minutes later Brian and Jillian walked into the house to find Caroline sitting in the living room with her purse in her hand and waiting impatiently.

"I've been trying to call Jim for the last hour," Caroline said curtly.

"He probably just has his cell off. You know, the hospital rules, and all," Brian replied.

Jillian and Brian shared a quick glance and then looked back at Caroline. Jillian said, "We, uh, came back to see if you wanted to go to the hospital."

"Thank you so much." Caroline took a step toward the door.

Brian stammered, "You're ready now... We need a few minutes before, um... Can I make you some breakfast or something?"

"Already ate, but thanks." After giving him a quick, polite smile, she began firing off questions, "How's the baby? What's going on at the hospital?"

Jillian replied, "She's doing well. They took her off the ventilator."

Brian began, "And they're working on pumping breast milk right about, uh..." He bit his lip fearing he had said too much.

"Who's they?" Caroline asked, concerned.

"Uh, Victoria and the nurse." Brian stammered as Jillian gave him a tired look.

"Where's Jim?"

"He's, uh, I'm sure he's waiting outside," Brian murmured with a hesitant smile.

Jillian smiled. "Could you give us a few minutes? I really —"

"She has diarrhea and uh needs to..." Brian blurted out. Jillian glared at him, horrified.

Caroline reacted with a sour face. "Oh, okay," and moved to the sofa.

After rolling her eyes at Brian, Jillian said sternly, "If you two will excuse me."

Bouncing up and down on his heals impatiently, Brian's gaze darted around the room. Caroline glanced up at him, their eyes met, and they shared an awkward moment. He bit his lip and then said, "I'd better see if she needs any Pepto or anything."

Caroline nodded uncomfortably, and he took off up the stairs.

Rushing into the bathroom, Brian discovered Jillian sitting on the toilet peeing.

She looked at him dumbfounded. "Seriously, diarrhea."

"I panicked."

"Couldn't you give yourself diarrhea instead?"

"Sorry."

Brian began unbuttoning his pants. "We'd better hurry up."

Staring at him with her mouth open and her eyes narrowed, she flushed and pulled up her underwear. She stood while still glaring at him, pushed down her skirt and headed to the sink. "You can't seriously still want to—"

"I'm still sorta hard, and we—"

"How can you be after all that intestinal distress talk?" She rolled her eyes. "Oh, that's right, you're a man. I almost forgot."

Brian pushed down his underwear and sure enough, he was almost at full staff. He smiled at her, and she glanced down, wearing a sickened expression. "What's wrong with you?"

"I'm just so hot for you."

"I'm hot for you too, but come on. I'll bet if I really had what you said I had, you'd still be chasing after me with that thing."

"Probably, but only if you showered first."

Jillian rolled her eyes as Brian widened his suggestively.

He began, "So what do you think? I mean, we—"

After interrupting him with a scoff, Jillian whispered, "Caroline thinks I'm up here pooping my brains out, and you still want to do it?"

"Well, we probably don't have time for all that, but maybe just a quick blowjob or a, uh—"

"Wait, and just where does Caroline think you are?"

"Um, helping you, I guess."

Jillian furrowed her brow. "Helping me."

"I came up to see if you needed Pepto." Brian shrugged. "I'm not thinking all that clearly, okay..."

"Obviously."

Glancing back down at his erection, she shook her head with a grin. "I'll give you three minutes."

Brian smiled. Jillian got down on her knees and brought her A-game. After ninety seconds she forgot all about Caroline and really lost herself in the experience. Brian struggled to complete the mission quickly, but it wasn't happening. After another minute, Jillian glanced up at him and then pulled away, winded, and tugging at her collar.

"You're not even close, are you?"

"Sorry, there's too much pressure. You know I can't perform when—"

"Finish now," she commanded.

He nodded quickly and she slipped back over him. Brian gritted his teeth and tensed every freaking muscle in his body as he fought to push it out. Getting up on his tiptoes, he held the wall with one hand for support as the struggle continued. A huge vein swelled up in his forehead, looking like it might explode before anything *else* actually did.

After forty more seconds Jillian pulled away from him and shook her head. "That's it."

"Really?" He gave her a disappointed look.

"Sorry, we're just going to have to do this later."

Checking her face in the mirror, Jillian grimaced. "I'm a mess now. Thanks."

"I think you look fine."

Brian stood with his underwear and shorts still around his ankles, his erection still pointing straight out and not making a move.

She glared at him. "Let's go."

"I can't."

"What do you mean, you can't?"

"I need to finish before—"

"You're actually going to jerk off now?"

He shrugged.

Jillian shook her head and breathed out deeply. "Here I was giving it everything I had, and you couldn't finish."

"Sorry."

"I'm getting out of here. Just get it done quickly."

"All right, all right."

Glancing down once more at his problem, she shook her head with a smile before she headed to the door. Stopping suddenly, she looked back. "Just make sure you think of me when you're doing it."

"Who else would I—"

"Right."

"Oh, and we're doing it later, so don't go tiring yourself out."

"I'll be ready later."

Jillian nodded skeptically before breaking into a grin. Moving to him, she kissed him on the cheek and smiled. "God, you are cute."

"Thanks."

Jillian slipped out of the room, and Brian quickly went to work.

45

Ten minutes later, Brian drove with a slightly red face as he was still recovering from his recent overexertion. Glancing over at him, Jillian shook her head while holding back a smile. Caroline sat in the back seat, staring out the window at the beautiful Miami skyline. She glanced down at her bare finger, where her engagement ring had been displayed proudly up until twenty-four hours ago. She could think of nothing other than Jim watching Victoria pump out breast milk from her huge, perfectly-shaped breasts.

Sighing, Caroline glanced at her purse. After a moment of reflection, she reached into her bag and pulled out the large diamond ring. She slipped it over her finger and turned the stone toward her palm as a slightly evil grin spread over her face.

In Victoria's room, Jim stood nearby, watching as the nurse demonstrated how to pump milk from Victoria's swollen breasts. He found it hard to look away as the gorgeous twins were now so much larger than he had remembered.

Jim stared at her cleavage as the gentle hum of the pump filled the room. Drifting away, his thoughts went to St. Barts and the amazing sex he and Victoria had enjoyed together. His mind went to the image of him hovering over her as he looked down while she was pleasing him so amazingly. He smiled as he stared at her breasts without really focusing. Glancing up at him, Victoria noticed his stare and smiled. "Jim."

Victoria called a little louder, "Jim."

He snapped out of it and looked at her face. "Sorry, I was daydreaming."

"About what?"

"Uh, just St. Barts. The wedding and other... stuff."

Victoria gave him a smile.

After turning off the pump, the nurse said, "I think that's enough for now."

Victoria placed the pump on the table next to her as the nurse left the room. She secured her top and smiled up at Jim. "That feels weird."

"Really?"

"It's just... I don't know how to explain it."

"You don't have to." Jim said, "Uh, you said your breasts were all veiny. I didn't see anything wrong with them at all. They look fine to me."

She quickly pulled her top and exposed both of the golden globes. Bending her neck down, she hefted one of them up and pointed to a tiny blue vein. "You see."

He narrowed his eyes and moved in for a closer look. "You're crazy. There's nothing wrong with those."

"Well, I don't know. I like the old ones better."

Jim moved back to a safe distance. "Sure, the old ones are great, but, uh... Sorry, why are we talking about this?"

She giggled. "You brought it up."

"Right. I just wanted to tell you the new ones are fine, and the old ones were fine, too." He looked away nervously. "I'll just stop taking about your breasts now."

"Okay," she replied casually. After covering everything up, she asked, "Can I see the bracelet one more time?"

"Sure." He pulled it from his pocket and handed it to her.

Just as Victoria held it up to admire it, the door swung open and Jillian, Brian, and Caroline walked in. Jim glanced at the visitors then back to Victoria as she dropped her hand to the bed and hid the bracelet under the sheet.

Breathing a sigh of relief, he looked at Caroline. "Oh, are you feeling better?"

She nodded and moved to him for a hug. They embraced for a little longer than necessary while Caroline splayed her fingers wide in front of Victoria as she wrapped her arms around Jim. The engagement ring was unmistakably visible, and Victoria's eyes quickly went to it.

Pulling away from Jim, Caroline brought a hand up and pushed hair from her face, which once again put the ring on display. Jim caught sight of it now, and his eyes narrowed. He glanced at Victoria and saw her staring at it.

Jillian noticed it as well but didn't say a word.

Victoria asked, "Is that... is that an engagement ring?"

Looking down in mock surprise, Caroline replied, "Oh, my God." She glanced at Jim. "Sorry, I totally forgot I had it on."

Jim frowned slightly. "We were going to wait to tell everyone, but yes, we're engaged."

"Congratulations," Jillian said.

Brian shook his hand before moving to hug Caroline.

After painting on a smile, Victoria said, "Congratulations. That's wonderful."

Caroline shook her head with a silly smile. "I'm sorry. We didn't want to take anything away from your big day."

"Don't worry about it," Victoria replied.

"So how's the baby? I hear she's breathing on her own." Caroline said.

Jim replied, "Yes, she's doing great."

"And you guys are now pumping?" Caroline asked in a bright, happy voice with her eyebrows raised.

"Uh, well yes, I mean Victoria is. I'm just..." Jim stammered.

Victoria's and Jillian's eyes met, and they shared an awkward glance. Feeling the bracelet still in her hand under the sheet, Victoria paused for a moment, thinking. She grinned slightly with the plan forming in her head. Putting it into action, she grimaced, clutched her stomach, and let out a groan. Placing one hand on the bed while under the guise of adjusting her position, she moved her other hand, dropping the bracelet off the bed right at Caroline's feet.

Jim's eyes followed it down.

Glancing down in surprise, Caroline picked it up. "Wow, this is pretty." She studied it closer. "Amethyst... that's Kaylie's birthstone, isn't it?" She furrowed her brow as she asked, "Was this a gift?"

Jim's jaw dropped. Caroline recognized the look of extreme guilt on his face instantly. She glanced at Victoria and saw she was wearing a slightly embarrassed smile.

Jim began, "I, uh, that is... just—"

"I bought it for myself as a little present from the baby," Victoria interrupted.

Lifting her chin up, Caroline appeared to consider that possibility. "But the baby was due in April, so why would you get February's birthstone? Oh, unless of course, you ran out to a jewelry store since you've been locked up in here." She let that statement sink in and then added, "But wait, you couldn't have. I'm so confused right now."

Everyone stared at Caroline, speechless, until Brian smiled and said, "Gee, what are you a cop?"

No one laughed as the tension hung thickly in the air.

Jim admitted, "Look, I bought it for her. It was just a little present, you know, for all she's been through."

Caroline did her best to smile. "Oh, it's lovely." She added sarcastically, "That was *so* nice of you, Jim."

An awkward silence fell over the room as Caroline's blood began to boil. After taking a deep breath, she said with an edge to her voice, "Is anyone else thirsty? I'm thirsty."

Brian, Jillian, and Victoria shook their heads no.

Caroline shot a deadly look at Jim. "Are *you* thirsty?"

He quickly nodded yes. Turning, Caroline rushed from the room.

Jim watched the door close as he remained perfectly still. He slowly turned back to everyone and announced softly, "If I don't come back in ten minutes, call 911."

Brian held back a laugh as Jim slumped from the room.

Jim found Caroline next to the nurses' station, red-faced and about to burst. She took one look at him and headed down the hall. Rushing after her, he caught up then followed as she walked ahead of him, looking down each corridor until she found one that was empty. Turning the corner, she quickened her pace and motioned from him to walk faster. Finally, she stopped at the end of a hallway. Turning slowly, she stared right through him, waiting.

Jim opened his mouth to speak, made a face as he changed his mind, then groaned softly before he began, "I just wanted to get her something."

"That's fine, Jim, but hiding it from me... that's not fine."

"We weren't."

"Oh, so she always keeps her jewelry under the sheets."

"Okay, so I didn't want you to know about it. I wasn't sure how you'd react."

Caroline shook her head. "I can tell you that I would have been much better about it if you had actually told me. I would have helped you pick it out. When did you get it?"

"This morning," he admitted sheepishly. "Sorry, I'm not thinking clearly. I'm worried about Kaylie and just wanted to do something nice for Victoria since she was so concerned about the breathing tube and everything. You know, this is—"

"I feel like you are sneaking around behind my back," Caroline interrupted.

"I'm not."

Turning toward the wall, she said, "I know you're not, and I'm hoping it's not, because she just gave birth. I mean, I suppose you guys couldn't be having sex already, I believe you need to wait for a while after... Jesus, what am I saying?"

Jim placed a gentle hand on her shoulder. "Look, I love you. I told you it's over between Victoria and me."

Turing to look deeply into his sincere eyes, Caroline shook her head. "I know. I know... I'm just acting crazy."

She moved into his arms. He pressed his lips to the side of her head and kissed her, drinking in the scent of her hair. He held her for a long time before he pulled back, and they shared a passionate kiss.

"Are we okay?" he asked.

She nodded. "Just tell me before you buy another woman an expensive piece of jewelry." Smiling, they both pondered that for a moment, realizing how odd it sounded.

"I probably won't be buying a lot of jewelry for other women," he said with a completely straight face.

"I should hope not," she replied, playing along.

After sharing a chuckle, Jim said, "We should probably get back. Do you want to hold Kaylie?"

"Yes." Caroline returned a genuine smile, pausing before giving him a serious look. "But let's not keep anything from each other anymore. I want to know everything you're thinking."

Jim thought, *Everything? Wow, you really don't trust me... Shit, I'm not sure I trust me.*

"Okay," He replied. "You also... we should be completely honest with each other."

"We should be," she replied.

They stood together for a moment not looking each other directly in the eye.

Jim took a deep breath and shrugged. "Good."

Turning, he opened his hand to her. She put her hand in his and they headed down the hall with their fingers intertwined.

As they turned down the main hall, Jim felt her engagement ring against his fingers and asked, "So, what's with wearing the ring?"

She didn't look at him. "Really, I forgot."

Jim wasn't so sure the complete honesty had kicked in quite yet.

Jim and Caroline returned to Victoria's room to find Adam Rawlings sitting next to Victoria and gently caressing her hand. They were alone. Jim gave him a *"Who the hell is this guy"* look. Caroline's face lit up when she laid her eyes on the handsome, brawny older gentleman who seemed to be getting pretty cozy with the one big problem in her world.

Victoria said, "Adam, this is Jim and Caroline. Jim's Kaylie's father."

Wearing a big smile, Adam got up and met Jim in the center of the room. As they shook hands, Jim stood tall, trying to match Adam's more-than-six-foot stature. Jim glanced down to see his tiny hand get swallowed up by the giant paw of the apparent ex-college football linebacker whose face probably graced the cover of GQ at least twice.

Jim gave Adam an uneasy smile and murmured, "Hi."

"Congratulations," said Adam.

Jim nodded as he replied softly, "Thanks."

Victoria added, "And Caroline is his fiancée; we just found out they're engaged."

Adam smiled at her. "Well, then, congratulations are in order for you, as well." They shook hands as she beamed up at him. Turning her ecstatic eyes to Victoria, Caroline said, "Victoria, you didn't tell me you had such a gorgeous boyfriend."

Jim watched closely as Adam and Victoria looked at one another, both unsure what to say. Adam began, "Well, we—"

Victoria interrupted, "He's my friend, but we're planning a date really soon, aren't we?"

"As soon as possible." Adam nodded.

Victoria smiled. "Definitely... Adam owns a few restaurants in the area."

Caroline's smile widened, if that were even possible, as she nodded, impressed. "Wow. Fantastic. We're going to go see the baby and let you guys visit."

Jim appeared to be in a trance as Caroline grabbed his hand and pulled him toward the door. He snapped out of it. "Yeah, um, nice to meet you."

"Great meeting you," Adam replied

Jim nodded with a slight frown as Caroline dragged him out of the room.

In the hall, Caroline glanced up at him, her mood now a complete shift from ten minutes earlier. She smiled. "Let's go see the baby."

"Okay," Jim replied weakly as he followed her down the hall.

46

A few hours later, Victoria visited Kaylie in the NICU, pumped out an ample supply of breast milk, and returned to her room for an examination before being released from the hospital. She was going stir crazy being trapped in her room, and as much as she wanted to be with Kaylie every second, she desperately needed a good meal and wanted just two hours away to recharge her batteries. Kaylie was in more than capable hands with the hospital's expert caring staff. After receiving discharge instructions, Victoria changed into clothes that Jillian brought for her.

Jim and Caroline were booked on a flight for later that night, and the group planned to go to dinner before Brian dropped them off at the airport. After dinner, Victoria intended to return to the hospital, staying as late as she could before checking in to a nearby hotel for the night.

As the group was heading through the lobby, Victoria's cell phone rang. She answered and her jaw dropped. Stopping in her tracks, she stammered, "They... want us back up there. The nurse wouldn't tell me what it is, but the doctor... He, um, needs to meet with us right now."

Jim and Victoria sat in Doctor Smyth's office as he began, "We noticed Kaylie breathing irregularly, and we were able to detect a slight heart murmur."

"Oh, my God," Victoria said.

Jim took hold of her hand as the doctor continued, "Kaylie has what we call patent ductus arteriosus. I realize that it probably sounds serious, but it is quite common and easily correctible. Let me explain... When a baby is first born the umbilical cord is cut, and the lungs take over to supply oxygen to the body. The lungs expand, their blood vessels relax to accept more flow, and the ductus arteriosus usually closes within the first hours of life. Sometimes and more likely with a premature baby, the ductus arteriosus does not close on its own, and this is referred to as a patent—meaning, open—ductus arteriosus. Are you with me so far?"

Victoria and Jim both nodded while wearing solemn looks. They barely comprehended any of that.

"There are several options available to correct this condition. A medication such as indomethacin can be given. The medications can constrict the muscle in the wall of the patent ductus arteriosus and promote closure. These drugs can have side effects, such as kidney injury or bleeding. So we checked Kaylie's lab values and found it would be too risky to attempt that course of action."

"So what other options are available?" Jim asked. With her lip quivering, Victoria glanced at Jim then back to the doctor.

"Surgery can be performed to close the ductus arteriosus."

Victoria said, "I don't understand. She seemed to be doing so well and—"

Giving her a sympathetic nod, Doctor Smyth explained, "Usually the symptoms of this condition do not present themselves until a few days after birth. I will assure you that this is very minor surgery, and the risk of complications is extremely low, especially since Kaylie is otherwise a very healthy baby."

"And if she doesn't have the surgery?" Jim asked.

"We could wait to see if it closes on its own, but Kaylie's blood pressure is already too high and putting a strain on her heart. I've consulted with Doctor Cardon who is one of the finest pediatric cardiac surgeons in the state. We both agree that the surgery should be performed as soon as possible. We would like to do it tonight."

Victoria looked at Jim. "What do you think?"

He widened his eyes. "I think we have to do it."

"Okay... okay," Victoria said as she gripped Jim's hand firmly.

"Good. Please wait right here. There will be some paperwork to sign."

The Doctor stepped out of the room.

Standing up, Jim walked over to the window and stared out. Victoria stared up at Jim, on the verge of losing it. Turning to her, Jim said, "It's going to be okay. She'll be fine."

He opened his arms to her. Victoria got up and moved to him. They held each other tight.

For the next three hours, Victoria, Jim, Caroline, Brian, and Jillian sat in the waiting room, worrying and struggling to cope with the weight off all that was going on. At just after midnight, Doctor Cardon came out wearing a confident smile.

"She did beautifully. The surgery went as planned. She responded well to the anesthesia, and we were able to close the ductus arteriosus. She has a tiny scar between the ribs on her left side, but as she gets older, you probably won't even be able to see that. That's a strong little girl you have there, and she's going to be fine."

"Thank you, Doctor," Victoria said with her voice cracking a bit. "When can we see her?"

"In about an hour. A nurse will come out to get you."

The doctor stood. Jim did also and shook his hand. "Thank you."

Handing Jim a card, Cardon said, "If you have any questions, please call me."

After the doctor left, everyone exchanged hugs. Caroline went from Jim to Brian and then even ended up embracing Victoria as they both cried tears of joy. Pulling away from her, Caroline said, "I knew she was going to be okay. I just knew it."

"Thank you for being here," Victoria said.

Jim smiled as he watched Caroline and Victoria finally getting along. Then his eyes widened as he said, "Don't you have that exam tomorrow?" He glanced at the clock on the wall. "I mean today?"

Caroline replied, "I do, but—"

"There's a 2:00 a.m. flight."

"I can't leave you. I'll just see if I can make it up."

Jim frowned, "With Professor Black, I don't think so. You should go; I'll fly back in a day or two."

"Are you sure?"

Jim nodded as Brian said, "We'll drive you to the airport."

"Okay, but call me after you see her," Caroline said.

"I will."

There were hugs all around again before Jillian and Brian left with Caroline. Jim and Victoria were brought in to see Kaylie in the NICU at just after 1:30 a.m. She was sleeping soundly, and they stayed by her side watching their baby girl for more than an hour with their hearts melting with joy.

At 2:45 a.m., a nurse informed the new parents that there was a room reserved for NICU parents, and it was available. They were told they would be just steps away from the baby and would be awakened if needed. Both were exhausted and they gratefully accepted the offer.

The room featured two small twin beds and an attached bathroom. Jim tried to call Caroline while Victoria was washing her face. He left her a voicemail since she must have still been in the air.

Victoria came out of the bathroom wearing only a sleeveless shirt and panties, since neither had a change of clothes. She slipped past him in the tiny room, and they shared an awkward smile. Making her way to the bed, she slipped under the covers.

Jim took his turn in the bathroom and came out in only his boxer briefs. Victoria stole a glance of his firm, muscular body and breathed out quietly. He moved to the open bed and got under the covers.

They each turned on their sides to face one another. Jim said, "She's going to be fine."

"I know."

"Goodnight," Jim said.

"Goodnight."

Jim turned off the night on the table between them, and the room was suddenly pitch black.

Rolling onto her back, Victoria stared up at the ceiling, wishing Jim were in the bed with her, simply holding her all night. Jim was thinking exactly the same thing about Victoria. Less than forty seconds later, both exhausted parents fell into a deep sleep.

47

The next morning, something pulled Jim from his sleep. He sat up in bed, groggy and confused and struggling to remember why he was in this strange room. Glancing over at the sleeping Victoria, he fought to clear his head. He watched for a few seconds, wearing a silly smile on his face, as she peacefully breathed in and out. God, she was pretty, he thought. And then it hit him; he actually was now a father. His smile faded. He quietly got dressed and headed out to see his daughter.

As the nurse led him to Kaylie's isolette, she told him the baby was doing fine. And although he could not pick her up yet, all signs pointed to a successful surgery and a speedy recovery. Jim stared down at his tiny baby girl. She was still sleeping peacefully with tubes and wires connected all over her.

In his heart, he knew she was going to be fine, but she looked so helpless lying there in that condition; he felt horrible for her. Fighting the urge to have an emotional breakdown, he gently stoked her skin.

Victoria made her way to the NICU about an hour later. She found Jim sitting next to Kaylie and softly talking to her. Jim looked up at Victoria, and they shared a smile.

"How is she?"

"She's perfect."

He stood and let Victoria take his seat. She leaned down and touched her daughter as Jim watched them both while smiling proudly.

Victoria glanced up at him. "Did you call Caroline yet?"

His eyes opened wide. "No, but thanks for reminding me. Are you okay with her?"

Victoria nodded. "Go."

Jim called Caroline and gave her an update on the baby's condition. There seemed to be no hint of jealously in her voice when she found out he had shared a hospital room with Victoria. She even asked how Victoria was doing. He promised to call her back later that day.

For the next three days, Jim remained in Miami at the hospital with Victoria and the baby as Kaylie's recovery progressed. Jillian and Brian visited every day. Jim needed to return to school and was scheduled on a flight that afternoon. Before he left, he and Victoria met with Doctor Smyth, and they found out that Kaylie probably could leave the hospital in about two weeks. She now weighed more than four pounds and was making remarkable progress for a premature baby whom only days before had had surgery.

In their hospital room, Victoria sat on the bed and watched as Jim packed his clothes. "I wanted to talk to you about something," she began.

After zipping up his duffle bag, Jim sat on the other bed across from her.

"I decided to build an office behind the house. They break ground in a few weeks. I'm going to open a couples' therapy practice and see how it goes."

He smiled. "That's really great."

"It's actually going to be a guest house with an attached office. I know you planned to move to Miami after graduation, and I'm not sure exactly what your plans are, but you and Caroline are welcome to live there, if you'd like."

Jim's mouth opened wide as he nodded in surprise.

She continued, "I always wanted to have a guest house, and I figured you could be close to the baby... really close... and have your own private place. It could work well."

"It sounds perfect. I'll talk to Caroline about it. I'm sure she'll love the idea." After he said it, he thought, Well maybe not.

Victoria's thoughts were in the same ballpark, but they each put on a confident smile, and she said, "Good. Just let me know... It all should be finished in May, but you know how these construction projects go sometimes."

"Sure." Pulling his phone from his pocket, Jim checked the time. "I should probably get to the airport." He stood and she followed suit. They stared at each other from less than a foot apart, both shaking their heads and wearing awkward grins.

"I don't want to leave her."

"I know."

"I'll fly down as much as I can."

"In less than four months, you'll be back for good, and..."

Jim nodded and said with his voice quivering, "Let's not talk about it. I don't want to lose it here."

Victoria gave him a sweet smile. She opened her arms, and he moved to her. They held each other for a long, long time.

48

Jim returned to school, and twelve days later, Kaylie left the hospital a nearly five- pound, perfectly healthy baby. Jillian and Brian drove the new mother and daughter home. Carrying the sleeping Kaylie into the house, Brian placed her in an infant rocking seat that was sitting on the sofa.

Kaylie stirred a bit. Jillian, Victoria, and Brian stared down at the adorable baby as she rubbed her little nose with her tiny hand before she drifted back to sleep.

Jillian whispered, "Do you want us to stay?"

"No. We'll be fine," Victoria replied softly.

"Remember, we want to babysit soon."

Victoria nodded with a smile as she sat next to the infant seat on the sofa. After taking a deep breath, she stared up at Brian and Jillian with a look of relief mixed with slight terror.

"Are you sure?" Brian whispered.

Victoria grinned semi-confidently and waved good-bye.

Jillian mouthed the word bye as she grabbed Brian by the arm and led him toward the door. The new mother watched, smiling as they slipped quietly outside.

Slumping against the cushion, Victoria stared at Kaylie. She took a deep breath, smiled, and fell quickly into an exhausted sleep.

Thirty minutes later, Kaylie woke crying. Popping upright, Victoria struggled to pull herself to consciousness as she gazed down at her wailing infant.

"Are you hungry? I bet you're hungry."

Victoria performed a quick diaper change, fed Kaylie a bottle, and then gave her a tour of her new home.

The first stop was Kaylie's room. The room was painted yellow with cows jumping over moons in a border around the center of the room, just above the lip of the natural pine wood crib.

"Do you like yellow?" Kaylie's drowsy eyes were glued to her mother's smiling face as Victoria added, "I wasn't sure if you were a girl, so we went with yellow. If you don't like it, we can change it. I think it looks nice, though."

Next they moved to the massage room. Victoria cradled Kaylie in her arms as she slowly spun around the room, showing her the wooden massage table, the selection of massage oils, and the matching cocoa-colored towels and sheets.

"Daddy surprised me with all this. Do you like it? Daddy is a very good guy."

She moved in front of the odd grass sculpture. "Now this... I'm not sure what the heck this is. But your daddy picked it out, so we love it, right?"

She winked at Kaylie, who waved her hand back at her. "That's it; you get it. Sometimes you have to say you like something when you really, really, really don't... I'll teach you all the things you need to know. I'll teach you all about clothes and shoes and purses... oh, and boys. But I don't want you dating any until you're at least twenty-five, okay?"

Kaylie placed her hand on her face, seemingly giving her mother a skeptical look, but most likely just fighting some gas.

"You think I'm kidding... no, I'm serious. I will not allow you to make the same mistakes that Mommy made. You get your college degree and then a good job, and *then* maybe you can go on a date."

Next she moved to the bowl of smooth rocks sitting in the decorative heating pan. "This is my favorite thing. Your daddy gave me a rock massage, and it was amazing. He has magic hands."

Victoria paused a moment, just staring at the rocks.

She smiled down at the baby and began in a happy baby voice, "You probably want to know why Mommy and Daddy aren't together and why Daddy is..." Her voice took on a condescending tone as she continued, "... engaged to a hot, little, young wh—I mean, woman." Her voice returned to her baby-friendly tone. "Sorry. She's nice, I guess. When you're old enough, I'll try to explain it all to you, but you see, Mommy is much, much older than Daddy. Mommy's hiney is going to start sagging very, very soon, and well, thanks to you, Mommy's tummy will never be the same." Victoria wagged her finger in Kaylie's face.

The baby stared up at her with her eyelids fluttering.

"So, you're happy about that. Well, maybe I am, too, because without it, I wouldn't have you. Mommy loves Daddy, and he loves Mommy, but he's also in love with Caroline and, well, she's his age, and when Mommy is ready for a nursing home, Daddy will be ready to buy some type of two seat sports car, probably a convertible, and be just entering into his mid-life crisis. Daddy's probably better off with Caroline, don't you think?"

Kaylie seemed to shake her head no. Victoria studied her face carefully and then asked again, "Is Daddy better off with Caroline?"

The baby contorted her face slightly then let out a bunch of gas before filling her diaper. Feeling it against her forearm, Victoria smiled. "Somebody needs their pants changed."

<u>49</u>

At the Grayson home the next afternoon, Jillian yelled down for Brian to meet her upstairs. He came into their bedroom, but when he didn't see her, he called her name. She replied from the bathroom, and when he went inside, he discovered her wearing a proud smile along with an old t-shirt and shorts. She had newspaper spread out on the floor and the "Copy-a-Cock" kit items on the counter.

He grinned. "What the hell is this?"

"Victoria gave the kit to me months ago, but we've been so busy, I completely forgot about it. I figured after all you went through on your first try, you might want to actually make one."

"No, it was a stupid idea."

Shaking her head, Jillian moved to him for a kiss. "It's a great idea. I would really love to have an exact replica of your perfect penis."

"Really?" He gave her a skeptical look.

She nodded with a sexy grin and then moved to her knees. While running her hand slowly down over his chest to his abdomen, she said slowly, "Victoria told me it's much easier to make one with two people."

Jillian trailed her hand down further and placed it over the already growing bulge in his gym shorts.

"I think... that's true," Brian stammered. "You're supposed to do the mixing while I get, you know."

She looked up at his face as she pressed both her hands along his cotton-covered length. "How about I get... *you know*... started for you, and then I'll take care of the mixing."

He nodded quickly. "Or we could do that."

Jillian pulled down his shorts and boxer briefs. She gasped when his nearly hard penis sprang out and then flopped down before her. While holding the backs of his legs, she moved her head forward until her nose was pressed against his shaft. Then she slowly turned her head left and then right to allow his now throbbing manhood to brush against her cheeks and nose. Brian leaned back, literally gasping for breath.

She slid lower, extended her tongue, and covered the head with licks. His manhood throbbed, rose up, and grew until it stuck straight out from his body. Pulling back, she grinned at her accomplishment. "Look, no hands."

"You're good," he murmured.

She plunged her mouth over him. Placing his hands behind his head, Brian gazed down at the amazing sight of Jillian pleasing him. He said, "This is not only easier... it's so much more fun with two people."

Jillian pulled away from him and chuckled as she looked up at his face. Then she took him back into her mouth and began moving faster and faster over him. He groaned loudly as he approached the brink of climax. They were both lost in the moment until he spotted the kit on the counter. He pulled away, and she looked up at him, confused.

"The kit." He steadied himself by placing a hand on the wall as he added, "I'm about to shoot."

She shook her head. "Sorry, I got so, uh... wow." Jillian stood and took a deep breath while opening her eyes wide as she fought to get her bearings. "Okay, you keep it big, and I'll get ready."

Brian nodded as he slowly massaged himself in order to maintain maximum size. Moving to the counter, she measured and checked the temperature of the water. She poured it into the bowl, which already contained the mix, checked the time on her smart phone, and began to stir.

She glanced over to watch him, as he worked his manhood, and smiled. "I wish I was doing that for you."

"So do I."

She grinned. "I'll finish you."

Jillian stirred and stirred as he maintained his erection. After two minutes, she poured the cast mixture into the precut tube and stood on the newspaper on the floor. Brian met her there, and she looked down, impressed. "Wow, you are big. Ready?"

She handed him the tube and he quickly slipped it over his superhard length. The excess mixture slipped out the sides of the tube and onto his thighs. They both looked down, chuckling at the sight.

Brian began flexing the muscles in his groin to attempt to maintain his best showing. Jillian checked the time. "Okay, just sixty more seconds."

"Okay."

"How you doing?"

"Good."

"Do you need me to show you my breasts or anything?"

"No, I think I'm good."

She gave him an angry look.

"Oh, sorry. Sure, I'd love to see them."

She looked away, feigning anger. "Forget it now."

"Sorry, just trying to focus. I would love to see them in about thirty more seconds."

They stood there for another fifteen seconds while Brian grimaced twice more as he continued to flex. Jillian checked the time and said, "Okay, it should be good."

He carefully slipped the mold off his erection and handed it to her. Jillian smiled as she peered inside the tube. "This is so cool."

"They make one for your... you know." Confused, she looked at him, so he elaborated, "Yeah, you can make a mold of your vagina. Victoria told me about it."

"Huh."

Brian said, "I'm not sure exactly what you can do with it once you make it, but they have it."

"I think yours will be more fun."

They shared a nod.

Jillian said, "We need to let this dry for twenty-four hours and then we can pour in the rubber stuff."

After placing the tube on the counter, she looked at him and broke into a smile. He was a mess, with the cast mixture dripping down and beginning to dry all over his legs. Brian scraped it off onto the newspaper as she watched, chuckling.

Jillian said, "You take a shower while I clean up here. When you're done, meet me in bed, and we can play some more."

He never showered faster. Ninety-seven seconds later, he met her in bed, and it was fucking amazing.

When Bridget and Rob returned from their cruise, they spent a few days in Miami. Rob introduced Bridget to Jillian, who more than approved of the new woman in his life. They spent some time visiting Victoria and the baby. When they returned to Orlando, Rob took a job with another investment firm in the city and moved in with his new F.B.I. agent girlfriend. For the first time in his life, he was really falling in love. Oh, and the sex was fucking amazing.

Over the next four months, Jim called every day and flew to Miami four times with Caroline as they watched Kaylie grow and thrive. Brian and Jillian spent a lot of time at Victoria's. They babysat when needed and were both growing very attached to the new addition. Jillian got back to writing and was working on her follow-up to *The Leg Thing*. It was still untitled, but she thought it was coming together nicely. After completing his tennis certification, Brian began teaching classes at a small local tennis club. He was never happier.

Victoria worked closely with the contractors to keep them on schedule, and the guesthouse and office were both finished on time. The new building consisted of a waiting area and large office with a bathroom and had a separate entrance from the guest space. The guest space featured a living room, a gorgeous, modern eat-in kitchen, a bedroom, and an opulent bathroom with a separate tub and shower.

In late April, Kaylie switched over to formula and gave Victoria's tired breasts a much-needed break. Weighing in at just more than ten pounds, there were no signs that Kaylie was premature, and she was quickly catching up in weight to other infants her age. Her eyes were still blue, but now a lighter shade. She was alert and curious, not all that fussy, and mostly sleeping through the night. She'd just learned to smile and was beginning to make those adorable baby sounds like grunts, gurgles, and coos. Mother and child were immensely enjoying life together.

Victoria dated Adam regularly. He was wonderful with the baby, and Victoria found herself growing fonder of him as she got to know him better. For the first time since she began dating after the death of her husband, Victoria was actually able to keep the relationship from becoming physical. They took it slowly, and it wasn't just because she needed to heal.

Victoria found herself not thinking about sex nearly as much as she did before the pregnancy. Although she spent most of her time doting on Kaylie, she was also consumed with getting her practice off the ground and preparing the guesthouse for Jim and Caroline. She and Kaylie shopped for all the furniture together, and she swore that the baby had quite an eye for interior design. Kaylie pointed to all the paint colors she liked, spit up on the ones she didn't, and when it was finally finished, the guesthouse looked like it should grace the cover of a decorating magazine.

Victoria was attracted to Adam, but something was different. She still craved the touch of a man, but she had too many other things to focus on now to worry about all that. Adam enjoyed spending time with her and also the baby. Figuring that when the time was right, they would take the next step, he decided he could wait.

Victoria was also fighting to get her old body back, or as much back as was humanly possible. She bought a few one-piece bathing suits and resigned herself to the fact that her bikini days were probably forever behind her, although she secretly vowed to one day get back into her see-through tiny bikini. To that end, she worked out harder than she ever had, and the results were not coming as easily as before, but she was still making progress.

Two weeks before Jim and Caroline were to graduate, Victoria was lounging out by the pool with Adam. Kaylie was sleeping in her playpen under a sunshade, and Victoria watched as Adam got up and walked to the pool. Drinking in his tall, muscular body, that old familiar feeling began bubbling up through her loins. She really wanted him.

Victoria watched as he dove into the pool. Coming to the surface, Adam discovered her grinning at him. She was trying to picture what he would look like with no clothes on. She shook her head in disbelief as she thought, How have I not wondered about this before?

Narrowing his eyes at her stare, he asked, "What is it?"

She grinned, and never one to beat around the bush, said matter-of-factly, "Oh, I was just wondering what you looked like naked."

"Really?"

Victoria nodded with a big smile. Climbing out of the pool, he made his way to her. She eyed him up and down and licked her lips as she felt a tingle throughout her body.

He slipped on his sunglasses. "At the risk of sounding a little full of myself, I look pretty damn good for a guy in his forties."

"Oh, really."

Standing before her, he put his hands on the waistband of his swim trunks. "You don't believe me, do you? Do you want to see? I'll show you right here."

"That's okay. I can pretty much see everything now."

He smiled. "I was going to show you my ass. You really can't tell if it's droopy or not, but I can assure you that—"

"I would like to see it tonight." Victoria gave him a sexy smile.

He slipped down into a chair next to her. "I think it's available."

"Good." She chuckled.

After pausing for a moment, Adam grinned. "I just want to be sure I understand... uh, is it just my ass you want to see, or are you also interested in seeing anything else?"

Hiding behind a smile, Victoria fought to put on a serious look. "Well, I was really hoping I could, uh, see everything."

He stared into her eyes. "I would really like to show you everything."

Standing, she leaned over him. She moved her lips to his, and they shared a quick kiss. She began, "Let me call Jillian and see if she can watch Kaylie for about two..." She kissed him harder, their tongues intertwining for a moment before she pulled back and then continued, "... no, maybe three, hours."

He just stared up at her with his mouth open and nodding yes very slowly. She smiled, turned, and headed toward the house. Captivated, he watched her go, with his trunks not fitting quite so well anymore.

That night, Jillian and Brian watched the baby. Adam had food delivered from his restaurant, and after the meal, he carried Victoria to her bedroom. There, he slowly stripped off her clothes and then his, and they made love for not three hours but a solid thirty minutes. Adam was right; he did look spectacular for a man his age, and he also performed like one much younger.

Victoria was a little self-conscious about her new body, but he made her feel like a supermodel as he explored every inch of her. It wasn't the best sex she had ever had, but it was pretty damn good. Afterward, she rested her head on his chest, took a deep breath and found herself thinking about Jim. She tried to push those thoughts from her head, but they refused to go away.

After Adam left, Victoria went to Jillian's to bring the baby home. Kaylie was asleep, and Victoria didn't have the heart to disturb her. The girls stayed up chatting, while Brian went up to bed. Victoria told Jillian all about her date, but she didn't mention how thoughts of Jim still filled her head. An hour later, Kaylie woke up for a feeding, and Victoria took her home with a lot still on her mind.

50

A few days later, Jillian sat in the viewing area for Court One at the tennis club, where Brian worked. Brian was giving a lesson to a set of twins. Brian had been working with the eight-year-old brother and sister for the last few weeks, and both fine tennis players for their age. This particular lesson was focusing on their serves. Brian glanced up at Jillian. Smiling, she waved down to him through the large glass window.

Sarah Jacobs, the club's owner, walked into the room. "Jillian, nice to see you again."

"Hi, Sarah."

Sarah joined Jillian at the glass, and they both watch Brian work with his students. Sarah said, "He's great with the kids."

"He really likes working here. It's a refreshing change to see him come home from work and not be in a bad mood."

Smiling, Sarah added, "What do they say...? Enjoy your job, and you'll never work a day in your life."

Jillian nodded. "That's how writing is for me."

"Oh, so how's the new book coming?"

"I'm about halfway there."

"Can't wait to read it," Sarah said. "Are you guys playing today?"

"Yeah. I've never played indoors. Brian tells me I'll love it."

"What's not to like? No wind. No sun. No scorching heat."

"Sounds too easy." Jillian smiled.

"You still have to hit it over the net and keep it in the lines."

"Aw... the hard part."

They shared a grin before Sarah asked, "Has Brian told you that I'm putting him in charge while I'm visiting my daughter in Vermont next month?"

"No, he didn't mention it."

"She having her first baby, and I'm going to stay with her for a couple weeks. Once I get up there, I'm not sure I'll want to leave."

"It's not easy being a new mother," Jillian said.

They shared a knowing smile.

Sarah began, "I miss Vermont... the change of seasons, the snow. I used to ski a lot. I've never gotten used to a warm Christmas."

"You grew up there?"

"Born and raised."

"So, why Miami?"

"I married Dale and followed him down here. Now that he's gone, I'm not sure why I'm still here. At some point, I'm sure I'll move back. I'd need to sell the club first. In this economy, that might not be so easy."

Returning an understanding nod, Jillian said, "We were just skiing a few months ago. It was fun, but I'm not sure I could ever get used to living in a cold climate."

After Sarah returned a sympathetic nod, she checked her watch. "I've got to run... Well, have fun playing."

Turning, Sarah headed toward the door. Jillian watched her with her mind racing and then called out, "Sarah."

Sarah turned back to Jillian. "Yes?"

"What if you could sell the club, uh, really easily?"

Sarah widened her eyes as Jillian gave her a big smile.

51

When you have two willing parties and money is pretty much not an issue, it's amazing how quickly a business transaction can be wrapped up. Jillian bought the club without Brian having so much as a clue about what she was up to.

A little over a week later, Jillian parked in front of the tennis club a few minutes after closing time and found only Brian's and one other car in the parking lot. Inside, she discovered an employee finishing up some paperwork and learned that Brian was in the locker room. Confirming that the club was otherwise empty, she sent the employee home.

Jillian locked the front door, turned out the lights, and made her way to the locker room. After opening the door, she grinned upon hearing the shower running. Jillian slipped off all her clothes, grabbed a clean towel from the shelf, and placed it on the bench in front of the lockers. She sat down and waited while wearing only a smile. Moments later, Brian turned off the shower, dried off, and then walked out with a towel wrapped around his waist.

Spotting Jillian naked on the bench, he did a double take. "What the hell are you doing here?"

"Waiting for you."

"Well, I can see that. I mean, I hope you were waiting for *me*, since you're all naked and everything... but Joe could come in here and see—"

"I sent him home."

"What do you mean, you sent him home?"

Smiling, Jillian spread her legs wide. Brian glanced down to her perfectly coifed pubic hair and cleared his throat. She commanded, "Just shut up and get over here."

He moved until he was standing two feet from her. There was a telltale lump rapidly growing under the towel. Reaching out, she grabbed him by the towel and pulled him closer. Jillian looked up at his face as she slowly pulled the towel end he had tucked securely against his body. She let it go, and it fell from him, exposing his nearly-hard penis.

She licked her lips, grabbed him with both hands, and pulled him closer. Placing her lips to his belly button, she kissed him there as his manhood hung down, pressing between her breasts. Jillian breathed in deeply. "God, you smell good."

Brian looked nervously at the door as Jillian took hold of his penis and planted a tiny kiss on the tip. Glancing down at the sight of her delicate hands wrapped around him, he shook his head and stammered, "Um, what about Sarah? She comes by to close up some nights, and she—"

Jillian glanced up at him and smiled. "Sarah won't be coming back."

"Oh, okay..." Brian muttered as Jillian slipped her lips around his shaft. He closed his eyes tight and swayed from side to side dizzily as Jillian worked her mouth over him enthusiastically.

Looking down, he enjoyed the show for about two minutes before his curiosity got the best of him. "Sorry, but what do you mean Sarah won't be coming back?"

Jillian ignored him and kept going. He let her continue for thirty more seconds before he just had to know. Shaking his head, he pulled away from her. Jillian gave him a disappointed look as she said, "Really?"

"What you are doing is totally amazing and everything, but I've got to know why you said Sarah won't be coming back."

"Now?"

"Yes, now."

"Okay, I... I mean, *we* are now the proud owners of this club."

Brian looked at her in completely shock. "What the hell are you talking about?"

"I was looking for something to invest some money in, and I figured, who better to invest in than you."

Reaching out, she grabbed his erection and pulled him back to her. She stared at his manhood, mesmerized, as she massaged it with both hands.

He asked, "Are you serious?"

She looked up at his face. "Yes. It's all yours to run. Hire whomever you want. Change whatever you want. Have fun."

"That's freaking amazing!" He beamed. "I feel like I should be giving you, you know... instead of you—"

"You can do me later. Are we done talking now?"

He nodded. Jillian quickly went back to work. Running his hands through his still wet hair, he stared down at her in disbelief of both the blowjob and his ownership of the club.

Just then, Victoria opened the door and walked into the locker room. She spotted the intimate act, and her eyes locked on Brian's penis. She grinned. Hearing a noise, Brian looked over in shock to their spectator. He turned away, pulling his manhood from Jillian's mouth.

Jillian looked up, slightly annoyed. "What the hell is it now?"

He pointed to Victoria. Glancing over at Victoria, Jillian quickly folded her arms over her breasts.

Victoria shook her head with a grin. "Isn't it against club rules to get a blowjob in the men's locker room?"

Brian glared at her. "What the hell are you doing here?"

"It's my club, too."

Jillian nodded. "Oh, I forgot to tell you. Meet our new partner."

"Really?"

"Yeah, she was also looking for an investment, and she figured Jim could work here with you."

Victoria smiled. "It'll be great."

Giving her a scolding look, Jillian said, "I told you I was coming up to surprise him and tell him."

"I figured I could help you." Victoria drank in Brian's body for a moment and then added, "but it looks like you don't need any help."

Jillian rolled her eyes and chuckled.

"You know, this is a great idea." Victoria said as she looked around the room. "We combine a tennis club with a sex club. You could have nude tennis and unisex locker rooms. Maybe even swinger parties."

Brian turned toward Victoria with his hands over his groin. Both he and Jillian stared at her like she was out of her mind. Narrowing her eyes, Victoria pointed at the wall across the room. "I wonder if that's a loadbearing wall. Isn't the ladies' locker room over on that side?"

Brian gave Jillian an incredulous look. "We're not going to have a unisex locker room, are we? We have some senior male members whose balls are nearly hanging to the floor. I know, I've seen them. It's not something that any woman would ever —"

"I'm just kidding." Victoria smiled.

"Thank God," Brian replied.

"We're in the middle of something here. So, if you don't mind..." Jillian said with her impatience growing.

"Just keep going. I've seen you guys do that before."

"Get the hell out of here." Jillian glared at her.

"All right." Victoria smiled. "Oh, before I go..."

"What now?" Jillian asked.

"I plan on taking a look around. Are there any other places I should avoid? Like, you two aren't planning on doing anal out on Court Three, are you?"

Holding back a laugh, Jillian pointed to the door. "Seriously, get the hell out of here."

"Okay, okay... geez." Victoria sighed, turned, and headed for the door. Brian put his hands up and ran them through his hair as he and Jillian shared a look. After opening the door, Victoria turned back. Brian quickly covered up again as Victoria widened her eyes and said, "Just think about the nude tennis."

"That sounds like an amazing idea," Jillian fired back sarcastically.

Victoria smiled. "Nice penis, Bri." Then she slipped from the room.

"Anal on Court Three sounds pretty hot," Brian quipped with raised eyebrows.

Jillian grinned up at him. "I'll think about it. Where were we...? Oh, yeah." Reaching out, she grabbed his erection and began pulling on it sensually. Brian tilted his head toward the ceiling in ecstasy. As his lovely wife slipped his quickly hardening penis back into her mouth, he grinned. For some reason, he began thinking about the logistics of nude tennis.

52

Jillian wore a sexy nightshirt as she cradled the adorable little Kaylie Wilde, who was currently enjoying a bottle. Her little eyes were closed and she was quickly falling asleep. Brian stood behind Jillian, wearing only boxer briefs and a big smile.

He whispered, "God, she's cute."

"I want one," Jillian replied in a whisper as she placed Kaylie gently down into her bassinet.

"You want to adopt?"

"Maybe, but I should make an appointment with my doctor. He didn't say it was impossible for me to get pregnant... just unlikely. Victoria was kind of in the same situation, and look what happened there."

They shared a smile as they each walked to their respective sides of the bed and climbed in.

"Yeah, but she had like an incredible amount of sex for, like, three years in order to get that lucky. Are you willing to really do the work?" he asked with a grin.

"I'm willing."

Brian's smile faded. "Oh, but I don't want a girl."

"Why not?" Jillian asked, completely taken aback.

"There is no way that I want to worry about her going on dates and all that. Boys are easier. They're monsters, but they're easier."

"I don't know... A little girl would be so cute."

Brian frowned. "Yeah, we already have a son."

She nodded casually until they both broke into a chuckle.

Jillian pulled off her nightshirt and Brian looked her over with a sexy grin as he pulled his boxers down and tossed them to the floor.

"Just keep it down," Jillian said.

"No, you keep it down."

Jillian smiled. "You're right, it is mostly me. I'll try."

Moving in to kiss her, he suddenly pulled back. "Aren't we forgetting something?"

"Oh, yeah. Yes, where is it?"

Brian glanced around the room and spotted the magazine. He rushed over, grabbed it, and returned to bed.

Jillian asked, "Now, you promise you didn't already look at it?"

"I swear."

Brian returned to bed with an issue of Playboy. On the cover appeared the sexy, somewhat truth-avoiding, man-manipulating, anal-loving, and incredibly flexible Miss Natalie Brookhart, now known as Miss June. They both looked with wide smiles at the cover picture of Natalie performing a somewhat difficult ballet pose while wearing some tiny, mostly see-through lingerie.

"I can do that," Jillian grumbled.

He nodded. "I've seen you do it. Actually, I think we did it once while you were *doing that*."

"We did," she announced proudly.

Flipping to the centerfold picture of Natalie lying on satin sheets wearing nothing but a red ribbon around her neck, Brian said, "Your tits are much nicer."

"You think?"

"Definitely."

Brian turned to the next page, which showed a picture of Natalie lying on her back with her legs curled up in some insane position, her head only a few inches away from her most intimate of parts. His mouth dropped open as Jillian made a slightly horrified face.

"But can you do *that*?" Brian asked.

Jillian scoffed. "No. Why would you need to do that?"

Smiling widely, Brian replied, "Yeah, I guess that's the position she was telling me about where she could lick, you know, a guy's balls while he was..." He stopped talking when he took in Jillian's expression. His smile faded, and he stammered, "We, uh, don't really need to do that... that just looks wrong and—"

"Oh, maybe I'll work on it," Jillian announced.

"Really?" A bright smile returned to his face.

"I said maybe... But for now, you'll just have to survive with regular... old... ball... licking." Grinning, she slipped down to his lap, lifted up his penis, and began excitedly exploring the twins with her tongue.

Brian tilted his head to the ceiling, tossed the magazine onto the bed, and reached back to put a death grip on the headboard. He exhaled deeply and simply said, "Wow."

Moving her head to his thigh, she glanced up and smiled. "Will this work for you?"

"Uh-huh."

Jillian went back to work. Brian's body shuddered as his eyelids slowly closed, and a huge smile spread across his face.

53

Victoria, Jim, and Caroline relaxed outside in Victoria's hot tub just as Jillian and Brian were moving into a sixty-nine position.

The new parents, along with Jim's fiancée, all wore swimsuits. Popping the top off a bottle of champagne, Jim poured everyone a glass. As they relaxed in the tub, the three quickly polished off the first bottle. After Jim opened the second and poured another round, he asked, "So when are you going to tell us what we're celebrating?"

"Not celebrating, really..." Victoria took a big sip and smiled. "God, this champagne is good. I haven't had a drink in weeks."

Caroline and Jim shook their heads in agreement and each took another sip.

Victoria continued, "I really want to thank you both for all your help with the baby. I never could have made it this far without you and, I, uh..." She began losing it as a tear rolled down her cheek. Caroline moved to her and said, "It's okay. You can always count on us."

After covering her mouth in an attempt to control her emotions, Victoria smiled. She took a big sip of champagne. "I'm better now." Then she let out a long, slow breath before continuing, "So, I wanted to ask you both if anything ever happened to me, I mean, God forbid, well, I want you both to raise Kaylie." Victoria curled her lip as she stared at Caroline's face. "Caroline, I would like you to raise her as if she were your own daughter."

"Don't talk like that." Shaking her head with her eyes welling with tears, Caroline continued, "But, of course, I would. She's beautiful and such a perfect baby."

"She is," Victoria agreed.

Jim gave Victoria a gentle smile. "Nothing is going to happen to you."

"I know. I know, but just in case, I want to know she'll be taken care of. That's why I've named you both as beneficiaries in my will, and there's a trust fund for Kaylie to go along with it, but I wanted you guys to have something."

Jim and Caroline shared a look with their hearts melting and it wasn't from the steamy water. They both turned their attention back to Victoria.

Jim said, "You didn't need to do that. Really, you should put all the money in Kaylie's trust. We don't need anything."

"There's more than enough to go around. Really."

He added, "Thank you, but I'm sure we'll — "

"Now, don't go murdering me or anything for the money," Victoria interrupted with a smile. "The police always look to the beneficiaries first. You'd never get away with it."

Jim shared an evil smile with Caroline. "You know, accidents happen all the time."

The three chuckled.

Jim refilled all the glasses, and everyone drank as they relaxed back in the tub.

"This feels amazing," Victoria said as she looked toward the starlit sky.

Gazing at Victoria, Caroline said, "I want to thank you for welcoming me into your home. You are incredible. I just really wanted to hate you, you know, but you're amazing."

Victoria smiled at her. "Honestly, I wanted to hate you also. I mean, I'm jealous of your teenage ass, but — "

"My ass... Your ass is spectacular and you've got those great breasts too! It's totally not fair."

"You are right about my tits." Victoria smiled and then shook her head in disbelief. "But your ass is beyond perfect. Mine is starting to sag and — "

"Okay, girls... enough with the love fest." Jim interrupted. "You both have great tits AND amazing asses."

"He's right," Victoria said as she moved her hand to Caroline's and held it along the edge of the hot tub. They shared a warm smile. As they continued to hold hands, their smiles slipped away, and a pulse of electricity shot through their bodies. Caroline pulled away first, feeling a little silly. After chugging her champagne, a sudden urge to empty her bladder came over her. She said, "Oh shoot. I really need to pee."

She stood, and the combination of the heat from the water and the champagne made her feel a bit woozy. When she lost her balance, both Jim and Victoria reached out to her. Ending up in both of their arms, Caroline sat back between them. The sexual energy now pulsed through the intertwined bodies of all three.

Caroline glanced into Victoria's eyes and sighed. Victoria felt her young rival's warm breath on her lips.

Caroline murmured, "Sorry, I just, uh —"

"Are you okay?" Jim asked.

"I just lost my balance." Caroline rose up. Standing with her, Jim guided her out of the tub. Both Victoria and Caroline's eyes locked on the growing bulge in his swim trunks. Glancing down, he noticed it as well. By the time he looked back at the two women, they had already turned away. He slipped into the tub as Caroline dried off and then wrapped a towel around her body.

"Um, does anyone need anything while I'm..."

Shaking their heads no with their eyes glazed over, they both stared straight ahead as Caroline headed toward the house.

After a long pee, Caroline stood in front of the mirror studying her supple body. Moving her hand down to her bikini bottom, she pushed it inside. She slipped a finger between her legs and upon discovering she was completely wet, let out a soft moan. She pushed her finger deeper inside, then brought it out, then back inside.

"Oh, wow," she murmured. Staring at her reflection in the mirror, she went on touching herself and running her tongue around her lips with her breathing labored.

Outside in the hot tub, neither Jim nor Victoria said a word. They just tried to avoid eye contact, and the awkwardness was almost as palpable as the building sexual desire. Jim motioned to Victoria with the bottle, and she nodded. He poured them each a glass, which they downed quickly with huge gulps.

"It's a beautiful night," Jim said.

"Gorgeous."

Inside, Caroline was now naked with one hand squeezing her nipples and the other slowly moving over the swollen lips of her vagina. Sighing, she pulled her hands away and stood frozen, contemplating while staring at herself in the mirror. She closed her eyes, swayed back and forth a bit, still feeling lightheaded from all the champagne. She turned and ran her tongue around her lips once more as she glanced toward the door. Closing her eyes tight, she took one long, deep breath. After she opened her eyes, she shook her head, determined, and headed out of the room.

Victoria spotted Caroline first, as she walked slowly, not wearing anything, toward the tub. Seeing Victoria's expression, Jim quickly turned his head toward the house.

When he saw Caroline, his jaw dropped, and he let out a big sigh. He stammered, "What, uh... what are you..."

Slipping into the tub, Caroline put a finger over his parted lips. Victoria watched mesmerized as Caroline pulled her hand from his mouth and leaned in to give him a passionate kiss. When she pulled away, she turned to Victoria and extended her hand to her. Victoria rose to her feet, and Caroline's eyes locked on her face first and then back to Jim's.

Caroline licked her lips and moved toward Victoria. Jim watched, wide-eyed, as the two gorgeous women shared a gentle, tentative kiss. He stared, unblinking, as the kiss deepened, and along with it, his erection grew to full size, testing the fabric of his swim trunks. Picking up a champagne glass, he found it empty. Without taking his eyes off the kiss, he reached for the bottle, brought it to his mouth, and tilted it high. Champagne spilled down his chest as he sloppily downed the rest of the bottle.

He moved the bottle from his mouth and watched as Caroline gently squeezed Victoria's breast through her bathing suit. He murmured, "Wow..."

Jim stared, entranced, as the two ended their kiss and stared into each other's eyes. Reaching up, Victoria pulled the straps of her bathing suit top off her shoulders and down until her full breasts spilled out. Caroline leaned in toward her, and their mouths connected once more with their bodies pressing together, breasts gently grazing and tongues intertwining.

Looking down at his enormous erection, Jim adjusted his trunks a bit to relieve the pressure. Caroline and Victoria turned their heads toward him, and when their eyes traveled down to his bulge, their mouths fell open. The women each extended a hand to beckon him closer. He placed the empty bottle on the edge of the patio and moved to them. The women returned to their kiss as Jim bent over and moved his mouth down between their breasts, parting them as he fought his way through. Extending his tongue to Caroline's nipple first, he captured it between his lips. He sucked on it carefully and then, after turning his attention to Victoria's, he did the same. The women kissed more passionately now as Jim released Victoria's breast and extended his tongue to carefully lick both women's nipples at once as they just barely pressed together.

The women looked down at him and then guided him back up, each using a gentle hand to his face. Jim stood, and they turned to him. Caroline kissed him first, a passionate kiss. Pulling back from him and using her hand, Caroline gently guided his head toward Victoria. Victoria stared at Caroline with a curious look as if she were asking for permission to proceed. Watching closely, Jim witnessed Caroline's approving nod; then he moved in to kiss Victoria. They kissed deeply as Caroline moved her lips down to his nipple and tenderly gnawed at it between her teeth.

She bit down harder. Jim pulled his mouth from Victoria and gasped. Glancing down at Caroline, Victoria grinned before slowly moving to his vacant nipple. She pulled it between her teeth. Jim stared straight ahead with his eyes rolling back in his head as the two women feverishly explored his chest with their mouths, teeth, and tongues.

A few seconds later, Victoria pulled away and climbed out of the tub. Caroline rose up, and both she and Jim watched as Victoria slipped her one-piece suit off her body and began drying off with a towel. Victoria extended her hand to them and they followed her out of the tub. Victoria used her towel to dry Caroline while Jim struggled to pull down the swim trunks over his huge erection.

Catching sight of him first, Victoria stopped working the towel over Caroline's body. Caroline's eyes traveled down next, and they both stared unblinkingly at his swollen manhood as it stood straight out from his body. Gasping, neither could remember it ever being this big.

Jim's eyes traveled back and forth from Victoria's then to Caroline's naked bodies as he picked a towel off the chair and dried himself. Victoria finished drying Caroline and then extended a hand to each of them. They moved to her, and Victoria led them into the house and then to her bedroom.

For the next ninety minutes, they took turns pleasing each other in all manner of erotic exciting positions. Caroline did things she never imagined she would, and even Victoria was able to knock an item or two off her Bucket List.

At one point, Jim smiled dreamily as he looked down at the sight of his two favorite women in the world teaming up to please his every nerve ending, which they did with unrestrained lust. It was an experience he had previously only seen in movies. Living it, he found, was so much fucking better. It went on and on and on until after a series of multiple intense and exhaustive orgasms, all three tumbled away into a deep sleep.

54

At 5:34 a.m. Caroline stirred from the midst of a sexy dream. She woke wearing a groggy smile and reached out to find Jim. Her hand slid from his shoulder, down his arm and around him, but instead of grasping his firm chest, her hand landed on Victoria's large, soft breast. Both Jim and Victoria groaned before returning to their quiet breathing. Caroline's eyes shot open with the realization that it wasn't a dream; it was real. She was in bed with both Jim and Victoria, and they had...

She sat up with the memories flooding back to her. She had done things with Victoria, things she never imagined she would do with a woman. Was she a lesbian? Was she a swinger? Did she really encourage this to happen, or was she seduced? She closed her eyes as she remembered; she was the one who walked outside naked after touching herself in the bathroom. She caused this. She did it; it was her fault. Caroline let the weight of all of it wash over her. Then she took a deep breath and closed her eyes.

Moments later, with immense guilt and regret swirling in her head, Caroline slipped out of bed and went to the bathroom. She stared at her face in the mirror, just shaking her head. What have I done? Oh my God. How can we possibly get married now?

After running water over her face, she returned to the bedroom. The light from the bathroom shone on Jim's naked body as he spooned with the also naked mother of his child. Caroline moved closer to see Jim's hand resting on Victoria's thigh and them both sleeping peacefully, nearly intertwined. Covering her face with her hands, she began to sob silently.

Two hours later, Victoria woke and left Jim sleeping as she made her way to the bathroom. She found it odd that Caroline was no longer in bed with them. When Victoria returned to the room, she noticed a note along with Caroline's engagement ring sitting on the nightstand. She froze for a moment, staring at the ring. While holding her breath, she moved to the nightstand.

Victoria held the ring in one hand as she read the note. A look of intense sadness overtook her, and she sighed. She stared across the room at nothing in particular for twenty seconds before a slightly evil smile crossed her lips. Just then, Jim began to stir. After quickly returning the note and ring to the nightstand, she rushed back to bed next to him.

Jim took a deep breath and rolled to his back. Groaning, his hand went to his head to fight off a slight headache. He opened his eyes and began struggling back to consciousness. Jim glanced at Victoria's perfect naked body as she lay on her side facing away from him. First he smiled; then a look of shock spread over his face as the memories came flooding into his brain. God, that was so hot, but how the hell did it happen?

He turned to his other side, expecting to find Caroline, but the bed was empty. Spotting the ring on top of the paper, he sat back against the headboard, grabbed the note, and began to read:

Jim,

I'm sorry. I don't know what to say. I just can't marry you. Last night was my fault. Don't blame yourself. You two belong together. You have Kaylie, and you should all be together as a family. Please don't try to contact me. I'm so sorry.

Caroline

Jim reread the note slowly as he took a long, deep breath. Victoria remained frozen in her fake slumber as Jim folded the note carefully and placed it on the nightstand. Victoria's eyes shot wide open when she heard him sigh loudly. A wider smile spread across her face. Closing her eyes, she turned toward him while taking a big sleepy breath. She rolled up on him with her head on his abdomen and her arm trailing down his long leg. His penis lay flaccid and rested against his thigh.

Jim glanced down almost in surprise to Victoria lying on him. He thought a moment about turning away from her, but her skin felt so good on his. She seemed to be in a sound sleep and he would hate to wake her.

Victoria opened her eyes and stared lovingly at his penis. It was only three inches from her lips and she wanted it again. Should she? Groaning, she stirred groggily, moving her hand up his thigh mere inches from his groin. She breathed out deeply.

He felt her hot breath all over him before feeling her hand gently tracing a line on his thigh. Next he felt the intense heat building up through his body as all his blood rushed to his groin.

Victoria watched closely as his penis slowly grew, expanded, and lifted up. She slid her hand up lazily over it until it flopped toward his belly button. Staring at the head, she watched as it throbbed and grew closer to her lips with every beat of his heart. Her hand still rested over it, and she adjusted her position a bit now, directing it toward her lips.

"Oh, no..." Jim murmured inaudibly as the guilt washed over his mind.

Victoria licked her lips and let out a sleepy sigh as she waited for his length to move into her mouth all on its own.

Staring down at her long, beautiful hair, he felt his erection continue to grow. He could feel her hot breath stronger on the head of his penis and her fingers as they gently brushed up against his shaft.

She felt him thicken under her palm as his length stretched to her waiting mouth. Victoria shut her eyes as the head slipped between her lips. Moaning happily, she began gently sucking at his flesh.

He groaned, "Oh, God."

Opening wider, she allowed him to slip deeper into her mouth. Staring down with his mouth wide open and his heart beating out of his chest, he exhaled. She held her head still as he slowly began thrusting his hips up slightly and then back as he drew his erection in and nearly all the way out of her warm, wet, perfect mouth.

She purred loudly as he moved in a slow steady rhythm. He shook his head with a sad expression, but he couldn't stop. After moving one hand to his lips to stifle the whimper he felt struggling to slip out, he moved his other to Victoria's head and began gently running his fingers through her hair. A lone tear streamed down Jim's face. Tumbling into ecstasy, Victoria's eyes rolled back in her head as she relished in the feeling of his girth sliding between her lips.

Suddenly, he stopped moving but his erection remained buried between her lips. Victoria sprung into action, lifting her head off his body taking his cock up along with it and then plunging her mouth up and down over him. Craning his neck up, watching her and struggling to catch his breath, he pulled his hand from her hair. He opened his mouth to speak, but nothing came out. He closed his eyes tight as she worked her lips over him faster and faster. Shaking his head, Jim opened his eyes wide, fighting for the courage to stop her.

"Victoria," he whispered.

She was so engrossed in her current assignment that she didn't skip a beat.

"Victoria," he repeated, louder.

Pulling up from him, she turned and glanced at his face with her lips parted and her eyes glazed over. "What is it?" she murmured breathlessly.

"Caroline took off, and I'm not sure—"

"I know," she replied unable to look him in the eye.

"What do you mean you know?"

Glancing back to his face, she moved to her knees and admitted, "I, uh, read the note."

He glared at her. "My fiancée leaves me because of..." He motioned to the bed and continued, "... all this, and you think a blowjob is a good way to celebrate?"

She stared at him, speechless.

"I can't believe you." He slipped out of bed. Tilting his head toward the ceiling, Jim exhaled a long, slow breath. He rubbed his hands over his face before he glanced back to her with his expression softening. "This is all my fault."

"No, it's not," She replied, her guilt washing over her.

He knelt to the floor placing his head on the mattress. Moving to him, she ran her fingers through his hair as she began hesitantly, "I... I'd be lying if I said I wasn't at least a little... happy about this."

The worst thing was that Jim couldn't help feeling the same way. This is what he'd been denying he wanted for months. Lifting his head up, Jim said, "I've never stopped loving you, you know that."

"I know."

Jim stared deeply into her eyes. "I can't start this again if... I mean I just can't do this if we're not going to be together for real, you know, forever."

"I don't want anyone else."

He returned a skeptical look. "In St. Barts, you said you could never settle down again... that, that you got bored easily, and —"

"I didn't know what I was saying... I mean, I knew, but I thought that was... I thought I was doing the best thing for you, turning you away, sending you back to Caroline. I'm sorry. I'm so sorry," Victoria broke down sobbing as he stared at her, barely able to breathe.

"Don't cry," he murmured.

Shaking her head and whimpering, she stared down at the sheets.

Jim climbed on the bed, moved his hand to her cheek and brushed away a tear. Slipping his hand under her chin, he guided her eyes to his.

Smiling weakly, she began, "I don't..."

"What?"

After sniffling, she wiped her eyes. "I don't want anyone else. I love you more than I thought I could ever love anyone again."

"I love you too."

Moving his lips to hers, he kissed her tenderly. He pulled back slightly, and they stared into each other's eyes for a long, long time.

She seemed to be asking him a question with her eyes. Eventually, despite his sadness at losing Caroline, whom he truly loved—although maybe not with the same desperate, reckless abandon he loved Victoria—he gave her the answer she wanted with a gentle smile.

He fell back slowly against the pillow and shook his head with a slight grin. Curling against him, she placed her head on his chest and sighed. It felt more than right, more than perfect. With their minds racing, they both thought about what lay ahead. As he ran a finger slowly over her lower back, she placed her hand on his chest and closed her eyes.

THE END...

Follow the continuing story of Victoria, Jillian, Brian, Jim and Rob in FRIENDS WITH WAY TOO MANY BENEFITS (An excerpt is included).

If you are a big fan of this series, want more Victoria and don't mind a little more spice in your reading, you will want to check out the series prequel released under my Ian Dalton pen name. DESPERATE THOUGHTS details Victoria's back-story — the super erotic, mostly tragic tale of how she moved on with her life after the death of her husband. Please be warned that the prequel contains descriptions of explicit sex with explicit language. Please note that the rest of the books released under my Ian Dalton pen name are expanded versions of my Luke Young books. Each Ian version contains approximately 7,000 more words in the form of more expanded and explicit sex scenes. It's a great way to revisit the series at some point in the future with a little more spice.

To find out more about the author and his work, see http://www.lukeyoungbooks.com/

To contact Luke or to be placed on a mailing list to receive updates about new releases, send an email to lukebyoung@gmail.com

ALSO BY LUKE YOUNG

SHRINKAGE
CHOCOLATE COVERED BILLIONAIRE NAVY SEAL
CHANCES AREN'T

The Friends With... Benefits Series:
FRIENDS WITH PARTIAL BENEFITS
FRIENDS WITH FULL BENEFITS
FRIENDS WITH MORE BENEFITS
FRIENDS WITH EXTRA BENEFITS
FRIENDS WITH WAY TOO MANY BENEFITS (releasing
12/17/2013)

FRIENDS WITH WAY TOO MANY BENEFITS

Jim, Victoria, Jillian and Brian sat around the dinner table after having just finished a delicious meal prepared by the famous author. The couple with the new baby hadn't been out of the house much in the last six months or for that matter enjoyed much sleep. With Victoria's parents watching Kaylie for the night, they were both ready to unwind. Now the hosting couple, the one with a twenty two year old child/best friend, had been humping quite regularly for the past four months in a frenzied, yet casual attempt to conceive in a, if-it's-meant-to-be-it-will-happen, sorta way. Unfortunately, they were unsuccessful so far.

The group headed to the great room to watch the DVD Victoria rented of the new independent movie starring Ben Affleck. It was a film the women were interested in seeing and the men half-heartedly agreed to watch. Ten minutes into, *To the Wonder*, everyone in the room wanted to hang themselves. With only a few scant words of dialog and pretty much nothing at all happening in the story during that time the four exchanged looks of boredom and confusion. Even with the promise of some gratuitous nudity at some point in the almost two hour epic it was unanimous that they bail.

Brian hit the stop button on the remote and slumped back on the sofa.

Jillian asked, "So what should we do now?"

Jim was busy looking at his iPhone. "We could go to a movie. The new Sandra Bullock movie starts at 10:20."

Victoria frowned. "I don't feel like going out. Does anyone else?"

"Not really." Jillian shrugged. "We could play a game. We have Trivial Pursuit, Monopoly, Scrabble... or maybe we could play cards."

"Scrabble. I love scrabble." Grinning, Victoria rubbed her hands together.

"Really?" Brian whined, "Scrabble."

"Come on," Victoria pleaded. "I'm really good at it and we can make it interesting."

"How?"

"Well, for starters double points for any dirty words."

"Woopie." Brian gave her a look.

"Okay, how about this. Low score for any round has to do a shot and... and..." Victoria widened her eyes. "Take off an article of clothing."

Brian perked up a bit. "Okay, but what happens when one of you girls gets naked — are you just out of the game?"

Victoria smiled. "First off, us *girls*... will not be the first ones naked. Let's just say we'll be seeing things hanging and swinging before you'll be seeing any of these." Putting on a smug look, she motioned with one hand to her own chest and with the other over to Jillian's stunning pair.

"That's right." Jillian nodded, smugly.

"Okay..." Brian held back a laugh. "Regardless of who gets naked first, what happens after that?"

"Then you choose a truth or dare. And the person with the high score from that round gets to ask the question or provide the dare."

"And the dare can be anything?" Brian asked.

"Well, within reason." Victoria put a finger to her lips. "How about the other two have to agree the dare is acceptable?"

"I sorta have a bad feeling about this," Brian cringed. "But yeah, I'm in."

"Me too." Jillian flashed her husband a smile.

Jim frowned. "This sounds really complicated."

"It's not." Victoria blew out a long, slow breath. "I'll tell you when to drink and when to strip..." She shook her head quickly and made a face. "Okay? Mr. Fun as a dishrag..."

"Hey, I can be fun."

"Well then go get the vodka."

"All right." Jim took off toward the liquor cabinet and Brian headed to the den.

When Brian returned with the board game Jillian set it up on the large coffee table. Everyone moved to the floor sitting around the table with their shot glass, wooden letter holder and group of letter tiles.

Victoria scolded the group. "And we all get exactly five articles of clothing, so if you don't wear a bra then you can count each of your socks separately, but no shoes or anything like that."

"For this dirty word thing who judges whether the word is dirty or not?" Brian asked.

"I think we'll know." Victoria shot the group a knowing look. "If it has to do with a fun body part or sex, then it's dirty."

"Is slang okay?" Jim asked.

"Yes, but only for dirty words."

"Ready?" Victoria said. "I'll go first."

"Why do you get to go first?" Brian complained.

"Duh, it was my idea."

After twenty minutes of game play, the boys were working on a decent buzz and were down to only their shorts and underwear. Jillian, the leader, was missing only her socks and Victoria was sockless and down to her bra. On the board appeared the words — *sex, nipple, cock* and a few less fun selections.

Smiling, Jim placed his letters on the board. "S. H. I. T. that's a double and the T is on a triple word score so that's —"

"That's not a dirty word." Brian scoffed.

"Is too." Victoria came to her man's defense.

"Um, you'd better check your rule book." Brian sighed. "The rule was the word had to be for a fun body part or sex."

"Yeah."

"Well, I don't know what you two pervs do in the bedroom, but please tell me poop is not involved."

Victoria cringed. "Oh, yeah, you're right. I'm into a lot of wild stuff, but S.H.I.T. is not one of them. Jim, no, you cannot double that."

"Okay," he sighed.

"My turn." Jillian ran her tongue over her teeth. "I'm going to use the 'I' in his shit for my TAINT." Grinning, she arranged the letters carefully and looked up to discover everyone giving her horrified looks. "Oh, sorry, that didn't come out right."

Brian winked. "Now that definitely is a double word, a fun body part and hers is so cute."

"Oh, that's sweet." Jillian put her hand on his arm, beaming.

"We're all happy for you," Victoria said with an edge to her voice.

"I didn't say a word when we all had to hear about how awesome your nipples were earlier." Brian sneered. "What? Can we not share in this game? I thought we were sharing."

"Oh, we will share." Victoria chuckled. "...but that's happening after we're naked."

Brian studied the board, cringing. "Crap, I don't have anything decent." He bit his knuckle and took one last look at the board before frowning at his awful letters. "Does anyone know of a word with four Es and a Q?"

"Hey, no cheating," Victoria scolded.

"You need a shot." Brian looked at her pointedly before returning to the board.

"Maybe we need a time limit," Jim said.

"Okay, okay." Brian placed his two letters down forming the word *bet*.

Victoria grumbled something under her breath.

"What's wrong?" Brian asked.

"Well, you took my space. I was going to put down BACKDOOR."

"Yeah, we all know you love that." Brian and Jillian shared a look.

"I at least knew how to do it."

"Your parents... they... must be so proud." Jillian cracked up barely able to get out the words.

"Go ahead, laugh it up. But you weren't laughing when I taught you both how to do it."

Jim's jaw fell open. "Wait, what are you talking about, you taught them how to do what?"

"Anal sex."

"What? How?"

Victoria shrugged. "Well, we were all high and they were having some trouble so I sorta walked them through it."

"You're kidding right?"

"No."

"So you watched them like doing it and... and everything?"

"Yep, until they threw me out for... what was it?" She placed a finger to her chin.

"You wouldn't shut up remember? The constant play by play."
Jillian shook her head. "It was awful."

"Ahhh…" Victoria looked to the ceiling. "Good times."

"Please, please…" Jim ran his fingers through his hair. "…tell me this was before I met you."

"It was. Remember, I said we were high."

"Still…" He looked at her like she was nuts.

"Hey, don't judge." Victoria turned her attention to Jillian. "Okay, score master, who is drinking and taking something off?"

"Um, sorry Brian," Jillian said, sympathetically.

"Really?"

"Yeah, your three letter word just didn't cut it."

Jim poured him one third of a shot. After the initial rounds when they each took a first full shot they all agreed to switch to the mini shot in order to prolong the game into its more enjoyable phases before they all blacked out.

After slamming it back, Brian stood and stripped off his shorts then as required performed a slow spin before sitting back down.

"Look at the cute little bulge." Victoria smiled. "I forgot that you're a grower."

Brian scoffed. "You didn't forget and you know how much it grows. Hell you held it in your hands more than once."

"Wait, you held it." Jim looked up from the board, stunned.

"Uh-huh. It's a long story."

"Don't tell it." Jim sighed, then poured himself a healthy shot and pounded it back. "And they ask me why I drink."

Twenty seven minutes later, all four were completely naked with Brian bearing the brunt of the punishment, of course. With about five full shots consumed, he'd been required to confess the most dangerous place he'd ever masturbated (waiting in a long line at a fast food drive-thru), his most horrifying sexual experience (a girl in college who bolted from his dorm room just after he dropped his pants) and during his third straight losing round he reluctantly chose dare.

Victoria put on an evil grin. "I dare you to try to perform oral sex on yourself."

"What?"

"Give yourself a blowjob."

"How?"

"Um, do I need to draw you a picture?" Holding her palms up, Victoria looked around the room to Jillian's and Brian's utterly confused faces.

"Yeah, in this case." Brian swayed back and forth with his eyes open like slits. "I think I'm going to need a picture."

Jim raised his hand. "I know I can't do it, she made me try a few weeks ago."

Brian shook himself awake, widened his eyes and slowly turned to Jillian wearing a horrified expression. When he turned back, he said, "You poor man. I don't want to know what other sex stuff, sex queeny over here makes you do."

"Uh..." Jim shrugged. "It's not so bad."

"So, let's go." Victoria folded her arms, staring Brian down.

"There is no way I can do this."

"How do you know?" Victoria asked.

"Well, for one thing, if I could do that, I probably wouldn't be here with you all, I'd still be living with my parents... at my parent's house with a chronic case of scholastics..." He chuckled. "...shit, I mean, scoliosis."

They all shared a laugh.

Brian turned to his wife. "I can't believe you're not going to veto this."

"You know..." She shrugged. "I think I'd like to see that. Come on give it a try."

"Jim?"

"Dude, I'm not going to watch, but I'm not standing in their way either."

"Gee, thanks. Just wait until your turn." Brian sighed. "All right, give me my shot and make it a full one... not one of those girly ones."

Jim poured then the victim took a deep breath and pounded it back, cringing and blowing his breath through his teeth. He stood up too quickly, leaned a bit and had to steady himself by extending his arms out. "All right... I'm okay." After shaking his head, he grabbed his *other* head, pulled it upward and half-heartedly bent down, opening his mouth slightly along the way. After two seconds he stood up and again had to steady himself. "See I can't... can't do it."

"AHHHTTT!" Victoria mimicked the buzzing sound of a game show wrong answer.

"What?" Brian said, covering his junk.

"Seriously?" Victoria rolled her eyes.

"What's wrong?"

"First you need a hard-on and second you need to be on your back. Then throw your legs up over your head and pull your hips down."

Shaking his head, Brian gazed at her dismayed. "How in the world do you know this shit?"

"You guys have internet, right?"

"Yeah, but I don't..." Brian looked like he might vomit. "...Google guys blowing themselves."

"Well..." She widened her eyes. "...maybe you should."

"Whatever." Brian sighed. "Really, you want me to do all that?"

"I could..." She shrugged and looked to the ceiling with a hand resting on her cheek. "...come up with something else for you to do."

"No." Brian looked at her alarmed. "No, that's ok. I'll do this."

"Good."

Frowning, he sighed, long and deep. "So, I guess I need to, you know, jerk off until it, uh..."

"Or, you could get a fluffer." Victoria smiled at Jillian.

"A fluffer?" Jillian returned a confused look.

"You know, those girls who get porn guys..." She made quote marks in the air. "...*ready*."

Maybe it was the booze or the nudity, or a little of both, but Jillian still maintained a deer-in-headlights expression. Victoria rolled her eyes before acting out a little oral action with a raised semi-closed-fisted hand and a few apt head movements.

"Oh..." The realization washed over Jillian's face. "So I should, um..."

"Well, you probably don't want me to blow him, do you?" Victoria asked.

"Uh, no."

Jim raised his hands in the air. "Don't even look at me!"

After mulling it over for a moment, Jillian said, "All right, I'll do it... But we don't have to do *that* in front of you two do we?"

"No." Victoria made a face. "You can go around the corner if you're shy."

"Um, I'm shy."

"Yeah, me too." Brian agreed.

"So go." Victoria waved them away. "But come back before you get too carried away."

The naked tipsy couple headed off down the hall.

Jim and Victoria held back their giggles as they listened closely to the whispering, short disagreement followed by soft moaning. Almost three minutes later Jillian returned wearing an embarrassed expression and covering up her parts. Brian followed behind her, wearing nothing but a stiffy and wearing it proudly. "Okay, let's do this."

"Now that's the Brian I remember." Victoria gave him a wink.

Jim made the mistake of glancing at him. He winced and covered his eyes. "I think I just threw up a little in my mouth."

Moving onto his back, Brian brought his legs up then over his head and wrapped his arms around his hips and pulled down. His full erection hung down, but about four inches short of success.

"He's not really trying," Victoria rolled her eyes. "Pull your hips down and stretch your neck up."

"I am. I am." He struggled to say.

"Come on baby. Come on baby," Jillian cheered him on.

Brian took one more shot at it, groaning and struggling getting no closer than maybe three inches from glory before he gave up. After letting out a loud groan, he released his legs and took a deep breath.

"Good try babe." Jillian gave him a sympathetic smile.

"You either need to be a foot long or really flexible to pull that off." Brian frowned and sat back down in front of the table.

"Probably both." Jillian replied.

"Yeah," Brian grumbled. "Who's turn is it?"

"That would be me." Victoria studied the board.

They played a few more rounds where no dirty words were spelled and the losses were spread evenly among the four participants with all choosing the truth option. Nothing too earth shattering was learned, although all were feeling no pain and starting to get a bit silly.

During the next round, Brian stunned the group by figuratively pulling the word *asshole* out of his ass. He won and Victoria ended up with the low score. She choose dare and after thinking for a moment, Brian whispered in Jim's ear. Jim nodded his head then returned a grin.

"I dare you to make out with Jillian and..." Brian pointed to her. "... and you have to feel her up at the same time."

Victoria looked at Jillian. "Any objections?"

Jillian asked, "Tongue?"

"Definitely tongue." Brian nodded.

"Oh, all right."

Turning her attention to Jim, Victoria asked. "Okay with you?"

He just stared straight ahead and nodded slowly. "Uh-huh."

She waited for Jim to pour her a shot, but he was apparently somewhere far away. Instead she sighed and filled her own glass.

After pounding it back, she scooted over to Jillian and slowly leaned into her, placing her lips softly on hers. The boys watched unblinkingly as Victoria reached up with both hands and gently caressed Jillian's firm breasts.

When the tongues got into the mix, the boys looked on mesmerized, with their jaws hanging open, barely breathing. After ten seconds of kissing and fondling, Victoria pulled away and shot her best-friend an arrogant grin. "Now, you're probably regretting turning me down for that threesome, aren't you?"

"Huh, what?" Jillian swallowed hard, blinking several times.

Victoria rose up to a kneeling position and glanced to Brian's lap and then to her boyfriends. Smiling proudly, she said, "Mission accomplished. They're both rock hard."

Jillian craned her neck to check out her husband's condition and her eyes widened. "I think I've, uh, had enough of this game. What do you all think?"

"I'm done." Jim popped up to his feet, grabbing his shirt and holding it in front of the problem area.

"Me too." Brian covered up with his hands.

Jillian stood and hid her intimate areas by facing sideways and using an arm draped across her body. "You guys don't mind showing yourselves out do you?"

"No." Victoria shook her head.

Jillian held her other hand out for Brian. "We're really tired. We've, um, got an early day tomorrow."

"Yeah, that's right." Brian stood up, held his hand in front of his groin and performed a fake yawn. Then he took off out of the room and up the stairs with Jillian right behind him.

"Good night," Jillian called back when they were half-way up the stairs.

Jim let the shirt fall to the floor exposing his massive erection. He glanced down to it then flashed her a grin. "Well, they didn't say we had to leave did they."

"No… they… didn't," she replied slowly.

"I'm coming over."

Lying back, she held her hand up for him to join her.

He slipped over her and it was on.

End of excerpt… Friends With Way Too Many Benefits is available now.

6126321R00182

Printed in Great Britain
by Amazon.co.uk, Ltd.,
Marston Gate.